JOSEPH'S KISS

Joseph turned to the woman at his side. Her golden head was next to his shoulder, her small hand rested in his. The clean scent of her herbal soap teased his senses and her breasts rose and fell with her accelerated breathing, no doubt caused by the exertion of the climb.

A feeling of love filled him, so strong that he could not withstand the urge to take her in his arms. The maneuver was awkward with the rifle in his hand, and he was scared of moving too fast, yet he managed. Annie Rose gasped, and her body stiffened, but again, she did not pull away. He touched his lips to hers, gently, tentatively, silently asking her permission to proceed. She made a single faint whimpering sound, and her eyes closed. Her hands crept about his waist, and Joseph deepened the kiss, pressing more firmly against her lips. They parted slightly, and he teased her with the tip of his tongue. She relaxed a little, leaning against him, her breasts soft against his chest, and even that hesitant response sent desire flaring through him like a wild prairie fire.

One of the hardest things Joseph Beaudine ever had to do in his life was to keep that kiss gentle, and after a moment, withdraw . . .

Books by Jessica Wulf

The Irish Rose

The Mountain Rose

The Wild Rose

Hunter's Bride

Joseph's Bride

Published by Zebra Books

Joseph's Bride

Jessica Wulf

Zebra Books
Kensington Publishing Corp.
http://www.zebrabooks.com

for Jesse,
my beloved goofball

Throughout your life, you amazed and inspired me
with your quiet courage and dogged perseverance.
Your great heart has been stilled,
but your indomitable spirit will live forever,
just as I will love you forever.

♥

Now you can truly dance.

I'd like to thank a few people for their contributions to this book:

Janet Grill, critiquer and proofreader extraordinaire—your fine-tuning made this a better book, and your encouraging comments (and the multitude of little stars!) kept me going.

Kathy Simillion and Karen Emanuelson—thanks for sharing your extensive knowledge of that most fascinating and sacred creature, the Horse.

Maggie Osborne and Annie Oakley—thanks for liking my work and for being willing to say so in public.

And a special thanks to Joe Brown, whose handsome likeness graces the cover of this book and whose kind and engaging manner inspired the character of Joseph Beaudine. Years ago, I made you a promise. It took awhile, but here's the book.

—J.W.

One

She was better. Aurora was better.

Annie Rose Jensen knew it at once, and relief flooded through her, so powerfully that her shaking legs threatened to fold under her. The hurried, three-mile trip on foot from her grandfather's house to the hidden meadow and its rough corral had left her weary and winded, but now, the rush of love she felt for the golden mare strengthened her, and she approached with slow, quiet steps, murmuring words of comfort, her extended hand carrying the gift of a carrot. The mare, as always, allowed her to close the distance between them, watching with liquid brown eyes that showed more interest than they had in hours. Aurora nickered a welcome, then daintily took the carrot from Annie Rose's hand.

"Oh, sweetheart, I'm so glad you're recovering." Annie Rose stroked Aurora's neck before she moved her hands to the mare's belly. The faint movement she felt there filled her with joy and thankfulness. "You can't be getting sick, honey. You have a baby to grow." She rested her head against the mare's side. This time her luck had held. At the first sign of colic—thank God she had been there to see it—she had given Aurora some of the medicinal herbs Sweet Water had vowed would help the dreaded condition pass. The Cheyenne woman's word had been true. But now Annie Rose's supply of the herbs was gone, and there was no guarantee the illness would not strike again.

Annie Rose looked up at the sky, which was rapidly darkening as much from the setting of the sun as from an approaching storm. Even now, the wind was beginning to rise. With a glance at the patient black mongrel who sat at her feet, Annie Rose considered her options. Sweet Water had promised to prepare more of the herbs; the package would be waiting. The distance to the cabin Sweet Water shared with her frontiersman husband, Jubal Sage, was the same as to Annie Rose's own home, but in the opposite direction. She could either play it safe and go home, only to retrace her steps the next day, or she could travel to the Sages' cabin and spend the night there if the weather worsened.

"What do you think, Maggie?" she asked of the dog. "Will Gramps worry too much if we're gone all night?" Maggie looked up at her, one ear endearingly cocked, and barked. The last few inches of her tail wagged in the dirt of the small enclosure that offered the mare and her grey companion horse protection from the elements. Annie Rose smiled. "You're right," she said affectionately. "Gramps never worries about me when I'm with you." She bent down to scratch the dog's neck. "I'll feel better with more of those herbs on hand. Let's go visit Jubal and Sweet Water."

The dog jumped to her feet and barked again. Annie Rose hitched up the too-big trousers she wore and turned back to the mare, lovingly stroking the pale blaze that graced the animal's golden forehead. "I'll be back tomorrow, Aurora," she promised. "All will be well." She pressed a kiss to the mare's velvety nose and, with a last backward glance, set off at a trot along the almost invisible trail that would lead her and Maggie to the creek and beyond to Sweet Water's home.

The three men huddled in the far corner of the small, neat cabin broke into raucous laughter. One swung a ceramic jug to his lips and drank deeply, allowing the whiskey to dribble down his bearded chin. Another punched his arm and chided him for wasting the liquor. At the rude wooden table in front of the fireplace, Joseph Beaudine eyed his brother, who was seated across from him. From the look in Orion's eyes, Joseph knew there was no need to voice his concerns about their companions. He was thankful for the long length of his Hawken rifle resting against the table near his leg.

A loud crack of thunder shook the sturdy cabin. Any minute now, the skies would open and vent their fury, fulfilling the threatening promise of the rising wind. Another ominous round of thunder rattled the wooden bowls on the rough plank table, as if to remind Joseph that it would be foolhardy to leave the protection of the cabin.

It was going to be a long night.

Orion pushed away his unfinished bowl of rabbit stew and swiveled on his bench to stare into the flames of the cheery, crackling fire.

"Is it that bad?" Joseph asked.

A moment passed before Orion responded. "What?" He looked back over his shoulder, his green eyes shining in the light of the candle that rested on the table in a pool of its own wax.

Joseph nodded at the bowl.

"Oh. No, no, the stew's fine. I'm just anxious to get back to Fort Laramie."

Another round of thunder shouted as if in defiance of Orion's worries. Joseph stroked his thick mustache and eyed his brother sympathetically. Sarah, Orion's wife, was expecting their first child, due to be born any day now, and she waited for him back at the fort. Although he had no woman of his own, Joseph understood Orion's need to be with Sarah. Even he felt concern for his pretty sister-in-law and the coming babe, the first of a new generation of Beaudines. But night was full upon them and the storm promised to be fierce; it would be unwise to travel in the potentially dangerous Laramie Mountains under such circumstances. Joseph again surveyed the unsavory group in the corner.

Unfortunately, there was danger in here, too.

He and Orion had reached the cabin of their good friends, Jubal Sage and his Cheyenne wife, Sweet Water, just as the sky darkened with both impending nightfall and the encroaching storm. Although Jubal and Sweet Water were not there, the closed cabin door had been unsecured in the unspoken but understood tradition of hospitality in the West, and neither Joseph nor Orion had felt any compunction about making themselves at home. In fact, the two stacked beds near the door sported straw-stuffed canvas mattresses and were intended for visitors, who, it was assumed, would have their own bedrolls.

Joseph had put together the simple but filling rabbit stew, and the two brothers had expected to spend a comfortable night waiting out the storm. The recent arrival of Abelard Baines—known in the Indian territories as Abby—also seeking shelter from the storm, along with his two cohorts, had ensured that the night would be far from comfortable.

His troubled thoughts were interrupted by a sudden knock at the door. The group in the corner fell silent as Joseph rose to lift the latch. Although he didn't open the door far, a powerful gust of wind and the first drops of rain forced their way in.

A boy—maybe fourteen or fifteen, judging by his slight build and smooth chin—stood there, hunched inside a too-big jacket and baggy pants, a floppy hat pulled low on his face. A large black dog sat patiently at his side.

Joseph peered past the boy into the night, surprised to see no horse.

"Is Mr. Sage here? Or his wife?" the boy asked in a hoarse voice.

"No, but you're welcome to shelter and some supper. Come on in." Joseph stepped back from the door.

The boy didn't move. "Do you know when Mr. Sage and his wife will return?"

"No." With curiosity, Joseph eyed the obviously nervous

boy. "Come in out of the storm, boy. The sky's going to break any minute, and it promises to be a real gully washer."

Still the boy hesitated, shifting his feet. From the corner, Baines muttered something, and his friends broke their silence with another round of boisterous laughter. At the sound, the boy looked over his shoulder toward the barn, then down at the dog. "I reckon we'll just stay in the barn. Thanks anyway." He turned away into the increasing rain.

Joseph glanced at Orion, who shrugged in puzzlement, then back out the door. The boy was halfway across the dirt yard. "At least have something to eat first," Joseph called. "Your dog might be hungry, even if you aren't."

A flash of guilt raced across what Joseph could see of the boy's face and was gone.

"Close the goddamned door!" Abby shouted.

The boy seemed to come to a decision and retraced his steps to the door, then edged inside. The dog silently followed. They both stood close to the wall.

"I'm Joseph Beaudine, and"—Joseph waved toward the table—"that's my brother, Orion, also called the Hunter."

The boy nodded at each of them. "Howdy." He did not remove his hat.

"Have a seat." Orion shifted along the bench, making room. "The fire'll warm your back."

"Thanks." The boy slid onto the vacated spot, while his dog laid down on the packed-dirt floor between him and the fire.

Joseph ladled some of the stew into a clean bowl. What on earth was a boy—a white boy—doing out in the wilderness alone? There wasn't another cabin or settlement of any kind for miles, yet the youth was alone and evidently on foot. Who was he? The fact that the boy had not introduced himself was not lost on Joseph. He turned and set the bowl in front of the boy, then laid a wooden spoon next to it. Orion pushed a fresh cup of steaming coffee toward the boy.

"Thanks," he whispered again. After a moment, he took the spoon and scooped up some of the stew.

Joseph exchanged another puzzled glance with Orion, then

refilled his coffee cup and resumed his seat, honoring their visitor's obvious wish to eat in silence. Trying not to stare, he watched the lad. Whoever had raised him had taught him some manners, for he ate almost daintily, and chewed with his mouth closed.

From the corner, the querulous voice of Painted Davy Sikes—so called because of the series of tattoos covering most of his plump, pock-marked face—rose above the sound of the now pounding storm. "How much more time are we gonna waste looking for that damned Golden Mare, Abby? I ain't even sure she exists."

The boy's hand stopped in midair, the spoon he held quivering. Joseph and Orion looked at each other again.

"She exists, all right," Abby assured Painted Davy. He swung the jug to his mouth and drank deeply, then scrubbed the back of one dirty hand over his lips as he passed the jug to Hank Westin, who was slumped in the corner. "My Sioux brothers told me she's been seen, somewheres in these mountains. The man who catches her'll be rich, indeed. Any of the Plains tribes will pay dearly for the mare, 'cause they figure her to be some kind of important spirit animal." He turned his head and pierced Joseph with an unfriendly glare. "Ain't that right, Beaudine? Or should I call you Captain?"

Ignoring the sarcastic second question, Joseph took a swallow of hot, strong coffee before he answered the first. "The Golden Mare is a legend, Baines, just like the White Buffalo. Your friend called it right—you're wasting your time, and theirs, looking for her."

"Told you so," Painted Davy whined. "I wanna head back to Fort Laramie in the morning, and hole up with one of them Injun whores 'til I can't walk. What'da you think, Hank?"

Hank Westin, a thin, wiry man wearing stained buckskins and clearly feeling the effects of too much corn liquor, struggled to focus his watery, bloodshot eyes. "Whatever you say, Painted Davy. I'm tired of roamin' these mountains lookin' for a spirit horse that don't exist." He emitted a loud belch and slumped lower against the wall.

"Shut up, the both of you," Abby growled. "The mare exists. And she ain't no spirit animal. She's a horse, like any other piece of crowbait, 'cept the damn fool Injun tribes want her real bad and are willin' to pay for her." He snorted in derision. "Spirit animal. There ain't no such thing."

The boy finally released his death grip on the spoon and laid the utensil on the table, then grabbed the almost-full bowl of stew and set it on the floor in front of the appreciative dog. He wrapped both hands around his coffee cup and stared down at the table, but not before Joseph saw a flash of fear cross his young, hat-shaded face. Then the boy's expression settled into a curiously resolute one.

"Hey, boy," Abby called. "Where the hell'd you come from?"

The boy did not answer. His knuckles whitened as his grip on the cup tightened.

"Didn't you hear me, boy?" With apparent difficulty, Abby climbed to his feet and lurched toward the fireplace. The dog sat up, leaving the nearly empty bowl in its place on the floor. Her ears were perked, her wary gaze upon the approaching man.

"It's not polite to pry, Abby," Joseph said mildly. "Leave him alone."

Abby's voice turned ugly. "I'm talkin' to the boy, Beaudine."

The boy released his cup and his hands disappeared under the table.

Joseph set his cup down and pushed back on the bench. "Now you're talking to me."

The two men in the corner fell silent.

"Let it be, Abby," Orion calmly advised, not turning to look at the man standing behind him. "The boy's entitled to his privacy, just like we all are. And you don't want Joe to get upset."

Abby glared at Joseph. "There ain't nothin' wrong with insistin' that a youngun be respectful to his elders, like answerin' when spoken to and takin' his hat off." Abby's hand shot out and knocked the boy's hat from his head.

Joseph stared in astonishment as a long golden braid fell forward over the "boy's" shoulder. It took a moment for him to realize that he was observing a young woman, one who came up off the bench in a quick, graceful movement and stood in a crouched defensive position with her back against the door, a wicked-looking knife in her hand, the growling dog at her side. Her narrowed eyes darted about the room, from man to man, and her lips pressed together in a tight, determined line.

The shocked silence was broken by an evil chortle of glee from Abby Baines. "Lookee what we got here, boys. We'll have us some fun tonight after all."

Painted Davy scrambled to his feet. "Will you look at that hair," he said in awe. "I wanna touch it."

"When I'm finished with her, you can touch whatever you want to," Abby promised.

Hank Westin made it to his knees and could rise no farther. His mouth hung open as he stared at the woman with naked longing.

"No one will touch her." Joseph's hard, angry voice echoed in the small room, holding its own against another clap of thunder. He now stood beside the woman, his Hawken in his hands.

"Don't interfere, Beaudine," Abby warned. "You'll have your turn with her." His meaty hand clutched the handle of the long knife stuck through the leather belt tied around his thick waist.

Without warning, Orion shot up from his seat and knocked Abby against the wall next to the fireplace. In an instant he stood at the woman's other side, a knife in his hand as well. The dog growled again.

"You don't know us very well if you think a Beaudine would stand by and allow you to abuse this woman," Orion said almost conversationally.

"Either that or you're stupid," Joseph added. As he watched, Abby's face flushed with rage. For some reason, he could not stop himself from baiting the frontiersman. A part of him hoped Abby would make a move, give him grounds to use his rifle. That the bastard could even conceive of doing to a woman what he obviously planned to do was enough to send the blood roaring through Joseph's veins in a flood of fury. "As long as she's here, the woman will be safe." He stared at Abby, then at Painted Davy, then at Hank, who fell back to the floor. "My brother and I will see to it."

The room settled into a tense silence, broken only by the sound of the fire inside, and that of the storm outside. Finally, Painted Davy spoke.

"C'mon, Abby." He crumpled to a sitting position next to Hank. "I ain't tanglin' with the Beaudines, 'specially when they're sober and we ain't. No woman is worth dyin' over, not even one with hair like that." He wrestled the jug away from Hank and took a swig.

"You're just like your pa was," Abby growled at Joseph, nursing the elbow that had hit the wall. "Always stickin' your nose in where it don't belong. Was me who discovered she was a woman—should be just between me and her."

"I'm like my father in many ways," Joseph agreed. "He would have felt that the match between you and the woman was somewhat uneven, just like I and my brother do."

"Gawddammit, I'll get you for this, Beaudine. Both you and your brother."

Joseph narrowed his eyes, struggling to control himself. "Anytime, Abby."

"Anytime," Orion echoed, his voice carrying a threat of its own.

With one last murderous glare, Abby lumbered to the corner and joined his companions.

The woman sagged back against the door. "Thank you," she whispered.

"You're welcome." Joseph rested the butt of the Hawken on the dirt floor next to his moccasined foot. "What's your name?"

She hesitated before she, with obvious reluctance, answered. "Annie Rose." Her gaze darted up at him, then away, and she knelt to put an arm around her dog, murmuring words of praise to the animal.

Joseph knew of no family in the territory named Rose, and they were too far south of the Oregon Trail for her to have wandered off from an emigrant train, even if any would have been so foolish as to be traveling through this late in the year. Apparently her name was not familiar to Orion, either, for he shook his head. Joseph crouched down next to Annie Rose. "Where did you come from?" he asked in a quiet tone. "How do you know the Sages?"

"I've known them for a long time," she finally answered. "Sweet Water had some medicinal herbs for me; I just came by to get them."

Joseph glanced up at the small cloth-wrapped bundle that rested on the stone fireplace mantel. He had found the bundle on the table and moved it when he and Orion first arrived.

"Do you live around here?" he persisted.

Annie Rose rested her head against the dog, not looking at him.

"You're prying, big brother," Orion gently chided.

Joseph bit down on his next question. Orion was right. Another unspoken but well understood rule on the frontier was to respect each person's privacy about their past. One had the chance to start over out here, to leave the past and all it contained back East. Most considered it the height of rudeness to press someone with questions they obviously had no desire to answer. He was guilty of the same thing he had called Abby on. Usually he was not so unmannerly, but he had been unable to stop himself from questioning the woman. He found her fascinating.

"My apologies, miss." He stared at Annie Rose, his eyes roaming over her golden hair. She nodded her acceptance of his apology, then raised her head and looked at him. Joseph's breath caught in his throat. Her eyes, touched with shadows of fatigue, were green, protected by long, surprisingly dark lashes, over which hovered delicately arched dark eyebrows. And even in the firelight, he could tell that her skin was pale and clear. Miss Annie Rose—if she was a miss and not a missus—was lovely. Joseph fought an absurd desire to touch her cheek, to see if it was as soft as it looked.

Who could she be?

"No harm will come to you tonight, Miss Rose." Joseph noticed that she did not correct the "miss" and for some reason was glad. "You take the lower bed," he continued. "My brother will take the upper one, and I'll sleep on the floor next to you. Between us and your dog, you will pass the night with no interference from that bunch in the corner."

"And if I have no wish to pass the night here?"

Her quietly spoken words startled him. "You can't go out in the storm," he protested. "I don't know where you've come from, but I do know that there is nothing out there for miles around."

"So you intend to keep me here against my will?"

Joseph shared an uncomfortable glance with Orion. "No, miss, we won't keep you here. But the weather is bad, and both you and your dog are weary. If you choose to stay, my brother and I will keep you safe."

She looked at him for a long, thoughtful moment, then up at Orion. She sighed, and her shoulders sagged. "I believe you, Mr. Beaudine. I'm sure Maggie has no desire to travel in the storm, and neither do I. We thank you for your protection."

"Good." Joseph straightened. "The packet you seek may be that on the mantel. It was on the table when we arrived."

Annie Rose nodded and straightened also.

"You didn't eat much," Orion commented. "Would you like more stew?"

"No, thank you. I'll finish my coffee, then turn in." Annie Rose picked up the bowl and held it out to her dog, who obligingly licked the bowl clean. "Is there water?" she asked.

Orion pointed to a cloth-covered bucket near the hearth. She dipped some liquid into the bowl and set it down for her dog, then wearily sank on to the bench and reached for her cup. Joseph could tell from the closed look on her face that she would not welcome any more questions. He bit down on his lip, wondering why he was finding it so difficult to honor her desire to be left alone. Usually, it was much easier for him to mind his manners. Shaking his head in self-disgust, he reached for his bedroll and loosened the ties.

"Orion and I have enough blankets to share, Miss Rose, unless you have a roll in the barn."

Annie Rose shook her head. "I came unprepared, I'm afraid."

Her mouth twisted in what Joseph interpreted as a grimace of self-reproach, much like he had just felt himself. He spread a large wool blanket on the lower bunk, then shook out a buffalo robe and laid it on the ground near the bed. After Annie Rose and Orion drained their cups, they came over to the stacked beds. Orion snapped open his roll and tossed Joseph a blanket, spread out another on the top bed, and clambered up. Annie Rose stepped around Joseph's buffalo robe, sat on the edge of the lower bed, and removed her boots before she crawled between the two halves of the blanket. She shrugged out of her coat and bunched it up to use as a pillow, then laid back, pulling her long, thick braid forward so that it lay across her chest. The dog looked at her expectantly, and she patted the bed. Maggie jumped up on the bed near her feet and curled into a tight ball against her legs, sighing with pleasure.

Joseph banked the fire, then grabbed his rifle and laid it on the robe. He glanced at the three men in the corner. Hank Westin was slumped against the wall, snoring softly; he would offer no threat to Miss Rose tonight. Painted Davy swilled from the jug one last time before Abby, with a curse, jerked the jug away. Painted Davy seemed to take no offense. He pulled a mangy-looking buffalo robe around his shoulders and curled up on the floor. Within seconds, his snores joined Hank's.

Abby drank long from the jug, then, not taking his furious gaze from Joseph, wiped the back of his hand across his mouth. Drops of liquor glistened in his matted beard. After a moment, he stumbled toward the neatly made double bed that rested invitingly in another corner.

"Don't touch the bed," Joseph warned.

Abby's face flushed red. "Don't push me no more, Beaudine. I'm warnin' you."

"Sweet Water doesn't like anyone else sleeping in her bed, Abby. You know that." Joseph refrained from adding that unbathed men wearing filthy clothes especially bothered the tidy Cheyenne woman.

The big frontiersman swayed drunkenly, hatred and impotent fury flashing from his red-rimmed, puffy eyes. He belched, then growled, "I'll send you to hell one day, you preachy bastard."

"I doubt it," Joseph said dryly. He crossed his arms over his chest and watched as Abby lurched back to his corner. After another string of muttered curses and a well-aimed kick at Painted Davy's robe-covered backside, Abby slid down the wall to a sitting position, cradling the jug against his chest. His malevolent, unblinking glare returned to Joseph and stayed there.

Deciding to leave the candle lit as a precaution, Joseph dropped to the buffalo robe and pulled Orion's blanket over himself as he laid down. His fingers closed on his rifle and he drew it closer. He also checked for the knife that nestled along his right calf inside his knee-high moccasin. It was fortunate the three frontiersmen were drunk. When they were sober, Joseph suspected that both Abby Baines and Hank Westin could hold their own against just about anyone, including him and his brothers. Tonight, thankfully, there would be no contest if Baines made a move toward Miss Rose. The man was hard-pressed to simply hold his head up.

Annie Rose's soft voice came from the shadows of the lower bed. "Good night, brothers. Again, my thanks to you."

"Good night," Orion murmured as he leaned over the edge of his bed, his long dark hair falling forward over his shoulders. He nodded at Joseph, but said nothing further.

Joseph nodded in return, knowing that neither he nor his

brother would sleep deeply that night. "Rest well, Miss Rose," he said in a low tone.

The room settled into an uncomfortable silence, broken only by the continuing storm and the snores of the two sleeping men in the corner. Joseph glanced up at the bed where Annie Rose rested, his mind burning with questions. Who was she? Where had she come from? She couldn't have come from too far away, for she had no horse, carried no gear or supplies, and yet neither she nor the dog was dirty, ragged, or starving. But Joseph knew the area for miles in any direction, and he knew it well. There were no homesteads out here, Fort Laramie was a two-day ride to the east, and the Oregon Trail snaked westward far to the north. It was as if she had dropped from the sky.

Then the thought struck him. She knew the Sages, so it would follow that they knew her. If, when morning came, the pretty Miss Annie Rose was no more willing to offer information about herself than she had been tonight, he would ask Jubal Sage. The cagey and wise frontiersman knew something about Annie Rose, of that Joseph was certain. He frowned. Would Jubal be willing to talk about a woman who was so determined to keep her secrets to herself? Joseph silently answered his own question: not if Annie Rose had spoken to Jubal in confidence. Wild horses wouldn't be able to drag a word from the man's mouth under those circumstances. And, Joseph grudgingly admitted, he wouldn't want Jubal to betray a confidence, even to him. He sighed. Perhaps the morning would bring some answers from Annie Rose herself.

He looked back at the three men in the corner. In the dim light, he could see—and hear—that Hank Westin and Painted Davy Sikes slumbered on. Abby Baines, however, still sat up, still stared resentfully at Joseph, his eyes glowing like those of some evil creature of the night. But it was obvious that the big man's lids were lowering, albeit slowly. No doubt his snores would soon echo in the small room along with the others.

Just the same, it would be a long night.

Two

How could she have been so foolish?

Annie Rose Jensen silently berated herself. No, not foolish. Her actions tonight bordered on the stupid. Driven by the threatening storm, eager to see her friends, she had pounded on the door of Jubal Sage's cabin without thought, never considering that the smoke rising from the stone chimney might belong to someone else's fire. Before approaching the cabin, she had not even bothered to check the stable, which no doubt held several more horses than those the Sages owned. Now, thanks to her own carelessness, her secret was threatened, and perhaps her family as well.

A shiver ran through her, and she pulled Joseph Beaudine's wool blanket up around her shoulders with one hand, still clasping the handle of her large hunting knife in the other.

Abelard Baines. Hank Westin. Both men she had seen from afar over the years, watching them warily from the safety of the forest as they traded with her grandfather, Knute, for horses. Both were men her grandfather did not trust, especially Baines. Knute Jensen had warned his granddaughter that Baines was lecherous and cruel, if not downright evil. Hank Westin wasn't as bad as Baines, but he was wily and conniving when he wasn't drunk, which, rumor had it, wasn't often. And although she had never seen Painted Davy Sikes, Annie Rose was certain he was the third of the motley bunch in the corner. His distinctive description as well as his unsavory reputation had long preceded him.

Had those three men been here alone when she foolishly rushed up to the door, she could have been in very serious trouble. Another shiver raced down her body.

Thank God for the Beaudine brothers.

She had not met Joseph and the Hunter before, but she had heard of them, and she knew their brother, Grey Eagle. Over the last few years, the tall, handsome Cheyenne warrior had purchased several horses from her grandfather. Since her name—as much of it as she had offered—was evidently not familiar to either Joseph or Orion Beaudine, Grey Eagle had kept his vow of silence regarding her presence in the secluded valley where she and her little family made their home. But then, Grey Eagle was a Beaudine, and the Beaudine brothers were famous on the frontier for their honor, and their courage. And their beauty.

Rightly famous.

Annie Rose had always found Grey Eagle to be a strikingly handsome man, and Orion Beaudine bore a great resemblance to the proud Cheyenne warrior. To any who looked, it was clear the two men were brothers, although she knew they were born of different mothers. Both were tall and lean, well-proportioned and strong; both had long dark hair and unusual green eyes. While Joseph was obviously a Beaudine—born of Orion's mother, she knew—his appearance differed from that of his brothers in a few subtle ways. He was as tall as they, and as powerfully built. He moved with the same grace that came from growing up with the wild land, although his proud stance still carried traces of his military background. His hair was long and dark, also, but more brown than black, his eyes a rich warm brown, and his upper lip sported a thick, neatly trimmed mustache. The few days' growth of dark beard covering his cheeks and chin did not detract from the strong line of his jaw. All in all, the package that made up Joseph Beaudine was very nice; very nice, indeed.

Annie Rose could not resist glancing down at where he rested next to the bed. In the flickering light of the candle, she could see that his eyes were still open, that he intently watched the shadowy, malevolent figure of Abby Baines. Then, as if he felt her gaze on him, Joseph turned his head and looked right at her.

Her breath caught in her throat. It seemed as if a powerful current passed between them, a strange, silent arc of awareness that caused Annie Rose's heart to jump with something suspiciously akin to pleasure. She tore her gaze from the mesmerizing eyes of Joseph Beaudine and faced the wall, clasping the sheathed knife more closely to her chest.

If Joseph Beaudine was making her heart jump, then her defenses were down, and she had to be more tired than she knew. Painful lessons had long ago taught her that a handsome man was nothing but trouble, and she already had enough trouble, with no one but herself to blame.

Through her own foolishness, she had exposed the fact of her existence to five men—two of whom could be trusted, three who could not. Not only could the three not be trusted, but they were roaming *her* mountains in search of the Golden Mare. Judging by what Abby Baines had said, Annie Rose had no doubt that the unscrupulous frontiersman would go to any lengths in order to find the legendary horse. She had endangered her grandfather, her brother, her cousin, and of course, Aurora. A wave of regret and guilt washed over her, so strong that it caused an actual physical pain in her chest and forced a small moan from her lips.

How could she have been so stupid?

Was her mistake serious enough to threaten all of her grandfather's planning and hard work—work that had kept her and her younger brother Thomas safe for so many years?

Restlessly, Annie Rose rolled over and pressed her back against the wall, gripping the knife with new determination. If any man tried to touch her this night, he would pay with his flesh. And come first light, she would slip away, as her grandfather had taught her. Like a drifting early morning mist, she would travel the forest on silent feet, leaving no trail of her passing. The secret of her existence had been exposed to five men, but the truth of who she was would remain hidden, at least for a while longer.

Determined to rest, she closed her eyes, for she would need her strength tomorrow. The certainty that she could trust Joseph and Orion Beaudine to keep her safe was of comfort to her, as was Maggie's solid warmth against her legs. The late summer storm blustered and raged around the snug cabin, the snoring of Abelard Baines joined that of his co-horts at last, and gradually, Annie Rose drifted off to sleep.

Several hours later, she awakened instantly and froze for a moment, gauging her surroundings. Maggie still lay next to her, head and ears up now, alert and watchful. The storm had evidently passed, for all she could hear was the discordant sounds of loud snores issuing from the corner. Suddenly, a pair of long legs encased in fringed leggings dangled down from the upper bed, and Orion Beaudine landed silently on the floor. He flashed her a quick, reassuring smile, then left the cabin without a sound. Annie Rose pushed up on one elbow, just as Joseph straightened from his previously hidden position between the table and the hearth. The sound of crackling flames reached her ears as the dark room lightened a bit. Joseph placed a finger over his lips and pointed toward the door. Annie Rose nodded and, moving as silently as the Beaudine brothers did, gathered her belongings—including the packet left by Sweet Water—and she and Maggie slipped out of the cabin, followed closely by Joseph. In the dim, early morning light, they joined Orion near the stable.

Annie Rose circled her long braid around her head and pulled her oversized hat down over the untidy mass of hair. What she wouldn't give for a basin of warm clean water and a brush! She looked from Orion to Joseph and, finding the gleam of obvious interest in Joseph's brown eyes too intense to deal with on an empty stomach, back to Orion. "Thank you both for your assistance," she said, speaking softly although there was little chance the three slumbering men inside would hear her.

Orion shrugged. "We didn't do anything."

"Yes, you did." Annie Rose met his gaze squarely. "You know what Baines had in mind for me. I would have fought, but I may not have been able to get away from him, from them. I am in your debt."

"You can cancel that debt."

Joseph's voice was warm and low, a voice as enticing as the man. Disconcerted that he would expect payment so soon, nervous about what he would want as payment, Annie Rose reluctantly looked at him, raising her eyebrows in question. "And how is that, Mr. Beaudine?"

"Tell us who you are, where you came from, where you are going."

"Joe . . ." Orion warned.

Annie Rose glanced at him, then back at Joseph. "It's all right. He can ask as often as he wants, but I won't answer." She met Joseph's gaze steadily, steeling herself against the disappointment she saw in his eyes, and softened her tone. "I *can't* tell you. I'm sworn to secrecy. My foolish actions of last night may have already endangered people I love." *And one special horse,* she added silently.

Joseph frowned. "What foolish actions? Seeking shelter from the storm?"

"Not checking the stable first." She flung an arm out in the direction of the small structure. "Had I simply looked, I would have known that Jubal and Sweet Water were not here, that others were." The whinny of a horse issued from within the stable, a whinny that sounded naggingly familiar to Annie Rose. She pushed away the thought. "I didn't think, and now others may suffer for it."

"I don't understand."

"I'm sure you don't." The horse whinnied again, calling to her. Annie Rose glanced toward the stable. "I know that horse," she whispered. She did not miss the puzzled look shared by Joseph and Orion, and chose to ignore it. Without another word, she crossed the yard to the stable and slipped inside, leaving the door wide for the little light the morning offered. The horse in the first of the ungated stalls nickered a warm welcome.

"Thunder." A rush of joy spread through her, giving Annie Rose a brief respite from the clutches of her tormented guilt. "Oh, Thunder. How are you, sweetheart?" She approached the animal, holding her hand out, and when she had closed the distance between them, put her arms around his neck, breathing deeply of his clean, horsey scent.

Joseph followed Annie Rose into the stable, with Orion on his heels. Both men stopped and stared at the sight of the slender woman embracing Orion's large stallion. The loving warmth in her whispered words to the animal sent Joseph's blood racing, and for a brief, insane moment, he fantasized that she was talking to him.

"Do you believe that?"

Orion's low words snapped Joseph from his reverie. "No," he replied, just as quietly. "Thunder doesn't let anyone but you get that cozy with him." As he watched, the stallion nuzzled Annie Rose, knocking her hat off and releasing the length of golden braid. Even in the dim light, her hair seemed to glow, laying as it did against the dark, ridiculously over-sized coat she wore. The soft sound of her delighted laughter warmed Joseph to the soles of his feet and caused his stomach to tighten in a strangely exciting way. Then he caught himself and shook his head in irritation. Surely his stomach was just telling him that he was hungry.

"How do you know my horse, Miss Rose?" Orion asked.

To Annie Rose, his voice seemed to come from far away, so in tune with the horse she was, so joined was the beating of her heart with that of the great stallion. Without thinking, she replied, "I raised him." Then she realized what she had said. Her heart slammed against her ribs, and she closed her eyes in anguish as she rested her forehead against Thunder's neck. *Why had she said that?* Such a remark would not be lost on the Beaudine brothers. She had carelessly given them another clue to her identity.

"How could you have raised him?" Joseph asked incredulously.

"My brother, Grey Eagle, gave him to me as a gift over a year ago," Orion added, sounding as surprised and confused as Joseph did.

She did not respond. Her arms tightened around the horse for a moment, then she pressed her lips to his neck. "Goodbye, sweetheart," she whispered. If she didn't leave at once, she might as well lead the brothers to her grandfather's house, for the way she was going, she would inadvertently give them enough information to find it themselves. She reluctantly stepped away from Thunder. "I must go." She snatched her hat from the hay-covered dirt floor and pushed past Joseph and Orion. To her surprise and dismay, Thunder trailed after her. Orion made no effort to detain his horse.

Annie Rose came to a stop in the yard and turned. Both Joseph and Orion had followed them from the stable and now stared at her in amazement. Thunder halted next to her and nuzzled her shoulder. "He'll follow me," she warned.

"I can see that," Orion said. "What I don't understand is why."

She hesitated, wondering how much she should say, knowing that whatever she said would tell them too much. "I can't explain it," she finally admitted. "We have a connection." Annie Rose could not resist rubbing her cheek against Thunder's velvety nose.

"Obviously," Joseph muttered.

In the growing light, Annie Rose looked Thunder over, pleased by his shining coat and evident good health. Then she frowned. "How did he come by this?" she asked, running her fingers lightly over a long, narrow scar marking the horse's left hindquarter.

"He and I were ambushed last fall," Orion explained. "A bullet or an arrow skimmed his rump." He slapped the horse affectionately. "He got off easy."

"What do you mean?"

"Orion caught two arrows," Joseph interjected.

Annie Rose looked at Orion. "Who would attack you? Why?"

"We never found out for sure, but we think it was part of a group of renegades bent on starting an Indian war." Orion shrugged. "It's long over now. The leaders were killed late last year."

"Bartholomew Cutler and Lieutenant Roger Fielding," Annie Rose murmured.

"How did you know that?" Joseph demanded.

Not liking the tone of his voice, Annie Rose turned to face him. "I know a lot of things, Mr. Beaudine. Just as I know it is time for me to leave." She turned away from him and quietly called out, "Maggie." A moment later, the black dog trotted from behind the cabin. Annie Rose looked from Orion to Joseph. "Once again, thank you both for your assistance last night," she said formally. "I'll trouble you no longer." She scratched Thunder's forehead one last time. "Don't let him follow me," she cautioned.

"Where are you going?" Joseph asked. "Surely you don't intend to walk out of here."

"That is exactly what I intend to do, Mr. Beaudine," Annie Rose said firmly.

"You've had nothing to eat," Orion pointed out.

"Both my dog and I will be fine." She glanced toward the cabin. "Watch your backs with them, especially Baines. No doubt he'll awaken with an aching head and a foul frame of mind."

"Miss Rose, allow us to escort you to wherever you are going." Joseph glanced at Orion. "Or let me," he amended. "My brother's wife is soon to be delivered of their first child, and he is most anxious to return to Fort Laramie. I've no pressing business, though. I would be happy to see you safely to your destination."

"I appreciate your kind offer, Mr. Beaudine, but there is no need." Annie Rose looked at Orion. "I've heard of your coming child. Congratulations. I will pray that both your wife and child come through the delivery safely." She thought briefly of another babe soon to be born—one with four legs—and was more anxious than ever to be on her way. The need to again check on Aurora was strong, and she would do so on her journey home.

"Thank you, Miss Rose." Orion's dark brows drew together in puzzlement. "Do you know Sarah?"

"I've heard of her, as I have heard of your entire family. Now, I really must go." She touched Thunder's nose in a last caress, then pulled her hat on again. "Farewell, brothers." She started toward the forest at the edge of the yard. Maggie trotted at her side.

"Miss Rose, you can't just walk out of here. We are miles from anywhere."

Annie Rose steeled herself against the concern she heard in Joseph Beaudine's voice and kept walking. "The miles are quickly covered, Mr. Beaudine, if one knows where one is going," she called over her shoulder. "There is no need to trouble yourself over me."

"Then think of the men in the cabin," Joseph argued. "All are experienced woodsmen who will have no difficulty tracking you. You'll have no chance if they catch you in the open. I'll not allow you to leave alone and on foot."

By the sound of his voice, Annie Rose could tell Joseph was coming after her. Angry now, she spun around to face him. "As I asked you last night, Mr. Beaudine, do you intend to keep me against my will?" Over Joseph's shoulder, she could see that Orion still stood next to Thunder, one hand resting on the horse's neck.

Joseph halted a few feet from her. "This time I will, if I have to. Those men are dangerous. You know what they'll do to you if they catch you."

"I assure you, sir, that I can take care of myself in the wilderness. Not only do they have no chance of catching me, but neither will they be able to track me." Annie Rose lifted her chin. "Nor will you."

After a moment's hesitation, Joseph spoke, his angry brown eyes a sharp contrast to his deceptively soft tone. "Is that a challenge, Miss Rose?"

Annie Rose hesitated a moment as well, plagued by sudden doubt. The Beaudines were famous for their wilderness skills, especially Orion. He was known as the Hunter for good reason. "It is a statement of fact," she finally said. "I was well taught."

"As were we."

"There is no challenge, Mr. Beaudine. I ask you to leave me in peace. While I appreciate your concern for me, it is misplaced." She met Joseph's burning gaze, feeling the heat of his anger, the stirring of his interest. His interest bothered her more than his anger did. Praying that she had not inadvertently thrown down the gauntlet, Annie Rose turned and darted into the woods.

She heard Joseph's startled exclamation, heard Thunder's whinny of farewell, heard Orion's calming voice. Conscious thought shut down and instinct took over. She felt as if she were flying through the dear, familiar forest as she ran. The sounds of pursuit faded. Whether Joseph Beaudine had lost her trail or merely honored her wish to be left alone, she did not know. On she ran, with Maggie easily keeping pace with her as she scurried over boulders that left no trail, doubled back through a shallow stream, scaled a steep incline covered with loose shale, trotted along game trails hidden under layers of dead pine needles. On she ran, toward her beloved home—the safety of which she may have compromised— toward her beloved mare, who also could be in danger. The guilt rose up within her, strong and relentless, burying the tiny, irritating, betraying hope that Joseph Beaudine would follow her despite her stated wishes to the contrary.

Joseph could not believe she was gone. She had darted into the forest as would a skittish deer, and had disappeared just as quickly. He had taken no more than a few steps when

Orion's voice called him back, when Annie Rose's request that he leave her be echoed in his mind, when he realized that the fleeing forms of the woman and her dog could no longer be seen. He listened closely, but could hear no sound of her.

Like a wraith, she had vanished.

The longing to follow her was so powerful that it affected Joseph physically—his stomach knotted, his hands clenched in frustration, and his weight shifted from one foot to the other, as if he were preparing for a foot race. Surely he would be able to track her.

"Let her go, big brother," Orion said quietly.

Orion's words calmed his frenzy. With a sigh, Joseph turned and retraced his steps to his brother's side. "Who is she, Orion?"

"I don't know, and she doesn't want us to know. She has the right to be left alone."

"But she's not alone. She spoke of putting others in danger." Joseph stroked his mustache. "She knows Baines for certain, because she warned us about him by his last name when we'd only addressed him as Abby. Maybe she knows Westin and Sikes, too. Yet they don't know her. How can that be? Surely they would have remembered meeting a white woman, if for no other reason than her incredible hair." He paused, deep in thought. "She knew the story of Cutler and Fielding. And, strangest of all, she knows Thunder, and obviously knows him well." He ran a hand over the horse's side. "She's been in this territory for a while."

"It's a mystery," Orion agreed. "One I suggest you leave alone."

"I don't know if I can."

"You don't have the right to pry."

Annoyed, Joseph glared at his brother. "Aren't you the least little bit curious?"

"About a beautiful white woman who dresses like a man and claims to have raised my horse? A woman who runs like a deer, who is obviously at home in the wilderness, who in all likelihood was not exaggerating when she said she couldn't be tracked? A woman we've never heard of, when we were raised out here? Of course I'm curious, Joe." Orion led Thunder back toward the stable. "But I'm sure she has good reasons for refusing to tell us more about herself, and we have to respect that." He waved toward the forest. "She's gone, and I'm certain she'll be fine." He jerked his head toward the cabin. "However, those troublemakers aren't gone yet, and I don't want to leave Jubal's cabin to their tender care."

"No, neither do I, especially since Baines is so angry with me. We'll escort them for a few miles—far enough to make certain they won't find the woman. I'll go rouse them." He looked up at the clear sky, then at Orion. "I know you're anxious to get back to the fort; it should be an easy ride today."

"Are you going with me?"

Knowing that Orion was really asking him if he intended to try to track Miss Annie Rose through the wilderness, knowing that Orion was right in saying her wishes for privacy should be respected, Joseph nodded, his heart strangely heavy with disappointment. "I'm going with you, little brother."

Three

Abby Baines, Hank Westin, and Painted Davy Sikes were not happy about being awakened at what they considered an ungodly hour, nor did they appreciate being forced to leave the comfort of Jubal Sage's cabin. But none had been in condition to press the issue with the very sober and very impatient Beaudine brothers, so, after a great deal of complaining and, on the part of Baines, outright threats, the three rode off. Joseph and Orion followed them for a few miles, then turned northeast in the direction of Fort Laramie.

The trip so far had been a mostly silent one. Aware that Orion's lack of interest in conversation stemmed from his worry about his wife, Joseph had been content with his own thoughts—all of which seemed to revolve around Miss Annie Rose. He hoped he could remember enough of her features to capture her likeness on paper.

Orion was correct in his insistence that Miss Rose, whoever and wherever she was, be left in peace, but Joseph still intended to do some discreet investigating. He was particularly eager to speak with Jubal Sage, and fervently hoped the mountain man could be found at the fort.

The astonishing possibility that a beautiful white woman lived somewhere in the territory—and had perhaps for years, her presence unknown within the surprisingly intimate group of those who made their home within an area covering several hundred square miles—intrigued him. So did the strange and wonderful communication she shared with Orion's stallion. Joseph recognized that connection for the unusual and profound one it was, for he felt it himself with some horses. As with his own mare, Grace, it was almost as if he could hear them thinking, not that horses thought in English. He simply understood them on a very deep level, one where words were not necessary.

So did Annie Rose.

In his heart, he knew it.

He had to find her again.

Somehow, some way, he would. Joseph Beaudine had no doubt of that.

"Where the hell have you been?"

The angry words greeted Annie Rose when she opened the door of her grandfather's snug cabin. Her cousin Erik, at twenty, was two years her junior, but he often acted as if he were her guardian. Even now, he stood across the room from her, his hands on his hips, his rage evident and inappropriate. Somewhere along the line, in the past several months, he had stopped treating her with easy brotherly affection and had become strangely hostile and proprietary. Not even her grandfather would have spoken to her in such a manner.

Annie Rose straightened her shoulders and fought down the irritation that would come through in her own voice. She had no wish for another argument. The disagreement with Joseph Beaudine early that morning would last her for a while.

"At Mr. Sage's cabin," she replied calmly as she took off the disreputable hat. "I needed to pick up some herbs Sweet Water prepared for me, and because of the storm, I decided to stay the night."

"What kind of herbs?"

Annie Rose frowned. "For the colic, if you must know."

"None of the horses has been troubled with colic."

Except Aurora, Annie Rose thought, but she couldn't mention that horse to her cousin. "It's always good to have some on hand. One never knows when it will be needed." Her gaze searched the neat cabin. "Where is Gramps?"

"He decided those five horses we've been working with were ready to go, so he and Tom took them to the fort. They left right after you did yesterday, and won't be back until tomorrow, or maybe the next day. If that wild herd is still near the lake, they plan to round up a few more horses on the way back."

Hurt-tinged surprise and genuine disappointment flooded through Annie Rose with astonishing force—hurt mingled with surprise that her grandfather would make such a decision about the horses without consulting her, disappointment that he and Thomas were away from home, and for so long. She missed her twelve-year-old brother, and was anxious to talk with her grandfather, to tell him what had happened the night before. He would know what to do, what steps to take in order to protect them all.

"You didn't tell anyone where you were going," accused Erik.

Annie Rose forced her attention back to her cousin, and could not help but notice that Erik's face was almost as red as his thick hair and full beard. Why on earth was he so upset? For the last several years, she had occasionally stayed out alone in the wilderness overnight, sometimes for two or three nights. They all did, even Thomas, for Gramps had taught them well. Erik knew she could take care of herself.

At the thought, a new wave of guilt washed over her as Annie Rose remembered that she hadn't done a very good job of caring for herself—or her family—last night. "I told Gramps," she said defensively. She moved farther into the room and set her hat on the cloth-covered table.

"You can't be going off like this, Annabella, not any more. It isn't safe. These mountains are beginning to crawl with people, thanks to that damned gold rush to California."

Annie Rose grimaced as she unbuttoned the oversized coat. She hated being called Annabella, just as Thomas hated being called Tom, and Erik knew it. However, in his present angry state, she let it pass. "There's no need to curse. You wouldn't talk like that if Gramps were here."

"Don't change the subject." Erik stepped closer, until he stood directly in front of her.

He wasn't much taller than she, but he was stocky and strong. Annie Rose did not like what she read in her cousin's pale blue eyes. Behind the anger, she saw his longing. She did not step back in time to avoid the thick hand that reached out to touch her braid.

"You've grown too beautiful," he said huskily. "It isn't safe for you to be away from home. Here, we can protect you, just as we have all these years."

"Don't, Erik," Annie Rose warned as she pulled away from him. She snatched the hat off the table and marched over to the row of nails that protruded from the wall behind the door. Her coat joined the hat on a nail a moment later. "I've told you before that it's not your place to tell me what to do, or where I can and cannot go. I am a woman grown, and capable of making my own decisions. Not even Gramps orders me about, not any longer." She turned and looked at him, ignoring the furious rush of color returning to his face. "I'll not take orders from you."

Erik stepped forward, his hand raised, and, for one stunned moment, Annie Rose thought he was actually going to hit her. Maggie came to her side and growled at Erik, something the dog had never done before. With visible effort, he caught himself, and instead wagged a finger in her face. "One day you will, cousin," he vowed, his tone as ugly as his mottled features. "One day you will." He kicked in the direction of the dog—who nimbly dodged his big, booted foot—and stomped out the door.

A chill of foreboding ran through her, and, with a shaking hand, Annie Rose pushed the door closed, fighting the impulse to lift the heavy bar into its brackets. What was she going to do about Erik? She recognized the look in his eyes for what it was: he looked at her the way a man looked at a woman he desired. She could not suppress a shudder. Over the past six months, she had brushed off his clumsy attempts at flirtation with amused tolerance, thinking his infatuation would burn out. However, it had not died a natural death, but rather had mutated into something possessive and ugly.

Annie Rose was no longer comfortable being left alone with Erik.

How could she explain that to her grandfather? With a weary sigh, she moved to the hearth, where she hooked the handle of the heavy iron kettle on the ingenious hinged iron arm her grandfather had rigged up. She swung the kettle over the flames, feeling anxious and almost desperate. Not only did she need to talk to Gramps about Erik, but she had to confess her folly of the night before. How strange that she could view the return of her beloved grandfather with both welcome and trepidation.

By early afternoon, the Beaudine brothers found themselves at a good-sized lake—known as Wild Horse Lake—that was no more than six hours from Fort Laramie. The lake was remarkable both for the freshness of its trapped water and for the herd of perhaps thirty wild horses that often grazed on the lush grass of a wide meadow on the far side. Although Orion was reluctant to delay their trip, Thunder and Grace needed to rest. The two men decided to stop for a short while to water their horses and eat.

Thunder let out a whinny, and, as one, the herd raised their heads. A large paint stallion pranced to the forefront, his long tail waving back and forth, his ears up, his stance challenging. He let out a warning cry.

"Would you look at him," Joseph breathed.

"He's beautiful," Orion commented as he climbed down from the saddle. "Has to be The Paint."

"You know it." This was the first time Joseph had seen the wild stallion he had heard of for years. The Paint enjoyed a legendary status among the frontiersmen and Indians in the territory. A clever and fearless guardian of his herd, he possessed a free and noble spirit that made men ache to own him. Each of the several attempts made to capture him—by both red men and white—had ended with someone other than The Paint being injured. Most men now left the stallion in peace, at least most wise men.

"Do you think he minds us being so close?" Orion asked. "I don't want to run the herd off."

Joseph squinted against the glare of sunlight on the water. "The Paint'll keep an eye on us, but I think it'll be all right."

A short time later, Thunder and Grace were hobbled nearby, grazing on the thick grass that surrounded the lake. Orion built a small fire, over which Joseph placed a battered coffeepot.

"It's good we're heading back, for more reasons than the coming babe," Joseph commented. "Supplies are getting low."

"We were gone longer than anticipated," said Orion. "I hope Colonel MacKay is satisfied with the report we're bringing back."

"He should be." Joseph hunkered down near the fire. "He suspected there was no easy way to cut time or miles off the route to Fort Bridger, and we merely verified that. Following the Platte is still the best way to go, as difficult as that is."

"Hello the camp!"

In one smooth action, Joseph slid his Hawken from its beaded leather scabbard and turned in a crouched position. His gaze darted about the area as a detached calm settled over him.

"Over there," Orion said quietly from his position near their horses. He also held a rifle. "In that stand of cottonwoods at the western end of the lake."

Joseph rose, his Hawken at the ready, his stance relaxed yet prepared. Two riders emerged from the shadows of the trees and closed the distance between them. Both were dressed in buckskin, both wore wide-brimmed hats, both cradled rifles in their arms. There the similarities ended. One was a skinny, strapping lad of perhaps twelve or thirteen, his age belied by the confident way he rode and by the wariness in his expression. The other sported a white mustache and long white hair that moved in the afternoon breeze, his tall body hunched over the saddle like an eagle prepared to launch into flight.

"Greetings," said the elder as he drew his horse to a halt. His sharp blue eyes perused Orion, then Joseph. "You'd be two of the Beaudine brothers, if I'm not mistaken."

His voice carried a curious lilting accent, the like of which Joseph had not heard before. He exchanged a questioning glance with Orion, then asked, "Do we know you, sir?"

"Might know *of* me, son, same as I know of you, through Grey Eagle. You"—he nodded at Orion—"bear a powerful resemblance to your Cheyenne brother. You must be the Hunter."

"I am." Orion waved a hand in Joseph's direction. "This is Joseph, the oldest of the clan."

The old man crossed his arms on the saddle horn and leaned forward. "Pleased to meet you both. I knew your pa well, long ago, before any of you boys were born. I'm Knute Jensen, known by some as the Norseman." He pronounced his last name as *Yensen*. "This here is my grandson, Thomas."

The boy nodded at each of the Beaudines in turn. "Glad to know you," he said in a voice that quivered on the edge of manhood.

The Norseman. Joseph had indeed heard of him, in fact had intended to search for him when his scouting expedition was finished. Knute Jensen was known by a few names—the Norseman, the Horseman, and, for the last several years, the Crazy Viking. Rumor had it that something terrible had happened to the man in his youth, something so terrible that it eventually took his mind, and he now lived somewhere in the wilderness with three young men thought to be his sons, or grandsons. The Indian tribes left them in peace, respectful of the old man who was "touched by the Great Spirit," and the four eked out a living through the capture, training, and selling of horses taken from the wild herds that roamed the territory.

No doubt Knute Jensen was the man reputed to have a special way with horses, the man from whom Grey Eagle had purchased Thunder as a gift for Orion more than a year ago.

Yet, Annie Rose had claimed to have raised the stallion, and there was no question that the horse knew the woman.

Joseph looked at Knute with renewed interest, then at the boy. His eyes narrowed. Was it his imagination, or did Thomas resemble Miss Rose?

"I have heard of you, Mr. Jensen," Joseph finally said. "Step down if you've a mind to. We're on our way to Fort Laramie, and stopped to rest the horses. Don't have much for the noon meal, but we're glad to share what we have."

"Don't mind if we do," Knute answered. He slid from the saddle. "We can contribute a bit of cheese and bread." He nodded across the lake. "We aim to get us a few of those horses." The herd had resumed its grazing, with the exception of The Paint, who stood watchful guard.

"You're going after The Paint?" Joseph asked.

"No." Knute loosened the cinch on his saddle, then hobbled his horse with a short length of rope tied to each foreleg. "He will not be captured, nor should he be. Some creatures are meant to be free." The old man shrugged. "The Paint, he is such a creature. But his herd periodically grows too large for the available forage, so we help him out and take a few off his hands every now and again." He settled in a cross-legged position near the fire and, with a nod of thanks, accepted the piece of buffalo jerky Orion offered.

"You speak of The Paint as if he were a business partner," Joseph commented as he poured a fresh cup of coffee.

"*Ja,* he is. We would not take his horses without his permission."

Joseph exchanged another glance with Orion, then handed the filled cup to Knute.

"Takk." The old man took a noisy sip and gave a satisfied sigh. "Good. Strong and good." He pinned his sharp gaze on Orion, who now sat across the fire nursing his own cup. "I hear you have a little one coming. This is good, too. The Beaudine name should go on."

Orion nodded. "Thank you."

"We met Captain Rutledge earlier this morning to drop off some horses," Thomas interjected. "He said Mrs. Beaudine is doing well."

"I'm glad to hear that." Orion heaved a sigh of relief. "I've been gone too long." He jumped to his feet and began to pace, occasionally taking a sip from his cup.

"We'll soon be on our way, little brother," Joseph assured him. But he did not want to go just yet. He still had not decided if he would ask the Norseman about a pretty blonde woman who claimed to have raised Thunder, for Orion's earlier scoldings weighed heavily on him. Then he made the mistake of glancing at the boy, and his breath caught. The light hair color, the cheekbones, the eyes—the resemblance was too strong. There had to be a connection.

"Do you know of a white woman living in these parts?" he blurted out.

Thomas sputtered a mouthful of coffee in the general direction of the fire. "Too hot," he mumbled at Joseph's questioning look. His young face was flushed red.

"Ja, there are several white women living in these parts," Knute said calmly. "Your brother's wife, for one, a few officers' wives, some laundresses. But this I think you already know, Captain Beaudine."

Joseph frowned. For being a reclusive hermit, Knute Jensen knew a lot about the Beaudine family. "I'm no longer in the military," he said.

"Ja, but you earned the rank. It can never be taken from you."

Was the old man deliberately trying to change the subject? "I'm talking of a specific woman, one named Miss Annie

Rose," Joseph explained. "Orion and I met her last night at Jubal Sage's cabin, and she claimed to have raised Thunder."

For the first time, Knute Jensen seemed taken aback. He avoided Joseph's gaze and did not answer. Thomas stared at his grandfather, his expression fearful.

The silence dragged on.

"Perhaps you're treading where you're not welcome, Joe," Orion said quietly.

"Clearly I am." Joseph fought down his irritation and disappointment. "Whatever Miss Rose's secret is, it would be safe with us, Mr. Jensen."

Now Knute looked at him. *"Ja,* of that I am certain, Captain Beaudine." He took another sip of coffee, then suddenly paused and closed his eyes. His face paled to the color of his white hair, and a small amount of coffee dribbled down his lightly whiskered chin.

"Gramps!" cried Thomas.

Knute held up a hand. "I'm all right, boy. Finish your jerky."

To Joseph, the Norseman did indeed seem to be all right. The color returned to his face, and he wiped the coffee from his chin with the back of his hand. Across the lake, The Paint whinnied, the sound easily carrying over the water.

"The Army wants more horses before winter sets in," Knute said conversationally. He glanced up at Orion, then settled his piercing gaze on Joseph, his weathered features set like stone, his expression deadly serious.

Upon first meeting the Norseman, Joseph had doubted the rumors of lunacy. He was no longer so certain. Throughout their entire conversation, Knute had jumped from subject to subject, not following any discernible train of thought, and now he sat immobile, staring at Joseph as if he had just sprouted horns.

"Mr. Jensen?" he finally ventured to say.

"Are you looking for work?" Knute barked.

Thomas choked on a piece of jerky. His grandfather calmly leaned over and slapped the boy between the shoulder blades.

It was Joseph's turn to stare. "I beg your pardon?"

"You heard me. The Army wants more horses before the snow flies, as many as we can provide. We need help." Knute glanced at Orion, who was also staring in amazement. "I do not ask you, Hunter, because a man should be with his woman when she bears his child." A strange vehemence filled his voice at the last sentence, and he jabbed a gnarled finger in Orion's direction. "You will go to the fort." The finger jerked toward Joseph. "You will come with me."

"Gramps," Thomas whispered, his eyes huge with what looked to Joseph like fear.

Why would the boy be afraid?

"Don't worry, boy. I'm not crazy." Knute cackled, a strange, eerie sound. "At least not yet!" The cackle turned into outright laughter. The loud, discordant racket set a flock of field sparrows to flight.

Orion and Joseph shared another look, this one more than a little worried. Orion slightly shook his head, offering his opinion on the matter.

Joseph wasn't so sure. Stroking his mustache, he eyed the boy thoughtfully. No doubt about it, Knute was a strange old coot. But Thomas, whom Knute had raised, seemed to be respectful, well mannered, clean, and, for someone his age, very self-assured. Knute couldn't be completely crazy, or surely his grandson would show some traits of lunacy as well.

Then there was Miss Annie Rose. Knute knew her, on that Joseph would bet his life. That alone was enough to sway him. Without examining the mysterious hold the woman had on him, he said, "I'll go with you."

Knute cackled again. His blue eyes seemed to gleam with satisfaction.

Thomas groaned, then turned to his horse, vaulted into the saddle, and rode off in the direction of the lake. Although he didn't know the boy well, Joseph suspected the display of temper was unusual.

"Don't scatter those horses, boy!" Knute yelled after him.

Thomas responded with a wave of one hand and pulled up at the shore to allow his horse to drink.

Joseph joined Orion at Thunder's side some distance away, holding the maps and notes he had made while on their scouting expedition.

"You're as crazy as that old man," Orion announced in a low voice, shaking his head as he tightened the cinch. His long dark hair blew in the rising breeze. "I know why you're going, Joe. You've been bewitched by a golden-haired woman in baggy clothes, and you hope he'll lead you to her." He looked at Joseph, his concern obvious. "I don't like this, not one bit. We don't know a thing about them, including where they've settled. How will we find you if we need to?"

"Grey Eagle knows him, Orion, and I would bet Jubal does, too. I'll be fine. You get back to Sarah. She needs you now."

"I don't like this," Orion repeated. He looked past Joseph to where Knute still sat next to the fire, sipping his coffee as if he didn't have a care in the world. "I'm going to get word to Eagle and Jubal both, see what I can find out." He tucked the papers Joseph handed him in his saddlebag, then climbed into the saddle and looked down at his brother. His green eyes seemed to burn. "Do you remember once warning me to watch my back when I set off from Fort Laramie for Fort St. Charles?"

Joseph slowly nodded, knowing what was coming next. Orion had been ambushed and nearly killed on that ill-fated trip to the now-abandoned fort.

Orion leaned down out of the saddle. "I'm saying the same thing to you now, big brother. I have a bad feeling about this. You watch your back."

"I will. I know what I'm doing." *Do I?* Joseph fought down a niggling feeling of doubt.

"Let's get to it, Captain Beaudine!" Knute's old voice came to them on the rising wind. "Weather's coming in!"

Joseph waved to him, then turned back to Orion. "Give Sarah my love. Your little one will most likely be born before

I get back to the fort. I'll pray for a safe delivery." He held up his hand.

Orion clutched Joseph's arm near the elbow, and Joseph held onto his brother as well. "I'd better see you again," Orion warned.

"You will, little brother. I promise."

They released each other, and Orion touched his heels to Thunder's sides. The stallion took off at a trot, the packhorse following close behind.

Joseph watched until Orion could no longer be seen, then turned back toward the dying fire. Knute Jensen was now standing, motioning to him again. Thoughtfully, Joseph watched the old man. His long white hair moved in the wind, as did the fringe on his worn but clean buckskins. He was a tall man, and held himself straight, considering his age. But he was thin, and Joseph wondered if he always had been. He suspected not, for the buckskins hung on him in places like the shoulders and the waist. Perhaps more was affecting the man than his age alone.

He did not regret his decision to go with Knute, but Joseph couldn't help wondering what he had gotten himself into. Orion's uneasiness concerned him, because his brother did not give such warnings lightly, any more than he himself did. If Orion said he had a bad feeling, he did, one that was powerful enough to voice, and that was definitely something to pay attention to.

Joseph resettled his hat more firmly on his head. He would pay attention.

Four

It did not take the three riders long to separate nine horses from the herd, but getting them tied together for the start of the journey west proved more difficult. The air was filled with the sounds of angry, fearful horses, and, with his prancing and calling, The Paint was of no help. Finally, Joseph dropped a lasso over the head of the most belligerent of the captured horses and forced the irate chestnut mare away. Three of the other recruits followed her, making it easier for Knute and Thomas to rope them together. One by one, the rest of the nine were tied to the group, and at last they were on their way.

The weather Knute predicted came in, offering a welcome respite from the heat of the August afternoon. An easy rain fell, pushed in a southeasterly direction by the wind. Joseph tugged his wide-brimmed hat lower on his head, grateful for the cooling wetness, and equally grateful for the buckskin jacket that offered some protection to his upper body.

Knute had said little since they started, only that they would travel for several hours before stopping for the night, and that they would reach their destination late the next day. Joseph warned both Jensens that Baines, Westin, and Sikes were in the area, and although neither said anything in response, he saw the brief look of concern grandfather and grandson shared. Then Thomas fell back to the tail end of the herd and kept to himself, seeming subdued and troubled. Knute had taken the lead for the still-skittish mare from Joseph and rode in the most forward position, to the left of the herd, guiding them in a westerly direction. Joseph rode to the right.

The crossing of the Laramie River went easily, for the water was low this late in the summer, and the land changed from the relatively open prairies which had surrounded the lake to the scrub-covered foothills of the Laramie Mountains. On they rode, periodically running the herd in a deliberate attempt to tire the new recruits. The sun sank behind the mountains to the west, and the sagebrush and juniper of the foothills gradually gave way to scatterings of ponderosa pine and Douglas fir. Joseph breathed deeply and appreciatively of the clean, pine-scented air. Even though he had been in the mountains for almost three weeks and had only left them this morning, he was glad to be back.

Dusk had fallen when Knute finally called a halt. Joseph noted that the old man had chosen the campsite with care. A small clearing, naturally enclosed on two sides by out-croppings of tumbled rocks and on the third by a steep ridge, offered thick, sweet-smelling grass for the horses. A spring of clean, cold water gurgled at the base of a huge boulder, forming a tiny pool no more than two feet across. The camp-site had been used recently, for sections of the grass were cropped and trampled, and fresh horse droppings dotted the area. The remains of a fire showed black against the base of another large rock.

"Did you stay here last night?" Joseph asked Knute as they worked on hobbling and picketing the anxious horses. Thomas remained in the saddle, ready to chase down any escapees.

"*Ja*. From here it is a long day's ride to Fort Laramie. Captain Rutledge saved us a full day of travel. It was fortuitous that we met his patrol where and when we did." He straightened slowly and held a hand to his back, then moved toward another horse.

"How far is your home from here?"

"A full day's ride again."

Joseph nodded and went after another horse.

Supper was a modest, mostly silent affair of buffalo jerky, hardtack, and strong coffee. Knute seemed tired, Thomas distracted. Joseph respected their obvious desire for quiet, content with his drawing pad and charcoal pencil. Not long after the last of the evening light faded to black, grandfather and grandson rolled into their blankets, yet Joseph continued to toil over his pad, squinting in the dying firelight.

Several small sketches shared space on the single page— The Paint; Wild Horse Lake as he and Orion had seen it that morning, with the horse herd beyond; Knute's lined face; Thomas's young one. And in the center, a sketch of Annie Rose. He lingered long on her likeness, struggling to remember the finer details of her pretty face. He had drawn her from the shoulders up, without the floppy hat she wore, her thick braid pulled forward over her shoulder. Finally, with a frown, he set the pad aside and rubbed his eyes. The fire was little more than coals, and he would either have to give up on the so-far-unsatisfactory sketch of Miss Rose or put more wood on the fire.

Because he felt he needed to see her again in order to do justice to any picture he drew of her, Joseph opted for going to sleep. However, much to his frustration, sleep eluded him.

The hours drifted by, the constellations travelled the dark heavens, and, try as he did, Joseph could not shake his persistent and annoying preoccupation with Miss Annie Rose. All day long, the golden-haired woman had plagued his thoughts, and now she threatened to hound his dreams. Never had he been so taken with a woman, and he had been afforded many opportunities.

The years spent as an Army officer after his graduation from West Point as a member of the elite Corps of Topographical Engineers had sent Captain Joseph Beaudine to posts around the country and beyond. He had been introduced to many beautiful, desirable, charming women in the ballrooms of New York, Philadelphia, Washington, Richmond, Atlanta, New Orleans, and even Mexico City. He had flirted with and danced with many of those women, and he had even been seduced—quite willingly—by a few. Yet none of them had affected him like the strange young woman who wore baggy, unattractive men's clothes, handled a large knife with confident ease, and spoke in gentle, compelling tones of a spiritual connection to a horse.

The trouble was, he knew exactly what she meant.

Under his single wool blanket, Joseph shifted again in a vain attempt to find a comfortable position. Finally, in exasperation, he rolled onto his back and again stared up at the infinite, calming stars.

What on earth was wrong with him? he silently demanded, as if the equally silent stars would answer.

Perhaps he was simply overtired, as was often the case when he finished a scouting mission like the one he and Orion had just completed.

Then again, perhaps he was as crazy as his brother had accused him of being.

Unknowing of his destination, he had gone off into the wilderness, in the company of people about whom he knew nothing, except that one was reputed to be a lunatic.

All because of a bewitching, green-eyed forest sprite.

Joseph shook his head against the clothing-stuffed *parfleche* he used as a pillow. Orion was right.

He was crazy.

With a sigh, he turned on his side, determined to sleep. Determined that he would have no dreams. Especially of a golden-haired enchantress.

Annie Rose paused, the fingers of her left hand splayed against the smooth, cool bark of a towering aspen. The night wind rustled through the distinctly scented leaves, creating a soft clatter not unlike that of a distant group of gossiping women. She fought to still her rapid breathing, to listen to the night, to hear any sounds of pursuit.

There were none.

Erik was an accomplished woodsman, but not as good as

she, even when she wore a skirt, as she did now. He could not track her any better than Abelard Baines could have. For tonight, she was safe.

She murmured a word of encouragement to Maggie, who had materialized from the darkness, and together they trudged on toward Aurora's refuge.

The change in the cousin for whom Annie Rose had always cared was disturbing—deeply so. Throughout the long, long day, Erik's smoldering fury had not abated. He had gone about his chores with a clenched jaw and flexing hands—large meaty hands that Annie Rose sensed he wanted to use on her.

In violence.

In passion.

She knew, deep in her heart, that with Erik, both would be the same.

Painful. Degrading. Sick.

Her cousin was sick, and she had no cure to offer him. So, when night fell, and he paced the packed-dirt floor of the cabin she had always before found safe, never taking his eyes from her, drinking—first tea, then Gramps's brandy— she waited until he lurched out the door to the privy. Then she snatched her coat and ran, not taking the time to exchange her petticoats and cotton skirt for the trousers she usually wore in the wilderness. Secure in the knowledge that Maggie would follow her, she prayed that she could outrun her cousin. And evidently she had.

She would spend the rest of the night in the safety of Aurora's refuge, then in the morning decide whether to return to the cabin or head toward Fort Laramie in the hope of meeting up with her grandfather and brother on their way home. There was also the possibility of returning to Jubal Sage's cabin, but, as she had no way of knowing whether Baines and his cohorts were still there, it was an idea she quickly discarded.

Annie Rose gave a sad, troubled sigh as she walked among the fragrant trees, her way illuminated by the pale light of a three-quarter moon. The secure, happy life she had shared for so many years with her grandfather, brother, and cousin in the hidden valley they called home was coming to an end. She could sense it. Gramps was aging, Thomas was showing signs of restless curiosity about the outside world, and Erik thought he had fallen in love with her, a love she could not return to a man she considered a brother.

Even the ancient land itself was threatened with change from the seasonal tidal waves of white men rushing to the gold fields of California. Lately Gramps had taken to complaining that the territory was getting downright crowded. She knew his underlying fear was that someone in the influx of people coming to and passing through the territory would know them, would know what had happened so long ago in Baltimore. A chill caused by that same fear rippled through her.

They simply could not be found out.

For seven years they had successfully hidden from her father's powerful family, had lived in peace with the Sioux and Cheyenne, had made a comfortable if modest life in the beautiful, secluded little valley her grandfather had stumbled upon in 1834, the year of the last great fur trappers' rendezvous. Knute had discovered the hidden valley by accident—or Providence, as he believed—and had taken his grandchildren there when the need arose. Now that sanctuary was threatened, from within as well as without.

Ahead, Annie Rose could make out the rough fence she had fashioned on one side of a shallow cave formed by the long-gone waters of a prehistoric sea. Her grandfather had shown her the imprints of delicate leaves and ferns and the bodies of tiny, strange-looking sea creatures embedded forever in the very rock itself. There they had constructed a stable of sorts for Aurora, in an attempt to offer her a haven from the men—red and white—who searched so relentlessly for the fabled Golden Mare.

The mare now welcomed her with a soft nicker, and a

warm love flooded Annie Rose's weary heart. For tonight, with Maggie and Aurora at her side, all would be well.

But a nagging worry poked at her. What to do about Erik?

Without warning, the image of Joseph Beaudine flashed in her mind. As he had the night before, he would stand at her side against any who threatened her, including her own cousin. Instinctively she knew that. But hadn't he looked at her much as Erik did—as a man looked at a woman? There was a difference, though, Annie Rose decided, a difference she found comforting. Erik's blue eyes were hot with lust, while Joseph's brown ones were warm with interest.

With a shake of her head, Annie Rose forced the tall, handsome frontiersman from her mind. There was no place in her life for such a man, nor would there—could there—ever be. She had to remember that.

She put her arms around Aurora's neck and breathed deeply of the mare's scent. Maggie stood at her side, her tail moving in the dirt. Here, with her animals, she was welcome. She was safe.

At least for tonight.

Joseph awakened, blinking into the chilly grey light of dawn. A quick glance about the campsite ensured him that all was well with the picketed horses. Knute and Thomas slumbered on, the old and the young deep in the sleep of exhaustion. Joseph rolled out of his blanket and, on silent, moccasined feet, made his way into the forest to gather firewood.

When he returned with the first armload, he saw that Knute was awake, although the old man had yet to venture from his blankets, and Thomas was bent over the small pool splashing water on his face. Joseph nodded a greeting to Knute as he set the sticks he had gathered near the fire circle.

"I'll collect a little more wood if one of you will get the fire going and the coffee on," Joseph said.

"*Ja*, we will."

Joseph nodded again and headed back into the forest. He worked his way up the sharp incline of the ridge that towered over the campsite to the north. A once-tall pine, long ago struck down by lightning, lay on the ground near the top, one end of the thick trunk blackened and crumbling. Several branches of varying thicknesses littered the area. Having amassed a good-sized pile, Joseph knelt in preparation to pick up the wood when he heard the unmistakable call of a stallion. He froze, his head lifted, sniffing the air, listening.

The call came again, from the far side of the ridge, he decided. Leaving the pile of wood, Joseph climbed the last few remaining feet to the top of the ridge, careful not to outline himself against the lightening sky. There was no telling who he might discover on the other side—red man or white, friend or foe. He paused behind a boulder, took off his hat, and cautiously peered around the night-chilled stone.

The stallion's call once again ripped through the cool morning air, and Joseph searched for the source. He saw that the ridge provided a protective barrier for another valley on the far side, this one wider at the base than the snug enclosure which comprised Knute's campsite. There, at the eastern end of the valley, atop a small, grass-covered knoll, stood The Paint. Joseph stared. Had the stallion come after the unwillingly drafted members of his herd?

The Paint reared up, pawing the air as he called again.

Now Joseph heard the faint sound of rapid hoofbeats. Yet The Paint remained on his knoll, prancing. Joseph turned toward the open western end of the valley.

What he saw stopped his breath.

From that direction a horse came at an easy lope.

A golden horse.

On its back rode a woman, her dark skirts bunched up around her thighs, her long golden hair streaming out behind her. She rode bareback, with no sign of even a halter. Like a goddess she was, as much a part of the golden horse as the horse was a part of the land over which it raced. The woman's slender body moved as one with the horse, which he could now see was a mare.

The Golden Mare.

Like that of the ancient Cheyenne prophecy.

Since he was a boy, he had heard the stories of the coming of the Golden Mare, and of the White Buffalo, around the campfires of his beloved stepmother, Morning Sky—Grey Eagle's mother.

Was he dreaming? Joseph rubbed his eyes and looked again. They were still there, the golden horse and the golden woman, even now drawing near to The Paint, who had deigned to saunter down from his throne-like knoll to greet them. Despite his assurances to Abby Baines that the Golden Mare did not exist, Joseph had long suspected that she actually did, simply because he had heard of too many sightings of her over the last few years.

The difference between a prophecy and a legend was a simple one, in Joseph's opinion. The weight a prophecy carried with any given person depended a great deal upon that particular person's belief in the prophecy. However, most legends were based upon tales of an actual being—human or animal—or event, and then, over time, were embellished to the point of fantasy.

But what Joseph saw before him was no fantasy.

In breathless wonder, he watched as the mare approached the stallion—who was clearly her mate—with little dancing steps, tossing her head. The faint sounds of her welcoming nickers reached his ears, carried on the teasing wind. The two horses nuzzled one another, and the woman slipped to the ground and stood beside them.

Annie Rose. Her name leapt to his mind. From where he was, Joseph could not make out the woman's features, and she wore a long skirt that rippled in the wind, but her coat resembled the one Annie Rose had worn, both in its color and in its excessive size. And that long, golden hair . . .

It was her. Joseph knew it in his heart. Without conscious thought, he straightened, and had taken no more than a step in her direction when a strong hand clapped down on his shoulder.

"Leave them be."

Knute spoke quietly, but there was a steel-like quality to his old voice that gave Joseph pause. He glanced over his shoulder at the Norseman.

"That's the Golden Mare, Mr. Jensen."

"*Ja.*"

Joseph found the calm response annoying. "And The Paint."

"*Ja.*"

"Who is the woman?"

Knute's grip on his shoulder tightened painfully. Joseph never would have guessed that the frail-looking man possessed such strength. "Soon you will know. Let us go."

Joseph pulled away from him. "I will know now." He turned toward the valley, determined to make his way to the woman's side. He stopped short when he saw that she was now looking in their direction.

"I think not," Knute said mildly from behind him.

Joseph saw the shadow of the Norseman's arm move in an arc over the ground in front of him. His gaze returned again to the woman, and as he watched, she gathered her skirts and gracefully vaulted onto the mare's back. She directed the mare back in the direction from which they had come, and, to Joseph's astonishment, The Paint followed them, now quite docile.

"It is of no use to follow them," Knute said, as if he had read Joseph's mind. "You'll not be able to find them."

You won't be able to track me.

Annie Rose's words rang in Joseph's mind. For some reason, he believed both her and Knute. His heart strangely aching, he watched as the woman urged the mare to a lope, and, with The Paint following closely, they disappeared from his view.

A curious depression settled over him; the sun may as well have sunk again behind the curve of the earth.

"Come." Knute's voice was kind. "All will be well, Captain Beaudine. You will see."

Joseph looked at him. The old man did not seem crazy now. He was calm and confident, and a genuine warmth lit his blue eyes. Warmth and something else—approval, perhaps? Why would Knute approve of him? Joseph had the sense that he had just passed some kind of test. He sighed in resignation, remembering that Knute had promised that soon he would know who the woman was. There would be no point in trying to pry any information from the stubborn Norseman before he was ready to share it; Joseph knew that for certain.

"I've collected a pile of wood near the lightning-struck tree," he said.

Knute nodded. *"Ja.* I will help with it. The coffee will be ready soon." He turned away and started down the ridge toward the fallen tree.

With one futile backward glance, Joseph followed him.

After a hurried breakfast consisting of the last of the Jensens' bread and cheese, chased down with strong black coffee, they were on their way. Following the night of enforced rest, the recruited horses were invigorated and difficult to manage. There was no time for talk—not that either of the Jensens demonstrated any inclination to talk about anything—for all three riders were kept busy controlling the excited horses. Finally, after perhaps two hours of hard work forcing the horses in a westerly direction, the herd settled down into some semblance of that—a herd—and the going got easier.

Even then, neither Jensen attempted a conversation with him. At one point, Joseph suspected that Knute and Thomas had an argument. He could not hear their words over the noise of the horses, but their gestures were easy to interpret. Thomas was very unhappy about something, and refused his grandfather's obvious attempts to convince and comfort him. Finally, his aged features rigid, Knute left his upset grandson's side and returned to ride point.

Aside from a hasty watering at a trickling stream in the early afternoon, Knute allowed no stops. Without complaint, Joseph ate the midday meal in the saddle, something he had done countless times while in the Army. That didn't mean he enjoyed it. Jerky and hardtack, although filling, were hardly tantalizing fare, and the water in his canteen was as warm as the day had proven to be. He suspected Knute's insistence that they keep moving was an attempt to reach the Jensen homestead by nightfall, a goal Joseph supported, and so he remained silent and obedient.

Late afternoon brought them into territory Joseph—for all his explorations of the area—had not seen before. He knew they were in the Laramie Mountains, and that Jubal Sage's cabin was to the south, but where exactly they were, or where they were headed, he wasn't certain. Knute seemed to be leading them straight toward a forbidding wall of rock that rose several hundred feet into the air and extended left and right for a combined distance of at least a half a mile. It was as if the sword of some ancient giant had cut into the earth and in one clean sweep took away half of a mountain.

Closer and closer to the solid barrier Knute led them, and Joseph found it increasingly difficult to hold his questions. When the small group of men and horses milled about in a dirt-covered clearing snuggled next to the rock wall, Joseph finally spoke.

"Where are we going?"

Knute settled his burning blue gaze on Joseph. Again, there was no sign of imbalance in the old man's intelligent eyes, nor in his somber, assessing expression. He pulled at one end of his white mustache and seemed to come to a decision.

"Well, son, we're going through that wall."

After a quick glance at the impatient, undisciplined horses, Joseph pushed his hat farther back on his head and looked up at the daunting heights. "I was afraid you were going to say that."

Five

The warm wind swirled down the rock face, carrying with it eerie sounds. Joseph could not suppress a shiver. The sounds reminded him of the low, keening moans of grieving women, and, strangely, of bones—bones?—clacking together. He glanced at his companions; neither Knute nor Thomas seemed disturbed by the sounds. In fact, they gave no indication that they even heard them.

Thomas slipped down from the saddle and pulled a length of cloth from his saddlebag, then lifted his looped rope from the saddle horn. "We blindfold the lead horse for this part of the journey," he said in an unfriendly tone at Joseph's questioning look. "It makes 'em easier to lead." He looped the rope around the neck of the chestnut mare that appeared to have taken over as the leader and handed the other end up to his grandfather. The rest of the horses nickered nervously but did not try to run.

Joseph looked around again, trying to discover the cause of the unearthly sounds. They seemed to be coming from the rock wall itself, and at the same time from the nearby trees.

Knute cackled, his strange laugh fitting right in with the other sounds. "Most men in these parts—red and white—are superstitious about one thing or another. If a little spooky noise keeps them away from our home, so much the better." He motioned toward a tall pine not far from the rock face.

There Joseph spotted the source of the sounds: hanging

from a high branch were a thin hollowed-out cylinder of wood perhaps a foot long, and, sure enough, two pieces of bone that knocked together in the wind. The wind moving through the flute-like tube caused the moaning sound, while the bones hitting each other caused the clacking sound.

"People tend to stay away from places they think are haunted," Knute said, as conversationally as if they were discussing the weather. "And because I'm not afraid of the 'ghosts,' they think I'm crazy, and they give me wide berth as well." He cackled again. "It's kept us safe for many a year."

Joseph shook his head in admiration. Knute was crazy, all right—crazy like a fox. If the Norseman wanted seclusion, he'd found a smart way to try to get it.

Thomas tied the length of cloth over the mare's eyes. When he climbed back into his saddle, Knute led the way toward the wall, urging the reluctant mare to follow. Joseph watched in amazement as Knute guided his own mount around a projecting slab of rock and disappeared. The mare did likewise.

Thomas nudged another horse to fall into step behind the mare, and when he understood the boy's intent, Joseph moved to help him. Working together, it did not take them long to get four horses around the slab of rock. Joseph was very curious to see what was on the other side.

With a surly jerk of his head, Thomas indicated that Joseph should go next.

"You won't need help getting the rest through?" Joseph asked with a glance at the four remaining horses.

"My gramps and I do just fine on our own," Thomas snapped. "I don't need your help."

Joseph now understood what Knute and Thomas had been arguing about. It was very clear that Thomas did not welcome his company; perhaps the boy's hurt stemmed from the fact that his grandfather had acted against his wishes. Why did Thomas resent his presence? What was the boy afraid of?

"No," Joseph said mildly. "I can see that." He nodded at Thomas, then guided Grace toward the slab of rock. To his surprise, he saw that there was a narrow rocky path behind

the slab, one that rose at an incline and disappeared around
another upended slab. He could hear the sound of the horses
ahead of him echoing off the rock. His gaze travelled up the
sheer walls of the narrow passageway. Fortunately, he did
not suffer from claustrophobia, for the walls seemed to almost meet overhead. The strange sounds seemed amplified,
too, whining down the passageway on the breath of the wind.

The sound of the other horses behind him reached his ears,
and he wondered how far the passageway went.

It went a surprising distance, and at a constant incline.
The narrow canyon would be impassable during the winter,
for surely it filled with snow. Joseph wondered again about
Knute's reputed lunacy. Being snowbound in the wilderness
each year for several months would go far in helping one
along the path to insanity. But then, he had his family with
him. Perhaps they helped each other stay sane. Finally,
Joseph guided Grace around a large, smooth boulder, and
pulled her to a halt. He drew a deep breath and gazed with
wonder at the sight before him.

Knute had led them out of the passageway to a relatively
level clearing high on the side of a mountain. Below spread
a pristine valley rimmed in on all sides by mountains of
varying heights, the tallest of which were devoid of trees at
the top. Some were so high that patches of snow still showed
in the deepest crevasses, even though it was August. Joseph
estimated that the valley was three, maybe four miles long,
and a mile or two across. A narrow river meandered the
length of the valley. Lodgepole pine and aspen trees lived
together in harmony, as did thick green grasses and patches
of colorful wildflowers. From his vantage point he could see
no sign of a homestead, but farther down the valley a thin
trail of smoke rose into the early evening air.

"Is that the only way in?" Joseph asked, jerking a thumb
in the direction of the passageway.

"No, but it's the only way coming from the east," Knute
answered. "It would take another full day to circle around
to the north or south. Then one must come over those moun-

tains." He waved to indicate the encircling peaks. "Few people know of our valley."

"I can believe that."

"We will go down now." Knute pulled the blindfold from the mare's head.

Taking a quick count of the horses, Joseph saw that the last four had followed him out of the passageway, but there was no sign of Thomas. "What about the boy?" he asked.

"He is watching for a time, to be certain we were not trailed. He'll be along soon." With that, Knute started down the mountain. The horses eagerly followed, perhaps enticed by the scent of water.

By the time they reached the valley floor, dusk had fallen and darkness was not far behind. Knute urged the small herd into a lope, and a few miles were quickly covered. There was still no sign of a homestead, but the smell of smoke grew stronger.

Questions swirled around in Joseph's head. Where was the house? Was there even a house, or did Knute live in a campsite? Was there a corral, or would they have to hobble and picket the horses again tonight? Would food be available? Most important, was Annie Rose here? With difficulty, he kept his questions to himself.

Finally, Knute led him around a bend in the river, and most of Joseph's unasked questions were answered. To his surprise, Knute's home was a well-developed homestead, with a tidy log house built into the side of a hill, a garden surrounded by a fence, a small barn, a few outbuildings, and several corrals. All were cleverly situated among scattered groups of trees, which explained why nothing but chimney smoke could be seen from a distance. Chickens clucked happily, and a cow's gentle call was answered by the bleating of a goat, testimony that farm animals were nearby. Deep in the wilderness, Knute had built a homestead as neat and complete as any to be found in the East.

"How did you accomplish this in the middle of nowhere?" Joseph asked in astonishment.

Knute shrugged. "This land is no more inhospitable than the mountains of Norway, of my homeland. With patience and hard work, it was done." He pointed toward the corrals. "We will put the new horses in the first corral."

A stocky young man with a red beard came from the barn to open the corral gate. He stared long and hard at Joseph, with no sign of welcome on his face. "Who is this?" he demanded.

"This is Captain Joseph Beaudine," Knute calmly answered. "Captain, this is my grandson Erik." The last of the horses trotted into the corral and Erik secured the gate.

Joseph shifted in the saddle, wishing Knute would not use his military title. He nodded at Erik, who little resembled his brother and sister. "Pleased to meet you."

"You're out of uniform," was Erik's curt reply.

"I'm also out of the Army." Joseph returned Erik's glare. Why were Knute's grandsons so hostile toward him?

Erik's eyes narrowed. "What's he doing here, Gramps?"

"He's here to work." Knute heaved himself out of the saddle and to the ground, his weariness evident.

"What?" Erik shouted. "You hired help? Without discussing it with me?"

"*Ja,* that's right." Knute pierced his grandson with a hard look. "I am still the head of this family."

"We don't need help." Erik clenched and unclenched his fists. "You shouldn't have brought a stranger here. You know the agreement."

"You will not chastise me, Erik." Knute pulled himself up, and his old voice rang with determination. "I raised you with better manners than to be so disrespectful to your elders."

If Knute expected an apology, Erik did not offer one. After a moment, with a tightened jaw, Knute continued. "I have my reasons for hiring this man, and he is not a stranger. He is the son of Jedediah Beaudine, and Grey Eagle's brother. Do you think I would bring an untrustworthy man here?"

"You should have consulted me." Erik turned and stomped

back into the barn. A moment later, a flood of lantern light came from the open door.

"I apologize for my grandson's rudeness," Knute said as Joseph stepped down from the stirrup.

"Think no more of it. He was caught by surprise." Joseph loosened Grace's cinch. "He'll calm down."

"Perhaps. Perhaps not." Knute led his horse toward the corral closest to the house. "Come. We will put our horses here."

For a few minutes the men worked in silence. When their horses were free of saddle and blanket, brushed, and turned into the corral, Joseph followed Knute, his rifle in hand, toward the house. Even in the rapidly fading light, he could tell the entire homestead was well cared for, and someone had made an effort to add a civilized touch to the rustic cabin. A scalloped trim of carved wood skirted the edge of the sod roof and the window ledges, and neat flower beds cuddled next to the house in both directions from the stout wooden door. There was no porch as such, but the roof extended out over the front of the cabin far enough to offer a little shelter from the elements. Joseph followed Knute up two stone steps into the house, where he was greeted with the delicious aroma of something wonderful cooking. His mouth instantly watered. The meals of jerky and hardtack had grown tiresome.

"This is the house," Knute said unnecessarily, with a note of pride in his voice. A familiar black dog jumped up from its place in front of the fire and, with tail wagging, approached Knute, then Joseph.

Knute raised a curious eyebrow, but said nothing. Joseph offered no explanation as he scratched Maggie's ears and looked around, trying to ignore the hope that flared in his heart.

The interior of the cabin was as orderly and tended as the rest of the homestead. Twin fireplaces built of stone stood at each end of the oblong main room, which sported a table with benches along two sides and a chair at one end, a bed built against the earthen back wall, a large, scarred worktable near the door, and a strangely out of place, delicately carved rocking chair. A rough bookcase filled with an assortment

64   *Jessica Wulf*

of books stood near the bed. Scattered about the smooth, level, packed-dirt floor were the hides of various animals—bear, buffalo, elk—now serving as rugs. Neatly hemmed gingham curtains covered the two windows—made of real paned glass—that flanked the front door, and a matching piece of cloth covered the long table, which was set with four places. On the far side of each fireplace, more of the gingham hung to the floor over what Joseph assumed were doors, leading perhaps to bedchambers.

As his gaze fell on one of the curtained doors, the length of material moved to one side and Miss Annie Rose stepped into the room.

Joseph's heart stopped, then restarted with a furious pounding.

She was obviously as startled to see him as he was to see her, for her unforgettable eyes widened and her lips parted. Joseph snatched his hat from his head, unable to take his eyes from her. She wore a black skirt and a white apron, and her long-sleeved white bodice was partially covered with an intricately embroidered red vest. Her blonde hair was braided and wrapped around her head in a simple, fetching style, and a delicate blush rosied her cheeks.

To Joseph, she was beautiful, much more so than he remembered. His sketch of her was truly inadequate. He wondered idly if she would be willing to sit for him, so that he might draw a likeness that was worthy of her beauty. Even as he thought the words, he knew he did not have the talent—indeed, it did not exist in the world—to do justice to her.

"Granddaughter, this is Captain Joseph Beaudine," Knute said quietly. "Captain, my granddaughter, Miss Annie Rose Jensen."

"We've met," Joseph replied. That was why he had not heard of her family—she had not given her full name that night in Jubal's cabin. If she had, he would have known she was related to Knute Jensen.

"Ja, I gathered that." Knute looked from one to the other. "That is a story I would like to hear."

Annie Rose dropped her gaze to her clasped hands.

"It's nice to see you again, Miss Jensen," Joseph said.

"Mr. Beaudine. You will forgive me if I am surprised. Grandfather rarely brings guests." She moved to a trio of shelves that decorated the wall above a chest and took down another plate.

"He's not merely a guest, Annie Rose," Knute explained as he slumped into the rocking chair with a weary sigh. He removed his hat and rubbed his forehead. "The captain has agreed to work with us for a time. The Army wants as many horses as we can provide for them before winter."

"And Mr. Beaudine is a competent horseman?"

Joseph met her inquiring stare. There was no hint of humor in her green eyes. She didn't seem to be as upset about his presence as Erik and Thomas evidently were, but it was clear she was not happy about it.

"I do all right," he answered before Knute could say anything.

"Let's hope you do better than that, sir. There is a great deal of difficult work to be done." Annie Rose set the plate next to another and rearranged the spacing between them. Her gaze fell on her grandfather, and lines of worry immediately appeared between her arched eyebrows. "Gramps?" she asked softly as she moved to his side. "Are you well?"

"Just tired, *datter.*" Knute took her hand and looked up at her, his blue eyes filled with love and, Joseph thought, a curious touch of sadness. "We brought nine horses back, given to us by The Paint."

Annie Rose nodded. "That will keep us busy." She patted the back of Knute's hand. "I was surprised that you took the last five so soon." There was a gentle chiding tone to her voice, a hint of injured feelings in her calm expression.

"They were ready." He released her hand.

After a moment, Annie Rose moved away. "Do you plan to get more before winter, in addition to these you brought today?"

Knute shrugged. *"Ja,* I'd like to. The Army pays well for saddle-trained horses."

"We don't need the money, Gramps. There's enough to stock us comfortably for the winter. One last trip to Fort Laramie is all it will take." She now stood at the fireplace nearest the table, a long-handled spoon in her hand. The hurt look Joseph had glimpsed on her face had changed to one of concern. "You're not so young anymore. It's more important that you husband your strength, and rest when you need to."

Joseph found the merest hint of Knute's accent in her voice to be most intriguing.

"Don't be fussing and telling me what to do, Annie Rose," Knute warned, not unkindly.

"Grump all you want to, Gramps." Annie Rose pointed the spoon at him. "You know I'm right." Her voice now was warm with affection.

"Hush, girl, and finish fixing my supper." Knute took a deep, appreciative breath. "Potato dumplings and venison roast, if my old nose doesn't deceive me. And cabbage with caraway. She's a good cook, Captain. You're in for a treat."

"I can tell that." Joseph audibly sniffed.

"Thank you, Gramps," said Annie Rose, smiling. "Supper won't be long now, if you all want to wash up." With a glance at the door, she added, "Thomas returned with you, didn't he?"

"Ja, of course. He stayed back at the rock wall to watch the trail. He'll be along any minute." Knute pulled himself out of the rocking chair. "Let's get your belongings, Captain. The boys sleep in there." He pointed to one curtained door, then the other. "That's Annie Rose's room. You'll bunk in here with me, on the floor for now, but we'll get you a bed made right away."

"The floor is fine, Mr. Jensen. There's no need to make a bed."

"Nonsense." Knute headed toward the door. "A man needs to be well rested in order to put in a full day's work, and rest comes easier in a bed."

"Gramps."

There was a troubled tone to Annie Rose's voice. Joseph stopped and turned toward her, as did Knute.

"*Ja?*"

She looked from Joseph to Knute, wringing her hands in her apron. "I need to talk to you later, alone."

Knute's brow furrowed. "This sounds serious, girl."

"It is."

"After supper, then. You and I shall take a stroll down to the stock pond."

"*Takk,* Gramps."

"We'll be in shortly."

Annie Rose nodded. Joseph smiled at her, but she did not smile back. He pulled the door closed behind him, trying to hide his elation. It didn't matter that she wouldn't smile at him.

He had found her.

Joseph Beaudine. Of all men, her grandfather had to bring him.

Annie Rose stirred the potato dumplings with more force than was necessary, sloshing some of the water over the side of the pot. The liquid sizzled as it struck the burning logs.

That he brought anyone at all to their sanctuary—other than Jubal Sage, Sweet Water, or Grey Eagle—was astonishing in and of itself, for Knute had broken one of his own long-standing rules. That troubled her deeply. That he chose Joseph Beaudine troubled her even more.

Her breath had caught when the tall captain stepped through the door, and it touched her, the way he snatched his hat off his head. He wore simple buckskins, his long hair needed brushing, and his cheeks and chin had not seen a razor for several days, but, Lord, he was handsome, with those warm brown eyes, that luxurious mustache. Her heart had taken to pounding, and she had to fight the gladness that welled up in her—the gladness that she had dressed nicely for her grandfather's return, that her hair was clean and neatly styled. She looked her best tonight, and she was glad, fiercely so, that Joseph Beaudine had seen her thus, after first meeting her in her dowdy boy's clothes.

Then she sobered. Why had Gramps brought him home? Where did they meet? Had Joseph already told Knute about her unforgivable transgression of the other night?

She closed her eyes and rested her forehead against the fire-warmed stone mantel, fighting the urge to run after her grandfather, to insist that they walk to the pond now, to talk *now*. For the past seven years, she had been able to turn to Knute in times of confusion and trouble, and she needed him tonight. Yet how to tell him what she had done? How to tell him what Erik had done?

Annie Rose absentmindedly rubbed the painful bruises on her upper arm, where a furious and hungover Erik had grabbed her this afternoon when she returned from Aurora's hideout. The only reason she had come home was because she had seen Knute on the ridge at dawn and knew he would be home tonight. She did not realize then, as she did now, that it was Joseph Beaudine on the ridge with her grandfather, not Thomas.

Her argument with Erik had been ugly, and had Maggie not interfered when he raised his hand to strike her, she did not know what would have happened.

The sad truth was, she could not be left alone with her cousin again.

And now *he* was here, too.

The presence of Joseph Beaudine in her valley, in her home, was the last thing Annie Rose needed. She looked at Maggie, who rested comfortably on her grandfather's bed.

"What am I going to do?"

The dog appeared sympathetic, but she did not answer, much to her mistress's disappointment. Annie Rose put a great deal more faith in the opinions of her beloved animals than she did most people. Unfortunately, those animals often remained quiet, leaving her nowhere to turn but to her own heart.

And right now, her heart was hurting.

Six

As they approached the corral, Joseph saw that Knute was correct in his prediction that Thomas would be home soon. Even now, the boy unsaddled his horse, with quick, jerky movements which indicated to Joseph that his mood had not improved.

"Annie Rose is ready to serve supper as soon as we've washed up," Knute said conversationally to Thomas.

"All right." The boy spit out the terse words.

Knute walked to the open door of the barn, from which came the pale light of a lantern. "Supper's on, Erik."

There was no reply. Knute shrugged and turned to Joseph. "The washbowl's on the right side of the house. Let's collect your things."

"There's little enough that I can get it myself, Mr. Jensen. I sent most of my things to the fort with Orion. I'll meet you at the washbowl in a minute."

Knute nodded his agreement. "Don't dawdle, boys," he called out to include everyone. "Annie Rose put a lot of work into making us a nice meal, and it would be disrespectful to keep her waiting." He headed toward the cabin.

Joseph made his way to the small pile of his belongings nestled against the side of the barn, which included his saddle, a bedroll, the *parfleche* containing a few articles of clothing, a fringed buckskin jacket, and a leather case fortified with thin strips of wood that held his precious papers and pencils.

"I'd like to put my saddle in the barn," he said to Thomas.

"You don't need my permission," Thomas snapped.

With a sigh, Joseph lifted the saddle and carried it into the barn. Just as he passed through the door, Erik came out of a stall. His jaw was rigid, his blue eyes filled with hate.

"He shouldn't have brought you here," he snarled. "The old fool must be losing his mind for real now." He pointed a finger at Joseph, practically shook it in his face. "I want you gone in the morning, Beaudine, with your solemn oath that you'll tell no one of this place, or of Annie Rose. Your half-breed brother can be trusted, so maybe a former Army officer can be, too."

Joseph fought down his rising temper. If Erik meant to goad him with his derogatory remark about Grey Eagle, he was succeeding. "Your grandfather hired me," he said firmly. "He'll be the only one to fire me." He shifted the weight of the saddle, not liking that his hands were not free, for there was no guarantee that Erik wouldn't come after him with the intention of using those large clenched fists.

"We'll see about that." Erik shoved by him, pushing him against the sturdy door frame. Then he whirled around. "Stay away from Annie Rose." After a moment of glaring, he turned again and stomped off in the direction of the house.

Thomas approached carrying his own saddle. He walked past Joseph and set his saddle over the top railing of a stall fence. Joseph followed, placing his saddle next to Thomas's. The boy took the lantern from its nail and moved toward the door, then paused and looked back at Joseph. His young eyes were hard and angry.

"I don't know why Gramps brought you here, sir, but I'm sure he had his reasons. So I'll put up with you for now. But don't be expecting me to be your friend." He pulled himself up straighter and lifted the lantern so the light fell more fully on Joseph's face. "Like Erik said, stay away from my sister. I know she's real pretty, and a white woman is rare out here.

You'll end up wanting her. But if you ever hurt her, in any way, I'll kill you." The deadly words seemed incongruous coming from the mouth of a boy on the verge of manhood. Thomas continued, his voice squeaking. "I don't care if you are a Beaudine, and your brothers will come looking for me. I'll kill you if you hurt her."

Joseph nodded, once. "That's a fair warning, Thomas. I'll pay heed to it."

Surprise flared in the boy's eyes, then he nodded, too, solemnly. "Just so we understand each other." He turned on his heel and walked away, taking the lantern with him, leaving Joseph to follow or not.

Joseph settled his hat more firmly on his head. He'd found his forest sprite again, and he'd found the fabled Norseman who was reputed to have a gift with horses, but it appeared that he had also found some trouble in the persons of Erik and Thomas Jensen. Considering that neither of them knew him well, their hostility was confusing in its intensity. He retrieved the small pile of his belongings and trudged toward the house with the hope that his coming to the hidden valley did not upset the balance of peace among the members of Knute's little family.

"Pass the dumplings, please." Knute's blue eyes sparkled in anticipation of another helping. As he accepted the wooden bowl from Thomas, he asked, "Why'd you leave the Army, Captain?"

The question caught Joseph by surprise, and with a mouthful of delicious venison roast. He hurriedly chewed, then swallowed. "I felt it was time to move on."

"You had a promising career—graduated near the top of your class at West Point, distinguished yourself on the battlefield during the Mexican War, made a name for yourself as a cartographer with the elite Corps of Topographical Engineers—and yet you walked away from it." Knute set the bowl of dumplings down and smoothed his mustache. "Seems strange. *Ja,* it does."

Joseph stared at him. "How do you know all that? If I understand the situation correctly, you and your family are completely isolated up here. I find it difficult to believe that I'm a topic of conversation when you make a rare trip to Fort Laramie."

Knute chuckled. "Jubal Sage keeps me up to date on all the important happenings. Your resignation last month caused quite a stir. I'd like to know why you resigned your commission." He pierced a dumpling with his fork, then paused with it halfway to his mouth. "The real reason." His eyes bored into Joseph as he guided the dumpling to his mouth.

Reluctant to respond, Joseph now had a new understanding for how Annie Rose must have felt that night when he kept asking her questions she did not want to answer. A stab of guilt flashed through him. He glanced across the table at her, found her gaze on him. She quickly looked away. Both Thomas and Erik watched him closely, clearly still antagonistic. Had he been alone with Knute, he would have felt more comfortable talking about things which to him were private and important.

"He has the right to keep his reasons to himself, Gramps," Annie Rose said quietly. Now she met Joseph's gaze straight on. "It's not polite to pry."

Joseph wondered if she was deliberately quoting his words to Abby Baines that night in the cabin. As he looked into her green eyes, suddenly he wanted to answer Knute's question. He wanted Annie Rose to know more about him, to understand some of his beliefs.

"It's all right. I'm sure he has his reasons for asking," Joseph said, in a paraphrase of Thomas's earlier words. And he sensed that Knute did have a reason for asking. Again, he felt that he was being tested. He set his fork down and faced Knute. "It *was* time to move on. Changes are coming to this territory, and I'm not going to like the Army's role in those changes, just as I didn't like the Army's role in fighting Mexican families in their own homes."

"But didn't you like going to war?" Thomas blurted out. "It seems to me that it would be exciting."

"Perhaps it is, in the beginning. The idea is exciting, especially to someone who's never been to war." He eyed the boy, who seemed to be struggling to contain his interest. After all, Thomas had sworn he would not be Joseph's friend, yet there he was, asking questions. Joseph continued. "But war is not exciting. It is dirty, and exhausting, and filled with hardship—weeks and months of travel, rarely enough water, often not enough food, never enough sleep, always the fear hanging over you that you will die, from sword, bullet, or illness."

"Illness?" interjected Thomas.

"In times of war, far more men die of dysentery, cholera, and infection than from wounds," Joseph explained gently. "And they die much slower. A cannonball explosion or a bullet that takes a man quickly is a far kinder death."

"Oh." Thomas looked down at his plate.

"Forgive me for bringing up the topic at the supper table."

"I asked, Captain," Knute said. He pulled his napkin from his collar and set it next to his empty plate. "Please continue."

Joseph shrugged. "I want no more of war."

"You're sure you're not just a coward?" Erik sneered.

"Erik!" snapped Knute.

"It's all right." Joseph calmly met Erik's gaze. "He's young, and doesn't know much about the ways of the world."

Erik gave a snort of disgust. "I know what I need to know to make my way in *this* world." He waved an arm to indicate the valley.

"Indeed?" Joseph fixed him with a stern glare. "Do you know that someday, some of those pilgrims hurrying to California and Oregon are going to stop and look around?" Now Joseph waved his arm. "They're going to like what they see, just as you and I do. And they're going to want to stay, just as you and I do. But there will be too many of them, and in the end, the same thing that happened back East will happen here." A hard edge came into his voice. "The white man will want the Indian gone. And the Indians will fight, not only because this is their home, but also because there is nowhere left for them to go, as there was when they were pushed from the East. There will be more war, Erik. But I will be free to choose which side I will fight for. I will not raise my sword against my Cheyenne brothers."

Erik glared at him a moment longer, then dropped his gaze. Annie Rose and Thomas sat quietly, staring at him. He again faced Knute.

"That is the real reason I resigned my commission, sir."

Knute's expression was sober. "I've been thinking, too, that the area is getting a little crowded. You think it will get that bad?"

"Why should this territory be any different than any other part of the continent?" Joseph could not keep a trace of bitterness out of his tone. "The widespread belief in the United States' Manifest Destiny includes this territory."

"Manifest Destiny?" Thomas repeated.

"The belief that God intends the United States to extend from the Atlantic to the Pacific, including all land between the two seas," explained Joseph. "Unfortunately, most people forget that there are other peoples already living in some parts of that land, peoples who may not share the same belief in the Manifest Destiny of the United States."

"Or they simply don't care that others were there before them," Knute added.

Joseph nodded in agreement.

Knute turned the conversation back to Joseph. "What did you intend to do when you left the Army?"

"Continue scouting for the Army, at least for a while. It gives me an opportunity to further explore this land. I heard Tom Fitzpatrick thinks along the same lines I do and wants to work as some kind of mediator between the white man and the tribes. I like that idea. I want to help, too, and I'll have more freedom to do that if I'm not in the Army." He met Knute's gaze. "I also want to meet whoever trained Orion's horse, Thunder. The rumor is, that person has a special gift with horses." His gaze shifted to Annie Rose. "I'd like to see if he—or she—has anything to teach me."

A blush colored Annie Rose's cheeks. She jumped up from her bench and reached for Knute's plate. "You promised to walk with me after supper, Gramps." She grabbed her own plate and carried them to the worktable. "It's after supper."

"Ja, so it is, girl. And it was a mighty fine supper, at that." Knute rose from his chair at the head of the table. "You boys clean up while I walk with Annie Rose. Captain, that corner there is yours. We have a few extra buffalo robes that'll soften the ground somewhat. Thomas can show you where they're kept if you want to lay out your bed." He joined Annie Rose, who had wrapped a thick black shawl around her shoulders, and they left.

The room settled into an uneasy silence. As he finished the last of his coffee, Joseph couldn't help but wish that he had been allowed to walk with Knute and Annie Rose, not only to escape the uncomfortable atmosphere of the cabin, but to hear what was troubling Annie Rose. He wanted to help any way he could, both her and Knute.

Hell. He just wanted to be near her.

"The buffalo robes are stored in Annie Rose's room," Thomas said sullenly. "I'll show you where."

Joseph nodded his thanks and slid off the bench. After setting his empty plate on the worktable, he followed Thomas, ignoring Erik, who still sat at the supper table, fuming.

Behind the gingham curtain, Joseph found a feminine sanctuary that seemed to welcome him, perhaps because it was *her* room. Thomas struck a match and lit a candle on the upended wooden vegetable crate that served as a nightstand. Grateful for the soft light, Joseph looked about eagerly, wanting to learn all that Annie Rose's room would tell him about the woman.

The little room was tidy and charmingly decorated. Curtains made of a red, pink, and green floral print covered the small, high window and more of the material had been fashioned into a covering for the narrow bed built into a boxlike structure next to the far wall. A thick red wool blanket, like those the fur trappers traded with the Indians for buffalo robes, was neatly folded at the foot of the bed, ready to warm Annie Rose's slender body. Ridiculous as it was, Joseph felt a stab of jealousy toward the blanket. He wouldn't mind keeping Annie Rose warm himself.

A thick buffalo robe covered a good part of the packed-dirt floor, and a few modest garments hung from nails along one wall. A large trunk, a primitive washstand—clearly homemade—and the crate which held the surprisingly elegant brass candlestick and a stack of three books completed the furnishings.

Thomas's querulous voice broke into his reverie. "They're on that shelf." Joseph looked back over his shoulder in the direction Thomas pointed. A long shelf built high on the wall held several neatly folded buffalo robes. He grabbed two and held them, looking again about the room, not wanting to leave.

"Sir?" Thomas held back the gingham curtain at the door, clearly waiting—with impatience—for him.

Joseph was reluctant to leave the room that belonged to Annie Rose, but there was nothing else to be done. With a sigh, he went back out into the main room and the uncomfortable silence that hung heavy in the air. He hoped Knute and Annie Rose would not be gone too long.

"I can't believe I approached Jubal's cabin without first checking to see who was there," Annie Rose said mournfully after telling her story. She pulled the shawl closer around her shoulders and waited for her grandfather's response. When it came, that response surprised her, and stung.

"It was bound to happen."

"That I'd get careless?"

"No, *datter*." Knute patted the hand that rested on his forearm. "That your presence would be discovered. Joseph Beaudine is right—change is coming to this land. We could not have kept you hidden forever, nor should we. You are a woman grown now, and a lovely one. You deserve to have your own life, and your own home, with your own man."

Annie Rose tightened her grip on Knute's arm. "Don't say such things, Gramps. My life is with you and Thomas, and, and . . ."—she could not bring herself to name Erik—" . . . and that is how I want it."

"Nothing lasts forever, Annie Rose," Knute said gently. "My time here in this world is running out, you and Erik are grown now, and Thomas is well on his way. You all have your own lives to lead, your own paths to follow. And that is how it should be. That is the way of life."

Annie Rose bit down on her lip to keep from protesting Knute's words, because she knew he was right. A great sadness washed over her. The tall grasses rustled against her skirt as they walked. "We've been happy here," she said quietly.

"*Ja*. This valley has been good to us."

"I don't want it to end, Gramps."

"No, child, neither do I. But we must face life as it is." He stopped and looked at her. Even in the pale moonlight, Annie Rose could feel his sharp gaze on her, seeing all, missing nothing. "There is more, isn't there?"

"Yes," she whispered miserably.

"Tell me." Knute's old voice was warm with love.

"It's Erik, Gramps. I cannot be left alone with him again." Knute's jaw tightened. "What happened?"

Annie Rose forced herself to say the words. "He wants me. I thought he would outgrow his infatuation, given time, especially if I took great care not to encourage him in any way, even innocently. But his feelings have only intensified, and there is an ugly side to them now." She rubbed the aching bruise on her arm.

"Did he hurt you?" Knute asked the question carefully, as if he were afraid of the answer.

"He grabbed me, nothing more. But I fear he would have struck me today, if not for Maggie. He was furious that I left last night." Agitated, Annie Rose turned and began to walk again.

"Why did you leave?"

"I had to. Erik kept staring at me, all evening. Then he started drinking, Gramps, your brandy. I . . . I feared for my safety, so I went to Aurora." She stopped again, one hand on her forehead. "It all sounds so horrible. I can't believe it's Erik I'm talking about." She turned again to her grandfather, suddenly afraid that he wouldn't believe her. "He has changed."

"Ja, I know."

Tears filled her eyes at the sight of her grandfather's slumped shoulders. He looked so old! So weary! "I'm sorry, Gramps," she whispered brokenly.

"Oh, girl, it's not your fault." Knute placed her hand once more on his arm and led her on. "It's not your fault the Lord blessed you with your mother's beauty and your grandmother's gentle spirit, both of which will draw men like bees to honey. It's not your fault Erik has no other outlet for his affections, nor that there is a streak of rage in him which cannot be appeased. That's why I'll not allow him to work much with the horses anymore, especially in the beginning stages of training." He patted her hand again. "Fret not, Annie Rose. You won't be left with him again."

The tone of his voice concerned her, for—strangely—Erik's sake. "What will you do?"

"Erik is my grandchild, as much as you are. I love him, too. Don't worry about it, or him. All will be well." Knute took a deep breath. "All will be well. Now look at that moon. Have you ever seen a more beautiful sight?"

Annie Rose obeyed and raised her head to look at the moon, so recently risen that it still hung low over the mountains to the east. It *was* beautiful, shining so bright in the impossibly clear night sky.

"When you are troubled, *datter,* look up at the sky." Knute's voice softened. "From time immemorial, those stars have shined, that moon has followed its path across the heavens, regardless of the little turmoils of mankind here on earth. I know our troubles are not little to us, but in the greater scheme of the Creator, how important are they? Some are important, some are not. Some we can do something about, some we cannot. It is important to know the difference." He looked at her now. "The coming tide of emigrants, the changes threatening this land we love, the fact that I will die—those we cannot stop. The problem with Erik—that we can exercise some control over."

Annie Rose moved into her grandfather's welcoming arms and held him tightly, disturbingly aware of how thin he was. "I love you, Gramps."

"Ja, I know, just as I love you. Remember my words." His hand moved on her back in the ageless gesture of consolation. "When I am gone, as I will be one day, if ever you feel lost, or lonely, or confused, look to the stars. I shall be watching over you, as surely as they do. Take comfort from their constancy, for my love is as undying as the stars."

A sob caught in Annie Rose's throat, and she clung even tighter to her grandfather.

They stayed awhile longer at the pond, not speaking. Words were no longer necessary.

Seven

Joseph was disappointed that Annie Rose immediately disappeared behind her bedroom curtain when she and Knute returned to the cabin after a lengthy walk. Erik and Thomas had retreated to their own room the instant the last of the dishes was dried and put away. No sound had issued from the room since. Either the Jensen boys had already gone to bed, or they weren't speaking to each other any more than they were speaking to him. The tension between the members of the family created an uncomfortable atmosphere, one Joseph hoped would lighten in the morning.

The buffalo robes had enabled him to make a comfortable bed on the floor not far from Knute's bed. He sat there now, still fully clothed, his back against the wall, and watched as Knute pulled a bottle of brandy out of a drawer in the intricately painted chest near the fireplace. The old man held the bottle to the light and frowned, then grabbed something else from the drawer.

"Please come with me, Captain." He went out the door without waiting for Joseph's response.

Curious, Joseph got to his feet and left the cabin, closing the door quietly behind him. Knute was already halfway across the yard. By the time Joseph caught up with him, Knute had stopped near the farthest of the corrals, where the new horses milled about and nickered to each other. A thick length of tree trunk, perhaps two feet across and six feet long, lay on its side in front of the fence. The top had been leveled off to provide a flat seat. Knute sat there now, at one end. He pulled the cork from the bottle with his teeth and spit it away. When Joseph moved to retrieve it, Knute shook his head.

"No, we won't need the cork. There's not much left in here." He raised the bottle. "We'll finish it tonight." The moonlight revealed that he held in one hand two small handleless cups made of metal—pewter, Joseph guessed—with patterns or pictures engraved in the sides. Knute poured liquid into each cup and held out his hand. Joseph accepted one of the cups and took a seat at the opposite end of the log. Knute set the bottle down and wrapped both of his gnarled hands around his cup. For several minutes, he did not speak.

Joseph respected the old man's silence. He stared up at the heavens, marveling at the clarity of the night. The stars seemed so close that he felt he could reach out and touch one if he so chose. The almost full moon cast a pale light over the mountains and Knute's valley, creating shadows of the trees and the buildings. Aside from the shifting movements of the horses and the ever-present wind sighing through the trees and grasses, it was very quiet. Joseph took a deep breath, feeling a sense of peace steal over him. He was going to enjoy living here for a while, and not just because of a lovely, intriguing woman who knew how to cook.

"Annie Rose needs your help."

Knute's words startled Joseph as much as his voice suddenly breaking the stillness did. Annie Rose did not appear to need help of any kind, and she certainly would not welcome it from him. Before he could respond, Knute continued.

"I also need your help."

"I've already agreed to work for you, Mr. Jensen."

"Ja, ja, I know. This is different. I'm not talking about the horses now." He paused, taking a swallow from his cup. "I want you to call me 'Knute.' No more 'Mr. Jensen.'"

He needed Joseph's help in being called "Knute?" Was this request another sign of the old man's supposed mental imbalance? Confused, Joseph nodded. "Agreed, Knute. And no more 'captain,' I beg you. Joseph or Joe, please."

"Ja, all right, Joe." Knute took another swallow, then fixed his unwavering gaze on Joseph. "Annie Rose cannot be left alone with Erik. He fancies himself in love with her, and will not accept her lack of mutual feelings for him."

Joseph's stomach grabbed. "Erik is in love with his sister?"

Knute stared at him. "His sister?"

"You introduced both Thomas and Erik as your grandsons. I assumed they are . . ."

"Ah. I see why you would. Even their last names are the same. No, Erik is cousin to Annie Rose and Thomas, who are sister and brother. Erik was born to my son, the others to my daughter."

That explained why Erik did not look like Annie Rose and Thomas. Joseph also caught the fact that Annie Rose and Thomas went by their grandfather's—their mother's—last name. What of their father? He forced his mind back to Knute's statement that Annie Rose could not be left alone with Erik, and his jaw tightened. "Has he hurt her?"

"Not yet, and we will see that he doesn't get the chance. I will talk to him tomorrow, but you, I, and Thomas must watch out for her. Erik sometimes has terrible rages, and strikes out without thinking." Knute sighed, looking off into the dark distance. "There is bad blood in him, I fear. I warned my son away from that woman, beautiful though she was. But no, he had to have her, had to marry her. She was filled with rage, had bad, angry moods, like Erik. In fact, it was one of her moods that killed both her and my son."

Joseph could only stare at Knute, for he had no idea what to say.

"Ja, she liked to throw things when she was angry. One night, the nearest thing to hand was the lamp. My son was standing near the door, and she threw the lamp at him. He was afire in seconds, as was the door. My daughter-in-law could not escape the inferno she caused. Erik was in another

part of the house. The neighbors got him out; he was only a child, maybe eight years old. He stayed with the neighbors for a few years, until I returned from the frontier, then I took him with me."

For lack of anything better to say, Joseph asked, "When was that?"

Knute shrugged. "Over seven years ago, now, that I went back. I didn't know until then that my son was dead. That was when I learned that my daughter was dying as well. So I brought the children out here with me."

"What of your daughter's husband?"

The look Knute turned on Joseph was icy cold. "We do not speak of him. Ever."

Joseph was startled at the vehemence in the Norseman's voice. Evidently he had tread on dangerous ground. "Forgive me, sir."

"Ah, forget it." Knute waved a hand in the air. "I wish there was more brandy."

Another abrupt change of the subject. Joseph wondered how long this conversation was going to take.

"Try to get along with Erik, Captain—Joe. He is my grandchild, too, and I care for him. But he cannot stay here much longer." Knute threw his head back and drained his cup, then repeated, "He cannot stay here."

"I'll be careful with Erik, Knute. And I'll watch out for Annie Rose."

At that, Knute turned to face him once again. "Don't watch her too closely." His voice was very serious. "Annie Rose has good reason to distrust men. She is much more comfortable with her animals. Do not crowd her, or push her. I can see your interest in her, as I'm certain she can. Don't be surprised if she keeps her distance."

Now all three of the Jensen men had warned him away from Annie Rose. Joseph fought down a surge of irritation. "Do you think I'm not worthy of her?"

"On the contrary. I would be delighted if you and she were

to develop an affection for each other. That was one of the reasons I brought you here."

Joseph was startled. The old man was playing matchmaker for his granddaughter? As intrigued as Joseph was by the golden-haired woman, that didn't mean he wanted to marry her. He didn't know whether to feel flattered or used.

"But the final decision is Annie Rose's to make," Knute added. "Is that understood?"

"I'll force no woman to endure my company," Joseph said stiffly.

"Of course you won't. That's another reason I chose you."

Joseph was beginning to feel like a pawn in some crazy, solitary game that Knute Jensen was playing. It was an uncomfortable feeling, one he didn't care for at all. "We've known each other for less than two days, Knute, and yet you are prepared to bless a union between me and your granddaughter? You know nothing about me, except what you've heard."

"I knew your father well, and so I know something of you. And, despite what you may have heard about me, I'm no fool. I haven't survived on this frontier for over twenty years by being stupid, or blind, or crazy. I can size a man up real quick." As if he had suddenly wearied of the conversation, Knute stood, snatching up the empty bottle as he did. He met Joseph's gaze. "I don't know what will happen between you and Annie Rose. Whatever happens—if nothing happens—it will be for the best. But I do know I can trust you, Joseph Beaudine."

He paused for a moment, and even in the pale moonlight, Joseph could see that his features softened.

Knute continued. "Your father did a fine job with his sons. He was proud of you, and rightly so. I know you'll treat my granddaughter with respect, and you'll protect her if the need arises, just as you did that night at Jubal's cabin. By the way, for that I thank you and the Hunter. Baines!" He spat. "That bastard is a blight on the frontier. He must never get his hands on Annie Rose, or on the Golden Mare." He headed toward the cabin.

In the excitement of finding Annie Rose again, Joseph had forgotten about the mare. But now was not the time to attempt to pry answers out of Knute. *Patience,* he counseled himself. There was time to learn all. He decided to remain on the hard wooden seat for a while and finish his brandy. "Good night, Knute," he called after the tall, thin figure.

Knute waved over his shoulder. "Good night, Captain Joe." He disappeared into the cabin.

Joseph smiled. He might well be stuck with "Captain," at least as far as Knute was concerned. And from all Knute had told him, that could prove to be the least of his problems over the next several weeks. He took a sip of brandy, silently echoing Knute's wish for more, wondering if he'd been played for a fool. Only time would tell if he had been blindly—and, he had to admit, willingly—led into a hornet's nest by a beautiful young woman and a cunning old man.

Early the next morning, everyone gathered around the table for a filling breakfast of cornmeal-battered trout, fried potatoes, and strong coffee. Maggie's enthusiastic enjoyment of her meal was the only sound in the room. Joseph looked up from his plate to see Annie Rose pouring fresh milk for Thomas from a large, elaborately painted wooden tankard.

His artistic interest piqued, he decided to take a chance and break the uncomfortable silence. "The decoration on the tankard is beautiful. I've never seen anything like it before." He was thankful that Annie Rose did not hesitate to respond.

"The style of painting is a traditional Norwegian one," she explained with a touch of pride in her voice. "It's called *rosemaling.* The tankard was a wedding gift to my grandparents. Gramps brought it from Norway, as he did the chest." With a nod, she indicated the chest where Knute kept his drinking cups.

"May I?" Joseph held out his hand.

Annie Rose carefully gave him the tankard. Upon closer inspection, Joseph was even more impressed by the quality and originality of the artwork. Graceful swirls of pink and blue formed whimsical flowers on the red background, and the whole was highlighted by more swirls of green and black. The numbers one-eight-zero-four were painted in the front near the lip.

"Eighteen-oh-four." Joseph looked at Knute. "The year of your wedding?"

"Ja." A shadow of sadness passed over his face, then was gone. "It was a long time ago, and far away. Another life." Knute drained his coffee cup. "Now we have this life, and there is work to do." He pushed back his chair and stood up. "Thomas, Cap—Joe, please help Annie Rose straighten up in here. Erik, you come with me. Later we'll all meet at the corrals."

"We won't be long, Gramps," said Annie Rose.

Knute paused at the door, his hat in his hand. He looked at Joseph. "Annie Rose does the work of a man with the horses. Therefore, the men help her with the work of a woman. That is the way things are done here." His sharp gaze seemed to be offering a challenge.

"Seems only fair," Joseph replied. He meant what he said.

"Good." Knute clapped his hat on his head and left.

Erik followed, but not before he shot an angry look at Joseph. He pulled the door closed behind him with far more force than was necessary. Thomas glanced at his sister and rolled his eyes, then shoveled the last of his potatoes into his mouth.

"Mr. Beaudine, would you please fetch some water from the well?" Annie Rose asked politely as she stacked soiled plates in a wooden washtub. "The bucket is there by the door, and, from the front door, the well is off to the left near the stand of aspen, not far from the smokehouse."

"Of course." He drained his cup and rose from the bench, thinking how pretty Annie Rose looked this morning. It struck him as curious that she wasn't wearing her man's clothes to work with horses, but he liked the picture she presented in her dark blue skirt made of a serviceable material, an over-sized shirt of a lighter blue gathered around her narrow waist with a thick leather belt, the long sleeves rolled nearly to her elbows, and a clean white apron. Her hair hung in a long braid down her back, tied at the end with a blue ribbon, and her neck and cheeks were teased by golden wisps. She looked . . . cute. Joseph wanted to tell her so, but instead he said, "You're a fine cook, Miss Jensen."

His words seemed to have caught her off guard, for she hesitated a moment before she spoke. "Thank you."

She did not look at him, but Joseph would swear he saw the delicate coloring of a blush kiss her cheek. Pleased, he took up the bucket and stepped outside, leaving the door open to the glorious morning. Maggie followed him, to his surprise, and he almost started whistling. The day was off to a good start.

"You frightened your cousin, Erik, and there will be no more of it. Keep your distance from her." Knute spoke in a calm voice, fighting the urge to shout at his grandson, even though he knew the sound of his voice would not carry to the house from the barn, where he and Erik now stood facing each other, the antagonism thick between them.

Erik gaped at him. "You can't tell me to stay away from Annabella, Gramps. We—we live in the same house, we're together all the time."

"She knows how you feel about her," Knute said gently. "We all do, Erik, just as we know she does not feel the same way about you. You must accept that what you wish for will never happen. Even if Annie Rose returned your feelings, you are first cousins. You cannot hope to marry her."

"This territory is not part of the United States. There are no laws here against marriage between first cousins," Erik argued. "She loves me."

"As a cousin, yes; perhaps even as a brother. But not as

a mate, a husband. Many times she has told you this, and you have refused to believe her. Now *I* am telling you, and you *will* believe me. What happened here the other night will not happen again."

Erik shifted uncomfortably. "Nothing happened the other night. If she said something did, she's lying."

Knute glared at his grandson, beginning to lose control of his reined-in anger. "Annie Rose does not lie," he snapped. "If you loved her as you claim to, you would never even suggest such a thing."

His jaw tightened, but Erik did not reply.

"You drank my brandy the other night, without my permission. You let your rage settle upon you, take you over again. You stared at her, stalked her, frightened her. She did not know what you would do, so she ran in the night." Knute's voice rose steadily, and he pointed a finger at Erik. "Your cousin ran from her own house because she felt threatened by you, Erik. Does that not shame you?"

"I didn't touch her!"

"You did when she came back yesterday. You hurt her arm. What more would you have done if Maggie had not interfered?"

Erik's face flushed red, and his breath came in short gasps. His big hands closed into fists and opened, then closed again. "Annabella will be my wife," he ground out.

Knute felt the fingers of a too-familiar tightness spread across his chest. Sweat broke out on his forehead, and, as he stared into his enraged grandson's eyes, he wondered if Erik would actually use those flexing hands against him. Now Knute understood some of the fear Annie Rose must have felt, and a fresh wave of anger rose up in him. "I won't allow it."

A curiously cold look settled over Erik's features. "You won't live forever, old man."

Knute's hand whipped out and cracked across Erik's cheek, hard. "No," he whispered, then his voice grew stronger. "But while I do live, you will treat me with the respect I deserve as your grandfather, and you will treat your cousin with the respect any woman deserves. You will obey me while you live in my house, in my valley, or you will leave. Now. Today."

Erik's face paled.

"*Ja*, I mean it, Erik Jensen. Which will it be?" Knute ignored the pulses of pain flashing down his left arm.

Something akin to hatred flashed in Erik's blue eyes. "I'll do as you say, Gramps." He stomped toward the barn door. "For now," he shot back over his shoulder before he disappeared into the sunlight.

Knute leaned back against the wall, clutching at his chest. With deep, shaky breaths, he willed the pain away. "Please, not yet," he whispered, the plea as close to a prayer as he could come. He closed his eyes and rested, thankfulness flooding through him as the pain slowly withdrew once again, like a dragon backing into its cave.

That was how he pictured the thing that occasionally grabbed and tore at his chest—a fierce, fire-breathing dragon, like those of the old Nordic tales, lurking in its cave, occasionally coming out to attack him. One day the dragon would win, would still his heart and take his life; Knute knew that, and accepted it.

But not yet.

He had to see to Annie Rose and Thomas, ensure that they were safe from new threats—men like Abby Baines, the sick fury of their cousin. They could not be stranded here, in this beautiful valley they had all called home for so many years, alone with Erik.

Again, Knute was filled with gratitude, this time gratitude that he had listened to the sudden and powerful impulse that he offer Joseph Beaudine a job.

If nothing else, Annie Rose and Thomas had the captain.

Knute smiled, a satisfied, determined smile. Having one of the Beaudine brothers as his ace in the hole was more than most men could ask for.

* * *

With one hand balancing the filled water bucket on the lip of the well, Joseph watched Erik storm out of the barn. It wasn't difficult to figure out what Knute had probably told him. If he'd been unpleasant before, Joseph suspected Erik would cross the line to unbearable now. His suspicions were supported by the way Erik slammed the corral gate open so hard that it bounced back off the fence. The new horses milled about nervously, crowding against the far fence, away from the red-haired man. If Knute—or someone—didn't get out there quickly, Erik would have the horses so upset that it would take hours to calm them down.

Joseph anxiously scanned the empty doorway of the barn and was about to head in that direction when Knute appeared. The Norseman repositioned his hat on his head, then strode toward the corral, barking commands. At that distance, Joseph couldn't make out the words, but the meaning was clear. Erik left the corral as quickly as he had entered, closing the gate behind Knute with less violence than he had demonstrated when he opened it. Joseph noted with approval that Knute did not immediately approach the spooked horses, but stood, still and quiet, a few feet from the gate.

Assured that all would be well with Knute and the horses for a few minutes, Joseph lifted the bucket and headed toward the cabin, amused to see that Maggie again came with him. Apparently, Annie Rose's black dog accepted him as a friend. With luck, one day Maggie's mistress would also accept him as a friend, at the very least. As he approached the opened door of the cabin on silent moccasined feet, the sound of other voices reached his ears. This time, he could make out the words, although they were spoken quietly.

"Gramps had another of his spells, Annie Rose."

"When?" Annie Rose's voice was tight with fear.

"Day before yesterday, at the lake where The Paint gave us the horses."

Joseph found the belief—evidently accepted by all members of the Jensen family—that The Paint had "given" them the captured horses amusing, and somehow touching. It spoke

of a respect accorded The Paint that Joseph felt the magnificent stallion deserved. Then Joseph's attention was drawn
back to the conversation between Annie Rose and Thomas, a
conversation on which he had no right to eavesdrop. Yet he
did.

"Did the spell last long?" Annie Rose asked.

"No. It passed so quickly that I wasn't sure at first that it
happened. But it did, sister. I know it did."

"Did Gramps mention it?"

A snort of disbelief. " 'Course not." Then a pause. "Is he
dying, Annie Rose?" Thomas's voice cracked—from fear or
from puberty, or from both—yet there was strength there,
too. Joseph felt compassion for the scared man-child, trying
so hard to be strong for his sister's sake.

"I don't think he's actually dying right now, Thomas, but
he *will* die from this." Her tone was kind and loving. Joseph
imagined that she was touching her brother's shoulder or
hand, if not embracing him.

"When?" Thomas's voice was muffled, lending weight to
Joseph's imagined embrace.

"There's no way to know."

The incredible sadness in the voices of brother and sister
tore at Joseph's heart. He looked out over Knute's valley,
lovely beyond description in the early morning sun, and allowed the sadness to touch him, too.

Now Knute's actions made sense, as did some of his cryp-
tic words during their conversation the night before.

The Norseman was frightened.

Not of death; Joseph knew that.

Knute was frightened for his grandchildren, for what their
future without him would hold. Perhaps once, Knute had believed that Erik would take care of his cousins; now, knowing
that was not possible, Knute was frightened of Erik's unpre-
dictability and escalating violent behavior. He was frightened—with just cause—of the growing presence in the
territory of men like Baines, who had discovered the fact of

Annie Rose's existence. They would tell others. They would
search for her.

The thought made his blood run cold.

Now that Joseph understood what was at risk, he understood Annie Rose's anger toward herself that morning at
Jubal's cabin.

So many things made sense, now.

An affection for the strange old Norseman welled in
Joseph's heart. *You can count on me, Knute,* he silently
vowed. *You can count on me.*

Eight

"Maggie! Here, girl!"

Joseph deliberately called the dog, even though Maggie was only a few feet away. He wanted to alert Annie Rose and Thomas to his presence. Sure enough, the voices inside quieted, and he carried the bucket of water into the cabin.

"Thank you, Mr. Beaudine," Annie Rose murmured.

With quiet efficiency, the three worked together, and soon the main room was as neat as a pin. Thomas hurried off to the corrals, and Joseph and Annie Rose followed a minute later, with Maggie at their heels.

"Your mare sure is a pretty thing," Annie Rose commented as they approached the first corral.

So are you. Joseph had to bite down on his lip to keep from saying the words out loud. "Yes, she is," he said instead. "Grace and I have been through a lot together." Grace strolled up to the fence, nickering a welcome.

"Grace?" Annie Rose eyed him quizzically. "How did you come to name her?"

Joseph ran his hand down the mare's neck in an affectionate caress. "She saved my life on a battlefield in Mexico." Grace nuzzled the front of his shirt, and for a moment, he was back on that smoky, bloody battlefield. "Her sergeant was shot out of the saddle just after my mount was shot out from under me. Mexican soldiers were coming at me from all sides. In desperation, I whistled for her. By the grace of

God, she came, and we both lived to see another day. So I named her Grace." The intensity of the scene playing in Joseph's mind became unbearable, and he blinked several times to clear his vision, grateful to see Knute's valley and the distant mountains come into sharp focus before him. The horrors of that Mexican battlefield retreated to the past once again.

"It's a good name for her," Annie Rose said quietly.

Joseph glanced down at her, found her clear green eyes on him, soft with compassion. His stomach tightened, so grateful was he that he hadn't found pity in those green depths. "I think so."

"It's very curious that she would come to you when she was not your horse."

He shrugged. "Not so curious—I knew her. Her sergeant wasn't always kind to her, so I'd check on her." Grace nuzzled him again, and he couldn't help smiling at the mare.

"And your kindness to her had nothing to do with the fact that she came for you." A gentle sarcasm touched Annie Rose's words.

Joseph could think of nothing to say.

Annie Rose held her right hand under Grace's nose and, after a moment, stroked the mare's forehead with her left hand. "Hello, Grace," she crooned. "You're such a darling."

The warm, intimate tone of her voice sent a completely unexpected and surprisingly intense shiver of desire down Joseph's spine. He briefly closed his eyes, wondering what it would be like to have Annie Rose talk to him like that, then he looked at her, silently begging her to talk some more, even if only to Grace.

After a moment, Annie Rose glanced at him from under the wide brim of her felt hat. Joseph was struck again by the beauty of her face.

She frowned. "Mr. Beaudine?"

Joseph realized he was staring at her. Embarrassed, he looked in the direction of the meadow beyond Grace's corral, squinting against the bright August sun. Several horses grazed there, including the bay Knute had ridden from Wild Horse Lake. "Is that your family's herd?" he asked, for lack of anything better to say.

"Yes. The bay stallion is Gramps's Thoroughbred. He calls him Viking." Annie Rose rested a foot on the lowest fence rail.

"Was he Thunder's sire?"

"Yes. Gramps is experimenting with a breeding program. He breeds Viking with the finest mustang mares we can capture, hoping to blend the mustang's toughness and endurance with the Thoroughbred's greater size and speed. There have been seven foals born so far, and the experiment seems to be successful."

Joseph was impressed. "If all the foals turned out like Thunder, I'd say it was very successful," he said. "How big is your herd?"

"Over the years, we've sold several of our own horses, so there's only six right now, not counting Viking and the horses Erik and Thomas ride. We have a pretty little filly, born just over a month ago." She glanced in the direction of the farthest corral, where Knute, Thomas, and Erik were with the new horses. "We should go join them." With a final caress of Grace's nose, she turned, and they walked toward the corral.

"What is the Knute Jensen system of training horses?" Joseph asked.

Without looking at him, she answered, "Gramps and I work with the horses first, to get them used to being around people, to get used to a halter. When the horses are a little more settled, Gramps, Thomas, and Erik start saddle-training them."

The sounds of shouts came from the corral, followed by the neighing and whinnying of agitated horses.

Annie Rose frowned as she lifted a hand to the brim of her hat. "I wonder what's going on."

Although the volume of their voices had lowered, Knute and Erik seemed to be in disagreement about something.

"Erik and your grandfather had words earlier," Joseph said carefully. "I'm not sure what about, but it was clear they argued."

Her shoulders slumped, for only a moment, then Annie Rose straightened. "We have work to do, Mr. Beaudine."

"Let's get to it."

"No matter what you think you know about horses, you will take your orders from Gramps."

Irritated, Joseph looked at her, but she kept her face turned to the front. "I planned to," he said.

"Just so there's no misunderstanding. Also, absolutely no kind of abuse or cruelty toward any animal will be tolerated, no matter how unruly or stubborn an animal might be." She still didn't look at him.

Joseph's irritation grew. "That goes without saying, Miss Jensen. Aside from the fact that I find abuse of any creature abhorrent, a horse who is frightened of its trainer is very difficult to train."

"Again, I just want to be certain there is no misunderstanding. My grandfather's training methods might be considered unusual by some, but they are very effective." Annie Rose stopped at the fence surrounding the corral in which her grandfather, brother, and cousin worked. "We split the herd between the two corrals," she explained, waving an arm toward the empty middle corral. "For now, I'll work with one group, Gramps with the other. Thomas and Erik will see to other chores around the homestead. That pattern will probably last for two to three days, until we are ready for the saddles. I don't know what Gramps has in mind for you."

The set of her jaw and the tone of her voice indicated to Joseph that Annie Rose felt the same way Thomas and Erik did about his presence in their valley—he wasn't needed, or wanted. She evidently hadn't guessed the real reason Knute had offered him a job.

"Let's ask him." Joseph lifted the rope loop on the gate and allowed her to proceed first into the corral. They joined the Jensen men in the center of the enclosure. The nervous horses milled about, hugging the fence, their eyes wide and wary.

"Erik thinks we should divide the horses into three groups today, maybe even four," Knute commented, stroking his white mustache.

Annie Rose glanced at Erik. "We'd have to get the rest of our own horses out to pasture in order to free up that fourth corral."

"Tom can do that," Erik said.

Annie Rose saw Thomas's mouth tighten at Erik's use of the nickname her brother had never liked. Why did her cousin insist upon calling both her and Thomas names they disliked?

"We'll get more done in these first days if we each work with a smaller group," Erik explained impatiently. "Gramps said he wanted to get these horses trained as quickly as possible."

Erik's suggestion made sense to Annie Rose. "What do you think, Gramps?"

Knute shrugged. *"Ja,* that's fine with me."

There seemed to be no dissension between Knute and Erik on that subject. What had they been arguing about?

"Thomas, saddle up." Knute looked at Joseph. "Is it all right to put your horse out to pasture for today?"

"Of course. I'll help Thomas take them out."

Knute shook his head. "No, I want you to work with a couple of the horses."

"No!"

All eyes turned to Erik.

"Send him out with the horses. We don't need his help here."

Annie Rose silently agreed with her cousin, but she said nothing.

"Erik," Knute said, the warning very clear in his old voice. "I hired Captain Beaudine to work the new horses, and that's what he will do."

"You don't know what he *can* do!" Erik's blue eyes seemed to flash with rage. "Who says he knows anything

about horses? And even if he does,"—the contemptuous look
Erik threw in Joseph's direction indicated his opinion on the
matter—"the fact still remains that *we don't need him.* I say
send him on his way back to the fort."

"No." The word was spoken quietly, but it had the impact
of a cannonball. Knute drew himself up to his full height.
"That is my final word. Now let's get to work."

Annie Rose glanced at her brother. Thomas shrugged in
resignation, then headed toward the corral where the other
horses waited. Erik swore under his breath and, with a final
venomous look at Joseph, stalked toward the wild horses.

"Do you want the horses divided any special way?" Joseph
asked Knute.

Knute shook his head. "Put only one other horse with that
one, though." He pointed in the direction of the feisty chestnut mare they had used as the leader on the trip from Wild
Horse Lake. "She's got her dander up, that one does. She'll
be the most trouble."

Joseph nodded in agreement, then moved toward the
horses.

"Get the gate, Annie Rose," Knute ordered.

Annie Rose hurried to the gate that led into the neighboring corral. She lifted the rope loop from the post and stood
ready to swing the gate open when the time came.

"I'll keep these two back," Joseph called from the far side
of the enclosure. He waved his arms, causing two horses,
including the chestnut mare, to stay close to the fence. Annie
Rose could not see her grandfather and her cousin behind
the herd of excited horses, but they did seem to be having
some difficulty in getting the rest of the horses to move toward the gate.

She frowned, wondering what the problem was, then
Knute broke free from the pack, trotting toward her, urging
two horses in front of him. Annie Rose swung the gate open
just wide enough to allow them to pass through.

Suddenly, a horse screamed, the shrill sound splitting the
early morning air.

Annie Rose shared a startled look with her grandfather. What had happened? She peered into the swirling dust that had been raised by the pounding of hooves. Knute disappeared into the melee.

A length of rope snapped through the air and lashed a horse across the face. The animal screamed in protest and reared up, striking one of the other horses with its hoof.

Even through the dust, Annie Rose could see that Erik held the other end of the rope.

What the hell was he doing?

Annie Rose never spoke swear words out loud, and she rarely even thought them, but she was properly moved to do so now. If the horses were goaded into a blind panic and stampeded within the enclosure of the corral, someone was going to get hurt. Or killed.

"Erik! Don't use the rope!"

Knute's voice rose above the sounds of the horses, but Annie Rose could not see him.

Thomas ran from the barn toward her. "What happened, sister?"

"I don't know for sure. Watch the gate."

When Thomas had taken her place at the gate, Annie Rose ran along the corral fence toward Joseph. The two horses he had struggled to keep separate were once again with the main herd, but, thankfully, the other two were safely enclosed in the neighboring corral.

That left seven terrified and enraged wild horses to contend with, in a very small space.

Then she saw Joseph stride toward her cousin. The fury on the captain's face was almost more frightening than the threat of a stampede. He tore the rope from Erik's hand and tossed it over the fence, hardly pausing on his way to help Knute. Erik glared after him, making no move to offer assistance. Ignoring her cousin, Annie Rose hurried after Joseph. Working with care, she, Knute, and Joseph were able to herd the rest of the horses through the gate into the next corral. Thomas looped the gate closed.

"Is everyone all right?" Annie Rose asked the question in general, but she looked at her grandfather. His face seemed pasty, with a grey tone to his skin.

"I was knocked into the fence, that's all." Knute rubbed his elbow as he glanced over the fence at the nervous, milling horses. "That set us back timewise. It'll take them awhile to settle down."

Erik walked over to join them, a belligerent and defiant expression on his bearded face.

No one said anything for a long moment. Then Joseph casually crossed his arms over his chest. "It wasn't a good idea to use the rope, Erik."

Without warning, Erik turned and slugged Joseph in the jaw. Joseph staggered back a step, then caught himself and straightened.

"Erik!" gasped Annie Rose.

Knute grabbed Erik's arm and shook him, hard. "What are you doing? Apologize to the captain."

"Never!" Erik spat. "He had no right to interfere."

Joseph touched his bleeding lip with a leather-gloved finger, his hard gaze locked on Erik. Again, the expression on his face gave Annie Rose pause. Joseph Beaudine was a force to be reckoned with under any circumstances; when angry, he was downright dangerous. She shivered, then pulled out the handkerchief that was tucked in her belt.

"You're young and hotheaded, Erik," Joseph finally said, his voice deceptively calm. "So I'll let this one pass. But if you ever raise your hand to me again, you'd better be ready to go the distance." He paused. "And don't ever let me catch you abusing an animal again."

Erik strained against his grandfather's hold. "I'll take you on now, Beaudine. I'm not afraid of you."

"You should be, you fool." Knute pushed Erik toward the far gate. "Get out of here. Take our horses to pasture."

"Wh—what?" Erik stammered. "That's a boy's job, Tom's job."

Annie Rose saw her brother's jaw tighten. Was Erik as

unkind as that, or was he simply so upset and enraged that he didn't realize how insulting his words were?

"Today it's your job." Knute bit out the words. "You need some time to cool off. Take the scythe with you and go to work on the hay in the south meadow."

"But—"

"Go. Now. One of us will bring you something to eat at noon." Knute's tone brooked no argument. Annie Rose was thankful that Erik apparently realized that, for he stomped off and slammed the gate behind him, causing it to bounce against the post.

Knute turned to Joseph. "I apologize, Captain Beaudine," he said stiffly. "My grandson has shamed us all with his behavior toward you."

"Erik is responsible for his own actions, Knute. They are no reflection on you." Joseph accepted the handkerchief Annie Rose held out to him, smiling his thanks at her.

She looked away, quickly. If she watched Joseph Beaudine much longer, she'd be tempted to snatch the handkerchief back from him, to take his chin in her hand and dab the blood from his mouth herself. How she hated to see him injured, even slightly.

"I'm sorry, Gramps," she said quietly. Her gaze flicked to her grandfather, then to the horses. "This all started with me. Erik was upset because of me and took it out on the horses." Now she looked back at Joseph. "And on Mr. Beaudine."

"I told you last night that it isn't your fault. There will be no more talk of it." Knute hooked his thumbs in his belt and studied the group of horses in the next corral. "That chestnut mare is a feisty one. We used her as the leader on the way here. She'll be the most trouble."

Annie Rose dutifully turned her attention to the mare in question. "She has spirit, that's for sure."

Knute faced Joseph. "Let's bring her back in here, with one other."

Joseph glanced at Annie Rose, then nodded at Knute.

Thomas jogged to the gate that separated the two corrals and opened it just wide enough to let the two men through, one at a time. It only took a few minutes to separate the two horses from the herd and drive them toward the gate. As expected, the rest of the horses tried to follow, but to no avail. The chestnut mare and a black yearling colt with a white star on his forehead reluctantly trotted into the original corral, with Knute and Joseph on their heels. Thomas quickly secured the gate.

Angry now, the mare trotted around her corral, neighing her outrage and occasionally lashing out at nothing with her hind legs. At her antics, her companion became more agitated, as did the rest of the herd. The seven horses in the other corral stayed close to the dividing fence, offering neighs of worry and nickers of encouragement.

"Cap—Joseph."

At the sound of Knute's quiet voice, Joseph turned his gaze from the horses to the Norseman. Knute pointed toward the fence. Joseph nodded and backed up, watchful of the upset mare. Thomas and Knute climbed over the fence, but Annie Rose stayed in the corral.

"Miss Jensen," Joseph called softly.

Knute tapped his shoulder. "Let her be." He jerked his head, indicating that Joseph should join him on the other side of the fence. When Joseph frowned, Knute jerked his head again, his old eyes flashing.

Remembering Annie Rose's admonition that he follow Knute's orders, Joseph climbed over the fence. Neither Knute nor Thomas showed any sign of concern as they watched Annie Rose. Biting down on his words of protest, Joseph turned his attention to the slender woman in blue standing so calmly in the center of the corral.

Annie Rose took a deep breath, smelled the clean scent of sun-warmed horses, caught an occasional and not unpleasant whiff of droppings. Her eyes drifted closed. She focused on the sound of the disturbed horses, heard their trampling hooves and agitated breathing.

Then she went deeper.

She could *feel* their confusion and fear. Her heart started beating faster; her breath came faster as she fought against the contagious fear. Forcing her breathing to slow, Annie Rose searched for and found a place of calm deep within herself. She nurtured that calm, called it forth, and opened her eyes.

The yearling colt still moved about, as did the horses in the neighboring corral, but the frantic neighing had ceased. Only the chestnut mare remained defiant. That one pawed the dirt and snorted, making her feelings very clear. She watched Annie Rose with wildly rolling eyes.

Annie Rose glanced over her shoulder at the men on the fence. She ignored the look of bewilderment on Joseph Beaudine's face and spoke to her grandfather. "I think I need to work with Miss Troublemaker alone for a while. If I can calm her, it will help with the others."

Knute nodded his agreement, and he and Thomas clambered back over the fence. Joseph seemed to collect himself, and followed a moment later. Again, Thomas manned the gate between the corrals while Knute and Joseph separated the yearling from the mare. The mare screamed her outrage and began to race around the corral, every now and then veering toward Annie Rose, then away again. Thomas closed the gate behind the yearling, and the men left the corral once more.

Annie Rose could tell Joseph was reluctant to leave her alone with the furious mare, for his concern was evident in his facial expression and in his brown eyes. She was torn with conflicting emotions over that concern—a part of her was pleased that he cared, a part was irritated that he didn't trust her ability with the mare, a part was anxious to show him what she could do.

The mare thundered by again, very close this time. For the second time that day, Annie Rose silently cursed. She needed to put the handsome captain out of her mind and focus on the mare—before the hostile animal ran her down.

Again, she repeated the steps she had taken earlier—the deep, calming breath, the closing of her eyes, the intense concentration on the sounds the mare made. She heard them all. Pounding hooves. Tearing breaths. Furious snorts and whinnies.

Then deeper, to the hammering heart, the laboring lungs.

Then deeper still, to the wild fear, the desperation, the fierce need to escape.

Motionless, using only her soul, Annie Rose reached out toward the mare. The sounds of the world faded; she could no longer hear the hoofbeats, the calls of the other horses, the mare's snorting. All she could hear was the steady rhythm of the mare's heart, joined to the beating of her own heart, in perfect time. Beating fast now, very fast. Too fast.

Annie Rose willed her breathing to slow, willed her racing heart to slow. Of its own accord, her right arm raised from her side to extend in front of her, her hand held out as if in supplication.

Her heart rate slowed, as did the mare's. Her breathing slowed, as did the mare's. The pounding—of breath, of heart-beats, of hooves—quieted.

"Shh, baby," Annie Rose whispered. "It's all right." Slowly, she opened her eyes.

The mare stood near the far fence, her sides heaving, her muscles trembling. She shook her head and blew, watching Annie Rose intently. Some of the wildness, the hostility, had faded from her big brown eyes.

Annie Rose remained still, her arm outstretched. The connection of spirit had not yet been broken. She murmured patient words of endearment and encouragement to the mare.

Finally, after several long minutes, the mare took a step toward her. Then another. A quiet nicker. Another step. Then she touched her nose to Annie Rose's hand.

Love welled up in Annie Rose's heart. "Shh, shh, it's all right, sweetie," she whispered. "Everything's changed, hasn't it? You've been taken from your home, separated from your friends." She took a cautious step toward the mare, who threw her head back in warning. Annie Rose halted and stood perfectly still. "Shh. Shh." Again the mare pressed her soft nose into Annie Rose's hand. Moving very slowly, Annie Rose brought her other hand up to caress the mare's forehead. "Good girl. What's your name, sweetie?" She listened intently for an answer.

Calypso.

The name popped into her mind.

"Calypso," she whispered. "Yes. That's a good name for you, you irksome little nymph. You'd give even Odysseus trouble."

She moved along Calypso's side, finally looking back over her shoulder at the men on the fence. Knute looked proud, Thomas, impatient and ready to get to work. But Joseph . . .

Joseph looked thunderstruck.

Annie Rose didn't know if that was a good thing or not. Was he impressed? Amazed? Intrigued? Fearful?

Was he fearful that she was crazy, or perhaps in league with the devil?

Suddenly, his feelings were very important to her.

She turned away, disturbed. Why should she care what Joseph Beaudine thought? She patted Calypso's neck, fiercely determined not to care.

The decision was easy to make with her head; it was not so easy to convince her heart.

Joseph could not believe what he had just seen.

Without touching—or even going near—the mare, Annie Rose had calmed the wild-eyed animal. The souls of the woman and the horse had connected, and Annie Rose had been able to soothe the mare's frightened, troubled spirit. Joseph knew it not only because of what he had just witnessed, but because he had touched upon their connection himself.

He had felt their pounding hearts, the mare's fear and desperation, Annie Rose's struggle to throw off the negative force of that fear. He recognized the gentle power of Annie Rose's compassionate spirit, her genuine concern for the mare. She had touched his spirit as surely as she touched that of the horse.

The realization shook him. In his whole life—although his family had accepted it—no one else had ever truly understood the connection he had with horses, the communication, let alone shared that connection. As irrational as it seemed, he felt somehow violated, as if some deep defense had been breached. The feeling was intensely uncomfortable.

Joseph turned on Knute. "You're not the one with the fabled Gift, are you? She is."

Knute met his accusatory gaze. *"Ja,"* he responded calmly. "I have a touch of the Gift, but not like she does. She is blessed."

"So you keep her locked away up here in this valley and use her gift to support all of you." Joseph knew that wasn't fair, but he couldn't help himself.

"It isn't like that," Thomas snapped, his young face flushed with anger. He glared at Joseph. "There are good reasons we hide here." He waved toward his sister, who stood a distance away, still at the mare's side, her forehead resting against the mare's neck, her hands moving over the glossy chestnut coat in calming caresses. "Part of the reason is to *protect* her."

"To protect her from what? You've been hiding for seven years."

"To protect her from men like Abelard Baines," Knute interjected.

"And you," Thomas added heatedly.

Knute shot his grandson a warning look, then returned his attention to Joseph. "She is a young, beautiful, white woman. You know what would happen if the men in the territory were to learn of her presence. *Ja,* they'd be crawling all over the place looking for her, sniffing at her skirts. It would be worse if they also knew of her gift. That is why the few people who know of this place, who know of Annie Rose—

people like Jubal Sage and Sweet Water and Grey Eagle—are sworn to secrecy."

Joseph understood Knute's reasoning; he had seen the blind lust, the cruel desire, in the eyes of Abby Baines, Hank Westin, and Painted Davy Sikes. "The secret is out."

"I know. It was bound to happen." Knute's sharp eyes bored into Joseph. "Last night you claimed that part of your reason for coming here was to learn more about horses. Was that true?"

"Yes."

"I can teach you some things, Joe." Knute waved in Annie Rose's direction. "But she can teach you more. Are you willing to take lessons from a woman?"

Joseph studied the slender form of the woman, listened to the gentle murmurings as she continued to work with the horse. The bright morning sunlight streamed down on the horse and the woman and sparkled on the gold of her hair, now exposed because her hat hung down her back. The wind caused the material of her skirt to ripple and the long hair of the mare's mane and tail to dance, while the mountains rose in silent majesty behind them, thrusting up against the impossibly blue sky.

His heart grabbed, and Joseph knew that for as long as he lived, he would never forget the incredible beauty of the sight before him. He longed for his sketch pad, but knew it would be impossible to capture on paper what he saw. The fear caused by Annie Rose Jensen's innocent breaching of his defenses faded. "I can learn from her," he said quietly.

Knute nodded in satisfaction. "And she will learn from you, I think." After a moment, he continued. "Now we must all get to work. We've lost a lot of time this morning."

"What will you have me do?" Joseph asked without taking his eyes from the woman and the mare.

"You claim to know something about horses. What are you particularly good at?"

At that, Joseph looked at Knute. "I'm good at everything to do with horses."

Thomas rolled his eyes. "Sure you are."

"Thomas, I think you'd better go chop some firewood and contemplate the meaning of good manners," Knute ordered.

"Gramps, he just wants Annie Rose, like Erik does, like they all do!" Thomas cried. "Erik was right. Send him away, before he hurts her."

Joseph was startled by the fear in the boy's voice. "I won't hurt your sister," he said firmly.

Thomas turned on him, his hands clenched at his sides. "You'd better not. Just remember what I told you last night."

"I remember, Thomas."

With one last furious glance at his grandfather, Thomas stormed off toward the large woodpile.

Knute raised a curious eyebrow. "What did he tell you last night?"

"That he would kill me if I hurt Annie Rose in any way."

Knute stroked his thick white mustache and stared after his grandson, who now was venting his righteous, youthful fury on an unlucky log. "He's young, Joe, and he loves his sister very much. He won't hesitate to stand up to you."

"I know, and I respect him for it. He's a fine boy, Knute, and he'll be a fine man. I won't give him any reason to follow through on his threat."

"I know you won't." Knute started toward the gate between the two corrals. "We run the horses around the corral, again and again in a circle, periodically forcing them to change direction. Tired horses are more easy to manage, and they begin to learn to obey our commands, even such a simple one as changing direction. We'll bring the yearling back into this corral. He's young, I know, and if it turns out he's not strong enough yet to carry a man, we'll wait until spring to saddle-train him. For now, Annie Rose will work with him and the mare, I'll work with three, and, since you are so good at everything to do with horses, you can have four." He eyed Joseph. *"Ja,* we'll see how good you really are."

He was being tested again, but this time Joseph knew he had asked for it. He had stated his claim as fact, not as a brag. With a sigh, he repositioned his hat more firmly on his head and followed Knute, wondering if he would ever please any member of the Jensen family.

From the top of a small rise a distance from the corrals, Erik watched the distribution of duties with angry, disbelieving eyes. The old man had actually given Beaudine the responsibility of some of the new horses! A jealous rage flared up, so powerful that Erik wanted to scream. Fury pounded through his veins in the old familiar dance, causing his head to ache ferociously.

His plans had been so perfect. He and Annabella would marry and at last he would move into her room, into her bed, as he had dreamed of for the last year. Gramps would die sooner or later—sooner, with any luck—and Tom would grow up and go off to find his own way in the world.

Then he would have her all to himself.

Annabella's long golden hair and curvy, fascinating woman's body would be his to touch when and as he pleased. With her Gift, they would make a fortune training and selling horses. He would force her to tell him where the Golden Mare was hidden, and they would sell that animal to the highest bidder. Yes, he had it all planned.

But Annabella wasn't cooperating. She refused to return his love, pulled away from even his casual touch, ran out into the night when he might have found the courage to simply take her and force the issue. Then she would have no choice but to marry him. She would not admit that she knew the whereabouts of the Golden Mare, which was practically the same thing as lying to him. *Him,* her future husband!

Annabella was upsetting his plans.

So was Gramps.

And now that damned Joseph Beaudine was, too. He'd seen how the captain looked at Annabella—*his* Annabella. Beaudine wanted her, just as any man who laid eyes on her would.

Erik ground his teeth and jerked hard on the reins, forcing his horse's head around. The animal squealed in protest and sidestepped, then obeyed his master's unspoken command to head toward the mountains to the north.

His grandfather had ordered him to cut the hay in the south meadow, but Erik had no intention of swinging a scythe today, unless he could swing it at Joseph Beaudine's neck. However, preventative measures and revenge would have to be plotted with the same care he had taken to plan his future. All would be lost if he acted in haste. The pounding headache receded.

Today, Erik Jensen was going hunting—for mule deer, for elk, for bear—it didn't matter.

He affectionately patted the butt of his rifle, which protruded from its case, and smiled, a grim smile of anticipation. Soon he would feel better.

He always felt better after he killed something.

Nine

All through the long, long day, Annie Rose was aware of the tall man in the neighboring corral. Joseph Beaudine worked tirelessly, keeping the four horses on the move. As she did, he would periodically work alone with one horse while the others rested, and by late afternoon his patient efforts were showing.

In truth, he was as good with the horses as she was, and she couldn't decide if she liked that fact or was bothered by it.

Joseph Beaudine was encroaching on her home territory—sleeping in her house, eating her food, endearing himself to her grandfather and her horses—and she felt annoyed and threatened by his presence. It didn't help that whenever her gaze accidentally fell on him, her rebellious mind took pleasurable notice of the obvious strength of his tall, lean body and saw that his long hair blew in the wind, as did the fringe on his buckskin shirt. He moved with the natural grace of a mountain lion, and had infinite patience with the nervous, stubborn horses.

Again and again, Annie Rose found it necessary to force her thoughts back to the two horses she was responsible for, and she grew angry with herself, resenting the power Joseph seemed to have over her wayward mind. It became a point of pride that her horses be ready for the bridle as soon as Joseph's were, and so she worked until well after dusk.

At last, ready to drop from fatigue, she trudged toward the cabin, noting with satisfaction that Joseph had quit earlier than she had. At least she assumed he did, for he was nowhere to be seen. She pushed the cabin door open and, in the welcoming light of fire and candles, saw that Knute and Thomas had the table set for supper. A smile of gratitude curved her lips.

"Sure smells good in here," she commented as she loosened the strings of her hat and pulled it off. She felt gritty and dirty, and knew she looked it. Her blue skirt was grey with dust; no doubt her face was, too. The pounding hooves of the captured horses had churned up the dirt of the corrals, and, even now, a layer of dust hung in the cool evening air over those enclosures.

"Thomas made a stew of what was left of the venison roast," Knute commented from his rocking chair. He puffed on a primitive clay pipe, sending up a cloud of aromatic smoke.

Annie Rose smiled at her brother, wondering if his antagonistic mood had lifted. Thomas had avoided the corrals all day, whether by his own design or under orders from Knute, she didn't know. There was also no sign of Erik. When they had taken a short break for the noon meal, Thomas rode out to the hay meadow in search of his cousin, only to return with the news that Erik was nowhere to be found, and that his horse's tracks headed in the direction of the northern mountains.

Knute had made no comment on Thomas's report, but Annie Rose knew by the set of his jaw that he was not pleased. As for her, she was simply relieved that she had not had to face Erik all day. Now that Gramps had talked to him, perhaps her cousin would finally understand that she would never return his feelings for her.

"I'll make some biscuits to go with that stew as soon as I wash up," she said to Thomas.

"I was hoping you'd offer." Thomas flashed her a grin. "I

love your biscuits, Annie Rose. We all try, but no one makes them like you do."

"Not even me?" Knute demanded.

Thomas rolled his eyes. "Especially not you," he retorted affectionately.

"But *I* taught her how to make biscuits," argued Knute. There was a teasing twinkle in his blue eyes.

"Yes, and, lucky for us, she was a better student than you were a teacher."

Annie Rose gave a little sigh of relief. Thomas and Gramps were getting along again. The rare occasions when the two people she loved most in the world argued deeply disturbed her. "Where is Mr. Beaudine?" she asked before she thought to stop herself. Biting down on her lip, she fought the urge to stomp her foot in frustration. She didn't want anyone getting the idea that she cared anything about Joseph Beaudine, including where he was.

Then why did you ask?

Determined to ignore the taunting of her own mind, Annie Rose grimaced as she released the end of her dusty braid; her hair needed washing, as did the rest of her.

"The captain is at the bathing pool," Knute answered.

Then Annie Rose realized that both Thomas and her grandfather had wet, neatly combed hair. The men had obviously gone for a bath while she was still working. She thought longingly of the naturally heated pool that nestled against the base of a small rocky cliff a short distance from the cabin. The hot water bubbled up out of the ground on one side of the pool, while a clean cold waterfall cascaded down the rock cliff on the other side. One's position in the pool determined the temperature of the water—warmer near the hot spring, cooler near the waterfall. Annie Rose loved that pool, but there was no time to visit it before supper. Even if there was, she would not risk running into Joseph Beaudine. Her bath would have to wait.

"Any sign of Erik?" Knute asked her.

"No."

"He sure was in a bad mood this morning," Thomas commented as he stirred the stew. "I hate it when he gets like that." A frown furrowed his brow. "He's like that more and more, Gramps."

"I know, son."

"Sometimes I'm scared he's going to hit me." Thomas turned his troubled gaze on his grandfather. "I'm scared he's going to hurt Annie Rose, too."

Stricken, Annie Rose put her arm around her brother's shoulders. It shocked her to realize that her baby brother was almost as tall as she was, and that his shoulders weren't as thin as she remembered. "He won't hurt me, Thomas."

"We won't let him." Joseph Beaudine spoke from the open door. His pleasantly accented voice carried an undeniable tone of authority.

Annie Rose jerked her head around to look at him, aware of how disheveled she must look with her dusty clothes and her unraveling braid. Joseph's long clean hair was wet and slicked back, his cheeks and chin freshly shaved, his mustache trimmed and combed. He wore a clean white shirt, neatly tucked into his buckskin pants, and a beautifully beaded belt.

He looked good, standing there so calm and tall, in her house. He looked *real* good.

Suddenly it occurred to her—how long had he been there? Had he heard her ask about him? A hot rush of embarrassment flooded through her, and Annie Rose knew her face was bright red. She turned toward her bedroom. "I'll be out in a few minutes," she mumbled, and hurried behind the door curtain.

Furious with herself, she stomped over to the washstand, grateful for once that her bedroom floor was not made of wood. The sound of her stomping feet couldn't be heard on a packed-dirt floor. She could stomp as long and as hard as she wanted to.

What on earth was wrong with her? Annie Rose poured water from the beautiful porcelain pitcher she had inherited from her mother into the matching washbasin, set the pitcher on the floor, and slapped a clean washing cloth into the cool, clear water. Then she stared at her reflection in the small hand mirror that hung from a nail over the basin, searching for an answer to her own question. *What was wrong with her?* Every hour she was in his company, she discovered more about Joseph Beaudine to like, and her considerable willpower was helpless against the growing attraction she felt for him.

She would not succumb. There was no room in her life for a special man.

For *any* man, aside from her grandfather and her brother.

Except for Knute and Thomas, no man was to be trusted. Not even Erik, her own cousin.

In the end, they were all the same, wanting only one thing from a woman. Some, like her father, used pretty words, courtly manners, and money to get what they wanted; others, like Abby Baines, merely took it. Either way, they all strived for the same goal—to bury their selfish male appendage in a woman's body for a few fleeting moments of pleasure.

Then they left.

Joseph Beaudine wanted her, that she knew. Which method would he use to try to achieve his goal? It didn't matter; he would not be successful.

Annie Rose shrugged out of the dusty blue workshirt and dropped it on the floor, then reached for the washing cloth. The feel of the cool wet cloth was soothing as she ran it over her heated face and down her arms. She rinsed it out and applied it to her chest, pushing under the neckline of her chemise and between her breasts, then dropped the cloth back in the basin.

Still deep in thought, Annie Rose looked down at her chest. What was so special about a pair of breasts? Searching for an answer, she lightly placed her hands over her own breasts. Under the thin cotton of her camisole, they felt soft and warm. And, to her, not at all enticing. Yet, virgin though she was, she knew that men were fascinated by the female breast.

How could a man be so drawn to those soft mounds of flesh without caring a whit for the woman's heart that beat beneath?

Her hands fell to her sides. Men extracted too high a price for what little was received in return. Never would she pay that price, she vowed. Never would she sacrifice what her mother had sacrificed for the sake of a man.

No matter how nice a package that man presented.

Before Annie Rose stepped back into the main room a few minutes later—reasonably clean, her hair brushed and pinned up on her head, wearing a simple skirt and bodice made of matching brown calico—she schooled her features into a serene mask. Still, despite her best intentions, it was difficult not to notice that Joseph Beaudine presented a very nice package, indeed. His warm brown eyes seemed to follow her as she donned her apron and quickly made a batch of biscuits. She couldn't tell if the heat she felt was from the fire over which she cooked, or from his silent attention, and that uncertainty merely added to her sense of irritation.

Knute and Joseph carried the conversation throughout supper, for Thomas seemed no more inclined to talk than Annie Rose was. The boy ate quickly, then asked to be excused. He took a book from the shelf near Knute's bed and retreated to his room, declaring his intention to read another chapter in *The Last of the Mohicans*.

"That's a good book," Joseph said. "My stepmother read it while she was carrying my sister Cora, and named her after Cora Munro."

"Cora Munro was a courageous woman," Knute commented, once again puffing contentedly on his pipe. "It's a shame she died in the story."

Annie Rose began to clear the table, remembering the sadness she had felt in reading Cooper's book when she came to the part that described Cora's death, and that of Uncas, Chingachgook's brave and noble son.

"Have you read the book, Miss Jensen?" Joseph asked.

His words brought Annie Rose out of her reverie, and she

realized that Joseph had moved off his bench and was stacking dirty plates.

"Yes. I've read it several times. Up here, one has a lot of time for reading during the winter months." She snatched up a fork he was reaching for. "I'll clear the table, Mr. Beaudine. You and Gramps enjoy your tea."

"I was told that the chores are to be shared." Joseph carried his stack of plates to the worktable where two washbasins waited. "You worked with the horses all day."

"So did you," she retorted, wondering why she found his insistence upon helping her so annoying.

Because it's one more thing to like about him.

"You worked longer than I did, longer than any of us," Joseph said calmly.

Annie Rose ground her teeth and poured hot water from the heavy cast-iron kettle over the dishes piled in the larger basin. She turned back to the table to retrieve her cup and did not miss the smile her grandfather was struggling to hide. With pointed finger, she glared a warning at him before she grabbed the cup.

Joseph filled the rinse basin with hot water, then took up a towel, ready to dry the dishes. "Have you ever heard the story of how my father's children were named?" he asked.

"No." Annie Rose refrained from rudely adding that she had no desire to hear the story. She did not want to know anything more about Joseph Beaudine.

"Tell us the story, Joe," Knute urged.

Annie Rose attacked a dirty tin plate with more force than was necessary and, when it was clean, thrust the plate toward Joseph.

"Well, the story starts with my father." Joseph dipped the freshly scrubbed plate in the rinse water and began to dry it. "On his return trip to the West from Virginia where he had gone to visit his family, Jedediah Beaudine met two young women in a rough settlement somewhere along the Natchez Trace. He caught their pa beating on them, so Jedediah took the girls with him to St. Louis. He married Ellie, the oldest, and taught her to read and write before he returned to the frontier to continue his trading business with the Cheyenne. He also left her with child. During her confinement, Mama read the Bible from cover to cover, and when I was born, she named me Joseph."

Annie Rose handed him another plate, caught up in the story in spite of herself. As Joseph took the plate from her, their hands touched, and it seemed that a bolt of lightning flashed up her arm. Her breath caught. She jerked her hand away from his touch, steadfastly refusing to look up, fearful of what she might read in his eyes, more fearful that she might find no emotion at all in those brown depths.

Joseph continued as if nothing unusual had happened. "My father came home for the winter, and when he left in the spring, he again left her with child and Mama was working her way through the Greek and Roman mythologies."

"So that's where the Hunter got his name," Knute said.

"Orion, the Hunter," Annie Rose whispered, then blurted out, "what of Grey Eagle?" She knew Grey Eagle had been born to a Cheyenne woman. Had Jedediah been unfaithful to his beloved Ellie? Deep in her heart, Annie Rose hoped not. Some hidden part of her longed to hear that Jedediah was a good man.

"My mother died that next winter." Joseph spoke matter-of-factly as he reached for another plate.

Now she did look up at him, saddened that Ellie had died so young, relieved that Jedediah had been honorable, amazed that she felt such emotion for two people she had never met. "I'm sorry," she said sincerely.

"Thank you. I don't remember her, but I know my father was devastated. He took Orion and me with him to the Cheyenne encampments, where he always spent his summers, trading with the tribes. A year later he married a Cheyenne woman named Morning Sky. It was to her that Grey Eagle was born." Joseph paused. "His name did not come from a book."

Annie Rose smiled in spite of herself. "I guessed that."

Joseph returned her smile, his even teeth appearing very white beneath the dark brown of his mustache, laugh lines showing at the outer corners of his eyes.

Again, Annie Rose's breath caught, and she hastily returned her attention to the few remaining dishes in the basin.

"So finish the story," Knute ordered. "You have two sisters, *ja?*"

"Yes, sir." Joseph took a cup from Annie Rose's hand. Their fingers did not touch this time. "A few years later, Morning Sky died. Heartbroken again, Jedediah returned to St. Louis with his three sons and eventually married Ellie's younger sister, Florence. Ellie had taught Florrie to read, so she continued the tradition when her daughters were born, naming Juliet from her Shakespeare days, and Cora from her James Fenimore Cooper days." He glanced at Knute. "And that's the story."

"So Grey Eagle lived in St. Louis for a while," Annie Rose mused, scrubbing at a particularly stubborn bit of food stuck on a fork. "I always wondered where he learned to speak such flawless English."

"He would have learned it even if my father had not taken him to St. Louis." Joseph accepted the cleaned fork from her and rinsed it. "You see, Jedediah was a unique man, a Renaissance man, really. He came from a wealthy Virginia family, and was highly educated, but, as the youngest of four sons, his prospects for inheritance were bleak. Determined to make his own way in the world, he came West, where equal opportunity was available to any who were willing to work. My father insisted upon treating all of his children equally, with no regard for race or gender. We all speak Cheyenne as well as English, we know the sign language of the Plains tribes, we know how to stay alive on the frontier, and we all can safely negotiate the treacherous, high-society parlors of St. Louis and, if necessary, Washington and Philadelphia."

Incredulous, Annie Rose stared at him. "Even your sisters speak Cheyenne?"

"Even my sisters. They learned the language, although Mama Florrie wouldn't let her girls stay with the Cheyenne for the entire summer, like the boys did. Juliet and Cora were allowed to come for a month and a half, maybe two, and she always came with them. Mama Florrie knows her way around a Cheyenne village as well as we do." There was an unmistakable note of pride in Joseph's voice.

"I'd like to meet your Mama Florrie," Annie Rose said wistfully. "And your sisters."

Joseph looked down at her golden head, which was once again bowed over the washbasin. It suddenly occurred to him how lonely Annie Rose must be at times, with no women to talk to. She had lived in this secluded valley for the last seven years, had grown to womanhood here, surrounded by males.

True, Jubal Sage's Cheyenne wife, Sweet Water, knew Annie Rose and no doubt had visited the valley, just as Annie Rose no doubt had visited the Sages' cabin before that fateful night when he met her there. Sweet Water had been working diligently to learn English since her marriage to Jubal a year ago, but her command of the language was still rudimentary at best. And, if Joseph understood the situation correctly, even on the rare occasions that Knute allowed Annie Rose to accompany him on a trip to Fort Laramie to trade trained horses for supplies, she was forced to go disguised as a boy, for her own protection.

Few people knew of her existence at all; even fewer knew she was a woman.

His heart grabbed in genuine sympathy. *How very alone she must feel at times!*

Joseph allowed his gaze to wander about the snug, inviting room. Aside from the noticeable cleanliness, Annie Rose's charming feminine touches were obvious—the curtains at the windows and bedroom doors; the tablecloth, serviceable though it was; the handful of wildflowers slowly dying in an old brandy bottle on the mantel; the delicate lace edging the doily that covered the storage chest and the matching lace that edged her remarkably clean apron. He remembered the floral pattern on the coverlet protecting her bed, and the modest flower beds so cozily snuggled along the front of the house, and Joseph Beaudine looked at Annie Rose Jensen with awe.

In the middle of the wilderness, with no female companionship, she had made a welcoming home of the fiercely protected refuge Knute Jensen so lovingly provided for his grandchildren. Even now, after working in a dusty corral all day with a bunch of willful horses, Annie Rose looked soft and feminine, having taken pains to fix her hair and change her gown before she sat down to supper with her family.

"I think that fork is dry."

Her voice gently intruded upon his thoughts, but Joseph wasn't sure he caught all her words. "What did you say?"

"The fork." She nodded in the direction of his hands. "You've been drying it for some time." She met his gaze. "It isn't that big."

"No, it isn't." Feeling foolish, Joseph set the fork down, watching as Annie Rose untied her apron.

"I'd like a bath," she said to her grandfather. "I'll make a quick trip to the bathing pool."

Joseph closed his eyes, fighting the mental picture of Annie Rose in the soothing waters of the pool.

Naked.

Her golden hair down around her shoulders, her rosy lips parted, calling to him, inviting him to join her.

"Mr. Beaudine?"

He blinked, then forced his eyes to remain open. Annie Rose was looking up at him, curious, perhaps even a touch concerned.

"Yes?" he asked stupidly.

"Are you all right?"

"Uh, yes, I am." He glanced over Annie Rose's head, saw the knowing amusement in Knute's eyes, and felt even more foolish.

Annie Rose watched him closely for a moment, then turned away. "Where is Maggie?" she asked Knute.

"In with Thomas. Do you want her to go with you?"

"No. Let her be; I'm sure she's sound asleep. I won't be gone that long." She disappeared behind her bedroom door curtain, then reappeared a moment later with a bath sheet draped over one arm, clutching a bar of homemade soap and a silver-backed brush. "Shall I make more tea before I go?"

Knute picked up the beautiful *rosemaled* tankard and gently shook it. "I'll make more, *datter.* Go enjoy your bath, and when you return, we'll share a fresh pot before we turn in." When she hesitated, he made shooing motions toward the door. "Go."

"All right."

With a grateful smile—and no glance spared for him, Joseph noticed—she left. He stared longingly at the closed door.

"Captain Joe, you will sit with me," Knute commanded. "You are not the only one with stories to tell."

Joseph sighed and, stifling his baser impulse to follow Annie Rose to the warm, inviting pool—which by now would be sensually lit by the light of the newly risen moon—reluctantly obeyed the Norseman.

Ten

Annie Rose luxuriated in the warmth of the pool, feeling it rinse away the stress and fatigue of the long day in addition to the dirt. Her hair was now squeaky clean and floated about her bare shoulders. Moonlight played over the water, dancing on the ripples caused by her movements. She deliberately waved her arms again, sending a new dance across the water.

Joseph Beaudine had immersed his body in these waters only a short time ago.

The thought came unbidden to her mind. Annie Rose could not suppress a shiver of excitement at the mental image of Joseph revelling in the water as she was doing now, his intriguing male body as naked as her female one was.

With a low cry of anger, she slapped the water, sending the moonlight on a violent dance. Was she to have no peace? Would Joseph Beaudine continue to hound her as he had done since the night she first met him—invading her life, her home, even the deepest, most secret reaches of her mind? Would she ever be free of him?

Her mother had never been free of her father. Even after years of humiliation and ill treatment, Thora Jensen had remained true to Blaine Coburn, enduring the loss of her reputation, of her heart, of her very soul. Until death stilled her tongue forever, she swore that she loved him and he loved her, that the love they shared made it all worthwhile.

"Was he really worth it, Mama?" Annie Rose whispered

into the night, her eyes filling with tears. Then she answered her own question. "He wasn't. No man is."

Annie Rose ducked under the water one last time, rinsing the tears away, then started for the shore. If she had hoped to rinse her thoughts of Joseph Beaudine away as well, she failed. The man still teased the edge of her mind. She rose from the warmth of the water, her nipples tightening and her skin puckering into goose bumps as the cool night air hit her. A slab of smooth, relatively flat rock that jutted into the water served as a landing of sorts, offering a surface free of pebbles for her bare feet. Annie Rose stood for a moment in the moonlight, tall and quiet, her eyes closed.

Would Joseph Beaudine find her appealing if he saw her thus?

A moan of frustration escaped her lips as she bent down to snatch up her bath sheet. She refused to even like the man, and still he played on her mind.

How much worse it must be if one gave in to love.

She never would.

The bath sheet felt rough as she rubbed it mercilessly over her skin, but as least she warmed up some. She hurried into her chemise, drawers, and petticoat, then used the damp sheet on her still dripping hair, suddenly anxious to hide in the privacy of her own room.

A twig broke. Close by.

She froze, her heart pounding, the bath sheet clutched to her chest. A strange scent filtered through the night air. Annie Rose sniffed, her mind seeking the answer. The scent was familiar.

Blood.

She smelled blood, and the peculiar musky odor of raw meat.

A horse nickered quietly. The horse was very close.

Annie Rose grabbed her moccasins, skirt, and bodice. Her searching hand knocked her brush, sending it skittering across the slab of rock and into the darkness. There was no time to recover it now. Cautiously, slowly, she backed up to a thick cottonwood, thankful for the breeze that rustled through the leaves, covering any small sound she might make.

"You sure make a pretty sight, Annabella, with no clothes on." Erik's voice, heavy with lust, came from a short distance away.

Nausea boiled up in her stomach as Annie Rose slid around the tree, paying no heed to the rough bark that clawed at the tender skin of her shoulders and upper back. She had to get away from the pond, away from Erik.

"Don't run off, cousin," he commanded.

Judging from the direction of his voice, Erik had to be near the path that led to the cabin.

"Annabella Rosalie, where are you?" Anger rose in his tone and he no longer troubled himself to move quietly.

To Annie Rose, it sounded like an irate bear pursued her, lumbering along, mindless of the bushes and shrubs in its way. Why hadn't she insisted on bringing Maggie with her? Erik would not have been able to sneak up on her with Maggie on guard. How long had he been there? How much had he heard? How much had he seen?

She flushed, knowing he'd seen plenty.

In all her life, Annie Rose had never felt so violated, so unclean. She held her bundle of wadded clothes close to her roiling stomach.

"Annabella!" Erik shouted. "Get out here!" He was much closer.

She darted between two trees and crouched behind a large rock. There was a roundabout way to get to the cabin, but Erik would soon be at the cabin himself.

Joseph Beaudine was already there.

If Annie Rose returned to the cabin now, they would both watch her—blue eyes and brown, following her every movement. Erik, with a taunt on his face; Joseph, with genuine interest on his, interest she did not welcome or return.

She could not face either one.

Her breath rasped against her gritted teeth and her heart

hammered against her ribs as she peered around the side of the rock. Erik's horse waited a short distance away, heavily laden with a freshly butchered animal. What the poor creature had been when alive, Annie Rose could not tell in the dark, but at least the cloying scent of blood was explained. The horse blew gently and looked straight at her.

"Annabella!" Erik screamed.

She faded farther into the forest, praying that the horse's nicker of welcome did not register with Erik.

"You can't hide from me forever, cousin." Erik's voice took on an ominously patient tone. "Just like Gramps won't live forever. Thomas is only a boy, and Beaudine will leave— I'll see to that. Then I'll have you." He laughed harshly. "It's only a matter of time."

Annie Rose bit down on her lip to keep from crying out as a stone stabbed her bare foot. She limped on, desperate to escape Erik's cruel words.

"Run, Annabella, while you can. Soon you'll learn there is nowhere to run." Erik's malicious laugh again echoed through the woods, and she could tell he was moving away from her.

Had he given up?

Erik would not be able to track her in the dark, and she knew that he knew it. The hour was growing late, and he had a carcass to hang. It was safe to assume that her cousin was returning to the cabin.

Her body wracked with shivers, Annie Rose thought longingly of her warm bed, of the comfort of her grandfather's protective presence. But there was no sanctuary offered in her home tonight. She could imagine how Erik would look at her if she went back. His narrow eyes, staring at her in that insolent, predatory way of his, would have a new gleam of knowing. He had seen her naked.

Annie Rose stopped and bent over, holding her stomach, willing her supper to stay down. She needed the food for strength, for Aurora's hidden meadow was miles away. With shaking hands, she struggled into her skirt and bodice, impatient with the challenge presented by the numerous hooks. The moccasins did nothing to warm her cold feet, but they offered protection from the rough path she would follow. She folded the damp bath sheet and tucked it under one arm, then took a deep, calming breath. For several minutes, she stood completely still, listening to the sounds of the forest, sniffing the air, taking stock of her exact location in respect to both the homestead and to Aurora's haven.

Satisfied that no one pursued her, she set off, hoping to reach Aurora before the moon completed its journey across the night sky.

Joseph stood at the open cabin door, peering into the night. Annie Rose had been a long time at her bath. Too long, in his opinion.

Something was wrong.

He looked in the direction of the smokehouse, where Thomas and Knute helped Erik hang the mule deer he'd just brought back. Erik seemed almost cheerful, and Joseph found that disturbing. What had lifted the man's surly mood?

Without another thought, Joseph took the lighted lantern that hung on a nail next to the door and headed toward the pond.

"Miss Jensen," he called as he approached. "Miss Jensen?" He followed the path around a large rock that afforded the pond some privacy, then stopped just before the view of the pond would be revealed to him. "Annie Rose, are you there? It's Joseph Beaudine."

He listened carefully. No sounds reached his ears except those of the night forest.

"I'm coming around the rock," he warned, suddenly worried about what he might find. The pond was not deep in most places, but there were opportunities for a person to get into trouble—losing one's balance on the rocky shore near the waterfall, diving off of Thomas's favorite rock into water that was too shallow, slipping on the flat docking rock. Even as the thoughts raced through his mind, Joseph discarded them as ridiculous. In addition to having a good head on her shoulders, Annie Rose was an accomplished woodsman. She would not get into trouble in her own bathing pond.

Unless someone gave her trouble.

Joseph rounded the rock, holding the lantern high.

The pond was empty. The only ripples marring the smooth surface of the water came from the waterfall. Bent over, holding the lantern near the ground now, Joseph carefully and methodically surveyed the area. He found the flat rock where Annie Rose left the water. Judging from the size of the puddles on the surface, she had stood there for a few minutes, no doubt drying off. But she had stepped off the rock with bare feet. Why had she not put on her moccasins before she risked the rocky path back to the cabin? Why had she circled the cottonwood, so close to the tree that patches of wet showed in places on the bark?

His gaze fell on something shiny at the edge of the circle of light, and he reached for it. Her brush. Annie Rose left her beautiful, silver-backed brush?

With a worried frown, Joseph followed her footprints a short distance and realized they were leading away from the path. She had not even tried to return to the cabin. Why not? Where had she gone at this time of night?

The faint prints led to the east, into dense forest carpeted with a thick layer of pine needles. Even the use of the lantern would not enable him to track her across such terrain in the dark. Heaving a troubled sigh, Joseph turned back in the direction of the pond. Suddenly, he caught sight of hoofprints. Recent ones. Those of a horse carrying a man—a big man, judging from the depth of the tracks in the soft earth.

He crouched low, peering at the tracks, then swung the lantern in a slow arc around his body, searching. For what, he did not know. He spotted something—a dark spot in the dirt near a track. He touched it, found it damp, brought his finger to his nose.

Blood.

The blood of an unlucky mule deer, no doubt.

The horse had been carrying a carcass as well as a man. No wonder the tracks were so deep.

Erik had come this way.

Joseph's stomach grabbed as he straightened and looked around. What had happened here to send Annie Rose running into the night? His jaw clenched, he retraced his steps around the pond and strode down the path, slapping the back of her brush against his thigh.

The Jensen men were no longer at the smokehouse. Joseph shoved open the cabin door and found Knute and Thomas at the table, looking at him with startled expressions on their faces.

"Has Annie Rose returned?" Joseph barked, not realizing he had used her Christian name.

"Not unless she came in while we were at the smoke-house." Knute hurried to pull back the curtain at her bedroom door. "No." He faced Joseph. "What is wrong?"

"Where is Erik?" Joseph ground out. He set Annie Rose's brush on the table.

Knute looked from the brush to Joseph, and fear flashed across his face. "Putting his horse up."

Joseph turned on his heel and headed toward the barn, the lantern still in hand. As he approached the building, Erik disappeared inside, carting his saddle. When Erik came back out, Joseph almost ran into him. He halted and stared at the younger man.

Startled, Erik stepped back. Obviously uncomfortable with Joseph's continued silence, he finally blurted out, "What?"

"You returned by way of the pond, didn't you?" Joseph asked in a deadly tone.

A gleam of smug triumph shone in Erik's eyes; a smirk twisted his mouth. He said nothing.

Joseph grabbed the front of Erik's shirt with his free hand. "Where is she?"

"How the hell would I know?" Erik twisted out of his grip. "I've been gone all day, remember?"

"What is going on?" Knute demanded as he and Thomas hurried up.

"Annie Rose is gone," Joseph snapped. "And Erik knows why, don't you?" He glared at Erik, desperately wanting to smash his fist into the man's face. Only Knute's presence and the respect he felt for the Norseman kept him from giving in to his impulse.

"Where is she, Erik?" Knute advanced on his grandson. "What have you done?"

Some of the insolence left Erik's expression as he looked at Knute. "I didn't do anything. She went off into the forest, like she always does."

"She went into the forest *tonight?* With no hat, no coat, no bedroll? Without her knife?"

"Without Maggie?" Thomas shouted.

Joseph glanced at the boy. His eyes flashed with anger, but his face was pale with fear, no doubt for his sister.

"I didn't do anything!" Erik shoved past them, a horse brush in his hand. "I didn't touch her. I only spoke to her, but I don't think she heard me, because she didn't answer."

Deep in thought, Joseph watched Erik run the brush over his horse with long, smooth strokes. Annie Rose had heard Erik; of that, Joseph had no doubt. What had the brute said to her? What had he threatened her with?

She had hidden from her cousin. That explained her leaving the rock barefoot—there hadn't been time to put on her moccasins, or to search for her brush. She had clung to the cottonwood for protection, circling around it, dampening parts of the rough bark with her still-wet body and hair.

Had Erik so effectively blocked the way to the cabin that Annie Rose felt she couldn't safely get by him? No. There were other ways back to the cabin. There had to be. And Annie Rose would know them. She had *chosen* not to return.

Joseph looked at Knute. "He didn't touch her. I found her tracks, and his. They didn't meet."

Knute's shoulders slumped in relief. "Go to bed, Thomas."

Thomas appeared to be about to argue.

Knute shook his head. "Go, son. You know your sister can take care of herself in the wilderness. She'll return in the morning."

With a parting look of impotent fury directed at his cousin, Thomas stormed back to the cabin, whistling for Maggie to follow.

"There is nothing more to be done until we talk to Annie Rose," Knute said. He took a few steps toward the cabin, then paused near Erik's horse. Erik did not look at him. "If you are lying, Erik, the consequences will be dire."

Erik's only response to Knute's words was a hesitation in the brushing motion he used on the horse. Knute continued on to the cabin.

After a moment, Joseph started after Knute.

"I saw her."

Joseph stopped, at first not certain Erik had actually spoken. Then he wondered if he had correctly heard the words. "Excuse me?"

"I *saw* her." Erik looked at him, the smugness back in his expression, lustful gloating in his eyes. "All of her. Which is more than you'll ever see."

In one quick movement, Joseph carefully dropped the lantern so that it landed on its base and grabbed the front of Erik's shirt with both hands. He shoved Erik into the corral fence with such force that Erik's breath left his lungs in a sharp *whoosh,* his hat flew off, and the horse brush fell to the ground.

"You spied on her?" Joseph ground out. He noted with pleasure that all traces of triumph and taunting had fled Erik's features. Indeed, the man seemed to be struggling for breath, and his blue eyes were now wide with terror. Joseph shook him. "Did you?"

Erik stammered incoherently. Even with his full red beard, he looked surprisingly young—and pathetic.

"You disgusting excuse for a man." Joseph shook him again, hard. "She is your *cousin,* for God's sake, a woman you profess to care about." He could not bring himself to use the word "love" in connection with Erik's twisted feelings. "You will never again dishonor her; you will never again speak of her in such a way. You will not treat any woman disrespectfully, in action or word, not in my presence. If you do, I'll beat the hell out of you, Erik Jensen. You have my word on it. Is that understood?"

Erik merely stared at him, horror-stricken, as if Joseph were the Devil himself.

Joseph shook him one more time. *"Is that understood?"*

Now Erik managed a nod. "Y-yes, s-sir."

"Good." Joseph released him.

Erik sagged against the fence, gulping air in great gasping breaths.

Struggling to control the rage that still roared through him, Joseph picked up the lantern and walked slowly to the cabin. He hung the lantern on its nail next to the door, then stepped away from the house. He was tempted to return to the bathing pool, even though he knew Annie Rose was not there. Instead, he walked past the smokehouse, past the well, to a little rise that looked down on the homestead.

He took a long, slow breath in an attempt to calm himself, then breathed out the rage that made him want to pound Erik Jensen's florid face into the ground. Eventually, he calmed down, but he could not escape the truth.

Annie Rose had chosen to seek sanctuary in the forest rather than within the stout walls of the little cabin.

Did she doubt Knute's ability to keep her safe from Erik?

Joseph chewed on that for a while. True, Knute was aging, and he was ill. No doubt Erik knew of his grandfather's "spells," just as Annie Rose and Thomas did. But the Norseman still commanded the respect of his grandchildren.

No, Knute could protect Annie Rose. And he was not alone—Thomas had the protective instincts of a mama grizzly when it came to his sister. The boy was young, but Joseph had no doubt that Thomas would gladly give his life for Annie Rose. Erik could not prevail against the rest of his family.

Surely Annie Rose knew that.

She would have been safe had she chosen to return to the cabin. Uncomfortable in Erik's presence, perhaps, but physically safe. What else had she run from?

Him.

Joseph bowed his head as the truth slammed into his brain. He had played a role in her decision to run.

He had pushed her too far.

From the first night he met her, he'd known she was as skittish as a newborn foal around men, and still he had pushed her—asking questions he had no right to ask, prying into her past, teasing her, complimenting her, making no attempt to hide his interest in her, even though it so clearly made her uncomfortable.

No doubt she put him in the same class as Erik, and the thought shamed him.

Joseph looked up at the clear August night. The stars continued their slow and everlasting march across the heavens, unknowing and uncaring that he had acted like a selfish fool with a woman he had quickly grown to truly care about. But the stars paid no heed to the trivial problems of man, including his, and he found no answers there. With a sigh, he trudged back to the cabin. In the hope that she would come home, he would wait up for a while. Perhaps he would try again to capture her image on paper. His attempt would be inadequate, but the attempt itself would offer him some comfort, for he would be envisioning her.

Under the dusty horse blanket, Annie Rose shifted again, searching for a position that offered some relief from the sharp pricks of the hay that made up her rude bed. She was thankful for the old blanket she always kept in Aurora's shelter, but she had never dreamed she would need it to warm herself. Aurora and the grey mare both stood a short distance away, every now and then nickering quietly. Despite the physical discomfort offered by her makeshift bed, Annie Rose felt more sheltered and content here in this rude stable, with only a pair of horses for company, than she would have in her own home.

How sad that was.

Yet, as peaceful as this place was, she couldn't stay past morning, although Aurora was growing heavy with her foal, and Annie Rose knew the young one would come before too long. With the new batch of horses to be trained, there was too much work to do back at the homestead—even with the grudgingly admitted competent help of Joseph Beaudine— and for the sakes of Gramps and Thomas, she had to be there to carry her own weight.

Tonight, she would rest and conserve her strength, for to-morrow she would return home to do battle—with Joseph if necessary, with Erik for certain, and no doubt with her own heart.

Eleven

Annie Rose left the sanctuary of Aurora's enclosure as soon as the sun lightened the eastern skies. Her hair had finally dried, but with no brush or ribbon for it, the tangled blonde strands lay wildly about her shoulders and hung down her back. Bits of straw clung to her skirt and bodice, their occasional pricks and pokes adding to her overall feeling of unhappiness, as did her hunger and the stiffness of her chilled, aching body.

At first, she walked slowly, reluctantly, clutching the still-damp bath sheet, shivering in the nippy early morning air. She dreaded seeing Erik, and, despite the urgings of her traitorous mind to the contrary, insisted to herself that she had no wish to see Joseph Beaudine, either. On she plodded, one foot after the other, only the knowledge that her brother and grandfather would be worried pushing her forward.

As she got closer to home, however, Annie Rose's steps became faster and more resolute. Her humiliation of the night before and her fear of Erik transformed into anger, an anger so fierce that its momentum had her almost running as she approached the bathing pond.

No more. She would tolerate no more.

Down the path she went—the path Erik had kept her from last night—and to the cabin. A quick glance inside showed no one there. She stood on the step, shading her eyes with one hand, trying to ascertain where everyone was. Maggie approached with happy barks and a furiously wagging tail. Annie Rose bent down and absentmindedly scratched the dog's ears, still searching. Knute was in the far corral, Joseph in the middle one. Thomas was again working on the never-ending woodpile. Where was Erik?

Then she saw her cousin come from the barn with a few harnesses draped over one arm.

Where before she had been hot with anger and indignation, now Annie Rose was cold with determination and a surprisingly calm fury. "Stay, Maggie," she said firmly as she straightened her spine and her shoulders. She flung the bath sheet back through the cabin door and marched toward the barn, scattering indignant chickens. The disobedient Maggie happily followed her.

Thomas stilled his ax as she passed, his greeting frozen on his lips.

Knute waved to her from his corral. "Good morning, *datter!*" he called.

Joseph turned and took a few steps toward the gate of his corral, a look of relief on his handsome face.

She ignored them all.

Erik looked up from his task of untangling the harnesses. Annie Rose came to a stop in front of him.

"How dare you do what you did last night?" Even she could hear the loathing and rage in her own voice. She glared at Erik, mentally daring him to say anything, to so much as *look* at her in that sinister, leering way of his.

He was taken aback for a moment, then started to smile.

Annie Rose swung her arm back and slapped his face as hard as she could.

Suddenly, Erik wasn't smiling anymore. He dropped the harnesses and clapped a hand to his cheek. Above his beard, the skin reddened. "Why, you . . ."

"No more, Erik. No more!" Annie Rose saw him clench his fist, and remembered that once she had been afraid that he would hit her. Even if he struck her now, she was no longer afraid, and not because she saw from the corner of her eye that both Knute and Joseph had come through their respective gates, saw over Erik's shoulder that Thomas had come closer, clutching the ax in one hand, holding Maggie back with the other. "Will you strike me?" she demanded. "That's what it will take if you intend to have me, as you swore you would last night."

The rest of Erik's face flushed as red as his cheek.

"In order to fulfill your evil vow, you will have to beat me into submission, cousin, and then rape me. Are you prepared to go that far? Have you become that twisted inside?"

Now Erik's red face paled, and he took a step back. Nervously, he glanced at his grandfather, then at Joseph Beaudine, then he pinned his gaze on the ground.

Annie Rose again closed the distance between them. "I will tolerate no more, Erik; no more of your surly moods, no more of your predatory staring, no more of your attempts to touch me."

Again Erik took a step back; again Annie Rose took a step forward. "From now on," she continued, "when I go to bathe, Maggie will come with me, as will Gramps's rifle. Should you attempt to spy on me again, you will do so at your peril. You will not disgrace me again."

Knute uttered an oath and started forward. Joseph grabbed his arm and held him back, giving a slight shake of his head. Without taking her gaze from Erik, Annie Rose held her hand out in her grandfather's direction, motioning him to stay where he was.

"This is my battle," she said quietly. "Isn't it, Erik?"

Erik stared at her. There was no trace of lust or humor on his face now—just a smoldering anger. But Annie Rose could tell the urge to act in violence had left him.

"I will tell you this one final time," Annie Rose said firmly. "I care about you as cousin and friend, but no more than that. I do not return the depth of your apparent affection for me, nor will I ever. For your own sake, abandon any false hope you may harbor. Allow all of us to live here in peace together."

After a moment of tense silence, Erik exploded. "It's him,

isn't it?" He stabbed a finger in Joseph's direction. "I've seen how he looks at you, how you look at him. If he hadn't come, you wouldn't be saying these things to me."

How he looks at you—how you look at him. Annie Rose refused to let Erik's startling words steer her from her course. "Mr. Beaudine has nothing to do with my decision regarding you," she snapped. That much was true, anyway. "For over a year—far longer than I have known him—I have been telling you how I feel, but you have refused to believe me. Even Gramps has talked to you, to no avail. I beg you, Erik, listen to me now. Believe me now."

Erik gritted his teeth. His hands clenched and opened, clenched and opened. His furious, frustrated gaze raced from Annie Rose to Joseph to Knute, back to Annie Rose, to Thomas, back to Annie Rose. Then he leaned slightly forward. "I believe you, *Annabella Rosalie.*"

Annie Rose recognized the use of her hated full name as the deliberate insult Erik intended. It took a great deal of willpower for her to stand firm when everything in her cried out to step back. Erik continued to glare at her. She stood firm.

"Thank you," she said quietly.

"You can go to hell, *cousin.*"

Annie Rose flinched. Erik's last statement had been spoken so softly that no one else could have possibly heard it. Though shocked by the hatred in Erik's tone, in his eyes, she forced herself to stand her ground. Erik spun on his heel and stormed into the barn.

She blinked, and finally allowed herself to relax her rigid stance.

"What happened last night, Annie Rose?" Knute demanded as he and Joseph approached.

"It doesn't matter, Gramps. It won't happen again." Suddenly, she felt weary, so weary that her legs felt shaky, about to collapse under her.

"You're damn right it won't. Forgive my swearing, girl. You won't be left alone again, I promise you that." Knute put a supportive arm around Annie Rose's shoulders and led her in the direction of the cabin. He motioned to both Joseph and Thomas, who hurried to join them. Maggie trotted at Thomas's side.

No one spoke until they reached the cabin.

"Have you eaten?" Knute asked gruffly as he guided her onto a bench.

Annie Rose shook her head, noticing that all three men had removed their hats. She stared at Thomas. He was only twelve, but somewhere along the way she had started thinking of him as a man. Perhaps because he often conducted himself as one. She was filled with a sudden, fierce pride in her brother.

Without anyone giving instructions, Knute took her bath sheet from the table where she had blindly tossed it and draped the damp length of cloth over the back of his rocking chair, Joseph poured Annie Rose a cup of coffee, and Thomas fixed her a plate of the hotcakes they'd kept warm for her. Knute sank onto the bench at her side, pushed the treasured jug of Vermont maple syrup closer, then nodded his thanks for the steaming cup Joseph handed him. Joseph and Thomas took a seat on the opposite bench, each nursing a cup of coffee as well. Maggie sat at Annie Rose's feet, clearly hoping for a treat.

Knute began. "From now on, at least one of us must have either Annie Rose or Erik in our sights at all times. If Erik leaves the homestead, Annie Rose is not to be left alone. If Annie Rose leaves, even to go to the bathing pool, Erik will not be left alone."

Joseph and Thomas nodded their agreement.

"Annie Rose, always keep Maggie with you. She doesn't like Erik, and will give you warning if he approaches." Knute did not have to add that the devoted dog would also defend her against any attacker, man or beast.

"Today I will work on a door for your room." Knute waved in the direction of the curtain that separated her bedroom from the main room. "A stout door that you can bar."

"Oh, Gramps." Annie Rose set down her fork, giving up any attempt to eat. "I hate to have you take on the work. With all of us here, surely such a measure is not necessary."

"Yes, it is." Knute's tone did not invite further argument. "You will work with the horses today, Annie Rose, as will Captain Joe. Thomas, I want you to work with Joe. He is a good and patient teacher, much better than your cousin. Listen to him and do as he says." Knute gave no notice to the rebellious look that appeared on his grandson's face. "We must get these horses ready for trade as quickly as possible. I suspect Erik will want to leave us, at least for a while, and winter is not long off."

The serious repercussions of the confrontation with Erik struck Annie Rose with full force as she watched her grandfather. His voice was stern and strong, but his face was almost as pale as his white hair and mustache, and the hand that held his coffee cup trembled. *Oh, God.* Had he suffered another of his spells?

"I'm sorry, Gramps," she blurted out. "I don't understand how the situation with Erik got so out of control. I told him again and again how I felt—how I *didn't* feel—I was so careful not to encourage him, I even started avoiding him . . ." Tears threatened to form in her eyes. "And look where it all has led."

Knute covered her hand with his. "And I've told you again and again, *datter,* this isn't your fault."

Annie Rose's shoulders slumped. "I know that I did everything I could, but I still feel bad about it."

"We all feel bad about it," Thomas said quietly. "Things never should have gotten as bad for you as they did. We'll take better care of you now."

Knute's grip on her hand tightened. Annie Rose looked at the faces surrounding her—her grandfather's wise and aging one, her brother's young but surprisingly mature one—both of them watching her with love in their eyes. Then there was Joseph's handsome face, his expression concerned and protective, his eyes warm with . . . affection, at the least.

Suddenly, Annie Rose felt very blessed. "Thank you," she whispered. Her eyes found Joseph's again, locked on them. "All of you." After a moment, unable to bear the intense feelings that welled up in her, she broke eye contact with him and straightened her shoulders. "Well, like Gramps said, there's a lot of work ahead of us. Let's get to it."

"I'll take the first watch over Erik," Thomas announced. "Gramps'll be busy with the new door, and you both'll have your hands full with those horses." He glanced at Joseph. "I can watch him while you're teaching me." There was no mistaking the challenge in his voice, the belief that Joseph could teach him nothing of value.

Joseph shrugged. "Whatever you say."

Satisfied, Thomas rose, then hesitated. "Are you going to eat those hotcakes, sister?"

Annie Rose laughed. "No, brother. You may have them, on the condition that you share with Maggie. She has been a perfect lady, waiting so patiently, with so much hope." She roughed the dog's ears. "Haven't you, sweetie?"

"Oh, all right," Thomas grumbled good-naturedly. He took up Annie Rose's plate.

Even through the short discourse with Thomas, Joseph had not taken his gaze from her. "Your brush is on your bed," he said.

"Oh." Annie Rose ran a self-conscious hand over the unruly mass of her hair.

"I found it near the pool last night."

Now she stared at him, instantly suspicious.

"I went looking for you after Erik came in with the mule deer, Miss Jensen. You'd been gone too long." His tone was calm, reassuring. "I guessed some of what happened. I knew you went into the forest."

She didn't for a moment believe that Joseph would have spied on her as Erik had done, but still, Annie Rose had to force herself to relax. "Did you try to follow me?"

"In the dark, over a bed of pine needles, with you barefoot, at least at first?" Joseph shook his head. "Not even with a lantern could I follow that faint of a trail. Especially not yours." He paused. "After all, you once told me that I couldn't track you . . . under any conditions . . . ever."

Again, her eyes locked on him. Was there a note of teasing in his deep voice?

"You couldn't," Thomas boasted around a mouthful of hotcakes. "No one can."

"Not even the Hunter?" Joseph asked.

Annie Rose watched him closely. She was not misreading the teasing light in his eyes now.

"Not even the Hunter," Thomas loyally declared.

"Well, maybe the Hunter could," Annie Rose admitted. "I hear he's very good."

"He is." Joseph stood up. "And he's my little brother."

Thomas swallowed another mouthful of hotcakes. "So?"

"I taught him everything he knows." Joseph took up his hat. "I'll see you at the corrals in a few minutes." He smiled at Annie Rose—warm, friendly, nonthreatening, noncommittal?—then pinned Thomas with a no-nonsense look. "You, too, Thomas."

"Oh, all right," Thomas muttered as he set the plate down in front of the eager Maggie.

"I beg your pardon?" Knute's reprimanding voice stabbed through the room.

"Yes, sir," Thomas quickly amended, his face suddenly red.

Joseph smiled again, and left.

Annie Rose closed her eyes. Her cards were on the table with Erik. Not so with Joseph Beaudine.

Oh, Lord. What was she going to do about him?

Joseph paused on the front step as he adjusted his hat against the sunlight.

God, she had been magnificent.

He had been so relieved to see her coming—storming, actually—down the gentle slope from the cabin. She was unharmed. Alive and well. Beautiful.

Furious.

At him?

A part of him had been relieved when she confronted Erik. He didn't ever want Annie Rose Jensen as angry with him as she was with Erik. Then Joseph sobered. Of course, he would never behave toward her as the despicable Erik had done last night. *The bastard.*

She'd stood up to Erik and exposed him for the insecure bully he was. And a bully always backed down when confronted. She had been so clever to explain that assault and rape would be necessary in order to accomplish his goals—and Joseph doubted that Eric would resort to rape. He was young and cocky and possessive, and had confused adolescent lust for true love. But somewhere deep down inside, Erik probably still genuinely cared for his cousin; there was a chance he would come around.

Until he did, Joseph would be on full-time guard duty. He realized that his somewhat optimistic assessment of Erik's condition was based a great deal upon his faith in Knute's influence. Erik was Knute's grandchild as much as Annie Rose and Thomas were. The Norseman had done a hell of a fine job raising his grandchildren, caring for them, protecting them, under unbelievable circumstances, and for so long. *Seven years in the middle of Indian Territory. Not only unmolested, but undiscovered and thriving.*

Because of the wise and loving upbringing Knute had given all of his grandchildren, there was a possibility that Erik was not a lost cause. Given enough time, perhaps he would eventually remember who he was and find himself again. Perhaps Annie Rose's words had finally sunk in. Perhaps today Erik had been forced to face the truth and would eventually come to terms with it.

Perhaps Erik was the cowardly, abusive brute he had recently portrayed.

Until he knew for certain, Joseph would not let down his guard, not for a moment.

"I thought you said we'd meet at the corrals." Thomas's belligerent voice came from behind him.

"Yes, I did say that." Joseph hooked his thumbs in his beaded belt. "You caught me thinking instead of walking." He looked over his shoulder at the boy. "Let's walk now."

Without another word, Thomas pushed past him.

Joseph grabbed his shoulder. "I said, *'let's* walk.' That means together."

Thomas rolled his eyes as they headed toward the corrals, but he measured his step to match Joseph's.

"You love your sister very much, don't you?"

"More than anything in the world," Thomas snapped.

"Even more than your grandfather?"

Thomas hesitated. "It's a close call, but Gramps can take care of himself."

"And Annie Rose can't." Joseph deliberately made his words a statement rather than a question.

"She's a woman."

"Ah. And women can't take care of themselves."

At that, Thomas turned on him, his eyes spitting fury. "Women aren't as physically strong as men are. If they get caught, they're in deep trouble."

Determined to get to the root of Thomas's problem with him, Joseph deliberately debated with him. "But if a man were to get caught by the wrong people, say, the Apache, he'd be in as much trouble as any woman would be."

"No." Thomas shook his head in frustration, crossing his arms over his thin chest. "Deep trouble, yes, but different trouble. Men want different things from women than they want from men."

"What do they want, Thomas?" Joseph asked quietly.

"They want *them!*" he cried. "Like Erik wants Annie Rose!" He glared at Joseph, his green eyes filled with hatred, his voice low and filled with disgust. "Like you want her!"

Joseph stiffened. "I don't want her like Erik does."

"Yes, you do! I've seen how you look at her, how you follow her with your eyes all the time. Just like Erik, you're stalking her, hunting her, like she's a doe, or—or a mare, in heat." Thomas poked Joseph's chest, hard. "Stay away from her, *Captain*. For whatever reason, Gramps can't see through you, but I can. I meant what I said that first night you were here. I'll kill you if you hurt Annie Rose."

"As well you should," Joseph ground out.

Thomas blinked. "What?"

"If I were hunting your sister like that, you should want to kill me."

"I don't just *want* to; I *will*."

Joseph bit down on his rising annoyance. "Fine." He paused. "I'm not hunting your sister."

"Yes, you are."

"No, I'm not." Joseph grabbed Thomas's shoulders. "Look at me." He gave Thomas a little shake. *"Look at me."*

Thomas raised his gaze.

"Yes, I watch your sister sometimes." His jaw clenched at the flare of triumph in the boy's eyes. "Because I think she's pretty, Thomas, not because I want to possess her. Don't you think she's pretty?"

Thomas frowned, confused. "Yes."

Joseph released him. "I think Annie Rose is beautiful, and I like looking at her. That *doesn't* mean I want to hurt her. It means I admire her."

"But Erik watches her, too," Thomas insisted.

"Not the same way I do." Joseph met the boy's gaze, held it. "Not the same way I do," he firmly repeated. "There's a difference. You can see that difference, if you look."

Thomas stubbornly dropped his gaze to the ground.

Joseph placed his hands on his hips and sighed. "Look. Your grandfather told us to work together, and I intend to do as he says. I don't want Knute mad at me. How about you?"

"No, I don't want him mad at me, either."

"We're on the same side, son."

At that, Thomas jerked his head up to glare at him. "Don't call me that. I'm not your son."

Astonished at the boy's vehemence, Joseph held his hands up in front of him. "I apologize. I meant no offense."

Again, Thomas seemed taken aback, as if he had expected Joseph to fight. "All right," he muttered.

Joseph looked down at the corrals, where the horses waited, then back at the boy next to him, unsure how to proceed. "You and I are on the same side, Thomas," he finally repeated, quietly. "Like you and your grandfather, I'll fight in order to protect your sister. I intend to see that no harm comes to her from any side, and that includes from me."

"You don't love her like we do."

Maybe not yet, but I'll bet I could. I'll bet I'm already damned close to it. Joseph stroked his mustache thoughtfully, again at a loss for words. "I genuinely care about her," he said at last. "I give you my word, one man to another, that I will always treat Annie Rose with the utmost respect. I will fight for her honor and for her life, gladly giving my own life if necessary."

Thomas stared at him. "You mean it?"

"I gave you my word. Now I give you my hand, in partnership for your sister's sake, and in friendship." Joseph held out his hand.

"You mean it," Thomas whispered incredulously. He slowly reached out and took Joseph's hand. "Man to man?"

"Man to man."

They shook hands.

Thomas released him and stepped back, almost shy now. "Guess we'd better get to work, huh, Captain?"

"We'd better. Like I said, I don't want your grandfather mad at me."

Side by side, they started toward the corral.

"Thomas?"

"Yeah?"

"If we're going to be partners, call me Joe."

"Sure, Joe." Thomas smiled, a small, pleased smile.

Joseph smiled, too.

It was a start.

Twelve

Tension hung heavy in the air over the Jensen homestead for the next several days, but nothing flared up into outright confrontation. Knute kept Erik busy with chores around the homestead, preparing for the coming winter, as he did Thomas when the boy wasn't working with Joseph. Knute finished the door to Annie Rose's room—which further insulted Erik—and built a simple box bed for Joseph. Annie Rose harvested carrots, cabbage, and onions from her small, neat garden, all of which went into the cellar, and she used the cucumbers to prepare a large crock of pickles. Joseph chopped wood and made repairs to the sod roof.

In addition, with the exception of Erik, they worked with the horses every day.

Patiently, steadily, the animals were put through their paces. Halter, bridle, saddle, rider. Halter, bridle, saddle, rider. The new bunch progressed quickly and well, including the obstinate Calypso.

Twice over the course of those relatively quiet days Annie Rose disappeared for several hours. If Knute or Thomas knew where she went, neither would share that knowledge. Joseph was acutely aware of her absence, wondering where she had gone, and why. Never again did he want her to choose the forest over his company, and he was reasonably certain that her sojourns were not an attempt to escape from him for a while. Since the incident with Erik at the pool, Joseph had taken great pains to distance himself from Annie Rose, to treat her with casual friendliness. It had been difficult, for his attraction to her was stronger than ever, but she seemed to be more comfortable with him now.

A week later, they were all seated around the table—Knute at the head, Joseph and Erik on one bench, Annie Rose and Thomas on the other. They were sharing an excellent supper, in Joseph's opinion, of elk steaks, stewed wild plums, and fried potatoes, when Erik broke his customary sullen silence.

"How soon before the horses are ready to go to Fort Laramie?"

Knute glanced at Joseph. "Another week, perhaps ten days?"

Joseph nodded. "I think we'll have them ready by then."

"I want to take the Golden Mare and sell her, too," Erik said casually.

A stunned silence fell over the rest of the party.

Joseph watched Annie Rose's face drain of color, as if someone had emptied her of her life's blood. The small hand with which she clutched her fork trembled. She set down the fork and clasped her hands in her lap.

"I know you know where she is, Annabella," Erik said coldly. "We all worked to capture her; she belongs to all of us."

"She belongs to no one." Now two red spots appeared in Annie Rose's white cheeks. "She is free, Erik, as she was meant to be. And don't call me Annabella."

Erik turned to Knute. "Gramps, that mare is worth a lot of money, money that could make a difference to all of us. She doesn't have the right to keep the mare for herself."

"You think that's what she is doing?"

If Erik noticed the anger in Knute's voice, he paid it no heed. "She knows where it is! I want that horse!"

"So you can sell her to the highest bidder," Knute stated.

"Yes!" Erik's face became animated and his eyes took on a new fire. "The Sioux and the Cheyenne want her, Abelard Baines wants her, hell, probably even the Army wants her."

At Knute's frosty glare, Erik hastily added, "Sorry for swearing." The look on his face changed to one of entreaty. "There's so much we could do with the money."

"Like what?" Knute leaned forward, his eyes blazing. "We want for nothing. What is so important that you would condemn that beautiful animal to the likes of Abelard Baines for *money?*"

"The future, Gramps!" Erik scrambled off his bench and stood with his hands on his hips. "I have a future, even if you don't."

"Erik!" Annie Rose threw her napkin down.

Joseph reached across the table and caught Thomas by the arm when the boy tried to stand.

"No, no, Thomas, Annie Rose, it's all right," Knute said, holding his hand out in a placating gesture. He looked up at Erik. "Your cousin is right. We all know my days are numbered, while the rest of you do indeed have a future." His sharp gaze travelled around the table. "We will decide this as we have decided most issues facing this family. We will vote."

"No!" Erik ran a hand through his hair in frustration. "I'll be outvoted, like I usually am, like I was when Annie Rose took the mare away without my knowledge or consent."

"I took her away so you couldn't hurt her anymore." Now Annie Rose stood, also, glaring across the table at her cousin. "She wouldn't be broken, Erik, remember? No matter how you beat her, she wouldn't be broken. Nor should she be, ever. But you can't understand that. She is just an animal to you."

"They're all just animals, *cousin.* There's no such thing as a spirit animal, and that mare sure as hell isn't one, even though the stupid Indians think she is. If the tribes want to pay more for her, I'll gladly take their money or goods." Erik didn't bother to apologize again for his swearing. He placed his hands on the table and leaned toward Annie Rose, his eyes blazing with anger. *"I want that mare."*

"Never."

Joseph stared at Annie Rose. The indomitable strength in her voice made that single word a vow.

Erik waved his hand in disgust. "Fool!" he spat.

"Erik . . ." Knute warned.

After a moment of tense silence, Joseph said quietly, "Look around you, man. It isn't just Annie Rose you're fighting here. Your grandfather and your cousin agree with her. You were right—you're outvoted."

Without taking his gaze from Annie Rose, Erik stabbed a finger in Joseph's direction. "This is none of your affair, Beaudine. Stay out of it."

"By your grandfather's invitation, it is my affair. The answer is no. The Golden Mare will not be sold."

Erik turned on him. *"You* know where she is?"

"No, I don't. But I've been lucky enough to see her, once. Annie Rose is right, Erik. Some animals need to be free, *deserve* to be free. The mare is such an animal, and I will protect her freedom."

"We all will," Thomas interjected. Hatred burned in his green eyes as he stared at his cousin. "We won't let you hurt that mare or Annie Rose. We'll see that you don't get the chance."

Erik snorted in derision. "You'll take me on?"

Thomas met his gaze unflinchingly. "If I have to."

Again, silence descended on the room. Then Erik stomped to the door. "You're all fools," he snarled, and flung himself out into the night.

Annie Rose sank back down to the bench. "Is there a chance he'll leave here to go look for her?" she asked her grandfather.

"It's hard to say for sure, but I don't think so." Knute stroked his mustache. "He tried to find her right after you took her away, and he had no luck then. Why would he believe his luck would be any better now?"

"I don't know. With Erik, you can't tell anymore. He's changed so much."

"Ja, he has. But even if he does look for her again, *datter,* he won't find her."

Joseph saw the sorrow in the Norseman's eyes, heard the pain of betrayal in his tone, and his heart went out to the old man. "Is there anything I can do?" he asked.

"Just help protect my girl here," Knute said, patting Annie Rose's hand.

"Gladly." Try as he did, Joseph could not keep the warmth from his voice when he spoke. Evidently Annie Rose heard it, too, for an endearing blush crept up her cheeks, and she looked down at the table. Inwardly, Joseph groaned. After days of forcing himself to be cautiously polite to Annie Rose, he hoped he hadn't inadvertently pushed her away again with his sincere and enthusiastic pronunciation of one innocent word.

Early the next afternoon, Annie Rose again disappeared. One minute she was in the neighboring corral with Calypso, the next she was gone. When he realized it, Joseph frantically scrutinized the area, one hand held to the brim of his hat against the late August sun.

Maggie raced across the yard away from him and past the cabin, providing him with a clue. Sure enough, he caught a flash of brown—perhaps calico?—against the green of the willow bushes near the path to the bathing pool.

This time, he would follow her.

He gave a few quick instructions to Thomas, then let himself out of the corral. After making certain that Erik was nearby—the red-bearded man was helping Knute replace a rotting fence post—Joseph grabbed his rifle from its position against the fence and hurried off in the direction of the pool. Of course, there was a possibility that Annie Rose was merely indulging in a bath, but he doubted it. A cautious approach to the pool, complete with a few calls of her name, proved him right. She had gone into the forest again.

Joseph made his way to the place where he had lost her

trail the night of the incident with Erik. There, he crouched down and surveyed the area, perusing the ground with care before he moved a foot, not wanting to disturb any clue that might show him the direction Annie Rose had taken. His patience was rewarded near a stand of aspen, where he found a faint, partial imprint of her moccasin. With a word of thanks to the aspen trees for not yet shedding their leaves, he set off on her trail.

Something had changed in Joseph Beaudine's attitude toward her. Annie Rose strode through the trees, wondering what had happened. Ever since the day of the argument with Erik over the incident at the bathing pool, Joseph seemed almost withdrawn. Oh, he treated her with nothing but respect, was courteous and mannerly at all times. But the gentle teasing had stopped, and the compliments he gave now were restricted to her cooking or to her work with the horses; never about her appearance. She rarely caught him watching her, and when she did, he immediately looked away. Perhaps he finally understood that she did not return whatever interest he may have had in her.

She was relieved.

Annie Rose sighed and swung a stick at a tree trunk in passing.

No, she wasn't.

She missed the way Joseph had treated her before, missed his easy manner and the warmth in his brown eyes. Considering her deep-seated feelings of distrust toward men in general, she should have been relieved that his interest had waned, and it bothered her that she wasn't.

No, it went further than that.

Annie Rose was *frightened* that she missed his warmth, for it indicated that Joseph Beaudine had wormed his way into her affections much more deeply than she had realized. She longed for the day when the horses would be ready for the trip to Fort Laramie, for Joseph's job here would come to an end and he could go back to being a scout, or mediator for the tribes, or whatever he decided to be, and she could stop thinking about him.

Out of sight, out of mind.

She aimlessly swung at another tree. *Sure.*

"Come on, Maggie," she called, her voice sharp with irritation—at herself, not at the exploring dog. Aurora's secure meadow was not far now. Spending time with the beautiful mare would calm her and offer respite to her troubled spirit, as it always did. Annie Rose tossed the stick away and quickened her pace.

Joseph moved more slowly, and with more care. He wasn't far behind Annie Rose, and he heard the sound of horses in the distance. Every now and then, Maggie would bark, happy and excited, by the sound of it. His heart started pounding with anticipation, as if he were on the verge of some great discovery.

He was.

After cautiously weaving his way through yet another thick stand of aspen, he found himself atop a rocky cliff. Joseph's breath caught. Surely he had stumbled upon a small piece of heaven.

Before him spread a small meadow, pristine in its beauty. Aspen, spruce, and fir trees stood shoulder to shoulder around the perimeter, offering a barrier against the rest of the world. A bright rainbow of wildflowers dotted the lush green grass— blue lupine, red Indian paintbrush, white Queen Anne's lace, yellow arnica, delicate lavender-and-white columbine—and a clear creek gurgled cheerfully as it meandered down the middle of the meadow. The pleasantly cool wind rustled the aspen leaves over his head and set the flowers in the meadow to dancing. Joseph breathed deeply of the clean mountain air, taking delight in the scents of aspen, pine, and flowers. As far as he was concerned, he had indeed found heaven.

He had also found the refuge of the Golden Mare.

Joseph knew it, even before he spotted the evidence of a small corral directly below him at the base of the rock.

His heart continued its pounding. Where were they? He could no longer hear horses or Maggie, but the Golden Mare and the golden woman had to be close by. He could sense their presence.

With care, Joseph retraced his steps through the aspen, searching for a way down to the meadow. He found and followed a steep game trail, eventually coming out on the floor of the meadow. He made his way to the empty corral, which had been cleverly constructed to take advantage of a shallow cave dug by nature into the face of the rock. The shelter offered by the cave was augmented by a makeshift roof which extended perhaps six feet from the rock wall. Joseph saw that the grasses within the small enclosure had been trampled to dust, indicating that the mare had been here for more than a few days. A small, rough trough held a good measure of oats and Annie Rose's hat hung by its string on one of the fence posts.

Joseph leaned his rifle against that same fence post and, hands on hips, turned in a half circle, surveying the meadow. True, the place was isolated and therefore somewhat protected, but surely Annie Rose could not hope to keep the mare here indefinitely.

Then he saw her—them.

From the haven of the trees they came, the woman riding the horse, at a leisurely pace. A grey horse followed the golden mare, and Maggie bounded along in front.

Annie Rose rode the mare as she had that long-ago misty morning when he watched her from the ridge—bareback, astride, sitting tall and graceful, with nothing to cling to save the mare's long white mane. Her brown calico skirts were pushed up to her thighs, revealing white, lace-trimmed drawers and the handle of her long knife, which peeked from one of her calf-high moccasins. A great deal of her blonde hair had come loose from the chignon at the back of her head, allowing golden wisps to dance around her face and neck with gleeful abandon.

Again, Joseph was reminded of a goddess. Not only was Annie Rose lovely and regal, but she exuded an alluring, inexplicable power. He could not take his eyes from her as she guided the mare across the meadow toward him.

She was his.

The realization slammed into him with so much force that he almost staggered. His eyes widened and he stared even harder at her, mesmerized. She was his mate, the woman meant for him in this life, his destiny. Joseph knew it with a certainty that went beyond his heart all the way to his soul. Just as Orion had known Sarah was his soul's mate, Joseph recognized Annie Rose as his. He stepped out of the shadow of the corral roof, into the full sunlight, his gaze intent upon her, his heart pounding in anticipation.

Surely she felt it, too.

She *must* feel it.

Maggie barked an enthusiastic greeting and raced toward him. Annie Rose stiffened, wary and defensive, then he saw the light of recognition in her eyes, and she relaxed a little. In truth, she did not seem all that surprised to see him. The golden mare suddenly sidestepped, perhaps nervous at the sound of the still-barking dog, but Annie Rose kept her seat and easily controlled the animal. Joseph bent and scratched Maggie's ears in welcome, then straightened again.

His heart gladdened even more as Annie Rose drew near, and he fought the urge to reach out to her. His recent revelation made him want to run to her side, to pull her from the horse and take her in his arms, to share the joy of his discovery, to kiss her at last.

But he held back, waiting, watching. Annie Rose did not look joyous. She looked . . . well, angry.

"You tracked me." The accusatory words cut through the air like a whip, sharp and stinging.

"Yes."

"You had no right." Annie Rose slipped from the mare's back and faced him, her green eyes flashing in the sunlight.

Although she wore simple brown calico trimmed with only a bit of lace, she looked more like a goddess than ever, albeit an angry one. Joseph would not have been surprised if Annie Rose was suddenly able to command lightning and thunder with a wave of her hand. "Perhaps not, but I was concerned about you." He paused, then nodded at the mare. "And about her."

"Aurora is no concern of yours." Annie Rose guided the mare toward the corral. "Neither am I, for that matter. Don't use Erik as an excuse to make either of us your concern."

"He's only part of it." *She had called the mare "Aurora,"— the Goddess of the Sun. A perfect name for the golden animal.* Joseph watched as the mare docilely went into the corral, followed by the grey horse.

Annie Rose secured the gate and turned to him. "Your concern is not needed, nor is it welcome, Mr. Beaudine."

A little of the glow from his discovery faded in the face of her unrelenting hostility. "Why do you dislike me so?" Joseph asked quietly.

Her stern gaze faltered and she looked away from him, then down at the ground. "I don't dislike you," she finally admitted.

"Then what is it?" Joseph fought the urge to brush the fine golden strands from her cheek.

After a long minute, Annie Rose looked up at him, her expression defiant, yet sad and troubled at the same time. "Change is coming, Mr. Beaudine. My grandfather is dying, my cousin has turned against us, my existence has been discovered through my own carelessness, and, as you yourself said, our beloved land is being invaded. I have a young brother to care for and may soon be alone in that responsibility. All of these are unwanted and unwelcome changes. You are part of those changes."

"And therefore I am unwelcome as well."

Annie Rose shifted uncomfortably. "Yes."

That single word hurt. Joseph looked around the peaceful meadow, then back at the mare who waited by the corral fence, her ears pricked in curiosity. "Life constantly changes, Annie Rose, more often than not in ways we don't like."

"I know that," she snapped. She turned away from him, placing her arms around Aurora's neck.

As Joseph watched her, comprehension broke through, swiftly followed by an outpouring of compassion. Her whole world was being threatened. "You're frightened, aren't you?"

She whirled about to face him again. "No, Mr. Beaudine, I am *terrified.*"

Joseph was taken aback by the vehemence in her voice.

"My grandfather will die, probably with no more than a few moments' warning. His great heart will simply stop. He can't prevent it, and neither can I." Tears glistened in her eyes and she angrily blinked them away. "When that happens, my heart will be broken, as it was when my mother died. But there's more to it than the grieving—how am I to take care of Thomas, to see him through to manhood? How am I to protect this beautiful animal and her coming foal against the Sioux, the Cheyenne, Abelard Baines, and my own cousin?"

Startled, Joseph stared at the mare. He had been so taken with Annie Rose that he had not looked closely at Aurora. The mare was indeed with foal, and judging from the waxing of her udder, her time was not far off. He returned his gaze to Annie Rose. She stood with her chin up, her slender body held stiff and proud, yet he could see fear and vulnerability in her green eyes. "Thomas is closer to manhood than you realize," he said cautiously. "And I am here. I will not leave you and your brother and Aurora to face Erik and Baines and the Indian tribes alone."

"Why?" Annie Rose demanded, her voice not only angry now, but full of suspicion. "Why would you take on the responsibility for us all?" Her green eyes seemed to spit fire. "Why did you agree to work for my grandfather, Mr. Beaudine? What did you hope to gain? You came barging into our valley, wanted by no one but Gramps, and you have done a masterful job of endearing yourself to him. Why? Did you plan to one day take his place?"

"No!" Joseph snapped. "It wasn't like that."

One of her hands shot to her hip. "Then what was it like?"

His softly spoken answer slipped out before Joseph considered the wisdom of baring his heart to her in her present mood. "I would have done anything to find you." He regretted the words at once, for they seemed to only anger her further.

"Why?"

Joseph decided that he had nothing to lose by telling her the truth. "Because something in your soul touched my soul."

Annie Rose blinked, momentarily silenced. Clearly, she hadn't expected that answer. As she stared at him, hope began to grow within him that she would believe his words, but that fragile hope was short-lived. Her anger returned full force.

"Don't be ridiculous, Joseph Beaudine. We had only just met. Your coming here, your staying here, they have nothing to do with our souls. I think you will stay and offer your protection because you hope to win my heart, and therefore my body. Or, perhaps, like most men, you don't care about the heart that beats beneath these breasts." She laid her hands flat against her chest for a moment, then dropped them, balled into fists, to her sides. "It is my woman's body you want, not my mind or heart, or soul. That alone is reason enough for you to stay, isn't it? Perhaps you regard my body as a worthy reward for your efforts."

Now Joseph stiffened. Did she truly believe her own words? If so, what man had wounded her so deeply that she despised all men save her grandfather and her brother? Or was she merely trying to insult him in the hope that he would go away? "I will stay because I gave your grandfather my word," he finally said.

"So that's it." Annie Rose crossed her arms over her chest and some of the tension left her. "That's a good reason," she admitted. "I'm sorry Gramps placed that burden on you."

"I don't view it as a burden, Miss Jensen. I doubt any

man of honor would. It is a responsibility, yes, but one I took on freely." She looked so defensive, so wary. He wanted to reach out and smooth the lines of worry from her forehead. "You and Thomas are not alone."

Her shoulders slumped, in weariness or resignation, he could not tell. "I want to believe you," she said, her voice barely above a whisper. "I want to believe that you are an honorable man, that your feelings for me are those of friendship, that you have no ulterior motives—no matter what you say about our souls."

Her words took on a sarcastic tone at the end, and Joseph winced, sorry now that he had mentioned the word "soul." "You *can* believe that," he said.

"No, I can't. I don't dare." She turned away from him and stroked the white blaze that decorated Aurora's face. "But you are here to stay for now, and there's nothing I can do about it."

Troubled by her dejection, Joseph couldn't stop himself from asking, "Am I that bad?"

Annie Rose turned back to him. "No, Mr. Beaudine. You're not bad at all. That's part of my problem." She watched him for a moment, pondering, as if she were carefully choosing her next words. "I know you are different in many respects from most men, just as your brother Grey Eagle is. I do trust you to keep your word."

That's a start. Joseph did not dare say the words out loud. He meant them as the note of hope they were, but now was not the time to even hint that he wanted more than friendship from her. He would give anything to take back his honest but ill-timed comment about her soul touching his. Because she had found the idea so preposterous, she might have trouble believing anything he said.

After a moment, she continued, serious and intent. "You've given your word to my grandfather about Thomas and me. Now I must ask for your word about Aurora. You must swear not to reveal her whereabouts to anyone, or to even admit that you have seen her here. And you *must not* tell anyone about her foal." She stared into his eyes.

Grateful and relieved that she was willing to trust him about something—anything—Joseph met her gaze and spoke with no hesitation. "I swear to you, Annie Rose Jensen, that the secret of Aurora and her foal is safe with me. As I said at supper last night, I will do all in my power to protect her, to protect them both."

"Thank you." Aurora gently bumped Annie Rose's shoulder with her nose, and Annie Rose turned to again stroke the mare's face.

"Will she let me near?" Joseph asked, unable to keep the wonder and hope from his voice.

Annie Rose frowned. "I don't know. After Erik got rough with her, she hasn't let anyone but Gramps and me near—not even Thomas. And I'm the only one she'll let on her back."

"May I try?"

"Just don't upset her. If she protests, back off at once."

"Agreed."

Annie Rose stepped away, but Joseph made no attempt to move closer. Not yet.

Following Annie Rose's lead, he closed his eyes, as she had done that day in the corral with Calypso. After that, he wasn't sure what she had done, but somehow, she had connected with the horse's spirit. He wanted to do that now with Aurora. So he stood still and calm, listening and feeling.

Aurora nickered.

"Reach out to her with your heart." Annie Rose's words came to him from far away, so faint that he wasn't sure if she had actually spoken or if he had merely heard her voice whisper in his mind. Either way, he obeyed.

Breathing. Heartbeats. Then deeper. Calm curiosity. Welcoming.

He could feel Aurora's spirit.

Joseph held out his hand and took a step toward the golden mare. She nickered. He opened his eyes and edged closer. She blew and tossed her head. He moved closer still. She waited for him, then stretched her neck and sniffed the back of his hand. Her breath was warm on his skin, yet shivers ran down his spine.

Power. Joseph felt the raw power of her spirit, glimpsed the beauty and the wisdom of her soul, and was shaken to the depths of his own soul.

The Golden Mare was indeed a spirit animal.

Aurora nuzzled his shoulder. As he stroked her neck, Joseph remembered that she was also a flesh-and-blood animal, one that could be injured—and killed. His vow to Annie Rose became even more binding as he repeated it in a whisper to Aurora. "I will protect you and your foal." Aurora nuzzled him again with her velvet-soft nose and nickered, low in her chest, as if she understood his words. Joseph was certain that she did.

He glanced over Aurora's muzzle to Annie Rose, who stood near the rock wall. She stared at him, her face white, her eyes huge.

"You have the Gift, too." Even though she whispered, her voice cracked, indicating her shock.

"Not like you do. But yes, I have an understanding of horses that most men don't." As if to further clarify his point, the grey horse ambled up alongside Aurora and pushed her nose over the fence at him. Joseph obliged her with a good scratching on the forehead.

"Have you heard the legend of the Golden Mare?" he asked casually.

"Yes." Annie Rose slowly approached.

"The coming of the Golden Mare is supposed to herald the coming of a new age for the Plains Indians, a time of peace and prosperity. She is a powerful spirit animal to the tribes, Annie Rose. That's why Baines wants her, that's why Erik wants her—she is very valuable."

"She is a mare who happens to have a golden coat," Annie Rose said stubbornly.

Joseph looked down at her stiff stance, at her set jaw. "She is more than that."

Annie Rose remained silent, stroking Aurora's nose.

"How did you come by her?" Joseph asked.

"Gramps caught her with a small herd about a year ago. We didn't think anything of the legend. She was simply a horse, like the others, although a particularly beautiful one." Annie Rose fussed with the forelock of white hair that fell forward between Aurora's ears.

"But she wasn't like the others to you, was she?"

Annie Rose shook her head. "She was special. I knew it at once. The Paint even came for her, something he had never done with any other mare."

"He came for her?"

"Somehow he found our valley. He stood on the rise to the south, the one about a half mile from the cabin, and called to her. Aurora was frantic to join him. I begged Gramps to let her go, but Erik fought me. At that time, Erik didn't know about the legend, or if he did, he didn't believe it. He certainly didn't know how valuable she was. My cousin was angry because Aurora refused to let him ride her." Her tone turned bitter. "To break her became his personal mission. He didn't care what it took."

Joseph fought the anger that welled up in him, knowing that the mare would feel it. Indeed, she turned from Annie Rose and looked at him, her gaze calm. He reached over the fence and patted her shoulder reassuringly, noting the thin scar that ran along her side. His jaw clenched.

"I caught him using a board on her." Annie Rose shuddered, as if just saying the words was painful. "That night, she let me ride her, and, with my grandfather's blessing, I took her to The Paint."

"How did this come about?" Joseph waved an arm to indicate the corral.

"I'd see her every now and then, usually with the herd, but sometimes not. Once she was being chased by Indians, and I realized that her existence had become known."

"Like yours has."

Annie Rose's mouth tightened momentarily, and Joseph

again regretted his words. "Yes," she said. "I also realized a few months ago that Aurora was pregnant. She needed a safe place to grow her baby, a safe place to deliver it. So I brought her here, with the old mare for company."

Joseph raised a skeptical eyebrow. "You built this yourself?"

"Most of it. Gramps came once and helped with the more difficult tasks, like sinking the fence posts and constructing the roof."

"What of Thomas?"

"He feels as Gramps and I do, but he doesn't want to know where she is. He's afraid he'll let something slip. So he stays back and keeps an eye on Erik."

More impressed than ever with young Thomas, Joseph again looked around the enclosure. "Surely you don't keep her penned up all the time."

Annie Rose frowned up at him. "Of course not. The corral is mostly for shelter, although I would pen them and stay with them if I thought there was a real danger of discovery. She and the grey roam free, but they have yet to roam far from the meadow. It is almost as if Aurora knows that she is safe here. I come every few days to check on them and bring some oats. Aurora and I go for an easy ride, so she gets some exercise. The horses can retreat to the shelter of the cave if the need arises." She looked back at Aurora. "I just want to keep her safe." A wistful note, tinged with desperation, crept into her voice.

Privately, Joseph felt that Annie Rose had set an impossible task for herself. Both white men and red searched for the Golden Mare—she couldn't be hidden indefinitely, just as Annie Rose herself could not be hidden indefinitely. Word would get around of both the mare and the woman, especially with the big mouth of Abelard Baines spreading the news. Cautiously, Joseph reached out and lightly patted Annie Rose's shoulder, once. She stiffened, but did not pull away. "We'll keep her safe," he promised. *For as long as we can,* he silently added.

Annie Rose merely nodded. She slipped into the corral and put her arms around Aurora's neck, rested her cheek against the golden coat.

The Golden Mare and the golden woman.

As they stood in the sunshine, Joseph watched them. A mysterious aching need rose up within him, so strong that it took his breath away. He longed to join the mare and the woman, to put his arms around them both, to be a part of the love he knew they shared. *He belonged with them.*

Someday, Annie Rose would know it as surely as he did, just as she would know that their souls had indeed touched.

Thirteen

They had agreed that Annie Rose would lead the way back to the homestead, as she was more familiar with the terrain than Joseph was. Leaving Maggie and Joseph to follow as best they could, she hurried through the forest, unconsciously taking measures to hide her trail, for she was beyond conscious thought. Her mind was still reeling from the scene she had witnessed today.

Joseph Beaudine understood Aurora's power.

Not only did he understand that power, but he also felt it, and knew it for what it was. Aurora knew that he knew. The mare intuitively trusted the man.

I wish I could. I wish I could take Aurora's word for it.

But she couldn't. An animal's intuition was rarely, if ever, wrong, yet still Annie Rose wouldn't risk it, no matter how tempted she was to give in to Joseph's gentle allure. When he patted her shoulder in that friendly gesture of reassurance, she had longed to turn to him, to let him put his arms around her, as she instinctively knew he would have done. How nice it would be to rest against his strength, for just a while.

A part of her cried out to trust him, to believe that he was an honorable man where a woman was concerned, especially after his comment about their souls touching. But she would not. She had seen firsthand the payment exacted for misplaced trust in a man. Never would she open herself up to that kind of danger.

In heart and soul, her mother had trusted her father, and in the end had been betrayed in the worst of ways. Thank God Thora died before learning what her beloved Blaine had planned for their children.

"Miss Jensen!"

Panting, she came to a stop and looked behind her. Joseph and Maggie had kept pace with her, but both were breathing hard.

"Where's the fire?" Joseph asked.

Annie Rose blinked. "What?"

"You've been tearing along like the house is on fire. What's the hurry?"

"I'm sorry. I didn't realize I was moving so fast." She was tempted to tartly ask if he was having trouble keeping up, but she already knew the answer. He'd managed to stay right with her, even carrying his heavy rifle.

Maggie plopped to the ground, her tongue hanging from her mouth. A twinge of guilt assailed Annie Rose. She wanted to keep running. She needed to keep running. Running made it more difficult to think.

But no matter how fast she ran, she couldn't run from the fact that Joseph Beaudine had the Gift. Perhaps their souls had touched, if only through Aurora. The thought troubled her. Joseph was getting too close, in too many ways. "We'll rest a minute," she said, grudgingly.

Joseph nodded and moved a short distance away, resting the butt of his rifle on the ground. Annie Rose took off her hat and fanned her face with it, welcoming the cooling breeze that wafted over her head and through her tangled hair. She watched Joseph closely, let her gaze rove over him.

The dappled sunlight that filtered through the trees touched him here and there, making his white shirt appear to be very white, glinting off his thick mustache and highlighting his brown hair, which hung below his hat and lay about his shoulders. His eyes were shaded by his hat brim, so she couldn't tell for sure where he looked, but it seemed he was studying their back trail.

Annie Rose hated to admit it, but she took great pleasure in the sight of Joseph Beaudine. He stood straight and tall—a mark of his days in the Army, no doubt. His tanned, strong-looking hands clasped the long barrel of his rifle, the rolled-back sleeves of his shirt displayed equally tanned and strong forearms, his collar was unbuttoned and open in a vee that extended far enough down his chest to expose a small and tantalizing patch of dark hair. Her fingers itched to touch that hair, to see if it was soft, to see if the skin underneath was warm, to see how far down his body that hair trailed.

Lord.

She closed her eyes for a moment, her tingling fingertips pressed to her mouth, and fought the primal pleasure that coursed through her with such force that her breath was quickened from more than exertion. It did no good; the pleasure did not fade, no matter how firmly she willed it away. She opened her eyes. Joseph still stood there, and Annie Rose could not turn away from the sight of his narrow waist—accented by a beaded belt—the appealing curve of his taut flanks, his long, long legs encased in fringed buckskin pants, his knee-high moccasins.

Her eyes closed again. *Oh, Lord.*

"Miss Jensen? Are you all right?"

At the sound of his voice, low and soft, her eyes flew open, and she found him looking at her with an odd expression on his handsome face. Concern? Confusion? Amusement? Had he caught her staring at him like a moonstruck calf? The thought stiffened her spine, and raised her chin. Annie Rose reminded herself that Joseph stayed with them only because of a promise to Knute.

"I'm fine," she snapped. "We should be on our way. I need to get supper started." Annie Rose slapped her hat back on her head and set off at a fast pace, whistling for Maggie.

"We're not far from your home, Miss Jensen. Surely we can walk at a more leisurely pace." He paused, then added, "I won't bite." There was a definite teasing quality to his voice now.

Without slowing down, Annie Rose glared over her shoulder at him. "I never thought you would."

"Then why do you fear me?"

At that, she stopped and whirled to face him. "I'm not afraid of you."

"No?" One cocked eyebrow showed his disbelief. "Then walk with me, just as you would walk with Thomas or your grandfather."

"Very well, Mr. Beaudine," she said frostily. When he reached her side, she matched her stride to his, still careful of where she placed her feet.

A few minutes passed in relatively companionable silence. Then Joseph said, "Your grandfather taught you well."

"What do you mean?"

"Even now, this close to home, you watch where you put your feet. Even while running, you left very little to track." His voice was warm with approval.

"Yet you tracked me."

"I warned you that I could."

"Yes." That day at Jubal's cabin seemed like such a long time ago. "What did I do wrong?"

Joseph looked down at her. "You didn't do anything wrong. You feared for Aurora, and so perhaps hurried more than you would have under normal circumstances. I had a difficult time finding your path, Miss Jensen. I compliment you on your skill as a woodsman."

Coming from one of the legendary Beaudine brothers, Annie Rose took that as high praise. "Thank you," she said, turning her head away from him so that he could not see that her cheeks had flushed with pleasure. That was one problem with being blonde and fair-complected, she thought irritably. Her face turned red too easily.

A few minutes later, as they approached the bathing pool, Maggie suddenly took off toward the cabin, barking furiously. The plucky dog rounded the boulder and disappeared.

Joseph immediately shifted his rifle to a ready position, and Annie Rose bent and slipped her knife from the sheath in her moccasin without breaking her stride. Her heart in her throat, she walked faster, and Joseph voiced no objection. Maggie's barks changed to excited yips and yelps, which offered Annie Rose some relief as the cabin came into view.

"Jubal Sage!" Joseph called, his hand raised in greeting.

A smile curved Annie Rose's lips at the sight of Jubal and his wife, Sweet Water. Just as easily as she had removed it, she returned the knife to its sheath and hurried toward the group of people gathered in front of the cabin. Jubal had his arm draped around a smiling Thomas's shoulders, Knute was talking to Sweet Water, and Erik stood off to the side, glowering as usual.

"Sweet Water! Jubal! How good to see you!" Those words did not express the depth of feeling Annie Rose had for the couple. She loved Jubal and Sweet Water as if they were family.

Sweet Water waved, her round face split in a wide grin. "Annie Rosie!"

The two women embraced, then Annie Rose leaned over to plant a kiss on Jubal's weathered, grey-bearded cheek. "Welcome," she said sincerely.

"Let me look at you, girl." Jubal stood back from her and looked her up and down, then nodded in approval. "I swear, Annie Rose, you get prettier each time I see you. What are you doin' walkin' out with this rogue here?" He jerked his thumb in Joseph's direction.

The delicate blush that started in Annie Rose's cheeks at Jubal's compliment turned into a hot flush at his teasing words about Joseph. "We weren't walking out together," she responded, more harshly than she intended. A twinge of guilt grabbed her at Jubal's startled expression, so she flashed him an apologetic smile as she linked arms with Sweet Water. Ignoring the pleased look on Knute's face and the furious one on Erik's, she guided Sweet Water toward the house. "Let's get something cool to drink while the men see to your horses. Then we'll start supper."

"We bring fresh . . . sage gg-rouse," Sweet Water announced, clearly searching for the correct words. "My Jubal is . . . great hunter!"

A rush of affection for the stalwart Cheyenne woman filled Annie Rose. "I declare, Sweet Water, your English is getting so good, you'll soon speak it better than any of us."

Sweet Water beamed, and the two women went into the cabin.

Joseph watched them go, struck by the study in contrast they offered. Annie Rose was pale, tall, and slender in her brown calico, her hat hanging down her back, exposing her tangled golden hair. Sweet Water—darker, shorter, thicker— wore a beautiful buckskin dress, painstakingly decorated with shells and beads, her shining black hair tamed in two long, neat braids. Women from two different worlds, from two different cultures that often collided in violence, now with their arms linked and their heads together like two schoolgirls, talking about the things that brought all women together—cooking, housekeeping, family—and maybe later, men and children. The sound of their happy chatter was comforting to Joseph. He liked the sound of a woman's voice, especially Annie Rose's voice, and usually she was far too silent.

"Women." Jubal shook his head. "Always yakkin', ain't they?" The affection in his tone took any censure from his words.

Knute stroked his mustache. *"Ja,* but those two are mighty fine cooks. I'll gladly put up with a little female jabber in order to have a good supper."

All of the men laughed, with the exception of Erik. Knute motioned to his grandsons, then pointed in the direction of Jubal's three horses. "Like Annie Rose said, we'll see to the horses. You two say your howdies." The Jensen men led the horses toward the barn.

"Bring in those sage grouse and that small keg on the packhorse!" Jubal shouted after them. "I brought you some brandy!"

Knute grinned. *"Takk, min venn!* We were out!"

"You're welcome, my friend!"

With a happy wave, Knute followed Thomas and Erik, leaving Joseph and Jubal alone.

"It's good to see you, Jubal," Joseph said sincerely to the man he considered a second father. He shifted his heavy rifle and held out his free arm, which Jubal clasped at the elbow in a firm grip.

"You, too, Joe." He looked him up and down. "You look good out of that old uniform. I always thought it made you sorta stiff."

Joseph smiled. "Sometimes I miss it," he admitted. "But not often. Did you come from Laramie?"

"Yeah, about a week ago. We stopped by the cabin for a few days first."

"Orion and I were there."

"The Hunter told me. He also told me about Baines and his cohorts. Thanks for seein' that they left the place clean. Sweet Water can't abide filth in her home."

"I know. I thought I'd have to take Baines on to keep him out of your bed, but it didn't come to that." He narrowed his eyes at Jubal.

The lanky mountain man affected an innocent expression. "What?"

"Don't keep me in suspense, you old coot. What about Sarah and the babe?"

Jubal shook his head. "The babe hadn't come by the time we left, and he warn't givin' no indication that he wanted to leave his mama's warm belly anytime soon. Sarah is rarin' to have that kid, too, poor thing. I think she's about to start callin' the Hunter names."

Joseph frowned. "Why would she do that?"

"For gettin' her with child," Jubal explained, speaking very slowly. He punched Joseph's shoulder. "It's a joke, Joe. One you'll understand when your own woman is gettin' ready to give you a child. Womenfolk get powerful tired of luggin' a young'un' around in their belly, even when they love their man and they love their babe. It's hard work."

Joseph knew that Jubal was knowledgeable on the subject. Having been married not quite a year, Jubal and the much younger Sweet Water had no children as of yet, but Joseph remembered that his longtime friend had been married once before, to a lovely Arapaho woman. Sadly, Jubal's first wife and their two small children had died years ago of the smallpox, brought by a white man to a fur trappers' rendezvous.

One of Jubal's bushy grey eyebrows rose, and his knowing gaze sharpened. "What's goin' on between you and the lovely Annie Rose?"

"You sure don't mince words, Jubal." Joseph pushed his hat back on his head, steadied his rifle—which stood butt to the ground—with one hand, hooked his free thumb in his belt, and sighed. "Nothing's going on."

"Well, somethin' oughtta be. I never thought of it before I saw the two of you together just now, but you're a good match." Jubal slugged him again. "What's the matter with you, son? Go after that woman."

"She doesn't want me that way." Even to Joseph's ear, the words sounded mournful. "At least not yet," he hastily amended.

Jubal's distinctive eyebrows drew together in a puzzled frown. "But you both have somethin' special with the horses. And,"—he eyed Joseph critically—"I expect you ain't hard on the eyes, leastways to a woman, 'though I find you kinda ugly, like I do your brothers." He crossed his arms over his chest. "You and Annie Rose are a perfect match," he pronounced. "What's the problem?"

Joseph shifted his weight and brought both hands together on his upended rifle barrel. "She doesn't think we're a perfect match."

"But you do."

"I *know* we are."

"Women." Jubal shook his head. "The Hunter's Sarah was a mite slow catchin' on, too, as I recall. But her affections were all tangled up with that Captain Rutledge for a while. Nice enough fella, but not right for her, even if she did come all the way from Conn-ect-i-cut to wed up with him. Your Annie Rose, though, she don't have no such entanglements." He scowled at Joseph. "You messed up, didn't you?"

"She won't give me a chance to mess up," Joseph protested. "I'm serious, Jubal. Somewhere along the way, Annie Rose has been hurt by a man—hurt real bad."

"How can that be? She's been hidden up here for years, from the time she was young."

"I know that, but I'm telling you, aside from her grandpa and her brother, and you, I guess, and probably Grey Eagle, she thinks all men are bastards, after only one thing."

Jubal's eyes narrowed. "What about that cranky cousin of hers?"

Joseph shook his head. "Erik's caused some real trouble lately; he fancies himself in love with Annie Rose and won't accept the fact that she doesn't return his affection. We don't dare leave her alone with him."

"Damn." Jubal spat into the dust. "I never did like that boy."

"He's not the problem between Annie Rose and me. Well, he's a problem now, but I think this goes back much further than that. I'd bet money it has something to do with her father."

Jubal frowned. "I don't know nothin' about her pa."

"Exactly." Joseph smiled, a tight smile, with no humor to it at all. "They won't talk about him. Knute told me flat out the man is not to be mentioned. Annie Rose and Thomas carry their mother's name. What does that tell you?"

"That the bastard never did right by their ma."

"Based on the remarkable resemblance between them, I say that Annie Rose and Thomas have the same father. Yet there are probably ten years between their ages. That's a long time for a woman to stick with a man who wouldn't marry her."

"I'd have to agree with that." Jubal rocked on his heels and stroked his full beard. "There's a mystery here, Joe. Something made old Knute bring his grandkids out to hell-

and-gone and hide 'em. Had to be serious, 'cause the Norse-man ain't near as crazy as he lets on."

"He's not crazy at all," Joseph said quietly.

"No, he ain't." Jubal nodded in approval. "I figured you'd figure that out." He put his hands on his narrow hips. "So what're you gonna do about courtin' Miss Annie Rose?"

Joseph rolled his eyes. "I'm treading real careful here, Jubal. She's as skittish as a newborn foal around me." His words brought a picture of Aurora to his mind, and a feeling of warmth to his heart.

"Yeah, well, don't take too long to win her." Jubal stared past Joseph's shoulder, and Joseph turned to see what had drawn his friend's attention.

The sun was setting over the western mountains, coloring the everlasting sky with glorious shades of gold and red, sending luminous fingers of light through the wispy clouds. Joseph could not help but be moved by the silent splendor of the scene, his heart filled both with appreciative awe and with an artist's frustration in knowing that he could never duplicate that sight on paper, no matter how deeply it was imprinted on his soul.

"Don't take too long, Joe," Jubal repeated, his voice low and very serious. "Annie Rose's grandpa don't have too long. Her and that nice brother of hers are gonna need a man to watch out for 'em."

"I know, Jubal. I know."

Fourteen

The Sages stayed for several days. Because Annie Rose spent almost all of her time with Sweet Water, she rarely saw Joseph except at meals, and then she was grateful that so many people surrounded them. She did not want to give him an opportunity to speak privately with her, not that she could even imagine what he might say to her. It was better that they kept their distance from each other. Twice she went to check on Aurora, and she knew that he knew where she'd gone. Each time she returned, he would look at her, silently asking her if all was well, and each time she gave him a slight nod. Aurora's foal was evidently as reluctant to be born as Jubal said the Hunter's babe was.

One night at supper, Knute announced that the horses were ready to take to Fort Laramie. "We will leave at dawn."

Annie Rose's heart started pounding. Joseph would travel with the herd to the fort; would he come back? She set her fork down and deliberately forced her mind to another topic. "Gramps, I've been thinking," she said. "Calypso is a good little mare, young and strong. She'd make good breeding stock. I think we should keep her and mate her with Viking."

"No," Erik protested. "We need the money from selling her more than we need another brood mare. You only want her because you like her."

"Actually, Erik, I've been thinking the same thing as Annie

Rose," said Knute. "The mare has spirit and speed. She'll be a good addition to our own herd."

"I agree with Gramps," Thomas added.

"Of course you do." Erik's words came out in an ugly snarl. "Just like you always do. My opinion carries no weight in this family anymore." He shoved the bench back, jostling Jubal and Joseph, who shared it with him, and stood, throwing his napkin down on the table. "You can all go to hell." He stormed out the door and slammed it behind him.

Annie Rose stared down at her plate, her face hot with embarrassment. Innocent though her suggestion had been, she'd managed to spark another incident with Erik. Why hadn't she waited to speak to Gramps in private about Calypso? How could Erik speak in such a way, especially when they had guests?

His own face a dull red, Knute broke the uncomfortable silence that had settled over the group. "I apologize for my grandson's lack of manners."

"Think nothing of it, old friend," Jubal said calmly. "Erik was just statin' his thoughts on the subject. What do you think, Joe?"

"I'd keep the mare." Joseph offered Annie Rose a smile, perhaps of support. She looked away.

"*Ja*, we'll keep the mare," said Knute. "That will leave us with eight horses to take down, an easy task for five riders." His gaze settled on Annie Rose, as if he expected her to speak.

She did. "Five riders? Gramps, I can't go. Someone's got to stay and watch over things."

"Our own horses will be fine by themselves for a few days. I'll need all of you if we're going to capture more wild horses on the way home. I'd really like to get one more group trained and sold before winter."

"We're talking about more than a few days," Annie Rose argued. As much as she would love a trip to the fort, she could not leave Aurora now. "It'll be at least six days, more likely seven or eight, and even if the horses are fine—and

Here's a special offer for
Romance Readers!
Get 4 FREE Zebra Historical Romance Novels from the newest Historical Romance line- Splendor Romances!
A $19.96 value absolutely Free!
© ENNIS
Take a trip back in time and experience the passion, adventure and excitement of a Splendor Romance...delivered right to your doorstep!

Take advantage of this offer to enjoy Zebra's newest line of historical romance novels....Splendor Romances (formerly Lovegrams Historical Romances)- Take our introductory shipment of 4 romance novels -Absolutely Free! (a $19.96 value)

Now you'll be able to savor today's best romance novels without even leaving your home with our convenient and inexpensive home subscription service. Here's what you get for joining:

- 4 BRAND NEW bestselling Splendor Romances delivered to your doorstep every month

- 20% off every title (or almost $4.00 off) with your home subscription

- FREE home delivery

- A FREE monthly newsletter, *Zebra/Pinnacle Romance News* filled with author interviews, member benefits, book previews and more!

- No risks or obligations...you're free to cancel whenever you wish...no questions asked

To get started with your own home subscription, simply complete and return the card provided. You'll receive your FREE introductory shipment of 4 Splendor Romances and then you'll begin to receive monthly shipments of new Zebra Splendor titles. Each shipment will be yours to examine for 10 days and then if you decide to keep the books, you'll pay the preferred home subscriber's price of just $4.00 per title. That's $16 for all 4 books with FREE home delivery! And if you want us to stop sending books, just say the word...it's that simple.

4 Free BOOKS are waiting for you!
Just mail in the certificate below!

If the certificate is missing below, write to: Splendor Romances, Zebra Home Subscription Service, Inc., P.O. Box 5214, Clifton, New Jersey 07015-5214

FREE BOOK CERTIFICATE

Yes! Please send me 4 Splendor Romances (formerly Zebra Lovegram Historical Romances), ABSOLUTELY FREE! After my introductory shipment, I will be able to preview 4 new Splendor Romances each month FREE for 10 days. Then if I decide to keep them, I will pay the money-saving preferred publisher's price of just $4.00 each... a total of $16.00. That's 20% off the regular publisher's price and there's never any additional charge for shipping and handling. I may return any shipment within 10 days and owe nothing, and I may cancel my subscription at any time. The 4 FREE books will be mine to keep in any case.

Name _____

Address _____ Apt. _____

City _____ State _____ Zip _____

Telephone ( ) _____

Signature _____ SF0398
(If under 18, parent or guardian must sign.)

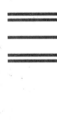

the goats—the chickens and the milk cow can't be on their own for that long. Besides, there's Aurora. Her time is coming, and soon."

Knute glanced at Joseph, then back at her, his eyes widened in warning.

"It's all right," Annie Rose said tiredly. No longer hungry, she pushed her plate away. "Mr. Beaudine knows all about her. He tracked me to her meadow."

"You followed her?" Knute demanded of Joseph.

"Yes, sir."

"You had no right!"

Joseph met Annie Rose's gaze. "That's what she said."

"I don't believe you could track her," Thomas interjected stubbornly.

"He did, Thomas," Annie Rose assured her brother. "Just like he said he could. What's done is done. Mr. Beaudine has sworn to help protect Aurora. I'd much rather have him know her whereabouts than Erik."

No one argued with that.

After a moment, Knute said gently, "You can't be left here alone, *datter,* not anymore. Not with men like Baines knowing about you."

Annie Rose fought down a surge of guilt. "But he doesn't know *who* I am, or where I am."

"Maybe not, but he's doin' his best to find you," said Jubal. "He was down at the fort askin' for any word of you or the Golden Mare. And that stupid Painted Davy is taggin' along behind him, and so's Hank Westin, when he ain't too drunk to ride. I always thought Westin had more sense than that."

Jubal's sober words caused a bolt of fear to stab through Annie Rose's stomach, and she stifled a groan of despair. She'd known there'd be a heavy price to pay for her mistake that night at Jubal's cabin; she hadn't guessed that payment would come due so soon.

"I'll stay with her," Joseph offered.

Thomas glared at him. "No, I will."

"I need both of you on the trail," Knute pointed out.

The group fell into a momentary silence. Then Jubal spoke again. "Sweet Water and I will stay with Annie Rose." He glanced at his wife, who nodded her agreement.

"Oh, would you?" Annie Rose cried.

"Sure." Sweet Water patted her hand. "You and me, we can make pemmican for winter here, same as at my house. Jubal hunt. We keep busy, watch chickens, protect gold horse. Protect Annie Rosie." She patted Annie Rose's hand again.

For Sweet Water, that was a long speech. Annie Rose smiled in gratitude.

"That settles it, then," Knute said. *"Takk,* my friends, for watching over my Annie Rose. Joe, Thomas, we'll move Calypso in with our stock and check the rest of the horses before all the light is gone. It'll save us time in the morning." He stood up. "I'll find Erik, get him to help us, and let him know what the plan is. Fine supper, ladies." He left the room, followed by the rest of the men.

Joseph, the last one out, paused at the door. "It was an excellent meal, ladies." His words included both women, but he looked at Annie Rose. There was an intensity in his brown eyes that Annie Rose hadn't seen for several days. She fought the hated blush that threatened to again warm her cheeks.

"Thank you, Mr. Beaudine."

"Yes, thanks, Joseph," Sweet Water echoed.

He smiled and left.

"Joseph, he like you, Annie Rosie," said Sweet Water.

Startled, Annie Rose looked at her friend. "You're imagining things."

"Hmmph." The Cheyenne woman's lips were curved in a knowing, almost irritating smile.

"You are," Annie Rose insisted. Sweet Water's expression did not change. Annie Rose rolled her eyes and reached for a dirty plate. "Well, you are."

In short order, the two women had the remains of the meal cleared away and the dishes washed, dried, and back in their places. Annie Rose had just filled the kettle with fresh water for another pot of tea when Joseph came back through the door. He removed his hat and held it in his hands.

"Miss Jensen, I'd be pleased if you'd walk with me for a short spell."

Annie Rose stared at him, her eyes wide, her heart hammering. Was Joseph asking her to go on a walk, like she walked with Gramps, or was he asking her to walk out with him, which signaled personal interest? There was a big difference. She felt her mental defenses slam into place as surely as if she had barred a door. Perhaps she had—the door to her heart. She opened her mouth to refuse, but Joseph spoke again before she could say anything.

"Please, Miss Jensen. There are a few things I want to tell you before I leave, and there won't be time in the morning." The grip he had on his hat seemed very tight, and Annie Rose was shocked to realize that he was nervous.

That was a revelation to her. The confident, sometimes arrogant Joseph Beaudine, nervous? Because of her? She stared at him, which she shouldn't have done. The pleading look in his brown eyes was her undoing.

"For a few minutes," she said, then, at the expression of joy that flashed across Joseph's face, wondered if she had made a mistake. She took off her apron and reached for her shawl.

"I tell you, huh, Annie Rosie?" Sweet Water asked triumphantly.

Annie Rose merely glared at her smiling friend.

"What did she tell you?" Joseph asked.

"Nothing of importance." Annie Rose threw her shawl around her shoulders and hurried out of the cabin, before Sweet Water could say anything more.

She automatically headed in the direction of the stock pond, following the path she always walked with Knute. Joseph stayed with her, not saying anything, and Maggie happily trailed along behind them. Annie Rose stopped at the edge of the pond and faced him, pulling the shawl more tightly around her shoulders. Although most of the light was gone from the evening sky, she could still make out his features, for he had not put his hat back on.

"What did you wish to speak to me about?"

"I wanted to assure you that I will watch out for your grandfather. I'll try to keep him from overexerting himself."

Annie Rose relaxed. Perhaps Joseph really did intend to just talk. "Thank you, but don't be surprised if you have a difficult time with him. He won't want to take it easy."

"I know." Joseph looked out over the calm water of the pond.

The silence grew long. "Was there something else?" Annie Rose prodded.

"There's so much more, Annie Rose Jensen, but now is not the time to tell you."

The passion in his voice shook her to her core. She turned back toward the cabin.

"Don't run away from me, Annie Rose. Please."

About to take a step, she faltered and looked back over her shoulder at him. Joseph was watching her now. She did not bother to deny that she had indeed been about to run. "If you have anything else to say, Mr. Beaudine, please do so."

"Keep an eye on Aurora. I know I don't need to tell you that, but you're right that her time is near. I hate to be leaving now."

Annie Rose could hear the genuine feeling and concern for Aurora in Joseph's voice. Had he come to love the mare so quickly? "Since Erik will be gone, I won't need to be so careful. I promise I'll check on her every day. Jubal and Sweet Water will be here if anything goes wrong."

Joseph nodded. "You're in good hands with them."

"I know."

Again, the silence stretched on. Joseph just watched her, twisting his hat in his hands. The urge to run grew stronger.

"Well, if there's nothing else . . ." she said, too brightly.

"Annie Rose." He hesitated. "I hope you don't mind my calling you that."

Oddly enough, she didn't mind. She liked the sound of her name on his lips. "No, I don't mind."

Joseph smiled in relief. "Good. It's such a pretty name." Another pause. Then he straightened and looked her right in the eyes. "What I want to tell you, Annie Rose, is that you don't need to be afraid of me."

"I'm not afraid of you," she hotly denied.

"Yes, you are." Joseph took a step toward her. "You're terrified of me." He reached out to brush a strand of her hair away from her cheek.

At his touch, her blood started racing through her veins.

"No," she whispered.

"I care about you very much, Annie Rose, and someday you'll believe that. Now I'm going to kiss your cheek."

She stiffened.

"That's all I'm going to do." He lifted her chin with one finger and pressed his lips to her cheek. His mustache tickled her skin in a very pleasing way.

Annie Rose allowed her eyes to drift closed. His warm mouth felt so good.

"Good night, Annie Rose." His breath caressed her cheek for a moment, then was gone. He backed up, still watching her, still holding his hat. Then he turned and strode purposefully toward the cabin.

Annie Rose stared after him until he disappeared through the cabin door. Finally, she turned to watch the last of the day's light fade from the sky over the mountains. "Oh, Maggie," she said to the dog who waited patiently at her side. "What am I going to do about that man?"

As always, Maggie didn't answer.

Early the next morning, everyone gathered in the yard. When the farewells were said, Thomas and Erik started the horses on the trail that led to the rocky passageway. Annie Rose stood next to Knute's Thoroughbred and looked up at her grandfather.

"I know it won't do me any good to tell you this, Gramps, but you take it easy. You're no spring chicken anymore."

"Don't be bossing me, *datter*," Knute scolded, his voice warm with affection. Then he sobered, and laid his hand on her head. "You be careful, too, Annie Rose. Always let Jubal know where you are, and don't go anywhere unarmed."

"I'll be careful, Gramps. I love you."

"*Ja*, and I love you, too." He waved to Jubal and Sweet Water, then followed the horses.

Joseph guided Grace to her side. "I'll watch out for him," he said quietly.

"I know you will, Mr. Beaudine. Thank you."

"There's no need for thanks, but you're welcome anyway." He hesitated, then looked down at her. "I'd be pleased if you'd call me 'Joseph' or 'Joe.' "

She met his intense gaze, knowing that to use his first name was to accept a new level of intimacy between them. But hadn't she given him permission to use hers last night? "I've always liked the name 'Joseph,' " she finally answered.

He smiled, and it seemed to Annie Rose that the early morning sky was lit by more than the sun. "You be careful, too," she added, shyly.

"I always am." Joseph adjusted his hat on his head and positioned his reins in his left hand. "Fare you well, Annie Rose Jensen."

"Joseph." Impulsively, she held up her hand to keep him from going, just for a moment. "Are you coming back?" she blurted out, hating to ask, but needing to know.

The expression on his face softened, and he leaned down to capture her hand before she could pull it away. "I'll be back. And not just because of a promise I made to your grandfather." He kissed her hand. When he released her, his gloved fingers brushed her cheek. He touched his heels to Grace's sides and chased Knute at a gallop. Maggie raced after him, barking, as far as the pond, then returned to Annie Rose's side and plopped in the dirt, her sides heaving.

Annie Rose watched until she could see nothing of the

horses and riders, not even traces of their dust in the clear air. Then she turned and went into the cabin, aware of how unusually quiet it seemed, thankful that Jubal and Sweet Water, who both sat at the table finishing their tea, did not tease her about Joseph.

"I'll straighten the boys' room," she said, and went through the curtained doorway into the bedroom Erik and Thomas shared. She smoothed the blanket on Thomas's bed, although he had done a good job of making the bed himself. Already Annie Rose missed her brother.

Then she turned to Erik's bed and found it stripped down to the straw-stuffed canvas mattress. She bent and opened the door to the enclosed space under his bed. Empty. With a frown, she perused the room. Nothing of Erik's remained.

Her cousin did not intend to come back.

Annie Rose sank down on the edge of the bed, her hands clasped in her lap. Where had it all gone so wrong? she wondered sadly. They had been a happy family for a long time, and she had thought they always would be. Erik had never been as companionable or as free with his humor as the rest of them, but she had enjoyed his company, and had indeed loved him as a brother. Annie Rose missed the old Erik. It hurt to admit that she was glad the changed Erik was gone. If he remained as angry and as threatening as he had become over the past year, she hoped he wouldn't come back. Ever.

Once the adventurous leg of the journey—that part through the narrow rocky pass—was finished, the rest of the trip to Fort Laramie was uneventful. They made good time, thanks to the fast pace they kept, and it was only a little after noon on the third day when the buildings of the fort came into view. Joseph heaved a sigh of relief. He had tried to ignore Erik's sullen mood and nasty remarks, but after three days, the young man was getting on his nerves. With the fort in sight, there was a chance that Joseph could complete the journey without giving in to the strong urge to slug Erik in the mouth just on general principle.

As they approached the fort, Joseph noted with amazement the changes that had been effected in the six weeks he had been gone, first on his scouting mission with Orion, then during his stay with the Jensen family. Neat rows of white tents showed where many soldiers still lived, but it appeared that the new two-story barracks was near completion, as was the building that would house the junior officers. Apparently the new parts needed to repair the saw mill—situated twelve miles away near timbered land—had finally arrived. The occupants of Fort Laramie would spend a more comfortable winter this year than the one before.

Following Knute's lead, Joseph helped guide the horses directly to the corrals situated on the eastern side of the fort. That done, his first order of business was to find Orion and Sarah and learn if the long- and eagerly-awaited baby had made its appearance at last. After seeing to Grace and arranging to meet Thomas and Knute for supper at Orion's house—Erik rudely refused to join them—Joseph hurried south across the compound toward the crumbling adobe walls of old Fort John, the original fort on the site.

When the Army had purchased the site a year earlier, the engineers from West Point deemed the old fort too far gone to be saved and had begun construction on a series of new buildings. However, Congress refused to allocate the funds necessary to build the enclosing wall envisioned by the architect, Lieutenant Daniel Woodbury of the Corps of Engineers, so Fort Laramie thus far boasted no outer bastions of defense. Joseph hoped that Congress's decision did not one day come back to haunt the soldiers stationed there.

The walls of old Fort John, which sat on a low bluff overlooking a curve of the Laramie River, had been abandoned to the elements. Joseph rounded a corner of the old fort and paused for a moment. The view across the river was stark; the cottonwoods and willows that had once grown along the banks had long ago been cut down. Treeless, barren hills stretched away to the south, the grasses not yet recovered from the hundreds of emigrant wagons that had been encamped there during the late spring and early summer. Now the emigrants and their animals—those who still survived— would be approaching the final stage of their journeys to the Promised Lands of California and Oregon.

Joseph silently wished the hardy emigrants luck, but he was glad they were gone. Someday—soon—too many of them would be stopping permanently.

A peculiar whining drew Joseph from his reverie, and he turned toward the sound. There, in front of the snug, two-room cabin Orion had fashioned from scavenged adobe bricks and logs he had hauled from the distant forest, stood a wolf.

"Dancer," Joseph called gladly, and the wolf came toward him with the playful, prancing steps that had given him his name. "How are you, boy?" he asked, affectionately roughing the fur on Dancer's neck. The wolf wagged his tail and yipped with pleasure. Joseph was surprised that he felt a pang of longing for Maggie. That sweet black dog had touched his heart, as surely as her mistress had.

"Who's bothering my wolf?"

At the sound of his brother's teasing voice, Joseph straightened.

"So, big brother, I see you survived your adventure with the Norseman," Orion said as he approached, his arms held out in greeting, a broad grin on his clean-shaven face.

"The first part of it, anyway." Joseph enveloped his brother in a bear hug, pounding him on the back. "Are you a papa yet?"

"Sure am." Orion stepped back but kept one arm around Joseph's shoulders. "Come and meet five-day-old Henry Jedediah, Uncle Joe." Orion's green eyes fairly shone with pride and love.

Joseph caught Orion in another rough hug. "Congratulations, little brother. How's Sarah?"

"Just fine. Her labor was long, but all went well once the little one finally realized he was going to have to come out."

"Was Sarah ever motivated to call you names?"

Orion's dark eyebrows drew together in a puzzled frown. "What?"

"Never mind." Joseph clapped him on the back. "I'll tell you later."

Orion stopped before the door, suddenly serious. "It was hard seeing my beloved woman in such pain, Joe, real hard. I love my son more than I thought it was possible to love anyone, but I hate what Sarah had to go through to give him to me."

Joseph frowned. "She really is all right?"

"Yes. She's wonderful. Seems to think it wasn't bad at all. But I was with her the whole time. It was bad."

"That's the way of the world, I guess, for human and beast. It doesn't seem fair, considering it's a two-man job to get things started—so to speak," Joseph hastily added at Orion's raised eyebrow. "But the female has the longest and most difficult part of the job, that's for certain. Oh, never mind." He slapped Orion's back again. "Let me say hello to your beautiful bride, then introduce me to my nephew."

Orion placed a finger to his lips as he reached for the door latch. "He's sleeping, or at least he was. Trust me on this, big brother: it's nice when they sleep."

Dancer whined and laid down near the door.

Both men quietly entered the house. The main room was empty. Orion pointed at his own chest, then toward the interior door, then motioned that Joseph wait where he was. Joseph nodded his understanding, finding it difficult to believe that his strong, confident, capable brother had been reduced to pantomime by a sleeping infant. He hung his hat on a hook by the door and looked about the comfortable room.

Some months ago, Orion had persuaded the commanding officer of Fort Laramie to allow him use of the abandoned site of Fort John and whatever materials he could scavenge. Joseph was impressed by the clever use Orion had made of what he had found. The cozy cabin faced the river and nestled against a reinforced section of the south wall, which offered protection from the north winds—protection that would be greatly appreciated when winter howled down upon them in a few short months. A sturdy table, flanked by several chairs and laden with what appeared to be the preparations for supper, stood before the massive fireplace, where a small cook fire now burned. Supplies were neatly arranged upon several wall shelves, and clean buffalo robes covered the packed-dirt floor. The home Orion and Sarah had made for themselves was a simple one, but comfortable and inviting. Perhaps the deep love the two shared permeated the very air, adding to the welcome Joseph always felt when he stepped through their door.

"Joseph." Like a living thing unto itself, Sarah's quiet, refined voice touched him and added to his sense of welcome.

He turned and faced her—and gaped.

The last time he'd seen her, Sarah was heavy with child. Joseph knew she no longer was, as the white apron tied about her again-trim waist attested, but the sight of her stunned him, and he was struck anew by his beloved sister-in-law's beauty.

Like Annie Rose, Sarah Hancock Beaudine was of average height and slender, but there the similarities ended. Where Annie Rose was blonde and green-eyed, Sarah's hair was a rich chocolate brown and her eyes a striking blue. While Annie Rose was unsettled in her heart and fearful for her future, there was a sense of peace about Sarah that clearly stated that she had found her place in the world and was content to be there. When Sarah looked upon Orion, when their eyes met and their hands touched, that peace grew and transformed into a passion that made the observer feel as though he had trespassed onto private and sacred ground.

Orion and Sarah belonged together, as surely as did the moon and the stars.

Joseph had always known that. But now, Sarah looked different—beyond peaceful, beyond happy. She was almost luminous. Had motherhood done that for her?

"Joseph." A small smile touched her mouth as Sarah repeated his name. She held out her arms to him, and Joseph gladly swept her into a heartfelt brotherly hug.

"I prayed for your safe delivery," he whispered. "I am so thankful both you and the babe are well."

"Thank you, dear brother." She stepped back and grabbed his hand. "Come and see him."

She led him into the next room, where Orion stood next to a carved wooden cradle, clasping a bundle of blankets to his chest. He faced Joseph and held out the bundle, which now squirmed and whimpered.

"Meet Henry Jedediah Beaudine, Joe, named for Sarah's father and ours," Orion said proudly. He settled the bundle into Joseph's arms and pulled the edge of the blanket back to reveal a baby's face. He then draped his arm around Sarah and beamed.

Joseph looked upon the child he held so carefully—the firstborn in a new generation of Beaudines. He felt the pride and love of young Henry's parents, sensed and understood their belief that the babe in his arms was nothing short of a miracle. He felt all that, knew all that, and to him, Henry was . . . well, red. And wrinkled. And bald.

Then Henry opened his eyes.

They were very blue, like his mother's.

They were filled with peace, like his mother's.

They were wise and innocent at the same time, like Dancer's golden wolf eyes.

Henry yawned, his small mouth moving in a way Joseph found absurdly endearing, and waved one little hand in the air. In an ageless, instinctive gesture, Joseph offered his forefinger, and when those tiny, perfect fingers closed around it, a connection was forged between the man and the infant that would last a lifetime.

Henry Jedediah Beaudine was indeed a miracle.

"You're certain you don't mind if I take your husband away for a while?" Joseph asked Sarah.

"Not at all. I'm sure you have 'brother' things to discuss." She sat in a rocking chair placed before the fire, with Henry asleep in her arms.

"We'll be here to keep her company," Thomas interjected, waving to indicate his grandfather. The boy seemed to be fascinated by the baby, and Joseph realized with a start that Thomas may have never seen an infant before meeting Henry today.

"*Ja,* we will, and we'll see to cleaning up the supper dishes, too," Knute said from his seat at the table, where he still sipped his coffee. Joseph was glad Knute and Thomas had accepted Orion's offer of shelter for the night, for the Norseman looked exhausted. Hopefully he would sleep well within the cool walls of Orion's cabin.

"We'll be over at the sutler's store, Sarah." Orion bent down to place a kiss on his wife's cheek.

"We won't be late," Joseph added as he went out the door. In the dusky evening light, he saw Dancer down by the river, picking his way along the water's edge, no doubt looking for some supper of his own. The strange cacophony of sound created by an orchestra of insects would cease as Dancer approached, then start up again after he passed. Even if Joseph could not see the wolf, he would have been able to follow his progress by the sounds—and lack of sounds—of the insects.

Orion joined him a moment later, and they set off toward the sutler's store on the other side of the compound.

"So, you're going back with the Norseman, huh?" Orion asked.

"Yes, at first light. He wants to capture another batch of horses and get them trained and sold before winter sets in. There was no sign of The Paint and his herd at the lake, which means we'll have to hunt for more horses along the way. Most likely, the return trip will take longer than two and a half days." Joseph paused, worry clutching at his gut. "We have to get back to his homestead as quickly as possible."

"Did you find her?"

"I found her."

When he said no more, Orion stopped and faced him. "Come on, Joe. I gathered you didn't want to bring it up in front of the Norseman, but it's just the two of us here. Baines won't shut up about her and that Golden Mare. If he lays eyes on Thomas, he'll see the resemblance between the boy and the woman, just as I do. It's plain as day they're related. The Norseman's secret about the woman is out in the open now, even if all the pieces of the puzzle haven't been found yet."

Joseph sighed, knowing Orion was right. If it hadn't been for Aurora, Annie Rose would have accompanied them on this trip, and the puzzle would have been complete.

"She's the Norseman's granddaughter. For some reason I haven't figured out yet, he brought his three grandkids out here about seven years ago and took them up into the mountains, to an isolated valley clear to hell-and-gone past the North Laramie River. You should see the place he built for them, Orion. It's like a little slice of civilization fell from the sky and landed in that valley. House, barn, corrals, smokehouse, hay meadows—all of it just as neat as a pin. Everything was either carried in on horseback or made by hand."

Orion stared at him, disbelieving.

Joseph spread his hands and shrugged. "I know. It sounds impossible. I wouldn't believe it myself if someone had told me. But Knute doesn't seem to think he's accomplished anything special. He said the mountains of Norway are far more inhospitable than these 'little hills' here."

"Is her name really Annie Rose?"

"Annie Rose Jensen. If she had given her last name that night at Jubal's cabin, we would have guessed that she had some connection to the Norseman."

Orion pierced him with a knowing gaze. "Do you still like her?"

"Yes," Joseph admitted. "I still like her."

"Does she like you?"

"A little. I think. Hell, Orion, I don't know. She doesn't think much of any man, save her grandfather and her brother. And Jubal and Grey Eagle, maybe. She won't let me near."

But she did let me kiss her cheek. The memory filled him with warmth.

They started walking again.

"So Eagle knows her," Orion mused. "I wonder why he never mentioned her."

"I'm certain he was sworn to secrecy, like Jubal was. Annie Rose has a real gift with horses, Orion, even more so than Knute. She did train Thunder."

"I knew that. Thunder made it very clear that morning at Jubal's."

"I've seen the Golden Mare, too."

Orion merely nodded. "I was pretty certain she exists. Are they hiding her, too?"

Joseph stared at his brother, amazed by his insight. "Yes, but I don't know how much longer they can." He paused. "Can you believe there's been no hint of a lovely white woman in these parts for seven years?"

"I have to hand it to the Norseman," Orion said in admiration. "He did a hell of a job protecting her." He looked at Joseph. "You didn't leave her up there alone, did you?"

"Jubal and Sweet Water are staying with her until we return."

"Good."

They approached the sutler's store.

"Just to warn you," Orion added. "Baines is still here. He might even be inside." He nodded toward the store. "He probably isn't going to be too happy to see you."

Joseph's jaw tightened. "I'm not looking for trouble. But if he is, I'll oblige him."

They walked around to the side door that led into a noisy, smokey back room. A short bar stood near the far wall across from the door, and several tables with accompanying chairs were scattered around the room. All but one of the tables were taken, and that one, unfortunately, was situated next to the table occupied by Abelard Baines, Painted Davy Sikes, and a third man whose back was to him.

"We could buy a bottle and take it elsewhere," Orion suggested in a low voice.

"Good idea," Joseph replied.

Several men called out greetings as the brothers made their way across the crowded room.

"Been gettin' any sleep, Hunter?"

"Good to see ya, Capt'n Joe!"

"Hey, Hunter, how's that young'un'? You need to get away already?"

A chorus of laughs followed the good-natured teasing.

Joseph approached the bar. "Hello, Miles. I'd heard you finally gave up on Fort St. Charles and took over the sutler's job here." He held his hand out to the burly, balding Irishman. "It's good to see you again."

Miles Breen wiped his hands on the relatively clean white apron tied around his portly middle, then, with a broad grin, pumped Joseph's hand. "Not enough folks coming up from the south for a man to make a living down at St. Charles, Captain Joe. Much more opportunity along the Oregon Trail." He released Joseph's hand. "Glasses should be coming with the next supply shipment from Fort Kearny," he said apologetically as he poured fine brandy into three tin cups. He handed one to Joseph and pushed another in Orion's direction, then grabbed the third one himself. "Here's to the newest Beaudine."

"Thank you, Miles," said Orion.

The three men emptied their cups. Even from a tin cup, the brandy tasted good to Joseph.

Miles leaned conspiratorially over the bar. "Watch out for Abby Baines, Joe. He sure is riled up at you."

Joseph shrugged. "I wouldn't let him sleep in Sweet Water's bed."

"He tried to do that?" Miles asked incredulously. "Everyone knows that woman don't like no one 'sides her and Jubal in their bed. Can't say as I blame her, 'specially with a slovenly ass like Baines. The only time that man bathes is when he gets caught in the rain." He snorted in the direction of the corner where Baines sat, his disgust evident.

Joseph fought a smile. "Give me a bottle of that good brandy, Miles. Orion and I'll take it with us. I don't want any trouble."

Miles snorted again and reached for an unopened bottle. "I'd rather Baines and Sikes left than you and the Hunter." He frowned. "I don't like them latching on to the Norseman's kid, neither."

"The Norseman's kid?" Joseph peered at the table in the smokey, dimly lit corner.

"The red-bearded one. He come in a bit ago, askin' after Baines." Miles shook his head. "That kid has a surly attitude, that's for certain. Maybe that's why he'n Baines are gettin' along." He set the bottle on the bar.

Joseph handed Miles a silver dollar and glanced at Orion. "I'll be right back."

"You want company?" his brother asked.

"Not yet, but watch my back." Joseph frowned. "I just hope Erik isn't as stupid as I'm afraid he is." He wove his way through the tables, shaking hands here and there, advancing on the table where Baines and Painted Davy sat. Sure enough, Erik was with them, his back to the room. Joseph could see the young man's red hair sticking out from under his hat. The three men were so engrossed in their conversation that none of them noticed Joseph's approach. He drew near enough to hear Erik's bragging words.

"I just might be able to help you find that Golden Mare."

Fifteen

A red fury roared through Joseph, pounding so hard that he could hear nothing save its savage call. He grabbed Erik by the back of his collar and dragged him out of the chair.

Erik yelped and struggled to escape. Joseph hauled him toward the door.

With a curse, Baines shot up out of his chair.

Joseph stabbed a finger at him. "Stay there, Baines. You won't get your claws into this idiot if I can help it."

"Let go of me!" Erik shouted.

An uneasy silence settled over the room.

Abby Baines drew his knife. "The kid don't want to go with you, Beaudine."

"Well, he's going anyway." Joseph shoved Erik toward the door with such force that Erik stumbled into a table and knocked it over. The men who had surrounded the table jumped from their chairs and backed up, their hands held out in front of them, their eyes wide.

"Beaudine!" Abby came around the table, knife in hand.

Orion stepped away from the bar, his own knife poised and ready. "Stay out of it, Abby."

"I'm tired of you interferin', Hunter," Abby growled, and waved the knife in Orion's direction.

Orion crouched to a defensive position, and Joseph was instantly at his side, leaving Erik sprawled over the toppled table.

The ominous sound of a rifle being cocked echoed in the room. Miles Breen held an old buffalo gun aimed at Abby's belly. "I've been lookin' for an excuse to shoot you for years, Abby Baines," he said conversationally, then his tone turned pleading. "Please give me one."

Painted Davy grabbed Baines by one shoulder and pulled him back toward his chair. "Let it be, Abby," he begged. "You're outnumbered and outgunned. That loudmouth kid ain't worth dyin' over any more than that yellow-haired woman was."

"Damn it, Painted Davy, shut up before you talk him out of givin' me an excuse," Miles ordered. "I want to shoot him."

Baines glared at Miles and slumped into his chair, laying his knife on the table.

Joseph turned and pulled the dazed Erik to his feet, then resumed the trip to the door.

"Thanks, Miles." Orion grabbed the bottle of brandy from the bar and flipped Miles another coin. "Sorry about the mess."

Miles touched his sweat-glistened forehead in a salute. "No trouble, Hunter. I was gettin' kinda bored." He pushed two of the tin cups toward Orion. "Bring 'em back tomorrow. Good night, Joe!"

Joseph waved over his shoulder and shoved Erik outside. With the bottle and cups in one hand, Orion backed out behind them and closed the door.

A scurry of whispers rushed around the room as men righted chairs and straightened tables.

Miles Breen easily held the buffalo gun with one arm while he poured a stiff whiskey with the other. Keeping the gun pointed at Baines, he marched over to the man's table and slammed the tin cup down in front of him, then snatched up Abby's knife. "You can get this from me when you leave tonight."

Abby snarled a curse and lunged for his knife.

"Uh, uh," Miles said, shaking his head, and held the gun

in Abby's face. "Are you slow or something, Abby? I said, 'when . . . you . . . leave.' And you ain't leavin' for a while yet. You just calm down and contemplate the foolishness of takin' on one of the Beaudine brothers." Miles started back toward the bar, then paused and looked over his shoulder. "I advise you to sip on that whiskey real slow, 'cause it's the last one you'll ever get from me, and I want you to enjoy it. After tonight, you're not to set foot in my establishment again."

"What about me, Miles?" called Painted Davy worriedly.

"Shut up, Painted Davy," Abby growled. "Just shut the hell up."

Joseph dragged Erik across the compound to the stables and pushed him up against the outside wall. He suspected that his hands clutching the front of Erik's shirt were all that kept the young man on his feet. Erik was either still dazed from his run-in with the table, or he was drunk. Joseph suspected a little of both. Somewhere along the way, Erik's hat had come off, and the moonlight showed Joseph the indignant expression on Erik's bearded face.

"You had no right to do that," Erik sputtered, his breath foul. He had definitely been drinking.

Joseph shook him. "What the hell were you doing, talking to Baines about the mare? Don't you know what kind of murderous bastard that man is? He'll stop at nothing to get what he wants."

"He wants the mare!" Erik shouted. "Just like I do. I wanted to offer him a fifty-fifty split if he'd help me find her."

"He also wants your cousin, you fool! Did you ever think of that?" Joseph shook him again. "Do you know what Baines would do to Annie Rose if he caught her? Do you?"

Some of the bravado went out of Erik's expression. "Leggo of me." He brushed at Joseph's hands.

Joseph released him, and Erik started sliding down the stable wall. He managed to pull himself back up and rested there, breathing hard. Orion approached, holding Erik's hat.

"Erik, if you value your life, and the lives of your family, stay away from Abelard Baines," Joseph warned, trying to keep the disgust he felt out of his voice. "That man will stick a knife between your ribs or shoot you in the back without a second thought, just as he would Knute or Thomas. And that would be pleasant compared to what he would do to Annie Rose. If you care anything for her at all, honor your vow of silence regarding her."

Erik glanced at Joseph, then clutched his stomach and leaned his head against the stable wall.

Orion thrust Erik's hat at him. "Knute and Thomas are staying with us. There's room for you, too."

Erik accepted the hat with a shake of his head, then groaned.

"I suspect you're not used to drinking whiskey, son," said Orion. "You'll soon be feeling poorly, and my wife has some herbs that might help."

"I can take care of myself," Erik ground out.

Orion shrugged. "Suit yourself." He walked away toward the old fort.

Joseph started to follow his brother, then hesitated and looked back at Erik. He was surprised that some of his anger had faded. "I know you hate me, Erik, but, for the love of God, listen to what I'm telling you. Baines is evil, through and through. Your grandfather is worth a hundred of Abby Baines. Follow Knute's teachings, and you can't go wrong. Just stay away from Baines."

Erik gave no indication that he had heard a word. With an exasperated sigh, Joseph followed Orion, catching up with him halfway across the deserted parade ground.

"He'll bring trouble on his family," Orion warned.

"He already has. In case you didn't know, Erik is cousin to Thomas and Annie Rose, not brother. He fancies himself in love with her, and his refusal to accept the fact that she doesn't return his feelings is tearing the family apart."

Orion pulled the cork from the bottle of brandy with his teeth and poured some into each cup without breaking stride.

He handed the cups to Joseph, recorked the bottle, and accepted the cup Joseph handed back to him. "There's a place by the river below the cabin where we can sit," he said. He waved at the sentry as they passed the unmarked perimeter of Fort Laramie and led Joseph down a path to the riverbank. A bench of sorts had been carved out of the dirt face of the bluff, the seat lined with a board. The brothers sat down, and for a while were silent, listening to the night. Joseph became aware of a rustling in the grasses to his right, and he was not surprised when Dancer appeared. The wolf whined a strange-sounding wolf greeting, then sat down between their respective pairs of legs. Joseph reached out and scratched Dancer's head, and Orion finally spoke.

"I think Mama Florrie and the girls might arrive with the next detachment, Joe."

Joseph started. "Are you serious?"

Dancer laid down and settled his muzzle on his paws.

"That's what I gathered from Ma's letter—the one that came last week with the dispatch. I'll let you read it."

"They're coming out here for the winter?"

Orion shrugged. "It surprised me, too. Maybe it really upset her that Sarah and I decided against the trip to St. Louis earlier this summer, but we just didn't want to take any chances, with the baby coming and all."

"Surely Ma understood that. She's had babies of her own."

"Still, I feel bad about it. I know she was powerfully disappointed." Orion took a sip of brandy. "Could be that I'm reading more into it than she intended. She wrote that she wants to see her grandbaby and help get this trading business going, and maybe that's all there is to it. Juliet and Cora won't have any choice about coming along, because you know Ma won't leave her girls in St. Louis alone."

Joseph glanced back up at the bluff, toward the cabin he couldn't see from where he was sitting. "Where are we going to put them?"

"I figured to add a third room on the other side of the main room."

"Damn." Joseph looked out over the river. "I wish I was going to be here to help you, little brother. But I gave my word to Knute."

"I know. Don't worry about it. I'll get word to Grey Eagle. He'll come if he can. If he can't, we'll manage, just like we always do." Orion eyed him. "When will you be back?"

"Four weeks, maybe longer. It'll be into October by then." Joseph took a long swallow of brandy, then faced his brother. "I don't think the Jensens should winter up in their valley, Orion. They'd be snowed in. Erik is no longer trustworthy, and Knute's doing poorly—heart trouble, from what I gather. He could go at any time, and he knows it. I promised him I'd look after Annie Rose and Thomas. I'm thinking the best thing to do is bring them all down here for the winter."

"Captain Rutledge told me the post has finally been assigned a surgeon. He's due to arrive with the next detachment from Fort Kearny."

Joseph relaxed a little. "That's comforting to know. Still, if it is Knute's heart, no surgeon will be able to help him."

"Bring the Jensens back with you. It'd be nothing to add on a fourth room, Joe, or even a fifth, if we all worked together." Orion jerked a thumb back over his shoulder. "That south wall of the old fort offers protection from the worst of the northern weather, even as dilapidated as it is now. We can shore it up to make sure it doesn't come down on our heads." He shrugged again. "It won't be fancy, but we can build something that'll see us all through the winter."

A rush of gratitude filled Joseph to the point where he had to clear his throat before he could speak. "I haven't discussed this with Knute yet."

"So? No matter what, you have to go back to that valley and get your woman. You'll talk to the Norseman when the time is right."

Joseph stared at his brother. "Annie Rose is not my woman."

"Yes, she is." Orion stood and stretched. "I should have known it that very first night, when you kept asking her questions you had no business asking. Even then, she was special to you. It took me awhile to figure that out, because it happened so damned fast. But that was the only explanation for your rude behavior."

"Well, thank you so much." Joseph glared up at Orion. It didn't help that his brother's expression was one of amusement.

That amusement faded to the utmost seriousness. "She's more than special, Joe," Orion said quietly. "She's in your blood. You love Annie Rose Jensen. I *know* it, just as you knew I loved Sarah, even before I was sure of it myself. Now go get your woman and bring her back here, along with all her family. We'll make do." He grabbed the brandy bottle and started up the path to the cabin. "Sarah will love the company," he called over his shoulder. Dancer whined and followed Orion.

Joseph stayed on the rough bench for a long time, watching the waning moonlight glint off the river, listening to the night creatures. Long after his brandy was gone, he lingered still, thinking how blessed he was in his family.

Annie Rose again gave thanks for the comforting presence of Jubal and Sweet Water in the room across from hers. Without them, she doubted she would have slept much the last few days. Perhaps all the dire warnings she'd heard from her grandfather and from Joseph had unnerved her more than she thought. Whatever the reason, she was glad for the company.

She rolled over in her narrow bed and punched her feather pillow before again plopping her head down in a futile attempt to get comfortable. Maggie huffed and shifted her position at the end of the bed to accommodate Annie Rose's restless legs.

"Sorry," Annie Rose muttered.

Maggie curled into a ball and sighed, a sleepy-dog sigh, and the room settled into silence again.

Annie Rose found the silence deafening.

Many times over the last seven years she had been alone; indeed, at times, she craved solitude—and silence—and had taken to the forest. No more.

She missed her grandfather's wise guidance and his loving, accented voice scolding her for "bossing" him.

She missed Thomas's youthful cheerfulness and honest affection.

She missed everything about Joseph Beaudine.

With a groan, Annie Rose threw back the covers and sat up, then leaned over to light the candle on the bedstand. Maggie opened her eyes without lifting her head, clearly exasperated.

"I need a drink of water," Annie Rose informed the dog in a whisper.

Maggie closed her eyes.

"Actually, a brandy would be nice," Annie Rose admitted. She clambered out of the high bed and draped a shawl over her nightdress, pulling her long braid free as she padded toward the closed bedroom door.

Although the hateful reason for its existence could not be denied, that stout wooden portal was still alien to her. Annie Rose had not barred it for days—not since Erik left—yet, in trying to be quiet so she would not disturb Jubal and Sweet Water, she missed her old door curtain.

Thankful that the lard she used on the hinges had been successful in silencing the annoying screeches that had first troubled them all, she crept into the main room. The meager light from the candle she had left on her bedstand was enough to enable her to see the cloth-covered water bucket resting on the worktable. Silently, she made her way around the dining table, past the hearth on which a few hardy coals still glowed. She was reaching for the water dipper when she heard it.

A giggle.

A giggle?

The sound was repeated.

A woman's giggle, followed by a whisper, then a moan.

Annie Rose's gaze locked on the gingham curtain that gave Jubal and Sweet Water whatever privacy they enjoyed in Thomas's room. They had rejected the use of Thomas's and Erik's separate beds and had instead made a larger bed of buffalo robes and blankets on the floor, a bed they could share.

A moan sounded again, and another.

Was Jubal hurting his wife?

Annie Rose was paralyzed. Surely Jubal wouldn't hurt Sweet Water. He couldn't.

The moans continued, low and soft. A rhythm developed, a steady rhythm that gradually increased.

Her fingers recoiled from the water dipper as if it were on fire. Annie Rose pressed her hand to her mouth and scurried back to her room, closing the wooden door with the utmost caution, leaning against its strength, panting, now grateful for its presence.

Jubal and Sweet Water were making love.

A hot flush of embarrassment coursed over Annie Rose's entire body. She flung the shawl away and dove under her blankets, mindless of the reproachful look Maggie threw at her as the dog grudgingly shifted her position once again.

Sweet Water giggled.

For the first time, Annie Rose considered the possibility that a woman could enjoy the act as an active partner, rather than submit as a willing—or unwilling—vessel for a man's passion.

Perhaps that was the true danger.

If a man could offer a woman genuine pleasure, perhaps that was how he actually wielded his power over her.

She frowned.

Had her father pleasured her mother? Did that explain the hold Blaine had over Thora all those years?

No.

Her father was too selfish.

Thora's pleasure had never been his concern, nor had her mother ever been a pleasure-seeker. Thora had merely wanted her lover to love her—enough to offer her marriage, enough to claim their children as his.

Annie Rose stared at the candle, as if the golden flame would offer her guidance.

It brought only memories.

Again, she felt Joseph Beaudine's lips upon her cheek, his fingers curled around hers. What would it feel like to have his lips pressed to her mouth, to have his strong, gentle fingers on her breast?

Heavenly.

She feared it would be heavenly. She *knew* it would be heavenly. And she would be lost.

With a moan, Annie Rose blew out the candle and buried her face in the pillow.

Joseph had been gone for almost a week. Rather than dying, as she had hoped and prayed it would, the flame of her feelings for him only burned brighter.

She loved him.

She was lost.

Joseph swore as the young bay mare swerved past him and galloped away. With only Thomas to aid him—as competent as the boy was—the capture of the horses Knute had chosen from the herd they had come upon was proving to be extremely difficult. He'd been surprised and relieved when Erik announced that morning that he was not returning with them, but they sure could have used the man's help now. Joseph glanced toward the trees at the edge of the clearing, where Knute rested in the shade. The Norseman had suffered one of his frightening spells only minutes ago, and Joseph uttered a silent prayer that the kind old man would still be with them when the time came to continue their journey.

"Sorry, Joe," Thomas called breathlessly as he rode up at a trot. "She got by me."

"No need to apologize." Joseph took off his hat and wiped his forehead with the back of his wrist before he resettled his hat. "She got by me, too." He looked again to the trees, and Thomas followed his gaze. Knute raised a hand in reassurance.

"Think he'll make it?" He tried to hide it, but Thomas's stark fear was evident in his voice.

Joseph crossed his forearms over the saddle horn and leaned forward. "I think he will today," he answered honestly. "But the day is coming when he won't."

"I know."

A fierce compassion welled up in Joseph as he watched the emotions race across Thomas's young face—fear, sorrow, resignation, determination. "I won't leave you and your sister alone, Thomas."

At that, Thomas looked at him. "I know," he repeated solemnly. "Thank you for that."

Joseph could find no trace of distrust or resentment in Thomas's eyes. Had he finally passed the test with the boy? He hoped so.

"Joe." Thomas's voice held a different note of fear.

Joseph slid his rifle from its casing at the same time he twisted in the saddle to look in the direction Thomas pointed, away from Knute. Two Indian braves rode from the protection of the trees, scattering a few of the wild horses. One lifted a rifle over his head in greeting, his long black hair flowing behind him on the wind.

"Grey Eagle!" Joseph shouted gladly. He touched his moccasins to Grace's sides and raced toward his brother. Before Grace had come to a complete stop, he was out of the saddle, clasping his brother in a bear hug. "It's good to see you, little brother!" he cried, although Grey Eagle was every bit as tall as he was. "How the hell are you?"

Grey Eagle smiled, revealing even teeth that looked very white against his bronzed skin. He looked so much like Orion, with his green eyes and black hair, that Joseph still marveled at the resemblance. The only real difference in their appearances was the length of their hair—Orion's fell past his shoulders, but Grey Eagle's reached almost to his waist.

Two thin braids behind his ears kept the hair back from his face and mingled with the long locks that flowed freely down his back. His signature lone eagle feather hung from the end of one braid and fluttered in the breeze, as did the fringe on his buckskin leggings and beaded buckskin shirt.

"I am well, big brother. And you?"

"I'd be a lot better if I could collect the horses the Norseman wants." He waved toward the scattered herd, then looked up at the Indian who joined them. "Raven's Heart, my friend." He held up his hand, which Raven's Heart leaned down from the saddle and warmly clasped. "How are Little Leaf and Sparrow?" Joseph asked, referring to Raven's Heart's wife and young daughter. He spoke in Cheyenne, but Raven's Heart answered in careful English.

"They are well, Joseph Beaudine."

"Well said! Grey Eagle has been teaching you English, huh?"

"No. Sparrow has." Raven's Heart grinned.

Joseph returned the grin. "Come and meet my friends," he said. Grey Eagle walked beside him as they led their horses toward Knute and Thomas, who had, Joseph noted approvingly, protectively joined his grandfather. Raven's Heart followed them, still mounted.

"Orion's going to need some help, Eagle," Joseph began.

"I know. We arrived at the fort soon after you left. He filled me in on everything."

"So you saw Henry."

Grey Eagle nodded, a gentle smile on his lips. "The miracle of life."

"Was that idiot Erik still there?"

"The red-bearded grandson of the Norseman? Yes—very hungover. No sign of Baines and Sikes. We found Hank Westin holed up in one of the Sioux tepees, drunker than a skunk. He couldn't or wouldn't say where Baines took off to."

"Probably 'couldn't say' is correct. He wasn't with Baines last night." Joseph squinted against the sunlight. "At least Erik didn't hook up with Baines."

"At least not yet."

Joseph looked at his brother. "Do you know something I don't?"

Grey Eagle shrugged. "Erik Jensen has alienated his family and has no friends and very little money. A desperate man can make desperate choices."

"That's true."

They approached Knute and Thomas, who were both standing now. Joseph looked Knute over carefully. Some color had returned to the man's face and he clearly felt better. The Norseman had survived another spell.

"Knute, you know my brother, Grey Eagle. This is our friend, Raven's Heart. Raven's Heart, meet Knute Jensen, the Norseman, and his grandson, Thomas."

"Thomas, I hardly recognized you, you've grown so tall," Grey Eagle said as he shook Thomas's hand. "You're a man now."

Thomas flushed with pleasure, then shook Raven's Heart's hand. "Glad to meet you, sir," he said.

"Do you two know anything about catching horses?" Knute demanded. "We're short-handed and I'm feeling a little under the weather. If you'll help us out for a few days, we'll give you a hand with a few horses for yourselves."

Grey Eagle glanced at Raven's Heart and spoke quietly in Cheyenne. Raven's Heart nodded. "That is why we came, Norseman," said Grey Eagle. "We will help."

Joseph frowned. As much as they could use the help, Orion would need it more if the women really were coming from St. Louis with the next detachment. "I think Orion needs your help more, Eagle."

"A rider came in ahead of the detachment." Grey Eagle swung up into his saddle. "Mama Florrie and the girls aren't with them, so we have a little more time to fix up a place for them. Also, only about half of the goods Orion ordered are being delivered. He won't be as busy as he thought he would be, and felt it was more important that I find you." He lifted his head, sniffed the air, nodded toward a flock of geese flying south in a vee-shaped formation. "Winter is coming, and there is much to be done."

"Ja, so let's get started with these horses," Knute said. He climbed up into his saddle.

"Be careful, Gramps," warned Thomas.

"Ja, ja, I be careful. Let's go."

Joseph stayed where he was while Knute and Thomas rode in one direction, Grey Eagle and Raven's Heart in the other. The riders would encircle the scattered horses and drive them together, then choose the ones they wanted. He watched Grey Eagle, grateful for his brother's company. Not only did they need his help with the horses, but the time might be coming—and soon—when they would need his help protecting Annie Rose and the Golden Mare.

Sixteen

Two days later, late in the afternoon, they drove a herd of twelve horses into the holding corral next to Knute's barn. Raven's Heart looked about in wonder at the orderly, developed homestead, and spoke in Cheyenne to Joseph.

Joseph smiled.

"What did he say?" Thomas asked.

"He said this is a magic place and wonders if Knute is a powerful medicine man. He cannot believe it has been here for years and no one knew of it."

Thomas frowned. "He'll keep the secret, won't he?"

"Yes, he will." Joseph climbed down from the saddle, unable to wait any longer to see Annie Rose. She had not come out of the cabin with Sweet Water when they arrived, and he could not help but wonder if she was avoiding him again. He hoped that the fragile beginning of something special between them had not been destroyed. But then again, there was no sign of Maggie, either, or Jubal.

"Sweet Water, where's Jubal?" Joseph asked as he pulled the saddle off Grace's back.

"He hunt, Joseph. Be back soon." Sweet Water came to his side.

"And Annie Rose?"

"Annie Rosie go to woods."

He led Grace to the corral that held Knute's own horses and let her in. "Has she said anything about a new foal?"

"No baby horse yet."

Joseph looked back at the others. All were involved in caring for their own mounts. "I'll go find her," he said to Sweet Water.

A wide grin split Sweet Water's face. "I tell Annie Rosie you like her."

Joseph cocked an eyebrow. "You told her that?"

Sweet Water smugly nodded.

"Well, you were right." He placed a kiss on Sweet Water's round cheek.

She giggled and pushed him away. "Go find your woman."

"Yes, ma'am." Joseph needed no more encouragement. With his rifle in hand, he headed in the direction of the bathing pool, and beyond, to Aurora's meadow.

Annie Rose murmured soothing words to Aurora and stroked the mare's belly. The foal inside was quite active. Aurora kept looking back at her flanks and shifting her hind legs, as if she was uncomfortable. Her time was upon her.

The grey mare nickered encouragement from her position outside the corral. As a precaution, Annie Rose had separated the horses, and had covered the ground of the corral with armfuls of fresh meadow grass. Although most horses gave birth in the field, she wanted Aurora to foal within the shelter of the corral, where she would be easier to restrain should anything go wrong. Also, both Annie Rose and Knute believed it was easier for the new foal to form a good bond with its mama if they were in a confined space. She wanted to take no chances that Aurora might reject her baby.

If all went well, the foal would probably come within the next two to three hours.

Annie Rose rested her head against Aurora's neck. "I won't leave you, sweetie." She hoped Jubal and Sweet Water would be able to guess what had happened and not worry about her, for she would not get home until after dark.

She glanced over at Maggie, sound asleep in the shade

offered by the shallow cave, and wished there was someone to talk to. With nothing to distract her, her thoughts constantly wandered to Joseph, and until she knew what his intentions toward her were, that was dangerous ground. Despite her vigorous attempts to resist doing so, she had been foolish enough to fall in love with him, but that did not mean she would throw away her heart and soul for him, as her mother had done for her father.

Still, she missed him, and wished he was there with her and Aurora. The men had been gone for over a week now. Surely they would be back soon.

"Annie Rose."

His low, lightly accented voice touched her, so delicately that she was certain she imagined it. She felt drowsy, with her cheek resting against Aurora's sun-warmed coat and the sun warm on her own back, so it was easy to believe.

Maggie barked.

Annie Rose jumped, startled out of her reverie, her heart pounding. Maggie squirmed under the corral fence and raced toward the tall man who strode across the meadow, his long rifle in one hand. Mesmerized, Annie Rose watched him come. He looked so good to her! Maggie joyfully threw herself at Joseph, something Annie Rose longed to do herself. She wanted to look away, afraid he would read her feelings in her eyes, but she could not, any more than she could keep her lips from curving in a shy smile.

After giving the persistent dog some attention, Joseph approached the corral and let himself in. He leaned his rifle against the stone of the rock face, while Maggie trotted back to her place in the shade and sat down, looking very pleased with herself.

"Hello, Joseph." Annie Rose clung to Aurora, hoping that would keep her from reaching for him, for he seemed to be devouring her with his eyes.

He felt that he was. He couldn't get enough of her. She again wore the brown calico skirt and bodice, and her golden hair was pinned up to the back of her head. She looked so lovely, standing in the sunlight with the mare. He would swear that he had seen the light of welcome in her green eyes. Annie Rose tried hard to hide it, but she was glad to see him.

"It's so good to see you," he whispered, no longer concerned about keeping his feelings out of his voice. She blushed, as he had known she would, and looked down. Joseph studied her, his heart swelling with love. He'd known she was his woman, and until now hadn't been quite sure what to do about it. Orion had told him to just go get her. Well, he was here to do just that.

"How is Gramps?"

"Tired, but well, for now."

At that, Annie Rose looked up at him again, all traces of shyness gone and replaced by concern.

"He had another spell, Annie Rose, the first day out from Fort Laramie. It was a bad one."

Her eyes filled with tears, making them appear very green. She blinked them away. "And Thomas?"

"Fine." He paused. "Erik didn't return with us, though."

"I knew he would not." She caressed the velvety softness of Aurora's nose. "He took all of his things when he left."

"It may be for the best," Joseph said carefully.

"There's no question that it is, not only for my sake, but for all of us. Erik badgered Thomas, was downright cruel to him sometimes, and he had become so disrespectful toward Gramps, always upsetting him. Erik's leaving may prolong my grandfather's life, at least for a while."

Privately, Joseph agreed with her. "Grey Eagle and a friend named Raven's Heart came back with us to help with the horses."

She did not seem to mind that even more people had come to her valley. "How many horses this time?"

"Twelve."

"That's a lot to train by winter," she said with a frown.

"Some will go with Grey Eagle."

"It will be good to see him again. I've always liked your brother."

"Do you like me, too?"

She looked at him, very seriously. "Yes, I like you, too, Joseph."

"That's a start."

She looked away, back at Aurora. "Has the Hunter's child been born?"

"Yes. I have a beautiful nephew named Henry Jedediah." His own words surprised Joseph. Days earlier, he'd found Henry rather funny-looking. Now he truly did think the baby was beautiful. "Both Henry and Sarah are well."

"I'm glad. New life is always cause for celebration."

Aurora nickered and stamped one foreleg, turning her head to scowl at her flank.

"We have new life coming here, too, don't we?" Joseph asked.

"Yes. I'd say within a few hours." She met his gaze. "I won't leave her until the foal is born and I know all is well, so if you came to escort me back, you'll go back alone." Her tone carried a definite challenge.

Joseph frowned. "Did you think I would insist that you leave her?"

"I don't know. Everyone is so concerned about my safety that I wasn't certain Gramps hadn't sent you to fetch me. Even if he did, I won't leave her."

"He didn't. I came because I wanted to see you. I'd like to stay, too."

Her shoulders appeared to relax, and she inclined her head. "If you wish."

Joseph reached out and lifted her chin so that he could look into her eyes. "I wish to be with you, Annie Rose, wherever you are."

The intensity in his eyes struck her like a blow. Annie Rose pulled away from his touch, suddenly very uncomfortable. Not knowing how to respond, she bent down to run her hand over Aurora's belly, anything to get away from the look in Joseph Beaudine's eyes. "This little fellow is really moving around. I wouldn't be surprised if her water breaks soon." Her eyes closed and she almost moaned in embarrassment. How could she have mentioned something so personal and . . . female . . . to Joseph, as if she were talking to her grandfather?

If he thought her forward or uncouth, he gave no sign of it. He hunkered down on his haunches on Aurora's other side and laid gentle hands on the mare's abdomen. Aurora nickered and shifted her back legs.

"I think she might want to lie down." Joseph straightened and stepped back.

Annie Rose did the same, and sure enough, Aurora settled down onto the grasses and then rolled onto her right side. Her legs stuck out in front of her, stiff, the top two elevated and perpendicular to her body. She was breathing heavily. Water suddenly gushed from under her tail.

"Here we go," Joseph murmured. He moved around to Aurora's rear and pulled her tail out of the way.

Annie Rose circled behind Aurora's head and sank to her knees, then sat back on her heels. With gentle hands, she stroked Aurora's head and neck, murmuring words of encouragement and endearment, knowing there was little more she could do to help the laboring mare. If all went well, Aurora would need no help from her or Joseph. The miracle of life would unfold as God intended, and the foal would be born within minutes.

All went well.

The head and tiny front hooves emerged first, then the rest of the wet body emerged moments later, the remains of the amnionic sac wrapped around it. The foal had inherited its sire's paint coat rather than its dam's golden one. The little one lifted its head, appearing somewhat bewildered, and scooted a short distance from Aurora. She sat up and brought her head around to sniff her baby. Apparently she was pleased, for she licked the foal's head.

Tears of joy filled Annie Rose's eyes as she watched the

foal struggle to its feet. The umbilical cord was torn by the foal's movements, which was to be expected, but she would watch and make certain it stopped bleeding within the next few minutes. If not, it would need to be tied off. The foal wobbled like a drunken man, fell, and stood again. Joseph peered under its belly.

"Aurora has presented The Paint with a fine colt," he announced.

"He's beautiful," Annie Rose whispered. "I've seen many foals born, Joseph, and yet I never fail to be moved by it."

"I feel the same way." Joseph moved to Annie Rose's side. She stood, and they stepped back as Aurora got to her feet. The mare sniffed her colt and licked him here and there, then guided him with her nose toward her udder. The colt nosed under her belly and finally found a ready nipple.

"We may need to tie off that umbilical cord," Joseph commented.

"I agree."

They waited for a few minutes, then Joseph steadied the colt while Annie Rose tied the umbilical cord with a piece of clean twine she had brought for that purpose. She frowned. "The tear is kind of jagged. I wish I'd brought some of Sweet Water's healing salve. I hate to think of him getting an infection."

"We'll bring some when we check on him tomorrow." He glanced at Aurora. "She's passed the placenta. Good. Now we just need to make certain this little fellow's elimination system is working. I don't want to leave until we know."

Annie Rose nodded her agreement. Joseph did know horses. It was critical that the mare pass the entire placenta, just as it was necessary for the foal to pass prebirth waste. Failure for either to do so would jeopardize the animal's life.

Joseph guided the colt's eager mouth back to Aurora's udder, then used the shovel Annie Rose kept in the cave to clean up the soiled grasses. Maggie sniffed the new colt curiously, and went back to her nap. Annie Rose left the corral to gather fresh, tall grasses from the meadow, feeling as if she could sing for the pure joy of being alive.

"We'll have to listen for his name," she called to Joseph.

Joseph rested both hands on the shovel handle and looked at her. "Listen for his name? Who's going to say it?"

"He will, of course, or Aurora will." Suddenly Annie Rose stopped. She stood there, her arms full of long stalks of grass, feeling utterly foolish.

"That's how you name the horses?" Joseph asked. "You ask them their names?"

Miserably, she nodded, certain he would laugh at her.

He didn't laugh. In fact, his expression softened with understanding. "You have a true gift, Annie Rose. Don't ever be embarrassed by it." He continued with his task. "But you'll have to do the listening. I don't think I'll be able to hear."

She approached the corral and tossed the fresh grass over the fence. "I think you could," she said. "If you tried."

"Maybe I could, at that." He looked back at the horses. "Ah, there we go, little fellow. Good for you."

The colt had passed the necessary waste, and it appeared that all was in good working order for both mama and baby. Joseph cleaned out the last of the soiled grasses and set the shovel back in the cave. His hands on his hips, he looked at her. "We won't get back until after dark even if we left now. Would you like to stay a little longer?"

"I want to stay all night with them, but I'm anxious to see Gramps," Annie Rose admitted. Then she paused. Joseph was staring at the colt with a strange expression on his face—one of shock, perhaps even awe. She glanced at the colt, saw nothing out of the ordinary, and turned back to him. "Joseph? What is it?"

"The markings, Annie Rose. Look at the markings." Joseph approached the nursing colt with slow, careful steps. He lightly touched the dark brown mark on the colt's left shoulder, the shape of which had become more obvious as the colt's coat dried. The mark was a perfect four-pointed star.

Annie Rose frowned. "There's one here on his other side

that resembles a lightning bolt, if you use your imagination. So what?"

Joseph came around the colt's rear. The brown jagged marking on his right side did indeed look like a lightning bolt. Joseph's heart started hammering, and he fought the urge to drop to his knees out of reverence.

"What is it?" Annie Rose placed a light hand on his forearm. "Joseph, you're frightening me."

He wasn't so addled that he didn't recognize that this was the first time she had ever voluntarily touched him. He fought the urge to draw her into his arms, to hold her while he tried to explain the unexplainable. He knew she had feared his ridicule when she admitted that the horses told her their names. Now he feared her ridicule.

"Like his mama, the colt is a spirit animal, Annie Rose, perhaps even a greater one than she is," he said gently.

Annie Rose stepped back from him. "No. He's just a colt. The markings on his coat are random."

"Perhaps they truly are random. But the Plains tribes won't see it that way. To them, he'll be much more than just a colt." Joseph pointed at the jagged marking. "Lightning represents power to the Cheyenne and the Sioux, and a four-pointed star, like that on his left shoulder, represents the four winds. To them, the gods have marked this colt." *Perhaps they really did.* Joseph would never lay claim to understanding the spiritual powers of the universe.

"But then he'll be wanted, too!" she cried. "He'll be hounded like Aurora is." She approached Joseph again, clutching his forearms. "They simply want to live in peace, Joseph, and they deserve to. If they are captured, they'll die, just like The Paint would die if he were not free. We have to hide the colt, too."

"For how long, honey?" He did not realize the term of endearment slipped out. He took her hands in his. "Do you plan to keep them here forever?"

To his surprise, Annie Rose did not pull away from him. "No, that would be impossible. I want to keep them here long enough for Aurora to recover and for Thor to grow strong enough to travel with the herd."

"Thor?"

"The colt," Annie Rose said, somewhat impatiently. "The Norwegian god of thunder. That's the colt's name. Joseph, listen to me. When Aurora and Thor are ready, I want to take them and The Paint far away, settle them in a place where no one has heard of the legend of the Golden Mare, or of a spirit colt born to her. I want them to live out their lives in freedom and peace."

Joseph found the desperate sincerity in her eyes and in her voice overwhelming. "Even if you never see them again?" he asked quietly.

"Yes."

"Does such a place exist, where the legend is not known?"

"I don't know," Annie Rose admitted.

"Aurora is a true spirit animal, Annie Rose. Those who have seen her will not forget her, just as any who set eyes on Thor will know him for what he is."

"No one has a right to either of them! They are living beings who deserve to be free, not religious icons to be manipulated and exploited for the advantage of whoever captures them."

"I agree with you." Joseph tightened his hold on her hands. "Woman, this is a difficult task you have set for yourself." *If not impossible,* he silently added. "But I will help you all that I can."

"Oh, thank you, Joseph." Annie Rose stood on tiptoe and kissed his cheek, then froze, as if she were shocked by what she had done. "We should, uh, probably get back," she said. Now she did pull away from him.

Joseph fought a smile. She was growing more and more comfortable with him, even if she didn't know it yet. "Yes," was all he said. He ran a hand over Thor's back, then patted Aurora's rump. "We'll see you two tomorrow."

He retrieved his rifle and they left the corral, propping the gate open so Aurora could get to the stream. Maggie followed without being called, and for several minutes, as they climbed the game trail, neither Annie Rose or Joseph spoke. The light was fading quickly now, and they had to pay attention to the steep, faint trail. Joseph neared the top and reached down with one hand to help Annie Rose. She placed her hand in his, and he pulled her up. For a moment, they stood, holding hands, looking down on the meadow. Aurora's pale form could be made out in the dim light, near the stream now.

Joseph turned to the woman at his side. Her golden head was next to his shoulder, her small hand rested in his. The clean scent of her herbal soap teased his senses, and her breasts rose and fell with her accelerated breathing, no doubt caused by the exertion of the climb.

A feeling of love filled him, so strong that he could not withstand the urge to take her in his arms. The maneuver was awkward with the rifle in his hand, and he was scared of moving too fast, yet he managed. Annie Rose gasped, and her body stiffened, but again, she did not pull away. He touched his lips to hers, gently, tentatively, silently asking her permission to proceed. She made a single faint whimpering sound, and her eyes closed. Her hands crept about his waist, and Joseph deepened the kiss, pressing more firmly against her lips. They parted slightly, and he teased her with the tip of his tongue. She relaxed a little, leaning against him, her breasts soft against his chest, and even that hesitant response sent desire flaring through him like a wild prairie fire. One of the hardest things Joseph Beaudine ever had to do in his life was to keep that kiss gentle and, after a moment, withdraw.

He was shaking. He fought to keep his voice even. "I've wanted to do that for a long time, Annie Rose Jensen. Thank you." He kissed her lips again, quickly, then moved away from her, before he gave in completely to the thundering hunger of soul-deep love and raw desire.

She turned away from him, her shoulders trembling, the fingers of one hand touching her lips.

He watched her, suddenly terrified. Was she crying? God, had he made her cry?

"Annie Rose?" he said fearfully.

"Shh."

Shh? She was telling him to hush? At least it didn't sound like she was crying, and Joseph took comfort from that. Only the palest light remained, and he could barely make out her expression. He waited, trying to ignore the snuffling sounds Maggie made as she snooted along the trail.

When Annie Rose finally spoke, it was in a whisper. "I wanted to savor this moment, Joseph Beaudine." She turned to him. "Aurora's baby has been born this day, in this most beautiful and holy of places, and, for the first time in my life, I've been kissed by a man." She smiled shyly. "I'm glad it was you."

His heart hammered painfully against his ribs. Joseph swallowed, feeling that he was the luckiest man in the entire world and yet strangely humbled at the same time. "I'm glad, too." He held out his hand to her. She took it, and in comfortable silence they continued on their way, with Maggie running ahead of them.

In his mind, Joseph relived the events of the afternoon—the joy of seeing Annie Rose again, the wonder of Thor's birth, the discussion about future plans for the horses, the magical kiss. All very pleasant, but something was nagging him, something important.

Annie Rose.

She was the only human he had ever seen be permitted near The Paint, and the stallion had actually welcomed her presence that misty morning in the valley when she brought Aurora to see her mate. Aurora allowed her near, but no one else, except him, and he suspected Aurora would not be so friendly if Annie Rose weren't there. Now there was Thor.

Annie Rose was the only one who could manage the little family of horses. Joseph knew it instinctively.

If that became known, Annie Rose would become just as valuable a commodity as the horses—to the Cheyenne, to the Sioux, to that scum Baines. Whoever had the horses would also need Annie Rose to manage them.

Wars had been started over less important things than spirit horses; in fact, some of the worst atrocities man visited upon his fellow man were done in the name of God. The Spanish Inquisition and the Crusades leapt to Joseph's mind. What chance would the brave, quiet woman who now walked beside him have against the sincere believers, the religious fanatics, and the unscrupulous horse traders who would descend upon them if the full truth became known? If all hell broke loose—and there was a good chance it would—Annie Rose would be caught right in the middle.

His fingers tightened on hers. Somehow, he would protect her and her beloved horses.

"Joseph?" she asked. She wiggled the fingers he had trapped.

"Sorry." He relaxed his grip, but did not release her.

"Is everything all right?"

"Yes." He brought her fingers to his lips for a quick kiss. "Everything is fine."

They lapsed into companionable silence again.

Everything *was* fine, for now. Joseph would do all in his power to keep it that way.

Seventeen

An hour later, Joseph and Annie Rose approached the cabin, still hand in hand. Knute waited in front of the open door, pacing, puffing furiously on his pipe. The welcoming light from the lantern that hung next to the door as well as that pouring out from inside allowed Joseph to clearly see the Norseman's expression. When Knute saw them, his glad smile changed to a puzzled frown to a thunderous scowl, in very short order.

Now Joseph frowned, too. What could be wrong?

Annie Rose stopped and pulled her hand from his. "Gramps?"

"Go inside, girl, and straighten yourself up. We have guests." He pointed the pipe at Joseph. "You will walk with me, Captain. Now."

"Yes, sir."

Annie Rose glanced at Joseph, her brow furrowed with worry. He offered what he hoped was an encouraging smile. She threw her grandfather an imploring look—one that did not soften Knute's rigid stance—then brushed some of the clinging grasses from her skirts before she hurried into the cabin.

Knute grabbed the lantern off its nail and marched across the yard toward the pond at such a pace that Joseph had to hurry to keep up with him. At the edge of the pond, he stopped so abruptly that Joseph almost plowed into him. Knute spun around and glared, holding the lantern high.

With no preamble, he snapped, "My instincts about a man are rarely wrong, Captain. I hope my trust in you regarding my granddaughter was not misplaced." He raised the hand holding the pipe when Joseph would have spoken. "After being separated for a week, you and Annie Rose disappear for hours, you return well after dark holding hands, both disheveled with grass stuck to your clothing, both wearing silly, satisfied grins. If there is an innocent explanation for this, I will hear it now."

"There *is* an innocent explanation, Mr. Jensen," Joseph calmly replied. He could see how Knute had reached his worried conclusion, but still felt the Norseman had jumped the gun. "Aurora foaled today, and neither of us wanted to leave until we were fairly certain all was well with mama and foal. The grass on our clothing is from that which Annie Rose placed in the corral. We were holding hands because we like each other, and the reasons for the smiles are many, the main one being the birth of the new colt." He paused. "I would not dishonor your granddaughter, sir."

Knute sighed and lowered the lantern. "No, you would not." He eyed Joseph thoughtfully. "You like each other well enough to hold hands?"

Joseph did not think it was necessary to mention the kiss he had shared with Annie Rose. That was too private, too special. "I thought you'd be pleased."

"*Ja,* I am. I'm just an old fool." Knute motioned toward the log seat they had shared once before. "I have a tale to tell you. Please indulge me."

Joseph followed the Norseman to the log and leaned his rifle against the fence before taking a seat. Knute sat down and placed the lantern on the ground between them.

"I am fiercely protective of my granddaughter, Joe, with good reason. It is time you knew that reason." Knute tapped the pipe on the end of the log, spilling the charred tobacco onto the ground, and clutched the empty pipe in both hands, his elbows resting on his knees.

Was the Norseman nervous about sharing long-hidden family secrets? "Anything you tell me will be held in the strictest confidence, Knute," Joseph assured him. "And nothing you tell me will diminish the affection I feel for Annie Rose."

Knute nodded, once, abruptly. "In 1825, a year after my wife died, I brought my two children with me from Norway, on the ship called *Restoration*. My son Olaf was nineteen, my daughter Thora—Annie Rose's mama—thirteen. There were just over fifty of us Norwegians, and we settled together in upper New York, on the shores of Lake Ontario. But I had wandering in my soul, and when the leader of our group of emigrants set off for the West to find a better place to resettle, I went with him. Because Olaf was grown and determined to marry that crazy woman, and Thora could stay with them, I saw no problem. Cleng Peerson and I traveled for many months. We found a new place to settle near Chicago, so he returned to our people, but I did not. Instead, I answered the siren call of the Western frontier. I am ashamed to say that I was gone for very many years."

Joseph shrugged. "Many men have heard the call of the West, Knute, my father among them."

"Your father did not abandon his family."

There was nothing Joseph could say to that.

Knute continued. "I've mentioned my son's wife to you before. What I did not tell you was that she made my daughter's life miserable, and finally, in desperation, Thora ran away, to the relatives of some Norwegian friends who lived in Baltimore. There, when she was but fifteen, she met Blaine Coburn."

Annie Rose's father. Joseph was certain of it. At last he was to hear the story of her father. He tried to appear nonchalant, but eagerly awaited Knute's next words. Perhaps they would offer some clue as to how he should court Annie Rose.

"He was ten years older than she, handsome, wealthy, sophisticated. He seduced my Thora when she was not yet a

woman, and I was not there to offer her a father's protection."
Knute's jaw tightened, as did his hold on his pipe. "When she
discovered she was pregnant, he set her up in fine style, not
as wife, but as mistress." Knute pierced Joseph with his harsh
gaze. "Annie Rose and Thomas are illegitimate, Joe, never
claimed by their father."

"I'd guessed that already," Joseph said gently. "It matters
not to me." He saw Knute's shoulders relax, but the old man's
bushy eyebrows went up in question. "Their last name,"
Joseph explained. "It's the same as yours, yet they are your
daughter's children."

"Ah. You are a clever man."

Privately, Joseph didn't think it would take a genius, or
even a clever man, to reach the same conclusion he had, but
he said nothing.

Knute took up the tale again. "I returned to the East in
January of 1843; a wagon train of settlers bound for Oregon
was leaving in the spring from Independence, Missouri, and
I had been hired as one of the scouts. I took the opportunity
to visit my children, only to find my son long dead by his
wife's hand, and Erik, my orphaned grandson, whom I had
never met, living with neighbors who did not treat him kindly.
I took him with me, and we went to Baltimore in search of
Thora." He stopped.

Joseph did not urge him on, for Knute straightened his
shoulders as if gathering his strength for what he was about
to say.

After drawing a deep breath, the Norseman continued. "I
found my beloved, beautiful daughter ensconced in an elegant town house, surrounded by every luxury, dying of con-
sumption and a broken heart. She had remained true to that
blackguard for years, even though he took her innocence,
ruined her reputation, refused to legitimize their children,
and used her at will." Knute turned on Joseph, his old blue
eyes blazing. "He visited that house often over the years
when he wanted a man's release, but he would not come to

see her when he knew she was dying. Coburn would not even offer her that much respect."

"Knute, calm yourself," Joseph urged. As angry as he was at Coburn—a man he'd never met—he fought to keep his tone soothing. The Norseman's hands shook, and Joseph not only feared for the safety of the clay pipe, but he feared that Knute's high emotions would precipitate another spell—perhaps a final one. "There's no need to tell me any more. I understand what the situation was."

"No, there's more." Knute grabbed Joseph's forearm with surprising strength. "You must hear it all. We had come from the cemetery, where my grandchildren, then fifteen and five, had just buried their beloved mother. We entered the front door and heard Coburn in the parlor with one of his friends, making arrangements to sell the town house with all its contents." His fingers tightened even more on Joseph's arm. "Including Annie Rose."

Joseph stared at him in horror. "He was setting up his own young daughter as mistress to one of his friends?"

"*Ja*. Thomas was to be sent to work in one of the textile factories owned by the family, though he was only a small boy."

"And they heard this?" Joseph's voice was barely above a whisper.

"*Ja*. Never will I forget the look on my Annie Rose's face when she realized what her father planned for her and her little brother. It broke my heart more than my daughter's death did. At that moment, I swore to be the parent for my grandchildren that I never was for my children. I spirited them away."

So much made sense now. Joseph's own heart broke for the young Annie Rose, for the child Thomas. He was tempted to go back to Baltimore himself and look up their villain of a father. "What happened to Coburn?" he ground out.

"When the children were away and hidden, and all preparations had been made to leave for the West, I went to Coburn's fancy mansion, where he lived with his proper, respectable wife and proper, respectable children. *Ja*, I told him in front of his wife what a demon he was. It was a terrible scene, one I enjoyed immensely." Under his white mustache, a grim smile twisted Knute's lips. "He swore he would track us down, and I hit him with all the fury of an outraged father. His head struck the marble mantel. I left him on the floor with his wife screeching over him."

"Did you kill him?"

Knute shrugged. "I don't know. I didn't stay in Baltimore long enough to find out." He looked at Joseph. "I didn't intend to kill him, but if I did, I don't regret it. The world is better off. I took my grandchildren and brought them here, far from the reach of their father, his money, and his family."

"And far from the reach of the law."

"Ja." Knute looked down at his pipe. "I am an honorable man, and would have stayed to face the consequences of my actions, but my grandchildren needed me. I would have done anything to stay alive for them."

Joseph allowed his gaze to wander over the quiet yard, the neat cabin, the sturdy barn, the clean corrals containing healthy, well-tended animals. "I admire what you have done, Knute," he said sincerely. "All of it."

"I never told the children I may have killed their father."

"If they are to be told, you will do the telling," Joseph assured him. "They won't hear it from me without your permission."

"Takk, min venn." Knute again turned his sharp eyes on Joseph and bluntly asked, "What are your intentions toward my granddaughter?"

Joseph returned Knute's gaze. "I intend to take your granddaughter as my wife, if she will have me. I ask for your blessing."

"You said you liked her, Joseph Beaudine. Do you also love her?"

"Yes."

"Your decision is not based on a sense of duty toward me, nor on a sense of pity toward her?"

Joseph shook his head. "She is the woman of my heart." The words came out with no forethought, and he felt foolish and vulnerable.

"This is good," Knute finally announced. It seemed that a great burden had been lifted from him. "This is how it should be between a man and a woman when they marry. I give you my permission to court my granddaughter."

"Thank you. I will treasure her."

"That is well and good. Be certain that you wed her."

"Yes, sir."

Knute sternly eyed him. "I mean what I say, Joseph Beaudine. I cannot forget the unhappy fate of my daughter. Do not betray my granddaughter. If you do, I'll come after you, and I will kill you."

"I would expect you to," Joseph calmly replied. "But it won't be necessary."

"Good, because I like you. I would not want to kill you."

Joseph smiled at that, and a companionable silence fell over the two men. Finally, Joseph decided to broach the subject of the coming winter.

"I don't think we should winter up here," he said casually.

"No, I don't either."

Joseph jerked his head around to stare at Knute. "You don't?"

Knute shook his head. "I have loved my life in this valley, the time spent with my grandchildren, and I hope I have made some atonement for my failings with my own children. But just as my life is coming to an end, so is the life here coming to an end. One cannot hide from the world forever, Joseph Beaudine."

"No," was all Joseph said in response.

"You thought of it once, entertained the idea of staying here, far away from the troubles coming to this land, content to make a life here with Annie Rose."

Joseph's eyes widened in disbelief. "How did you know?"

"What man would not want such a life?" Knute spread his hands, still holding the clay pipe in one. "To live in an isolated paradise, with a beautiful young woman to warm your heart and your bed?" He eyed Joseph. "You were world-weary, fearful of what you know is coming, feeling powerless because you can't stop it. But your destiny lies out there, Joe, not here, hidden away. You are one of few who can have real influence on the conflict between the white man and the Indian tribes. Tom Fitzpatrick is another, and also your brothers."

"Do you really think we can make a difference?" Joseph asked doubtfully.

Knute shrugged and spread his hands. "What will be, will be, son. But if anyone can make a difference, you can. You must try."

"I suppose you're right."

"Of course I'm right." Knute raised an eyebrow. "Now tell me why you think we should not stay here."

"Several reasons. Your health, for one. A surgeon has been posted to Fort Laramie, finally, and I think all of us will feel better if you are close to him."

"So you think we should go to Laramie."

"For this winter, yes. Orion and Sarah are there, and have agreed to help us with shelter." He looked at Knute. "My stepmother and two sisters may also be coming from St. Louis, so quarters could be crowded."

"What are your other reasons for wanting to leave?"

"I don't *want* to leave, Knute. I think we have to. If we stay here, we'll be snowed in. Erik is estranged from you, and determined to find the Golden Mare; there's no telling what he may do. Baines is out there, equally determined to find the mare, and he wouldn't mind taking a shot at me, either. Then there is Aurora's colt."

"Ah, the colt. The foaling went well?" At Joseph's nod, Knute added, "Tell me what is so important about the colt."

"He's a powerful spirit animal, even more so than his mother. Like his father, he's a paint. One shoulder carries a perfect four-pointed star, while a lightning bolt jags down his other side."

Knute stared at him. *"Min Gud."*

"You're right, 'my God.' Annie Rose is the only one who can manage The Paint and Aurora, Knute. What do you think will happen when that is learned?"

"We must go soon."

"Yes. My plan was to train the horses we have now as pack animals first. Then we'll load all we can carry and get to Fort Laramie. When we're settled for the winter, we'll finish saddle-training the horses and sell them. That should give us enough income to see us through the winter."

"What of Aurora and the colt?"

"Annie Rose wants to take them and The Paint far into the wilderness and set them free."

Knute stroked his mustache. "Where could we take them?" he mused. "We will ask Grey Eagle. Perhaps he knows of a safe place for them."

Joseph was glad that Knute felt comfortable taking Grey Eagle into his confidence. But then, Eagle had been friends with the Norseman far longer than he himself had been. There was much Grey Eagle probably already knew.

"It is decided then," Joseph said.

"*Ja,* it is decided. We will tell everyone in the morning." Knute stood up. "*Takk,* Joseph Beaudine, for everything. Should I die tonight, I shall die easy, knowing you are here to watch over Annie Rose and Thomas." He held out his hand, which Joseph took in a warm grasp.

"You're too ornery to die tonight," Joseph said affectionately. "You're going to stick around long enough to see my marriage to your granddaughter."

"Nothing would make me happier." Knute picked up the lantern, while Joseph retrieved his rifle. The two men began the walk back to the cabin.

"Why does Erik call Annie Rose 'Annabella'?" Joseph asked.

"It is her name—Annabella Rosalie Jensen. Her mother wanted the prettiest name she could think of for her beautiful daughter." Knute grimaced. "I found it a pretentious name, and Annie Rose always hated it. Thomas gave her the name

Annie Rose, when he was too young to pronounce the whole thing. Erik insisted upon calling her that only in the last year, because he thought it sounded sophisticated."

"Even though she hates it."

"*Ja,* even though she hates it. I told him that was disrespectful, to call a person by a name they don't like, even if it is their true name, but he would not be dissuaded, just as he always called Thomas 'Tom,' which Thomas hates." Knute shook his head. "I did my best for him, but Erik is a troubled young man."

Joseph silently agreed. "I'm going to the bathing pool before I come in, Knute. I need to clean up a bit."

Knute nodded and handed him the lantern, then waved him away. "*Ja, ja,* go along. We saved you some supper, and later we will drink brandy and discuss our plans."

"I'll be in soon." Clutching the lantern, Joseph made his way along the path toward the pool. His mind whirled with all that Knute had told him.

Now so many things made sense.

Knute's intense secrecy, not only for the sake of his grandchildren, but for himself as well if the law were indeed after him. Thomas's fiercely protective attitude toward his sister. Annie Rose's deep-seated mistrust of most men. It all made sense.

He wanted to take Annie Rose in his arms, to ease away her fears, to soothe her troubled spirit, to heal her wounded heart. Somehow he had to make her understand that she would be safe with him, in all respects.

Joseph approached the bathing pool, eager to finish his bath so he could return to the cabin and her. He set his rifle and the lantern on the flat rock and noticed drying footprints there. Someone else had recently bathed. Annie Rose, perhaps?

He looked about the area. The surface of the pool was smooth and calm, except near the waterfall. All was quiet. Whoever had been there was gone now. Joseph took off his hat, then his belt, laying both on the rock. With a sigh, he shrugged out of his shirt. It had been a long day, one that had started before sunrise with a herd of excited wild horses. Then had followed all the excitement of Aurora's foaling and Annie Rose's tentative opening up to him, then the long discussion with Knute. The warm water of the bathing pool would feel real good tonight. The only thing that was missing was a small glass of Knute's brandy.

And Annie Rose.

Joseph let the image of her lithe body and her long golden hair dance in his mind. What would it be like to share this lovely pool with her? Just the thought tightened his loins. He sat down carefully and removed his moccasins. Someday he would bring her to this pool, when she was his wife, when she understood that he wanted her woman's heart as well as her woman's body. Then he would show her that a man and a woman could share their bodies and experience only joy.

He groaned, hoping that the day came soon. His desire for her had flared to ungovernable heights today, and he knew it could not be brought back under control.

Something moved in the brush.

Joseph snatched up his rifle and waited, all his senses on alert. The rustling sound came closer and closer. Suddenly, Maggie broke free of the shrubs and climbed into his lap, her tail wagging furiously, her warm tongue lapping at his face.

Joseph put down his rifle and scratched the dog's ears. "Hello, girl. Where's your mistress? I'll bet she just took a bath, didn't she?" With a laugh, he set the excited dog aside and stood. "Let me take my bath, and we'll both go find her."

He loosened the lacing down the front of his buckskin pants and prepared to push them down off his hips.

"Joseph, stop."

Joseph froze.

Annie Rose's soft voice came from the direction of the tall cottonwood, where she had once hidden from Erik.

She cowered there, the hands that covered her eyes shaking. No longer could Annie Rose bear the wondrous sight of Joseph's body being revealed to her. She'd seen the approaching lantern light, but heard no sound, and had darted behind the tree half-clothed. Then she'd peeked out to see Joseph slowly disrobing in the revealing light. Unable to speak or move, she'd watched, paralyzed by his masculine beauty. Now she was ashamed. Hadn't Erik done exactly the same thing to her?

Although she wore only her chemise, drawers, and petticoats, and her freshly washed hair hung long and wet down her back, Annie Rose wrapped the damp bath sheet around her shoulders and stepped out from behind the tree, clasping her bundled moccasins, skirt, and bodice to her chest like a shield.

Joseph stared at her as she came into the circle of light given off by his lantern. "I heard you coming, and didn't know who it was, so I hid." She looked away from his magnificent, half-naked form. "I should have spoken sooner. I'm sorry." She flushed with shame. "I'm no better than Erik, am I?"

"Don't say that." Joseph hurried off the rock to stand in front of her. "Don't ever compare yourself to him. You did not welcome his attentions, and made that very clear to him. He violated you that night." He smiled at her. "I welcome your attentions. You can look at me all you want."

Taken aback, Annie Rose blushed more fiercely and murmured, "Thank you." She could think of nothing else to say.

His passionate gaze roamed over her, heating her, devouring her, yet there was a tenderness in his eyes also, a tenderness that unnerved her. "What is it?" she begged. "What are you looking at?"

"Oh, sweet woman, I'm looking at you." He reached out and touched her cheek. "You are so beautiful."

Annie Rose stared at him, her bottom lip trembling. "So are you," she whispered. Her grip on the bath sheet loosened.

Joseph's hand trailed down her neck to her shoulder, pushing the sheet out of his way. His other hand grasped her other shoulder and he stepped closer. Through the sheet, his hands lightly stroked her upper arms, then he bent his head and kissed her, his mouth gentle and searching.

Annie Rose clung to her bundle of clothes for dear life and

opened herself up to the wonder of his kiss. Her lips parted, and he moaned, low in his throat, before he plunged deeper with his questing tongue. After a moment, her hold on the bath sheet loosened even more, and finally she let it and the clothing fall, and wrapped her arms around Joseph's waist.

The feel of his warm skin under her hands was the most wildly exciting thing she had ever known. Instinctively, she tilted her head and angled her mouth across his. She pressed her breasts against his warm, naked chest, fighting the urge to throw off her damp chemise so that nothing would come between them.

Joseph caught her to him, one arm wrapped tightly around her waist, the other hand tangled in her hair. He ravaged her mouth until she was breathless, then his wondrous lips moved across her cheek to one ear, where his warm breath and nibbling teeth caused a bolt of lightning to shoot through her body, raising gooseflesh on her arms and causing her nipples to tighten into hard little buds. A strange, tingling fire burned low in her belly. She gasped and tilted her head even more when his mouth began to travel down her throat. The soft tickling of his mustache provided an intriguing follow-up to the gliding warmth of his mouth. Annie Rose's toes literally curled with pleasure.

Joseph's mouth travelled along her shoulder until it encountered the wide strap of her chemise. Then he raised his head and looked into her eyes. "My beautiful woman," he whispered.

Annie Rose stared at him. His chest rose and fell with the same agitated breathing as hers did. His hips were pressed to hers, his arm holding her so tightly against him that she could feel his male hardness. She knew she should be afraid, and yet she wasn't. Why wasn't she? It was clear what he wanted. Why did she want so desperately to give it to him, here, and now, with no words of love spoken between them, with no promises for the future? Her eyes filled with tears. Was she doomed to follow in her mother's unhappy footsteps? Why did she have no power to withstand the allure of this man?

The look in Joseph's eyes changed from one of heart-stopping passion to one of deep concern, and he laid his fingers gently on her cheek. "What is it, Annie Rose? Talk to me, sweetheart. Help me understand why I frighten you so when all I want to do is love you."

"You make me feel things I don't want to feel, Joseph." Annie Rose pulled her hands from his waist and gently laid them against his chest, then closed her eyes. Too late, she realized she had made yet another mistake, for all she wanted to do now was allow her fingers the freedom to explore the muscular contours of his chest, to comb through the soft, intriguing mat of hair, to touch his dark, masculine nipples, to rejoice in the powerful, steady rhythm of his heart. "I am helpless against you," she whispered sadly, "and I despise myself for that weakness. All of my vows to protect myself against the trap my mother fell into with my father blow away under the gentle force of your kindness and your desire." She pushed lightly against him, and Joseph released her.

"Your grandfather told me the story of your mother and father," he said.

"He didn't tell you everything, because he doesn't know everything." Annie Rose angrily blinked her tears away. "He didn't tell you how my mother would wait at the window and watch for him night after night, ignoring her lonely daughter for a man who rarely came to her, crying long into the night for a man who wasn't worthy of cleaning her boots. In the name of love, she gave up her soul, Joseph Beaudine. I'll not do that for any man."

"I would never ask you to."

With an agitated sweep of her arm, she brushed away his words. "I had every luxury money could buy—a beautiful home, dresses of the latest fashion, an exemplary education at the finest girls' school in the city, where somehow everyone knew that my mother wasn't really a widow. Gramps didn't tell you that I would have given up all of the trappings of wealth for a kind word from my father, for a show of genuine interest from my mother. A man has a responsibility to his children, as does a woman, yet neither of my parents accepted theirs. I, a mere child myself, was more a mother to Thomas than our mother was. In return, my brother saved my life, or at least my heart, for he truly loved me when no one else did."

"Annie Rose, listen—"

"No, you listen, Joseph Beaudine." Annie Rose poked his chest, his warm, wonderfully masculine chest. "I have always sworn that no man will know my body until he stands up with me before a preacher. But you make me want to give you anything you ask for, right here, right now. That is why you frighten me!" Her words ended on a cry.

"Marry me."

She blinked. "What did you say?"

Joseph dropped to one knee and grabbed her hand, sandwiching it between both of his. He looked up at her, his eyes burning, the lantern light shining off his bare chest. "Be my wife, Annie Rose Jensen. Let us make a home together, where your grandfather and your brother will also live, for as long as they want to. I want no sacrifice from you, save to give up your grandfather's name and take mine."

"You'll marry me?" she repeated, disbelieving. "Why? Because of the promise you made to Gramps?"

A look of exasperation flashed across Joseph's face and he stood up, still holding her hand. "Your grandfather has nothing to do with it, although I'm grateful he gave his blessing."

"You've discussed this with him?"

"Annie Rose, now you *will* listen to me." Joseph gently took her chin in one hand and looked into her eyes. "I am asking you to marry me because I want to spend my life with you. I believe you are the woman of my heart, meant for me as I am meant for you. I love you."

She could not look away. "Dare I believe you?" she whispered.

"If you'll examine your heart with just half the effort you put into connecting with the spirits of the horses, you'll find that you already do believe me." Joseph released her and stepped back.

His eyes were mesmerizing. Even when he reached out a hand toward her, she could not pull back. Slowly, so slowly, his hand advanced. She knew he was giving her the opportunity to step away, and yet she couldn't. She couldn't move. She didn't *want* to move.

Joseph's hand covered her left breast, pressed lightly, held her. Her breath stopped and her eyelids fluttered. Her heart pounded against her ribs so strongly that surely he could hear it.

"I care about the woman's heart that beats beneath this breast, Annie Rose." He drew closer, snaked his other arm around her waist once again, pulled her so close that his bold hand was trapped between them. His mouth took hers, softly, gently, while his hand moved the same way over her breast. Again her nipple hardened, thrust itself outward as if it were reaching for his touch.

Annie Rose leaned against his strength and did as he suggested. She searched her heart. The answer was swift in coming.

She did believe him.

Something in her stance, or in the way she opened her mouth to him, must have told him something, for he pulled his mouth from hers and whispered again, "Marry me."

"I will," she responded.

Joseph seemed surprised. He stepped back, releasing her waist and her breast, and took her hands in his. "Why?" he demanded.

"Because I love you, Joseph Beaudine. There is no other reason."

"That one will do." He grinned. "We're betrothed."

She smiled shyly. "I guess we are."

He swept her up into an exuberant hug, turning in a circle. Maggie started barking, as if they played a game and she wanted to join in. "I suppose Maggie is part of the deal," Joseph said.

"Absolutely." Annie Rose laughed with pure joy. She wore only her underclothes and her hair was wet, tangled, and hanging down her back, yet she gladly allowed a man—who wore only a pair of unlaced pants—to whirl her about on the banks of a seductive, inviting pool. Had she completely lost her mind?

Yes. Just as she had completely lost her heart.

Joseph set her down and gave her a quick, hard kiss. "Go now, woman, and let me bathe in peace, before I drag you in that water with me."

Annie Rose's eyes widened at the tempting picture that leapt to her mind at his words. *Some day* . . .

Joseph laughed. "We think along the same lines, Annie Rose." He scooped up the clothes she had let fall and held out her skirt, his voice dropping to a sensual whisper. "We'll share this pool one day."

She shivered as she pulled the skirt over her head and fastened it. Was she really dressing in front of Joseph Beaudine? He held out her bodice and she slipped into it, then allowed him to close the row of hooks down her back. She accepted her moccasins and decided against putting them on for the short walk to the cabin.

Joseph picked up the bath sheet and shook it out, holding it back when she reached for it. "I didn't bring anything to dry with," he said. "May I use this?"

"But it's damp," she protested.

"With water that touched your body. I'll treasure the dampness." A teasing light came into his eyes.

"You are addled," she said tartly as she started on the path toward the cabin. "Come, Maggie."

"Send Grey Eagle and Jubal out, would you?"

"I will." She waved over her shoulder and proceeded to the cabin. When she stepped in the door, she found everyone but Knute seated around the table, involved in a lively conversation. From his rocking chair in front of the fireplace, her grandfather looked up at her, his expression concerned, hopeful. She went straight to his side and bent to place a kiss on his cheek. "We are to wed, Gramps," she said softly, for his ears only.

Knute nodded his approval, his eyes shining with joy. "He will love you well, *datter.*"

"He already does. And I love him."

"*Ja,* I know."

Annie Rose laughed. "Of course you do." She kissed him again. "I must brush out my hair. I'll be back soon." She moved toward her bedroom, clutching her moccasins. "Grey Eagle, Jubal," she called. When she had their attention, she said, "Joseph asked that you join him at the pool."

"Well, la-ti-dah," exclaimed Jubal. "He sent for us, huh? Any idea what's so all-fired important?"

Annie Rose opened her bedroom door and spoke without turning around. "He and I just became betrothed. I think it might have something to do with that." She stepped into her bedroom and closed the door, needing some time alone with the wondrous joy she felt.

Out in the great room, a stunned silence settled over the group. Then Thomas gave a cheer, and Grey Eagle and Jubal bolted for the door and were gone. Knute puffed on his pipe and stared into the fire, a satisfied smile on his face.

Eighteen

The next morning, an animated discussion took place over breakfast regarding the recommendation that the Jensens spend the winter at Fort Laramie. At first, the very thought of leaving her home distressed Annie Rose, but the knowledge that a surgeon would be available should Knute need one and the idea of not being snowed in for the whole winter quickly persuaded her that the proposal was a good one. Her only real concern was for Aurora and Thor. Who would see to them if not her? The horses would have to be taken to a safe place before she would consent to leave for Fort Laramie. She would discuss it with Joseph later.

Plans were made to begin working with the new batch of horses immediately, and to train them as pack animals. Everyone agreed that Jubal would make a run to Fort Laramie and inform Orion of all that had been decided, while Sweet Water would stay with the Jensens and help with preparations for the move. Annie Rose felt that a new closeness had developed among the members of the group, literally overnight; they seemed to have all drawn together, even the silent Raven's Heart. Once again, she could not help but be thankful that Erik was not there. His sullen presence would have tainted the atmosphere of camaraderie that filled the cabin.

Annie Rose also felt a new closeness with Joseph. They sat next to each other, and she loved it—loved the feeling of his thigh pressed alongside hers, loved how his hand searched for hers under the table, loved the warm expression in his eyes when he looked at her. She was filled with a new joy, one that not even the unhappy prospect of leaving her beloved home could diminish.

She also loved how at peace her grandfather seemed this morning. Evidently, her betrothal to Joseph Beaudine had taken a great weight of worry off of Knute—a weight Annie Rose had not realized was burdening him so much until she saw that it was gone. Knute looked better this morning than he had in weeks. She squeezed Joseph's hand in silent thanks for his role in Knute's improved condition. Joseph looked at her questioningly, and she gave him her warmest smile.

When the meal was finished, Knute, Thomas, Grey Eagle, and Raven's Heart went to the corrals, Sweet Water and Annie Rose washed dishes and straightened the cabin, and Joseph helped Jubal prepare for his journey.

Down in front of the barn, Joseph tightened the cinch on Jubal's saddle and slapped the horse's rump. "What else do you need?"

"Can't think of anything." Jubal scratched his beard. "It ain't like I'm gonna be gone forever, 'though you'd think it, with all the food them women loaded me up with." He waved a hand toward his bulging saddlebags and rolled his eyes.

"They don't want you to starve," Joseph said with a grin, knowing full well that if Jubal Sage were ever to find himself alone in the wilderness, on foot, with no weapon but a hunting knife, the wily mountain man would eat like a king, never suffer from the weather, dodge all enemies, and live to tell his grandchildren—if he ever had any—the tale.

Jubal snorted. "Starve, indeed." He settled his hat on his grey-haired head. "I'll go find that woman of mine and say my goodbyes, then get on the road."

"You have my letter for Orion?"

"Right here." Jubal patted his chest, indicating that he had put the letter inside his buckskin shirt. "I'll see to all that other stuff you mentioned, too. Don't worry about a thing."

"The only thing I'm worried about is Erik hooking up

with Abby Baines." Joseph's gaze travelled the valley as he unconsciously looked for trouble. "He's the only one who can lead Baines here, and he just might be angry enough, desperate enough, and stupid enough to do it."

"Let's hope he ain't. Let's hope he has some respect left for his grandpa, who is one of the finest men I've ever had the honor of knowin'."

"That's the truth." Joseph saw Sweet Water come from the cabin. "Here comes your woman now, Jubal, so I'll leave you two alone. Watch your back out there."

"Likewise, Joe. You never know where trouble might come from." He touched the brim of his hat in a gesture of farewell. "See you in a week or so. Take good care of my woman." He draped his arm around a smiling Sweet Water's shoulders.

"You know we will." Joseph touched his own hat brim and left them. He hurried back to the cabin, hoping Annie Rose would be alone.

The door to her room was open wide, and he found her there, leaning over the bed as she smoothed the blankets. A few bunches of drying herbs hung from the ceiling near the small window, which was open to the early morning air. A breeze swayed the herbs, releasing a heady scent that would always remind him of Annie Rose and her homemade soap.

She turned and saw him, and her mouth curved in a shy smile.

"I was hoping to catch you alone," Joseph said. "May I come in?"

"Of course. I was just finishing up in here." She looked at him, her eyes wide and green, her hands clasped demurely in front of her neat white apron. Her hair was dressed in two braids and wrapped around her head in the Scandinavian style he found so fetching, and a delicate blush colored her cheeks.

Joseph couldn't believe that she was to be his—that the day would come when Annie Rose Jensen would take his name, that together they would explore the physical joys of love, that every day from then on he would awaken with her beside him. She would make him a home as warm and as inviting as she had made this one, and perhaps one day she would give him a child, as Sarah had given one to Orion.

"I am the luckiest man in the world," he said softly, and advanced to take her in his arms. A tiny frown drew her eyebrows together, and Joseph instantly halted. "Please don't fear me, Annie Rose," he pleaded.

Her brow cleared. "Joseph, I don't." Annie Rose stepped toward him, her hands held out. "I'm just not used to such open affection between a man and a woman. I have seen it only between Jubal and Sweet Water, and I see them so rarely." He reached for her fingers and she held onto him. "Be patient with me," she implored him.

Joseph drew her into his arms. "I will, sweetheart. I'll show you that love can be fun." He had intended to kiss her with all the passion that was pent up in him, but instead, he kept the kiss light and chaste, almost teasing. She responded eagerly, and Joseph knew he could have pressed the kiss further, but he left it at that. "We should go check on Aurora and Thor."

"I'm ready." Annie Rose followed him out into the main room, exchanged her apron for her hat, put an oilskin packet of Sweet Water's medicinal salve in her skirt pocket, and they left.

"I don't like this." Annie Rose examined Thor's umbilical stump, her stomach knotted with worry. She removed the twine that had stopped the bleeding, relieved that the bleeding did not resume, but the jagged edge didn't look right. "I think it might be getting infected."

"Let me see." Joseph hunkered down beside her and squinted at Thor's stomach. "Let's lay him down." Together they maneuvered the colt down, and Joseph frowned. "He should have fought us more." He lifted one of Thor's eyelids and examined the eye, then turned his attention to the stump. "You're right, Annie Rose. Something's wrong. He's not as spunky as a new colt should be." As if to lend weight to his words, Aurora sniffed her baby's head and licked him.

"He was suckling when we approached, so he's not too bad yet." She looked at Joseph, her heart pounding with fear. "But if he stops eating, we may not be able to get him started again."

"I know."

"What are we going to do?"

Joseph rested back on his heels. "I think we should take him to the homestead." He waved toward Aurora and beyond to the grey horse. "All of them."

Annie Rose stared at him. "We can't do that."

"He needs constant watching for a while, Annie Rose. You can't stay up here and nurse him."

"Yes, I can," she stubbornly insisted. "It isn't safe for him and his mama away from here."

"If this little fellow really gets sick, he won't be safe here either," Joseph said gently. "Erik is gone, so the main threat to Aurora is gone, too. All those now at the homestead can be trusted."

"I know Grey Eagle can be, Joseph, but what about Raven's Heart? Yes, he is kind, and honest, but how devout is he when it comes to the spiritual beliefs of the Cheyenne? What will he think when he sees the Golden Mare, and the markings on her colt's coat? However sincere he may be in his feelings of loyalty toward you and your brother, is he possessed of equally sincere beliefs which might lead him to betray us?"

"I don't know," Joseph admitted.

"We can't risk it," Annie Rose said firmly.

"Allow me to fetch Grey Eagle and bring him here. We'll discuss it with him."

Annie Rose nodded. "That's a good idea. I'll stay here." She looked at Thor, who had not tried to regain his feet. Aurora nudged her colt, as if urging him to stand, and Annie Rose's worry grew. "I'll clean the stump and use Sweet Water's salve." She looked up at Joseph as he straightened. "Hurry," she urged.

"I will." He nodded toward the rifle leaning against the

rock face. "I'll leave that with you, and I want you to keep Maggie here, as well. She'll let you know if anyone or anything approaches." He paused, looking down at her, clearly worried.

"Joseph, go. I have lived in these mountains for seven years, and know them well. I'll be fine." Annie Rose smiled in what she hoped was a reassuring manner. Joseph nodded again and took off at a run through the meadow grasses, his moccasined feet making no sound. She watched him scramble up the game trail, marveling at how quickly he could travel when unencumbered by his heavy rifle. He paused at the top of the hill and waved. She waved back, and he was gone.

Although she was surrounded by her beloved animals, Annie Rose felt very alone all of a sudden. She took up the bucket and made her way to the stream, and it occurred to her that Joseph—a man—had become as important to her as her animals were. Annie Rose found that astonishing. Even a month ago, she would have never guessed that any man could capture her heart so completely that she would sorely miss his presence when he'd only been gone for a matter of minutes.

But Joseph Beaudine had. Not only had he captured her heart, but last night she had freely surrendered it to him with her promise to wed him, and now, in paradox, she felt strangely free.

How odd.

Annie Rose had always thought of love as being restrictive, something that required sacrifice. Granted, some sacrifice— or perhaps compromise was a better word—was required whenever two or more people chose to live under the same roof. That had been true even with Thomas and her grandfather. She had never considered the possibility that love between a man and a woman could be joyful and liberating, and the idea was astounding.

She filled the bucket with clean cold water and returned to Thor's side, where she settled into a sitting position. Aurora stood guard over her baby, nickering and tossing her head. The colt had fallen asleep, and Annie Rose caressed the dark, four-pointed star on his small shoulder with gentle fingers. Thor did not stir at her touch, which caused her even more concern.

"Hurry, Joseph," she whispered.

Grey Eagle followed his brother through the forest, amazed at Joseph's endurance. He had just run the entire way to the homestead—from where, Grey Eagle did not know—and now he set a killing pace on the return trip. Joseph had not told him what the emergency was, only that he had to come at once. Grey Eagle had not hesitated, nor had any of the others questioned them. That was one nice thing about working with people who all trusted each other. They'd figure that Joseph had a good reason for whatever he did, and that he'd tell them about it if and when he deemed it necessary.

The brothers ran on, not speaking, until Joseph led Grey Eagle to the top of a hill that dropped off to a rocky cliff. There, Grey Eagle stopped, stunned by the sight before him. He looked down on one of the most beautiful mountain meadows he had ever seen, but there was no time to enjoy the view, for Joseph had started down a steep, barely visible game trail and clearly expected Grey Eagle to follow. He did, wondering again what the hurry was. In the distance, a dog barked excitedly.

At the bottom of the trail, Joseph paused, breathing hard. Maggie ran up to him, overjoyed, whimpering a happy greeting. He patted the dog, then looked at Grey Eagle, his expression deadly serious. "Prepare yourself," he said. "You are about to witness the handiwork of God."

Grey Eagle stared at his brother, puzzled. The handiwork of God? Was Joseph talking about the beauty of the little valley?

Walking now rather than running, Joseph led the way across the meadow. Maggie trotted at his side. Grey Eagle saw a corral fence built close to a rock wall. A grey horse grazed in the meadow a short distance away. In the shadow of the wall, inside the corral, another horse stood, watching them approach, alert, her ears pricked. A golden horse.

The Golden Mare.

Stunned, Grey Eagle stopped, not quite believing what he saw.

"Come, little brother," Joseph said quietly. "There's more."

Mute and obedient, Grey Eagle followed his brother. As they drew close to the corral, he saw Annie Rose sitting on the ground, watching them as intently as the mare did, Joseph's rifle across her lap. Next to her lay a paint foal, a very young foal.

"Aurora foaled yesterday," Joseph explained. "Perhaps obviously, The Paint is the sire."

Aurora neighed a shrill warning as the two men approached the gate.

"She doesn't know you, Grey Eagle," Annie Rose warned. "It might be best if you stayed back."

Grey Eagle stared at the woman sitting so calmly at the feet of a nervous, protective, wild, new-mother mare, and his amazement at the whole situation grew. *The handiwork of God.* Joseph had not exaggerated.

"We'll both stay back, Annie Rose," Joseph said. He closed the gate and secured it. "How is Thor?"

Thor?

As if he had heard Grey Eagle's silent question, Joseph said, "The colt—named for the Norwegian god of thunder."

Annie Rose spoke in a soothing tone, one she might use if speaking to a sick child—or about one. "I cleaned the umbilical stump and coated it with Sweet Water's salve. Later, he stood and suckled, but not for long." She stroked the colt's neck. "See how he accepts my touch? He's weary, Joseph, yet Aurora keeps trying to get him to stand. I'm very concerned."

Joseph turned to Grey Eagle. "We fear he may have the beginnings of a navel infection. I think we should take him to the homestead, where we can watch over him day and night. Annie Rose thinks it too dangerous, for, of course, the mare will have to come as well. Erik, the greatest threat to the safety of the mare, is gone, but Annie Rose worries that Raven's Heart may be torn between his spiritual beliefs regarding the Golden Mare and his loyalty to us. I don't know him well enough to guess where his most powerful feelings would lie. We agreed to seek your advice."

"*My* advice." Grey Eagle leaned on the gate, feeling like a fish out of water. There were forces at play here that he could only imagine. *The handiwork of God.*

"I should tell you about the colt's markings, Eagle," Joseph said. "You can't see them from here, but his left shoulder bears a perfect four-pointed star, and his right side is decorated with a lightning bolt."

Grey Eagle gaped at him.

Joseph nodded. "He is a spirit horse, more powerful even than his mother, I suspect. When word gets out about him, as it most certainly will, both Annie Rose and I fear for the mare and her miraculous colt."

"Aurora's miraculous colt can die of an infection, just as any other foal can," Annie Rose put in, somewhat sharply. "All that spirit stuff is fine and good, I suppose, but I just want to keep Aurora and Thor alive and free." She glared at the brothers. "I'm not certain the best way to achieve that goal is to take them to the homestead, where they will be in great danger of discovery and perhaps even betrayal."

After a moment of silence, Grey Eagle spoke. "Raven's Heart is as close to me as a brother, for his mother was my mother's sister. He respects and adheres to the spiritual teachings of the Cheyenne, but he is no fanatic. I can say with all confidence that he will not betray us. And"——he glanced at Joseph——"I agree with my brother. The colt is not well. He should be brought to the homestead, where we can better watch over him. Spirit animal or not, his young life should not be further jeopardized."

Annie Rose stared at him for a long time, then looked at Joseph, her green eyes shining with trust and love. "It is decided, then," she said softly.

* * *

In Knute's barn, bathed in golden lantern light, Thor rested comfortably on a fresh bed of straw, his mama standing guard over him. Neither animal seemed bothered in the least by the number of people who watched them from behind the stout stall rails. Neither did the grey mare, who nickered contentedly from her neighboring stall.

"*Ja,* the colt, he looks better," Knute commented.

Annie Rose had to agree with her grandfather. What had made the difference, no one knew—Sweet Water's herbal salve, the vigilant care of seven devoted people, the comfort and security of the barn, the simple remedies of mama's milk and nature's own healing. Whatever the reason, Thor's condition was clearly improved, and Annie Rose knew in her heart that a crisis had been averted. She rested her forehead against the top stall rail.

"I'll stay with him tonight," Thomas volunteered. He eyed Annie Rose. "You need some rest, sister."

For the last two nights, Annie Rose had insisted upon sleeping in the barn with her beloved horses. Grey Eagle and Raven's Heart had offered to move from the Army tent they had raised near the smokehouse, just as Joseph and Thomas had begged that she allow them to stay with the horses, but she wouldn't hear of it. In truth, she would have loved to have Joseph stay with her, but felt that was not entirely proper and, no doubt, would place great temptation on them both. Sweet Water had loyally insisted upon sharing the barn with her, to which Annie Rose had finally agreed.

The Cheyenne woman had slept peacefully, secure in the knowledge that the horses would awaken her should any genuine need arise. Not so with Annie Rose. She had awakened at the slightest sound—quiet nickers, the rustling of straw, the most subtle shifting of weight, the gentle sounds of suckling—let alone the outright changing of position in which horses, like all creatures, indulged during the course of a night. As a result, she was exhausted.

She gave her brother a weary, grateful smile. "You may stay with them tonight."

Thomas stood a little taller, his young face flushed with prideful pleasure. "As a precaution, I'll keep Maggie with me, just like you did. Sleep in peace, Annie Rose."

"I will, Thomas. Thank you." She started toward the door, with Joseph at her side.

"I sleep in peace, too," Sweet Water announced.

"You always do," Annie Rose retorted affectionately.

"Not always when my man is away," protested Sweet Water. "But here, with Maggie and horses and Annie Rosie, I sleep good. I sleep good in Norseman's cabin, too." With that, she set off up the incline to the cabin, leaving no doubt in anyone's mind that her destination was the comfortable pile of buffalo robes that had been moved from Thomas's room to the floor in Annie Rose's room.

"That woman, she has the right idea," Knute said. "Good night, all."

A chorus of "good nights" followed Knute as he trailed after Sweet Water. Thomas sprinted to the cabin, Maggie at his heels, and returned in a moment with his arms full of blankets, while Grey Eagle and Raven's Heart made their way to the white tent that gleamed in the dark. Joseph and Annie Rose found themselves unexpectedly and delightfully alone.

"Do you think that was planned?" Joseph asked.

Puzzled, Annie Rose frowned up at him. "Was what planned?"

Joseph drew her near with an arm around her shoulders. "Never mind, sweetheart. You're worn out."

"I *am* tired," she admitted.

"Then I'll keep you up only a little while longer." Joseph led her toward the log bench. "Sit with me for a bit."

"I will sit with you forever."

Joseph laughed. "That's sweet, my dear, but unnecessary. Just for a bit will do tonight." He guided her to a sitting position, then took a seat next to her, very close. Again, he draped his arm around her shoulders.

"Did you want to talk about something?" asked Annie Rose.

"No. I just want to be with you."

She smiled. "Now, *that* is sweet." She leaned her head against his shoulder with a sigh of contentment.

Joseph kissed the top of her head and took one of her hands in his free one. He said nothing, happy with the sense of peace he found in her presence.

"You were right," she said suddenly.

"Of course I was." He raised the small hand he held to his lips for a quick kiss. "About what?"

Annie Rose slapped his thigh with her free hand. "Arrogant rogue."

"That's why you love me."

Surprisingly, Annie Rose grew serious. She straightened, lifting her head from his shoulder, and looked into his eyes. "No, it's not."

Joseph kissed her hand again. "I was teasing, Annie Rose."

She sighed and dropped her gaze. "I'm sorry. I'm too tired to be clever tonight." Then she looked up at him. "You were right about bringing Thor here. It probably saved his life."

"Well, maybe I was right about that, but it doesn't mean you weren't right, too."

"What do you mean?"

He toyed with her fingers. "Aurora and Thor are not safely away. Your fears about bringing them here may yet prove to have merit."

"It won't matter if they do. The important goal was Thor's recovery from his infection. That has been achieved. We will go on from here."

Joseph brought her fingers to his mouth. "Where will we go from here?" he whispered suggestively.

Again, Annie Rose leaned her head against his shoulder. "Don't tease me," she pleaded. "I'm too tired."

"Then just feel." He took her forefinger into his warm, wet mouth.

Annie Rose felt.

He sucked gently on the length of her finger, sending a powerful shudder of desire through her body.

From my finger? she wondered dully, then she quickly grew numb to conscious thought, and her eyes drifted closed.

As if he were enjoying a most delectable feast, Joseph licked, nibbled, and sucked his way up and down all four fingers and the thumb of her hand, then started on the palm. By the time he reached her wrist, she was shaking.

"Imagine my mouth," he whispered, "doing these very things to your lovely neck, Annie Rose." He kissed her palm.

She shuddered again.

"Imagine my mouth on your beautiful breast." He nibbled on her thumb, his mustache tickling her sensitized skin, then drew it into his mouth.

Her nipples tightened, hungry for his touch. She moaned and pressed her head more firmly against his shoulder. She couldn't believe he was touching only her hand.

His erotic whisperings continued. "Imagine my mouth traveling all over your exquisite body, doing just as it is doing now."

As if his words had triggered it, a warm wetness grew in that mysterious, fascinating, woman's place deep within her. Annie Rose could not believe how desperately she wanted Joseph to act on the images he had planted in her mind. Her free hand gripped his thigh. "What are you doing to me?" she whispered.

"Oh, woman, I am telling you some of the ways I will one day love you." At long last, Joseph released her hand. His arm tightened around her shoulders and he cradled the side of her head with his free hand.

Annie Rose cuddled closer to him and tried to calm her breathing. "And will I one day love you the same way?"

To her immense surprise, a shudder rocked Joseph's body. He cleared his throat. "That would be nice."

She placed her hand over his heart. "Then I shall do so." Under her hand, his heart leapt, and his breathing became agitated. Annie Rose felt a surge of feminine power such as she had never known before.

"Do you promise?" he asked hoarsely.

Annie Rose smiled against his shoulder, exhilarated by her effect on him, excited by the truth in her next words. "I promise."

Nineteen

Annie Rose placed her hands on her hips and studied with satisfaction the growing stack of boxes, crates and canvas-wrapped bundles in the barn. A week had passed since that memorable night with Joseph on the bench, and much had been accomplished. Knute announced at breakfast that the new herd of horses had taken well to the training and were ready to serve as pack animals. They would leave for Fort Laramie the next morning, and none too soon, Knute had added, for the aspen in the high country had already begun to turn.

With a sigh, Annie Rose left the shade of the barn and went into the yard. Her gaze fell on the snug dug-out cabin at the top of the rise, the grasses on its sod roof as dried and brown as those on the hill beyond—another indication that fall was on its way. They hadn't left yet, but already the little cabin looked forlorn. A sadness washed over her.

Now that the leaving was upon her, Annie Rose found herself grieving the loss of her life as she had known it. So much had changed in the past few months, and so quickly, that she felt she hadn't had time to adjust, or to prepare for the additional changes that were coming. She remembered how she had felt that day seven long years ago, when Knute had taken her from Baltimore and the only home she had ever known. Then she had been glad to leave, anxious even.

Not so now, for she had been happy here. Perhaps there was no way to ever be fully prepared for the future.

"Annie Rose!"

She turned and saw Joseph wave to her from the far corral. With a smile, she walked to join him. He was inside the corral with Aurora and Thor, leaning on the fence, reaching for her hand, which she gladly gave him.

"You looked so sad a minute ago, honey," he said, lightly squeezing her fingers. "Is everything all right?"

"It will be." She nodded at Thor, who pranced around the corral, trying to get his mother to play with him. "He is doing so well!"

Joseph nodded. "He's completely recovered, and growing stronger every day. The coming journey will be hard for him, but I think he'll be fine."

Another wave of sadness washed over Annie Rose, this one more powerful and more painful than the last. Aurora had grown so comfortable with both Joseph and Grey Eagle that it had been decided that the brothers would take Aurora and Thor, and The Paint, if they could find him, to the Medicine Bow Mountains, close to one hundred miles south of where they were now. They all would travel together as far as the North Laramie River, then Joseph and Grey Eagle would turn south while the others continued on to Fort Laramie. "I wish I could go with Aurora and Thor," Annie Rose said sadly.

"I know how difficult this is for you." Joseph kissed her fingers. "This place Grey Eagle knows of sounds perfect for them, though—exactly what you had in mind."

"If we were already married, I could go with you."

Joseph shook his head. "I'd still think it best for you to go to Laramie and help your grandfather get situated. However, you have *no* idea how much I wish we were already married." He smiled, slowly, wickedly, his teeth even and white under his dark mustache. "Sweet Water would find herself tossed out of your bedroom so quickly, she wouldn't know what happened."

"Joseph!"

"You're so cute when you blush, Annie Rose."

She slapped his hand. "Be off with you!"

Joseph laughed. "Yes, ma'am." He looked toward the other corral, where Grey Eagle and Raven's Heart had just finished saddling their horses. Grace, already saddled, waited patiently near the barn, her tail flicking against a few annoyingly persistent late-season flies. "Knute's horses drifted to the north end of the valley. It shouldn't take too long to round them up. I fully expect we'll be back by noon or shortly thereafter."

"All right." Annie Rose pressed against the fence and rose up on her toes, intending to plant a kiss on Joseph's cheek. He turned his head at the last second, and her mouth connected with his. When her initial surprise faded, she was glad he had moved. "Rogue," she whispered against his mouth.

"Yes, ma'am," he whispered back.

"Do you intend to kiss that woman all day?" Grey Eagle called. He and Raven's Heart, both mounted now, waited with Grace.

"I'm coming, I'm coming." Joseph winked at Annie Rose, passed through and secured the corral gate, then hurried to join his brother. He vaulted into the saddle, waved at her, and the three men rode off.

Annie Rose trudged toward the cabin, where she and Sweet Water would soon be busy with the stack of willow branches they had collected the day before from along the stream bed. Cages were needed in order to transport the chickens, and she and the Cheyenne woman planned to work on those this morning.

Thomas passed her, carrying a bucket of ash from the fireplace. "Oh, thank you for cleaning that out for me, Thomas," she said.

"I'll just have to do it again tomorrow before we leave," he grumbled. "You know how Gramps is about leaving everything clean." He shook his head in disgust. "Even when we might never come back."

"I know, brother," she said soothingly "But the ash was high, and I plan to roast a big venison haunch this afternoon." She looked closely at Thomas. Was the leaving of the valley hard on him, too? He didn't act as if it were. More than anything, he seemed eager to go. He had found the routines of the soldiers at Fort Laramie fascinating, and he still spoke of the Hunter's infant son with wonder. Thomas was probably excited about the opportunity to see something of the world he'd been hidden from since he was a small boy. "Would you like to brush Thor down?" she asked, knowing how much her brother loved the colt.

"Would I!" Then Thomas hesitated. "Will Aurora let me?"

"She will if you take him in the barn and leave her outside. Shall I help you?"

"I think I can do it." Thomas's mood had definitely lifted. "I'll yell if I need help."

"All right."

Thomas took a few steps, then stopped and turned back to her, his expression very serious. "Do you think he's still looking for us?"

"Who, Thomas?"

"Our father."

Annie Rose blinked, then let out a thoughtful sigh. "I don't know. It's hard to believe that he would be, after all this time." She spread her hands. "Gramps did such a good job of hiding us that perhaps our father thinks we're dead. If not, and he is still looking for us, what can he do if he finds us? We are grown now. He can't force either of us to go back."

"Do you think Gramps is worried about him?"

"Not anymore."

"Why not?"

"For the same reason I'm not—the Beaudine brothers. Do you think they would let anyone hurt us?"

Thomas slowly smiled. "No."

Annie Rose smiled, too. "Neither do I. We're safe now, Thomas. The truth will come out about my existence, and all the hiding will be over. I, for one, am glad."

"So am I, sister." He ducked his head shyly, then looked at her again. "I'm also glad you're going to wed up with Joe. He's a good man." With that, Thomas turned away and hurried toward the barn, taking the bucket of ash with him.

" 'Wed up with Joe'?" she repeated in a whisper. Obviously, her brother had been spending too much time with Jubal lately; his grammar was beginning to suffer. Annie Rose shaded her eyes, watching Thomas closely. Why didn't he take the bucket on to the manure pile? She hoped he didn't intend to take the still-warm ash into the straw-filled barn.

Thomas didn't. He set the bucket down outside the barn door and disappeared inside, no doubt eager to spend some time with Thor. Certain that her responsible brother would dispose of the ash later, Annie Rose continued on up the incline. Knute came out of the smokehouse just then and fell in step with her.

"Most of the packing is done, *datter*. I want to work on the smokehouse roof and a few other things, just to tighten them up. The winter will be hard on the buildings with no one here to tend to them." An expression of sadness flashed across his old face.

"Gramps, are you certain you want to leave?" Annie Rose stopped walking and placed her hand on Knute's forearm. He halted, also. "We've made it through seven long winters here. We can survive one more."

"No, no, it is best, what we have decided."

Annie Rose bit her bottom lip, not certain how to ask what she needed to ask.

"What is it, *datter?*"

She looked into her grandfather's old eyes, saw the weariness and age there. "You love this valley, Gramps. If we leave, you may never see it again. Are you certain you wouldn't rather stay here?" She could not add the words *to die*.

Knute's expression softened with love. "No, child. If I do not again see this valley before I die, still I will die a happy man, knowing that you and Thomas will be safe and well cared for." He looked around the homestead and shrugged. "I'll just come back as a spirit and truly haunt the place."

Although her eyes had filled with tears, Annie Rose could not keep from smiling. "I love you, Gramps."

Knute pulled her into a tight embrace. "And I love you, Annie Rose. Now, is there any tea left? I need some fortification before I go to work on that smokehouse roof."

Two hours later, Annie Rose critically eyed the four cages she and Sweet Water had fashioned from the pliable willow branches. "I think these will be enough," she said to her friend.

"How many chickens?"

"Fourteen, including one rooster."

Sweet Water shook her head. "Bad rooster need his own cage. I make small cage for him, you make meal."

Annie Rose smiled at her friend's assessment of their cranky rooster. "All right." She slipped off her bench and stretched, then took two of the finished cages off the table. "This will be a strange meal," she warned. "I'm trying to use all the food that won't travel well."

Sweet Water shrugged. "It's all right."

The sound of approaching horses reached Annie Rose's ears; they were coming fast. Maggie started barking. Could the men be back so soon? Perhaps the horses had not been as far away as Joseph thought. With a happy smile, she went to the open door, still carrying the cages, and stepped outside.

Her heart stopped.

Erik rode into the yard at a gallop, scattering frantic chickens, followed by several men on horseback.

Annie Rose turned horrified eyes to the corral where Aurora had been earlier. Relief shot through her when she did not see the mare, but at best, that only bought them a little time. "My God, Erik," she whispered. "What have you done?" She flung the cages away and hurried back inside.

"What is it?" Sweet Water asked.

"Trouble," Annie Rose answered grimly. She snatched Knute's rifle from its place over the door and moved out onto the top stone step, where Sweet Water joined her. Annie Rose took quick stock of the situation.

Erik and six other mounted men milled about in the yard. She recognized Abby Baines, Painted Davy Sikes, and Hank Westin. The other three were Indians—Sioux, she thought—perhaps recruited from those who loitered around Fort Laramie hoping for work or a handout.

Joseph, Grey Eagle, and Raven's Heart were not due back for at least another hour.

Knute was on the roof of the cabin, where he had been securing one of the two chimneys for the winter, no doubt armed with nothing more than his knife.

Thomas was still in the barn with Thor—and perhaps Aurora. He would be as lightly armed as his grandfather, but with more at hand to use as weapons, such as the pitchfork and shovel.

Maggie raced in and out among the riders, barking furiously, exciting the horses, causing the men to swear. *Good job, Maggie!*

Annie Rose and Sweet Water had one rifle and a few knives and forks at their disposal. That was it.

Two women, a boy, an aging man with a bad heart—all of them poorly armed—and one feisty dog against seven ruthless, well-armed men.

They were in real trouble.

"We've come for the Golden Mare!" Erik shouted. "That's all we want! Take us to her, Annabella, and no one will get hurt!"

"Never!" Annie Rose cried, praying that it would never occur to her cousin that the mare they sought was as close as the barn, directly behind where he and his cohorts now stood.

"How dare you, Erik?" Knute shouted from the roof, his voice shaking with rage. "How dare you betray your family to scum like Abby Baines?"

"I told you long ago I wanted the mare, Gramps! Annabella had no right to keep her for herself! It's her fault things have come to this, hers and yours!"

"Where's Beaudine?" Abby demanded.

"He didn't come back with us," Knute responded.

"Yes, he did!" shouted Erik. "I saw him leave Fort Laramie with you."

"He met up with his brother, that Cheyenne, a day out of Laramie. They rode off together."

Annie Rose was impressed with her grandfather's ingenuity. There was a possibility Joseph and Grey Eagle would return in time; it would be to their advantage if Erik and Baines didn't know of that possibility.

"But he's sweet on Annabella," Erik argued.

"Not anymore," Annie Rose snapped.

"Gawddamn it, Jensen, the damned dog bit my horse!" Painted Davy Sikes pulled his pistol. "I'm gonna shoot it!"

Before Annie Rose had a chance to position the heavy rifle to fire, Erik shouted, "No! We agreed no one would get hurt, and that includes the dog." He climbed down from his saddle and caught the snarling Maggie by the scruff of the neck, then dragged her toward the barn.

Annie Rose's eyes widened in horror. If Aurora was in there—and there was nowhere else she could be, unless she truly was a spirit animal and had spirited herself away—Erik would discover her.

Her cousin disappeared inside the barn.

Knute scrambled off the sod roof and came into the yard.

Annie Rose started down the incline toward the barn, lifting the heavy rifle as she went.

Shouts came from inside the barn—Thomas and Erik—then a triumphant yell.

A horse screamed. Thomas yelled. Maggie barked.

A second later, a horse burst out the side door of the barn into the corral closest to the cabin, running in a frantic circle along the fence. Annie Rose stopped and stared. The mare resembled Aurora, but there were huge splotches of grey on her golden coat. Maggie howled from inside the barn.

Erik ran out into the yard. "I found her! I found her! That's her!" He pointed toward the mare in the corral. "And there's a foal!"

"Jump the fence, Aurora," Annie Rose whispered. "Run." But she knew the mare wouldn't, not without her colt.

"You won't have that mare!" Knute yelled as he ran toward the corral.

Abby Baines turned in his saddle, a malicious smile on his bearded face, and without hesitation, fired his pistol.

Knute stumbled and fell, clutching his leg.

"No!" Thomas's cry rang from the barn door.

A cold fury swept through Annie Rose at the sight of her grandfather lying on the ground, his blood seeping into the dirt, and that fury overcame any shock and horror she felt. She raised the rifle to her shoulder, took quick aim, and fired. Abby Baines fell from the saddle, away from her, out of her sight. The recoil of the rifle caused the butt to slam painfully into her shoulder, numbing her arm, but she held onto the weapon, although there was no means at hand to reload it. She glanced at the barn, saw Thomas's scared, bloody face at the door, motioned him back inside, and ran toward Knute.

An eerie silence fell over the people in the yard, broken only by Maggie's frustrated howling. Annie Rose dropped to her knees at her grandfather's side, thankful to see that he lived, was still conscious. Blood flowed from an ugly wound in his left thigh. Annie Rose tore her apron off and wrapped it around Knute's leg, then looked up and was stunned to see Erik at Knute's other side, a horrified expression on his bearded face. Sweet Water stood protectively over them, brandishing a wicked-looking knife.

Then Abby came from behind his horse, blood running down one arm, his hate-filled eyes spitting fury. "Get that mare," he snarled. Hank Westin and one of the Sioux men moved toward the corral. "And get those gawddamned women." With a grin, Painted Davy stepped down from his saddle. The remaining two Sioux followed him.

Erik jumped to his feet and hurried toward Abby. "No!

You said all we came for was the mare. Leave the women be."

Using his uninjured arm, Abby backhanded Erik with such force that the younger man was knocked to the ground. Abby kicked him viciously. "Did you really think I'd leave that yellow-haired bitch behind? My dick's been itchin' for her since that night those damned Beaudines kept me away from her. I'll have her now, for as long as I want her, and she'll pay dearly for puttin' a hole in me. The others can have the squaw." He kicked Erik again, then once more before he turned away. Erik groaned and lay still.

Annie Rose scrambled to her feet and crouched in a defensive stance, holding the empty rifle like a club, regretting like hell that she wasn't wearing her trousers; they gave her so much more freedom to move. Sweet Water stood at her side, knife poised and ready, a determined expression on her brown face. Knute pulled himself to a sitting position, but the nasty wound in his leg prevented him from rising farther. Painted Davy and the two braves advanced upon them.

"You stay away from my sister!" Thomas screamed as he ran full speed from the barn with a shovel in his hands. He swung at one of the braves, striking him in the leg. The brave swore and struck out at Thomas, connecting with his chin. Before the boy could fall, Abby Baines grabbed him from behind with an arm around his neck and held him securely. "Shut up, boy," he growled.

"Get to the house, Annie Rose," Knute ordered in a low voice.

"I'm not leaving you, Gramps."

"They don't want me. For God's sake, do as I say."

Annie Rose glanced down at her grandfather, saw his hand closed around the hilt of his hunting knife. Knowing he could protect himself somewhat with the weapon, she started backing toward the cabin. Sweet Water stayed close beside her. Aurora's furious screams came from the corral, punctuated by men's frightened curses and shouts, and Annie Rose took grim pleasure in knowing that Abby Baines had underestimated all of the females he sought to capture today.

"Don't let 'em get to the cabin!" Baines shouted.

Painted Davy motioned with one hand, and he and the braves rushed them.

With all her might, Annie Rose swung the rifle butt at Painted Davy. He ducked away, so she missed his head, but she caught him full on the shoulder. Her whole body was jarred from the impact. He swore viciously and jerked the rifle from her grasp, flung it away, and grabbed her arm, pulling her against his rank-smelling body.

One of the Sioux braves cried out and fell to the ground. Annie Rose caught a glimpse of her grandfather's knife protruding from the man's stomach. The other brave tried to stop the flow of blood from the wound Sweet Water had inflicted on his arm.

Annie Rose deliberately went limp in Painted Davy's arms, which elicited a string of curses from the man. She searched under her skirts and pulled her knife free from its moccasin, then, in one swift move, straightened and struck behind her, burying the blade in Painted Davy's buttock.

He screamed and released her. Still clutching her now bloody knife, Annie Rose raced for the cabin, glad to see that Sweet Water was just ahead of her. She darted through the door, Sweet Water pushed it closed, and together the two women forced the heavy bar into place just as the brave with the wounded arm threw himself against the solid wood. Abby's curse echoed across the homestead.

Quickly, the women closed and barred the stout shutters Knute had built for each of the four windows in the cabin— two in the great room, a very small one in each bedroom. The sound of breaking glass could be heard as the frustrated men outside tried to find a way in, but Knute's sturdy, well-planned defenses held.

Annie Rose leaned against the door, panting. She looked at Sweet Water, unable to tell in the dim light if her friend had been injured. "Are you hurt?"

Sweet Water shook her head as she wiped her knife blade on the damp cloth used for washing dishes. "You?"

"No." Annie Rose cleaned her own blade, then peered out the rifle slot in one of the shutters. Knute still sat on the ground, with Thomas now at his side. Erik had rolled over, but had not risen from his prone position. The brave so grievously wounded by Knute's knife lay on the ground, his hands clasped on the bloody hilt that still protruded from his stomach, shifting about in obvious agony. Abby Baines was again in the saddle, shouting orders, insisting that all of the men help control Aurora. Finally, they dragged the kicking mare from the corral, but it took four men with ropes to do it. She stood exhausted, her head hanging, her sides heaving, blood trailing down her coat from several small wounds. Annie Rose's heart broke at the sight. Thor had come from the barn, searching for his mother, and stood in the corral. At least she thought it was Thor; the young horse looked very strange—dark all over, not like the paint he was. Annie Rose prayed they ignored the colt.

Suddenly, Baines stared off across the pasture to the north. The other men did likewise.

"Let's ride!" Abby shouted.

Hope swelled in Annie Rose's heart. Were the Beaudines and Raven's Heart returning?

"Who's coming?" Hank Westin shouted as he tried to catch his spooked horse.

"Probably Beaudine, gawddamn it," answered Abby. "The bitch lied. Get that mare out of here!"

"What about the foal?"

"Leave it! It'll just slow us down!"

"But what about the women?" Painted Davy whined. "I want that one who stuck me."

Even through the rifle slot, Annie Rose could see that blood ran down the back of the man's leg.

"There's no time, you idiot!" Abby shouted. "The mare is more important. There'll always be women to take." He urged his horse toward the cabin, coming up to the door at a trot.

Annie Rose could no longer see what he was doing. She backed away from the shuttered window, tightly clutching her knife, straining to hear.

"What he do?" Sweet Water asked in a worried whisper.

"I don't know, but I don't like it." Annie Rose heard a tinny bumping sound against the door. "Oh, my God," she whispered in horror. "The lantern."

From the yard, Thomas cried out a warning, a protest. A strange whooshing sound came from the door, and smoke curled in under it.

Annie Rose stared at Sweet Water. "He used the oil in the lantern to start the cabin on fire."

"Burn in hell, bitch!" Abby shouted from outside. "I'll send your lover to join you as soon as I can! I'm sick of those gawddamned Beaudines interferin' with my plans!"

Sweet Water hurried into Annie Rose's bedroom. Annie Rose followed her and stood on tiptoe to look out the rifle slot in the high window shutters, trying to see through the smoke outside.

What she saw terrified her.

Abby Baines rode away from the cabin, laughing like a maniac. He said something to Painted Davy, accepted that man's pistol, then turned and took aim at Thomas and Knute, who still huddled together on the ground. Thomas threw himself over his grandfather, knocked Knute back, covered him as best he could. Baines fired, laughed again, and kicked his horse to a gallop, following on the heels of the rest of his men. Because of the ropes around her neck, Aurora had no choice but to run with them.

Through the thickening smoke, Annie Rose desperately looked back at her brother and grandfather. Both lay still. Erik had pulled himself up on one elbow. Thor thrust his nose through the corral fence, clearly distressed. Like a banshee, Maggie still howled from the barn. Annie Rose realized that Thomas must have tied the poor dog for her own protection.

"Annie Rosie, the fire grows bad." Sweet Water's calm voice pierced the horror that gripped her mind.

"Yes," she muttered, turning away from the window that was too small for either woman to fit through. She took a deep breath, and started coughing violently. The smoke was almost as heavy inside now as it had appeared to be outside.

She and Sweet Water were in trouble. Again.

Newly energized, Annie Rose ran back to the great room. The smoke was very thick, and flames licked around the edges of the door. She realized in an instant that no matter how many men outside were still alive—and able to move— no matter how many buckets of water they could rush from the well, no matter how desperately they tried, the fire would win the battle for the cabin.

She looked wildly about. There wasn't much time. What could she save?

Thank God the books, so treasured by her grandfather, were safely wrapped in canvas and rope and stored in the barn. Her frantic gaze fell on Knute's rocking chair—one of the few pieces of furniture they had planned to take with them. There was no way to save it now, nor the beautifully carved chest that had come from Norway.

"Annie Rosie!" Sweet Water's worried voice came from the bedroom.

Annie Rose saw Joseph's bed, saw the reinforced leather bag that held his treasured papers and pencils. She grabbed that, and the *parfleche* he used as a pillow, then ran to the doomed chest and yanked open a drawer. Her grandfather's pewter drinking cups nestled in their ancient bed of velvet, and she snatched them up and stuffed them into Joseph's *parfleche*. She seized the *rosemaled* tankard off its shelf, and finally, struggled with the small keg of brandy Jubal had brought as a gift in happier times. Then she lurched through her bedroom door, struggling to breathe.

Sweet Water slammed the door closed and dropped the bar into place, as if the stout piece of wood could hold a raging fire at bay. Once again, Annie Rose was grateful for that door.

She dropped her treasures on the bed, picked out the keg of brandy and handed it to Sweet Water, then hurried to the window and opened the shutter. Through the broken window panes came a blast of heated air. She grimaced when it hit her face, then she took the keg from Sweet Water and threw it out the window. Annie Rose slammed the shutters against the heat and turned to face her friend, who looked at her as if she had gone mad.

Perhaps she had. She shrugged. "Gramps so relished that brandy. If he is still alive, and if the keg didn't break when it hit the ground, and if we don't get out of here, he will have something with which to toast our memory." She grabbed Sweet Water's hands. "And bless him for building that blasted door. It's bought us a little more time."

Joseph rode as if the demons of hell chased him. However, he feared they waited for him ahead, at the homestead.

He, Grey Eagle, and Raven's Heart had been on their way back with Knute's horses when they heard the first shots. Now, after hearing several more shots, an ominous cloud of black smoke curled up to stain the afternoon sky—too much smoke for a cook fire, too dense a smoke for a grass fire. A building burned at the homestead. Joseph did not dare guess which one. Instead, he bent lower over Grace's neck and urged her on.

As they drew nearer, Joseph saw a group of riders racing away from the homestead, toward the south end of the valley. He also saw that the cabin was in flames. His heart stopped. *What the hell had happened?*

A single name slammed into his brain. *Erik.* Erik had happened. *And Baines.*

Grey Eagle pointed in the direction of the fleeing riders.

"Leave them!" Joseph shouted. "We have to find out what happened!"

They tore into the yard and pulled their mounts to a stop. Joseph leapt from the saddle, his primed rifle at his hip. His military training took over, and he approached the scene as he would a battlefield, which the yard evidently had been not very long ago.

The cabin was engulfed in flames. The dried grasses of the sod on the roof had caught fire; the ravenous flames now covered the entire roof and marched up the hill beyond, creating an unearthly roaring sound. A small keg—the brandy keg?—slowly rolled down the incline toward the barn.

Knute and Thomas huddled together in the yard, both battered and bloody, but both still alive. The white cloth wrapped around the Norseman's thigh was blood-soaked, and Thomas was covered with dirt and bleeding from cuts on his face. Erik crawled toward his grandfather and cousin, clearly hurt himself. Maggie's frenzied barks came from the barn.

Where was Annie Rose? Where was Sweet Water?

"Where are the women?" Joseph shouted as he ran toward the injured men.

Mutely, Thomas pointed toward the cabin. Tears streaked the filth on his face.

Joseph staggered to a stop, and his rifle slipped from suddenly nerveless fingers. He stared in horror at the engulfed cabin.

"Annie Rose!"

Twenty

Joseph lunged toward the cabin. It took both Grey Eagle and Raven's Heart to hold him back. He knew there was no hope of the women coming out of that conflagration alive, but still he fought to go to them.

"Joseph!" Grey Eagle locked his arms around Joseph's shoulders. "Brother, it's too late!" His voice cracked with emotion—fear, rage, sorrow. Joseph sagged in his brother's arms, and, as they watched, the roof over the great room collapsed with a roar, sending up a shower of debris and ash.

"Annie Rose!" Joseph cried brokenly. He felt as if his heart was being torn from his chest.

No longer able to bear the sight of the triumphant flames, Joseph glanced down at the Jensen men. Why had none of them tried to save the women? Even now, they didn't seem very concerned or upset. Granted, they were all injured, but still . . . he would have died, gladly, trying to save Annie Rose.

Thomas struggled to his feet. With the back of one hand, he wiped at the blood that trickled from his cut mouth. "Come with me, Joe," he croaked, swaying slightly.

"What?"

Thomas grabbed his hand and pulled him in the direction of the cabin. "Come."

Grey Eagle released him, and Joseph followed the stumbling boy, who guided him not to the cabin, but to the path that led to the bathing pool. "Thomas, where are we going?"

"Come," Thomas gasped, tugging on Joseph's hand. Past the pool they went, then they cut back to the right, toward the base of the hill that rose above the cabin. Thomas fought his way through a thick clump of brush and dropped to his knees in front of a small pile of rocks under an overhanging ledge. He grabbed a rock and tossed it away, then another.

Numb and beyond feeling, Joseph stared at him, wondering if the boy had been addled by the horrors he had witnessed this day. Thomas paused and glared at him over his shoulder, then, with an exasperated motion of his hand, indicated that Joseph was to help him. Understanding why wasn't important. Suddenly, Joseph couldn't wait to throw those rocks away, to do something, anything, to try to ease the unbearable pain that threatened to overwhelm him. He crouched down and eagerly grabbed a rock.

In a matter of minutes, a wooden wall was revealed, perhaps three feet across and the same distance up and down, lodged solidly in the earth. The outline of a smaller door could be seen, complete with aging leather hinges on one side.

"Indian tunnel," Thomas explained breathlessly.

A wild hope flared through Joseph's chest. Could the women have possibly escaped the inferno?

Thomas continued. "Gramps dug it out that first year we were here, said that although we were getting along with the Sioux and the Cheyenne then, one never knew when things might turn sour."

"Or when Abby Baines might show up," Joseph added. With renewed strength, he shoved and tossed the last of the rocks out of the way. Using his knife, he dug out the dirt-filled cracks around the door, and saw that the leather hinges were cracked and disintegrating.

"We've never had to use it," said Thomas. "The last time we checked it was in the spring—I hope there haven't been any cave-ins."

Joseph wrestled the door out of its frame—tearing the old hinges in the process—and pushed it aside. A rush of dank, damp air came out of the pitch-black tunnel that looked much too small for anyone to crawl through. He caught a scent of smoke, but could not tell if it came from the tunnel or was that which permeated the outside air. Had there been a cave-in? Were the women trapped? Had they been overcome by smoke and, even now, did they lay unconscious somewhere along the route of that narrow excavation?

"Annie Rose!" Thomas called. "Sweet Water!"

Both Thomas and Joseph listened intently.

"Toe-moss?" The curiously accented word seemed to come from very far away.

"Sweet Water!" Joseph shouted joyously. He tore his hat off and leaned closer to the opening. "Is Annie Rose with you? Can you see daylight? Have you run into any barricades?"

"We come, Joseph."

He glanced at Thomas, who flashed him a wide grin. The boy's teeth looked startlingly white against the dirt and blood that covered his face. Unable to contain himself, Joseph grabbed Thomas and gave him a quick, hard hug. "They live," he whispered thankfully, tears pricking his eyelids. "Your grandfather is a wise and clever man."

Thomas patted his shoulder and wearily leaned against him for a moment.

Grey Eagle pushed his way through the brush. "The Norseman told us of the tunnel." He crouched down and peered past Joseph to the dark opening in the earth.

"They're coming," Joseph assured him. Now the sounds of the slowly advancing women could be heard. Something materialized from the depths of the tunnel, and Joseph recognized the red blanket that had been folded at the foot of Annie Rose's bed. When he pulled it out, he realized something was wrapped in the blanket, and he passed the bundle to Grey Eagle with care.

Next he saw a hand, then another, and Sweet Water inched out of the darkness. Joseph eagerly reached for her, held tightly to her hands as he guided her into the daylight, held her briefly before helping her stand. She was filthy—her doe-

Jessica Wulf

skin dress covered with damp dirt, her face smeared with soot—but she smiled broadly and drew Thomas into a quick hug before she allowed Grey Eagle to assist her through the brush.

"I'm here, Annie Rose," Joseph called. "Come to me, honey."

"I'm coming." Her voice sounded weary and breathless, but it was the sweetest sound he had ever heard. Another bundle appeared, and Joseph was startled to recognize his *parfleche*. He pulled it out and reached for her again. Instead of touching her hand, as he longed to do, another item was pressed toward him, the leather bag which held his papers and pencils. Deeply touched that she had saved that for him, he handed it to Thomas, then at last he saw his beloved.

Like Sweet Water, Annie Rose was covered with dirt and soot, but she was alive, and his heart sang at the sight of her. Joseph practically dragged her from the lifesaving tunnel and carried her up with him as he stood. He held her, one hand at the back of her head, his other arm tight around her waist. She clung to him.

Joseph could not speak. He still had not recovered from the horror of believing her trapped in the fire, and to hold her warm and wonderfully alive body against him now was overwhelming.

Thomas managed to get to his feet. Joseph reached out and pulled the boy into their embrace.

"Gramps?" Annie Rose whispered.

"He's alive," Thomas and Joseph said in unison.

Annie Rose sagged against Joseph, her relief evident. "I saw Baines shoot at you, Thomas, just as he rode out. I feared . . ."

"He missed," Thomas assured her.

"Erik?"

Thomas's young voice turned deadly cold. "He lives."

"Let's go," Joseph suggested. He led the way through the brush, holding branches out of Annie Rose's way. Maggie came tearing around the boulder near the bathing pool, and her frantic panting turned to whimpering cries of joy.

Annie Rose fell to her knees and gathered the dog close. "My brave girl," she crooned. "It's all right."

After a moment, she allowed Joseph to help her up, and they hurried back to the yard. Grey Eagle and Raven's Heart had placed Knute in a sitting position against the barn wall, and the old man reached for Annie Rose with eager hands. Again, she knelt, and they embraced, holding each other close.

Another section of the cabin roof collapsed, drawing the attention of all. Surprisingly, the fire had died down considerably, before it had a chance to consume the outer bedroom walls. Joseph realized that the sod roof had helped smother the flames when it fell in. The front part of the great room had been completely destroyed, but it was possible that some things could be salvaged. Thank God Knute's treasured books were safely stored in the barn.

Joseph watched dispassionately as Erik struggled to his feet. The man stood alone in the center of the yard, facing them. His red beard was caked with dried blood, and he held himself stiffly, bent slightly to one side at the waist, one arm wrapped around his middle, the other hanging down. His breathing seemed labored. Erik was injured, perhaps badly.

He stared at the group of people near the barn with no expression on his face—not defiance, not regret, no sign even of the physical discomfort he surely had to feel. No one spoke, and the silence grew long.

Finally, Knute cleared his throat. "Are you hurt, Erik?"

Apparently surprised by the question, Erik shook his head. Then his features twisted with anguish, and his haunted gaze shifted from Knute to Annie Rose. "I'm so sorry," he whispered.

With a feral cry of rage, Thomas raced across the yard and hurled himself at his cousin. They both tumbled to the ground.

"How could you?" Thomas screamed. "How could you

bring them here?" He swung at Erik with more intent than with actual results.

"Thomas, no!" Knute shouted.

Erik made no attempt to defend himself from his cousin's flailing fists. Joseph hurriedly pulled Thomas away, while Grey Eagle helped Erik to a sitting position. One of Thomas's strikes had apparently found its target, for fresh blood trailed down into Erik's beard from the corner of his mouth.

"I just wanted . . . the mare," Erik mumbled. "Baines promised . . . no one would get hurt." He glanced up at Joseph. "You were right about him."

Joseph took no pleasure from that. He only wished Erik had heeded his warnings.

"You could not know the mare was here," Knute said sharply. "What did you think to do?"

Erik dropped his gaze.

"You were going to force Annie Rose to lead you and Baines to the mare, weren't you?" Joseph asked, his jaw tight. He still held Thomas, and could feel the boy's body tense, as his own did.

"We were going to sell the Golden Mare for as much as we could get—in cash or trade goods—and split the profit," Erik explained desperately. "I needed a stake for California."

"California?" Knute repeated.

"To start over. It was obvious I couldn't stay here any longer."

"Do you realize the price your family would have paid for your stake, Erik?" Knute demanded.

Erik lowered his head.

Knute glanced at Annie Rose, who sat at his side, holding one of his hands, then back at Erik. "The only way Annie Rose would have revealed the whereabouts of the mare was if Baines threatened someone she loves. Only for us would she have given up the mare, even though it would have broken her heart. Then, when he had what he wanted, do you know what Baines would have done to your cousin? Do you know that most likely he would have killed all of us? Do you know that he would have killed you?"

"I know!" Erik screamed. "I know!" He buried his face in his hands. His voice fell to a whimper. "I know."

"Then let us hope you do not ever forget." Knute lapsed into a weary silence.

Again, Joseph's military training came to the fore. "How seriously is everyone injured?" He released his grip on Thomas's shoulders. "Thomas?"

"Not bad," Thomas said, glaring at Erik. "I only got hit a couple of times."

"Sweet Water?"

"No hurt. Just dirty."

"Annie Rose?"

"I'm not hurt, either. Gramps has a serious bullet wound in his thigh, and he admits that he had another of his spells a few minutes ago, but it passed."

"I think Erik may have some broken ribs," Grey Eagle commented from his position at Erik's side. Erik did not respond in any way.

"Baines kicked him," Annie Rose put in. "Several times, hard."

With Thomas on his heels, Joseph crossed the yard and hunkered down in front of Knute and Annie Rose. "More than anything, I want to go after them," he said. "I want to kill Baines with my own hands and bring that mare back to her colt." He waved a hand toward the corral, where Thor waited by the fence, neighing piteously for his mother. Joseph placed his hand over Annie Rose's and Knute's joined ones, and looked into his beloved's eyes. He steeled himself against what he might find in Annie Rose's expression as he spoke his next words. "But I think we need to get your grandfather and Erik to Fort Laramie first. They both need medical attention."

The only emotion that appeared on Annie Rose's face was grief. "I agree with you," she said quietly. "Their well-being is more important."

Relieved, Joseph shifted his full attention to Knute. "Is there any possible way we can see to the wounded, get the horses loaded and packed, be on our way, and make it through that rock canyon pass before dark?"

Pensively, Knute looked up at the sky. "It's after noon already. No, we won't make it by nightfall."

"I don't want to try it in the dark," said Joseph. "Not with two seriously injured men and a bunch of heavily loaded and newly trained pack animals."

"No," Knute agreed.

"Then we'll get you and Erik as comfortable as possible, and stay here tonight. In the morning, with any luck, the ruins of the cabin will have cooled enough for us to salvage whatever is left. We'll pack and leave."

Knute nodded. "*Ja,* your plan, it is a good one. And we will have to see to the colt."

At his words, Annie Rose looked at Thor, but Joseph could not take his gaze from her. Tears formed in her eyes, her beautiful eyes that appeared so green in her dirty face.

"One of our own mares foaled earlier this summer," Annie Rose said. "She may have enough milk for two. I know it's a long shot, but we can try Thor with her. If she won't take him, I'll bottle-feed him goat's milk."

Joseph nodded. "I know which mare you mean. We'll get her and her filly into the corral with Thor right away." He straightened and gestured toward the strangely dirty colt. "What happened to him?"

"Ashes," Thomas answered.

"Ashes?" Annie Rose echoed.

Joseph looked at the boy, as did everyone else.

Thomas shrugged. "As soon as I realized who'd come, I took the bucket of ash I had cleared from the fireplace and covered Thor's markings. I didn't have time to cover all of Aurora. I wanted to make her appear to be a grey." He looked at Annie Rose, his eyes filled with sorrow. "I'm sorry, sister."

"Oh, Thomas." Annie Rose got to her feet and drew her

ash-covered brother into her arms. "You were *so* clever! There's nothing to be sorry for. If Baines had seen those markings, he would have taken Thor, too." Then she set him back and frowned. "But I saw you set the bucket of ash down outside the barn."

"I sneaked it in the door when everyone was watching Erik yell at you."

Annie Rose stared at him in wonder. "You are also very brave. Joseph was right—you have become a man."

Thomas turned to Joseph and gaped. "You said that?"

Joseph shrugged. "Something awful close to that, and I meant it, too. Your sister is right, Thomas. You did yourself proud today. I'd be pleased to have you at my side in times of trouble. You're a man who can be counted on when the going gets rough."

"*Ja,* you are, grandson," Knute added. "I'm proud of you."

Thomas beamed.

Knute looked up at Annie Rose. "You did yourself proud, too, *datter,* just as Sweet Water did. You women bought enough time for the Beaudines and Raven's Heart to get back here."

Annie Rose brushed his words of praise aside. "We all worked together, Gramps. I want to doctor that leg of yours, then see to Erik."

Joseph looked over his shoulder at Erik. The young man had not moved. He still sat in the dirt at Grey Eagle's feet, his chin slumped down on his chest.

"We'll make up beds in the barn," Annie Rose announced. "Joseph, there's a bucket in the barn, and another at the well. Would you mind bringing me some water from the hottest part of the bathing pool?"

"Not at all. Eagle, give me a hand, will you?"

Grey Eagle nodded. The men collected the buckets and set off for the pool.

When they were out of earshot of the rest of the party, Grey Eagle said, "Raven's Heart and I could go after Baines."

"Thanks, little brother; I thought of that." Joseph shook his head. "But I think we need you here, at least until we get packed up and out of the valley. The trip through that rock canyon is going to be difficult. Perhaps after that you can trail them." He stopped at the side of the pool and stared into the inviting waters. Here, it was so peaceful, in the little glade where he had once dreamed of sharing the warm waters of the bathing pool with Annie Rose. Here, it was difficult to believe that such awful violence had transpired just a short distance away. Joseph shrugged away the thought. "I don't think we're going to have any trouble finding Baines," he said to his brother, "no matter how long it takes to get after him. He'll spread the word about the mare so he can get the best price for her. I wouldn't be surprised if he arranges to hold an auction."

"Which could lead to war between the Sioux and the Cheyenne, because both tribes are going to want her," Grey Eagle commented soberly. "At any price."

"I know, Eagle. I know."

Annie Rose sat on the banks of the stock pond with her smoke-scented red blanket wrapped around her shoulders, alone in the darkness. The rest of the day had passed quickly, and now a smokey quiet reigned over the homestead.

Never before had the warm, cleansing waters of the bathing pool been as welcome as they had been that afternoon. Everyone was bathed and wearing whatever clean clothes could be found, a satisfactory supper had been scrounged from the smokehouse and cooked over a fire in the center of the yard, and beds had been fashioned from the blankets and robes that had been saved. Ravaged by the pain in his leg and exhausted, Knute had long ago taken to his bed in the barn, and Thomas had also turned in.

Grey Eagle and Raven's Heart sat in front of their tent—their gracious offer to turn the shelter over to the women had been refused, as Annie Rose wanted to be near her grandfather in case he needed anything in the night—and she assumed that Joseph was with them. Erik had arranged his blankets across the way from the barn, making it very clear that he wished to be left alone. He was in terrible pain from the beating Baines had given him, yet he would accept no nursing beyond a washing and a tight bandage wrapped around his middle to support his ribs.

Annie Rose's makeshift bed in the stall she shared with Sweet Water awaited her, but she could not sleep. She looked up at the clear night sky and remembered her grandfather's words about taking comfort from the timeless stars.

Tonight, those little sparkles of light did not offer much comfort.

Terrible things had happened today, and nothing could lessen the pain of it. Her heart ached—for Knute and the pain he must be suffering from Erik's betrayal as well as the physical pain he endured from his wound; for Erik himself, and the tearing guilt that would not allow him to speak or eat; for Thor, so confused and scared without his mama; for Aurora, separated from her baby and out in the wilderness with ruthless, cruel men.

Aurora. Thoughts of what Baines might be doing to the mare tormented Annie Rose. She derived a small amount of solace from the knowledge that Aurora was of no use to Baines dead. There was some assurance that he would not kill her, at least not deliberately. But Aurora was a fighter, and Baines didn't like it when his intentions were challenged. Anything could happen.

"Annie Rose?"

She welcomed the sound of Joseph's voice and looked up at him with a gentle smile.

"May I join you?" he asked.

"I'd like that." She spread out part of the blanket, silently inviting him to sit close to her.

He did, but he did not touch her. "Are you all right?"

"No," she answered truthfully. "I feel so bad about everything—about Erik, and Gramps, and Aurora." She glanced toward the ruins of the cabin. Even now, wisps of smoke still curled up occasionally, like tiny ghosts in the darkness. "The house."

"I'm sorry Aurora was here. Your concerns about the danger in keeping her here were valid, as I feared they might be."

Annie Rose looked at Joseph, barely able to make out his features in the darkness. "Surely you don't blame yourself for that."

"I keep trying to blame myself, even though I understand the reasons for every decision we made concerning Aurora and Thor. You didn't want to bring them here, and I keep wondering what we could have done different."

"Nothing." Annie Rose took his hand. "We could have done nothing different. Please don't blame yourself, or think that I blame you. The important thing was to ensure that Thor did not become truly ill. We accomplished that. We go on from here."

Joseph sighed with relief. "I was afraid you'd be upset with me."

Annie Rose placed a kiss on his hand. "No, my love. I'm thankful we're all still alive."

Now Joseph touched her. He placed an arm around her shoulders and drew her near. She rested contentedly against him.

"Grey Eagle and I will go after her as soon as we can," he said. "We'll find her, Annie Rose. I'll bring her back to you, then help you set her free."

"I know you will, Joseph." The strange thing was, Annie Rose *did* know he would. She knew it in her heart, felt the deep connection between her and Joseph and Aurora, and now Thor. They were all bound together somehow, engaged in a sacred dance of love. "I love you," she whispered.

His hold on her tightened. "Oh, woman. And how I love you." He kissed her forehead. "You have no idea what I felt when I thought you were in that burning cabin. It was as if the light had gone out of my world. I don't want to live without you."

"You won't have to." Annie Rose put her arms around his middle and lifted her face for his kiss, a reverent kiss rather than a passionate one. Never had she felt so treasured.

They did not speak again, but simply held each other, grateful to be alive, grateful to be together.

Twenty-one

The morning light revealed that little could be salvaged from the ruins of the cabin. Annie Rose found it very depressing to pick through the remains of her house, searching for anything of use that might have survived. She felt as if she were searching through the remains of her life, and she supposed that in some ways, she was.

Not surprisingly, the greatest damage was to the front of the great room. The rear sections of all three rooms fared the best, due in part to the earthen walls that would not burn, and in part to the fact that the roof had fallen in and smothered the flames before much damage had been done back there. Most of the bedding had escaped unscathed, as well as some of Knute's and Annie Rose's clothes, but all were smoke-saturated, and Annie Rose knew it was a smell that no amount of washing would ever remove. Thomas had lost all of his clothes, except those winter clothes that had already been packed for the journey.

Knute's rocker had been destroyed, as well as the Norwegian chest and the other furnishings in the front of the room. Sweet Water found the cast-iron kettle in the ruins of the fireplace, and several of the cooking pots had survived, but little else in the kitchen had. Ironically, the pieces of furniture that had survived, besides Annie Rose's washstand, were the beds—which they had no intention and no way of taking with them.

Of everything that was lost, Annie Rose felt the worst about the chest that had come from Norway, for it could not be replaced. She was very grateful that she had grabbed her grandfather's drinking cups and the *rosemaled* tankard, and Joseph's bag with his artist's supplies. Sweet Water had saved some of her things and Annie Rose's brass candlestick and brush set by wrapping them in the red blanket and carrying them through the tunnel. Thomas had made the startling discovery that Annie Rose's washbasin had survived, although the pitcher had been broken.

They had not lost everything, but they had lost much.

The leaving was easier now.

They set off for the pass in midmorning. Knute led the way, holding a rope that pulled a reluctant Thor along, while Joseph, Annie Rose, Sweet Water, and Grey Eagle rode alongside the pack animals at spaced intervals, alert to any sign of trouble. The packhorses did well, tied together with lengths of rope and encouraged to walk single file, but the milk cow fought the rope tied around her horns and bawled, while the two goats bucked and kicked, bleating angrily. The caged chickens fussed and squawked, clearly unhappy with the state of affairs, and Maggie's excited barking did nothing to calm the farm animals. Thomas and Raven's Heart herded Knute's six horses at the back of the caravan, while Erik rode at the very end, still not speaking to anyone.

At the level clearing near the opening to the narrow canyon, Annie Rose pulled Calypso to a stop and looked back at the lovely valley that had been her home and sanctuary for over seven years. Would she ever come back? Would she ever want to? The burned shell of the cabin would always be a reminder of the sad way her family's life in the valley had come to an end.

Joseph leaned out of his saddle and patted her hand, his eyes warm with love and understanding. "Everything will be all right, sweetheart."

"I know." She smiled at him, secure in the knowledge that with him at her side, everything would indeed be all right.

She turned away from the valley and toward her future with Joseph Beaudine.

With the exception of a minor incident with a mare who panicked when her pack caught on a rock, the journey through the rocky passageway went smoothly. By the time they came out on the other side, however, Knute swayed in the saddle, and his lined face was grey with pain. They halted in the clearing, where the mournful sounds of the wooden tube and the bones still echoed off the face of the rock wall.

Joseph insisted upon building a travois for Knute, and he, Grey Eagle, and Raven's Heart went to work cutting and stripping two young and relatively straight-growing aspens. Annie Rose and Sweet Water put together a hurried meal, then prepared one of the smokey buffalo robes to be stretched between the poles. Erik appeared to be faring little better than his grandfather, but he refused Joseph's offer to make him a travois as well, just as he refused Annie Rose's offer of pemmican and smoked fish.

"You must eat, cousin," she said gently.

Erik did not look up from his sitting position on the ground. "I'm not hungry."

"But you need the nourishment, Erik. You are injured."

"No!" he barked.

She did not push him any further, but could take comfort from the fact that Thor and his substitute mother got along surprisingly well together. The colt clearly longed for Aurora, but at least he would not starve.

They did not get far that day; the travois, the farm animals, and Thor slowed them considerably. Annie Rose chafed at the crawling pace, for Baines was taking Aurora farther away with each passing minute. But there was nothing to be done.

Shortly after noon the next day, they came upon the body of the Sioux brave who had caught Knute's knife in his belly. Baines had not bothered to see to a proper burial, nor had the other Sioux taken the body with them, which Joseph and Grey Eagle found peculiar. Although it was not the Sioux way, they buried the dead man, figuring it was better to do that than leave his body to the elements and the wildlife.

That night they camped at the box canyon where Knute always stopped with the horses. Joseph remembered the first night he had stayed there with Knute and Thomas, when he had struggled to capture Annie Rose's likeness on paper, when he had climbed to the top of the northern ridge and saw her riding Aurora, like a free spirit, like a goddess, in the mist of early morning. It seemed like so long ago. Now he could look upon her beauty whenever he wished, and he did so often.

The third day, as they approached the lake where The Paint sometimes kept his herd, it became clear that they would not have their campsite entirely to themselves. Long before they could see the lake, a great deal of noise carried on the air, audible from a half a mile away. Men shouted—many men, from the sounds of it—and horses neighed and screamed.

Annie Rose's heart started pounding. Were The Paint and his herd at the lake? Was someone again foolishly trying to capture him? Had they succeeded? She saw the concerned look Joseph and his brother shared, understood why Grey Eagle rode ahead. Joseph halted the little caravan, and they waited behind a rise that overlooked the lake, out of sight of whoever was there.

Grey Eagle came back over the rise at a gallop. He joined the group gathered around Knute's travois, his gaze on Annie Rose.

"The Golden Mare is there," he said quietly.

Annie Rose needed to hear no more. She gathered her reins, prepared to ride.

Grey Eagle grabbed the bridle. "Wait, little sister. Let me speak."

Little sister? He had never called her that before. "Speak," she said impatiently.

"Baines is there, too."

"I don't care."

"And his group of men, and representatives from the Sioux and Cheyenne nations. And a detachment of cavalry led by

Captain Rutledge." Grey Eagle glanced at Sweet Water, then at Raven's Heart. "And Jubal Sage."

Joseph frowned. "A regular party. It sounds like Baines is holding his auction."

Annie Rose looked at him. "His auction?"

"To sell Aurora to the highest bidder," Joseph explained.

"He stole her from us," Annie Rose snapped. "He has no right to sell her. Let's go claim her."

Joseph and Grey Eagle exchanged a glance.

"What is it?" she cried.

"The tribes want her, Annie Rose," said Joseph gently. He reached from his saddle to take her hand. "If we go in there now and try to simply take her, it could start a fight—a real battle. People could die."

Annie Rose pulled away from him. "With an Army detachment there? I think not, Joseph."

Grey Eagle spoke. "Perhaps you do not understand the importance of the Golden Mare to the Sioux and Cheyenne, Annie Rose. A warrior who battles for her will consider it a great honor to die in that battle, for he will have died for the good of his people. The Sioux and the Cheyenne together outnumber Captain Rutledge's detachment. This could easily turn into a bloodbath."

"Well, we have to do something!" she cried.

"Let's go ask for her," Knute suggested from his travois, where he kept Maggie at his side. *"Ja,* and see what happens then. We can't just ride past the whole mess."

Annie Rose flashed her grandfather a tense, grateful smile.

"The colt's markings aren't disguised any longer," Joseph pointed out. "If he is seen, that will cause a whole new problem."

"Tie my blanket around him," Annie Rose suggested. "It will cover him enough to buy us some time."

"Good idea."

That was quickly done.

Annie Rose looked at Joseph, then at her grandfather. "Let's go," she said quietly.

She and Joseph led the way. When they topped the rise, Annie Rose struggled to make sense of the melee she saw before her.

Near the lake, a circular arena of sorts had been formed by a flimsy fence made of rope and supported by a series of waist-high branches that served as stakes. Perhaps forty men surrounded the arena, many pressed close to the rope, many shouting. The soldiers stood together at one end, their blue uniforms standing out among the buckskin worn by the Indians and frontiersmen. Aurora pawed the ground in the center of the arena. Two warriors in buckskin leggings lay prone near her, neither one moving, as far as Annie Rose could tell. There was no sign of The Paint or of his herd. The only other horses there belonged to the gathered men.

Aurora reared up and pawed the sky now, screaming her outrage. Baines shouted in fury. Some of the men pulled back from the rope fence. A few checked their rifles.

Surely they did not intend to shoot the Golden Mare.

If Aurora had harmed or killed those two men on the ground, they might.

Annie Rose kicked Calypso to a gallop, and was relieved when Joseph urged Grace to stay with them. He did not try to stop her. Perhaps he knew he would not have been able to.

Men turned to watch them approach, and Annie Rose saw astonishment run through the crowd like a wave. Then she remembered that she wore a skirt, that few of those men had ever seen her, that none, save Baines and his cronies, had seen her as a woman. A slow, grim smile curved her lips and was gone. For the first time in her life, she would deliberately use her femininity to her own advantage.

Annie Rose took her hat off and hung it over the saddle horn, then pulled free the pins that held her hair in place. Her hair tumbled down her back and over her shoulders, strands blowing on the wind. An eerie silence spread over the scene. As she drew closer, she saw that all of the men—soldier, frontiersman, and Indian alike—gaped at her. Some men's mouths actually hung open.

Joseph rode straight and tall at her side, his Hawken cradled in one arm, his mouth pressed in a line of determination below his thick mustache. Again, she was grateful that he said nothing, that he did not try to stop her. He glanced at her and slowly nodded. Her heart soared at that small sign of his belief in her.

As they approached, Annie Rose stared over the crowd at Aurora. The ash had been washed from her golden coat, as had the blood, but she looked awful. She was covered with cuts and rope burns, and her white mane and tail were matted. Nervous and aggressive, she pranced, neighing and snorting, occasionally kicking and bucking. If a man attempted to go under the rope after the two injured men, Aurora turned on him, forcing his retreat. Of it all, though, what Annie Rose found the most worrisome was the wild look in the mare's normally placid brown eyes. What had Baines done to her?

A cold rage built up in Annie Rose, empowering her with its force. She pulled Calypso to a halt at the edge of the crowd. "Release the Golden Mare to me!" she demanded. The sharp, clear words echoed over the lake.

The hate-filled voice of Abby Baines reached her. "Stay outta this, you bitch!" he shouted. Murmurs of disapproval ran through the crowd as men parted and revealed Baines standing at the rope, one sleeve stained with blood, his rifle in hand, his bearded face mottled with fury.

"Watch your mouth, Abby Baines," Joseph warned, leveling his rifle. "You won't speak to my woman like that in front of me, or to any woman, for that matter."

"Nor in front of me." An Army officer pushed through the crowd and stood between Annie Rose and Baines. He nodded to Annie Rose. "I am Captain Adam Rutledge, ma'am." He said no more, clearly waiting for her to introduce herself.

She nodded in return. "Captain. My name is Annie Rose Jensen. I am granddaughter to the Norseman."

A murmur of surprise ran through the crowd as her words reached the soldiers and frontiersmen, and were translated for the Indians. She glanced back over her shoulder, saw that the rest of her party had arrived and waited directly behind her. Jubal had joined them and stood beside his wife. Annie Rose returned her attention to the captain. "Abby Baines stole the mare from me. I want her back."

"I fought you for her, fair and square, and won!" snarled Baines.

"That's right!" shouted Painted Davy Sikes. "We won her! If you want her, you have to buy her, just like anyone else." He came to stand next to Baines, and Annie Rose took perverse delight in seeing how badly he limped.

She pointed at Baines. "I accuse you, Abby Baines, in front of this congregation. You and your men attacked my homestead, shot my grandfather with no warning, beat my cousin and my brother, fired my house with Sweet Water and I barricaded inside when we refused to go with you, and took the mare by force." She paused, waiting for the murmured exclamations and mutterings to die down. "You did not win her fair and square."

"She's mine!" Baines screamed. "Mine to sell!"

"Who's gonna buy a rogue mare, Baines?" someone called out.

"She killed them two Injuns!" another man shouted.

"If she's yours, then you ruined her!" a third man said. "She's a wild rogue, a killer horse. I say she should be shot!"

Annie Rose opened her mouth to shout her protest, but Joseph touched her arm and shook his head, once, just as an elderly Indian stepped forward, motioning Grey Eagle to his side. He spoke in Cheyenne, and Grey Eagle translated, his voice deep and strong, easily reaching across the crowd.

"Spotted Crow, a great Cheyenne medicine man, says that the Golden Mare is a spirit animal, sacred to the People of the Plains. But she has injured two men who wished her no harm. If they lie dead, she must be killed to atone for their lives. If they live, and her spirit cannot be calmed, she must be killed so that no others die."

Jubal Sage spoke in a different language, and the Sioux warriors nodded in agreement.

"She's mine!" Baines screamed. No one paid him any attention.

Instead, all eyes turned to the arena. Aurora now raced around the outward edge of the rope enclosure, still snorting and blowing. As she passed, men drew back, then moved closer again. One of the two men on the ground raised his head, but stayed where he was. The other remained motionless. Annie Rose could see that blood came from a wound on the side of his head. She prayed that he was only unconscious.

She stepped down from the saddle.

Instantly, Joseph was out of his saddle as well, and standing beside her. "You can't go in there," he said.

"I can calm her spirit," she responded, and pulled off her gloves, tucking them into her waistband. When—if—Aurora let her get close, she wanted the mare to be able to smell her skin.

"Annie Rose." Joseph grabbed her hand and spoke in a low tone, his words meant for her ears only. "They're right. She's gone rogue wild."

"She won't hurt me."

Joseph stared at her, his deep concern obvious. "How can you be certain?"

"I just am. I'd bet my life on it."

"That is exactly what you're doing." He clung to her hand. "And I can't stop you, can I?"

She looked into his brown eyes, so filled with love and pride and fear. "No," she gently answered, squeezing his hand, hoping that her answer did not cause her to lose him.

"Come safely back to me, Annie Rose."

Love for him welled up in her heart, so powerfully that her breath caught. "I will." Annie Rose released him and started walking toward the makeshift arena, grateful that Joseph stayed at her side. After seven years of isolation, it felt strange to walk past so many people, especially with all of them staring at her. An unfamiliar anxiety struck and caused her stomach to knot. She focused on the agitated mare and fought to calm her own breathing. At the rope, she paused and faced Abby Baines, who stood about six feet from her.

When she spoke, her voice was harsh with loathing. "I curse you, Abby Baines, for what you did to my family and to that precious mare. How dearly I wish it was you lying in the dirt at her mercy, for that would be a fitting punishment."

Baines lunged at her, but got nowhere. Painted Davy grabbed him, Captain Rutledge shoved a hand against his chest, and Joseph cocked his rifle. Panting and cursing, Baines turned away, favoring his wounded arm.

Captain Rutledge looked down at Annie Rose, a frown on his bearded face. "Surely you don't intend to approach the horse, Miss Jensen."

"I do, Captain." She easily ducked under the rope, causing another tide of murmurs to ripple through the crowd.

Aurora screamed a warning at her and raced by.

That gave Annie Rose pause.

"Reach for her heart, *datter*." Knute's loving voice touched her.

She glanced over her shoulder and saw that her grandfather stood close to Joseph, supported by Thomas and Jubal Sage. With a nod, she stepped farther into the arena. A wave of murmured protests swelled over her, and she heard some of the comments.

"What the hell's that fool woman doin'?"

"That horse'll kill her."

"Christ, Beaudine, if she's your woman, get her out of there!"

Aurora ran by again, closer, frantic and snorting.

Annie Rose stood completely still. She drew a deep, calming breath and closed her eyes. She focused on the feel of the wind against her face, on its cool, clean scent, on how it blew her skirts and her hair about. The crowd grew quiet, or perhaps she simply could not hear them anymore.

All she could hear was the pounding of hoofbeats—coming closer, pulling away.

She went deeper.

Pounding, pounding, a different pounding now, that of Aurora's heart.

Much too fast.

Annie Rose fought its seductive contagion. Like a geyser welling up inside her, Aurora's terror and rage threatened to overwhelm her. It would be so easy to give in to the rising tide, to go with it. But Annie Rose had never allowed herself to ride that tide of fury, for she feared it would kill her.

She forced her breathing to stay calm, and went deeper.

With her heart, with her soul, she reached out to the maddened animal. "Aurora," she whispered. "Come to me." Her brow furrowed with the effort she made.

The pounding of the hoofbeats slowed, then stopped. Only the pounding of the heart remained.

A power infused her, such as Annie Rose had never known before. It was as if she was being strengthened from somewhere outside herself. To that tide she did give herself up.

The connection was made.

Her eyes flew open. Aurora stood perhaps twenty feet away, her head hanging, her sides heaving. She watched Annie Rose with wary, weary eyes.

So slowly, Annie Rose moved through the grasses, toward the two men on the ground.

Aurora raised her head and pawed the ground, suddenly more alert.

Annie Rose stopped beside the man she had seen move. Without taking her eyes from Aurora, she bent and touched the warrior's bare shoulder. He jerked. She glanced down at him, saw the astonishment in his brown eyes. She motioned him toward the rope. His frightened gaze darted between her and Aurora, then he rose and hobbled off. A low roar of approval went up from the crowd when he safely reached the rope.

The mare raised her head to the sky and neighed, loudly, then again pawed the earth. Annie Rose straightened and closed her eyes, determined to strengthen her connection to the mare. She shivered at the force of the power that seemed to sing through her very veins. Aurora blew, then softly whinnied.

The other warrior lay somewhere behind her. Step by slow step, Annie Rose backed up, not taking her eyes from Aurora except to glance about for the fallen man. At last she reached him. Now her own fear—that Aurora had killed the warrior—threatened. With a prayer that the man still lived, she pushed his long hair out of the way and laid her hand on his back. After a moment, she felt the beating of his heart, and relief flooded through her.

"He lives," she called quietly as she straightened. Again, a murmuring of voices moved through the crowd.

Only one task remained.

Annie Rose stared at the trembling mare, and her eyes filled with tears. "Aurora," she whispered. She held her hand out and advanced.

Aurora backed up and tossed her head.

"Sweetheart, don't fear me," Annie Rose begged, suddenly understanding something of what Joseph must have felt when she had at first resisted his kindness to her. With a fierce and silent vow to spend the rest of her life making it up to him, she took another step forward, then another. At last she was close enough to touch Aurora's nose, if the mare would allow it.

But she did not try.

In a flash of insight, Annie Rose realized that she had to give Aurora the freedom to come to her, just as Joseph had given her all the time and the freedom she had needed, just as he still did. Patiently, Annie Rose held her hand out, determined that she would stand there all day and through the night if it took that long for Aurora to come to her.

It didn't.

Aurora nickered, quietly. She pushed her nose against Annie Rose's hand. At the feel of the mare's warm breath on her hand, Annie Rose's eyes overflowed, and this time she let the tears fall. "Oh, sweetheart," she whispered. Aurora nuzzled her chest, and Annie Rose put her arms around the mare's neck. For a long time they stood there, the woman and the mare, head to head, heart to heart.

When at last she looked around, Annie Rose saw that the unconscious man had been taken from the arena. Other than that, no one had moved, not even Abby Baines. No one moved now. They stared at her, all of them, eyes wide with wonder, some wide with fear. Not a sound reached her ears, except that of the wind as it whispered through the grasses and blew her skirts and hair and Aurora's tail. One of the soldiers crossed himself when her gaze fell on him, and she wearily wondered if he thought her to be a witch.

She found Joseph. Like the others, he, too, watched her, but his eyes were on fire with love and pride. Her heart swelled, and it was as if the love they shared shimmered between them, alive and beautiful in and of itself. Aurora nickered again. Perhaps she felt it, too.

Suddenly, Annie Rose knew the mare did feel it, just as she knew that the surge of power she had experienced earlier had been Joseph's. He had reached for them both, sending his strength, trying to help. He had connected, as he did now. That connection called her.

Annie Rose grabbed a handful of Aurora's mane and, in one swift movement, threw herself up on the mare's back. Aurora sidestepped, but did not try to throw her. A roar of astonishment rose from the crowd. Annie Rose regretted that her drawers were exposed, as they always were when she rode, especially in front of all those men, but there was nothing to be done about it. Keeping Joseph in her sights, she nudged Aurora to a slow walk, and they crossed the arena, coming to a halt a short distance from the medicine man.

Knowing that Joseph would translate for her, she spoke to Spotted Crow.

"The Golden Mare has chosen me to be her guardian," she firmly stated.

Joseph translated loud enough for the rest of the Cheyenne to hear, while Jubal Sage repeated her words in Sioux.

Annie Rose stared at Spotted Crow, daring him to challenge her. He did not. When he did not respond, she continued, extending her message to all there.

"From this day forward, if any of you see her, she is to be left in peace. As Spotted Crow said, she is a spirit horse, and her spirit needs to be free. Otherwise, she will die, and her great, powerful spirit will be lost to all of you."

An uneasy silence settled over the crowd.

Then Spotted Crow spoke. Grey Eagle and Jubal translated.

"The golden-haired woman has spoken, and I hear her words as truth. She and the Golden Mare are to go in peace."

Twenty-two

Joseph cut the rope barrier and motioned people to stand back. No one argued with him. Annie Rose urged Aurora along the wide path that opened for them and stopped some distance away, then slid off the mare's back with the same grace she had exhibited in her unexpected mount. Joseph led the blanket-covered Thor to his mother's side and took great delight in the happy reunion.

A completely different creature from the maddened and dangerous hellion he had witnessed not an hour ago, Aurora now nickered gently and often, nuzzling her baby—the perfect mother. Meanwhile, Thor, like all children, was able to tolerate only so much maternal affection before he decided he was hungry. He nosed along his mama's belly and greedily began to suckle.

"There's nothing quite as good as home cooking, is there, boy?" Joseph asked, patting the colt on the rump.

Then he spun around, and without another word, gathered his woman in his arms. Annie Rose did not seem surprised, nor did she resist in any way. He held her close, not caring that many, many people watched them. For such a large crowd, they were surprisingly quiet . . . still.

"I felt you," she whispered. "So did Aurora."

He stroked her windblown, herbal-scented hair, wishing he could wrap himself in its golden length. "I know. I felt it, too."

They rested against each other for a moment longer, then Joseph reluctantly said, "We must speak to the family." She nodded, and again he had the uncanny sense of instant and flawless communication. Somewhere along the way, "family" had come to mean not only his family—which included Jubal and Sweet Water—but hers as well, and he knew that she felt that way, too.

Hand in hand, they approached the group that had gathered around Knute's travois, where the Norseman once again rested. Thomas knelt on one knee, holding Maggie, and Erik stood off by himself, close enough to hear, too far away to participate in the discussion, not that he showed any desire to do so.

"Baines took off like a bat out of hell, with Painted Davy and Hank Westin right behind him," Grey Eagle reported. "I'm not certain what happened to their two surviving Sioux buddies."

"If they was smart—which they ain't, or they wouldn't've hooked up with Baines in the first place—they hightailed it back to Fort Laramie," Jubal said with a derisive snort. "And they counted their blessin's all the way back that they ain't as dead as that friend of theirs that y'all buried."

Evidently, Sweet Water had filled her spouse in on all that had transpired since his departure for Fort Laramie a little over a week ago. Joseph caught himself. Had it only been that long? Surely a lifetime had passed since the decision had been made to winter the Jensen family at Fort Laramie.

Jubal rested the butt of his long rifle in the dirt and leaned on the barrel. He eyed Joseph, suddenly very serious. "What's your plan?"

"To get Knute and Erik to Laramie for medical attention. That is the most pressing. Get the Jensens situated with Orion and Sarah for the time being. Then Eagle and I are going to take Aurora and Thor south."

"Part'll do, part won't." Jubal shook his grey, shaggy head. "I'm afraid I got powerful bad news." He turned sad eyes on Raven's Heart, who stood next to Grey Eagle.

Joseph felt Annie Rose's grip on his hand tighten. He understood, for his own stomach knotted. If Jubal called news bad, it was.

"Out with it, Jubal," Grey Eagle ordered.

Joseph translated to English the Cheyenne in which Jubal—who directed his words to Raven's Heart—now spoke.

"A renegade band of Crow have been raidin' far south of their usual territorial lands. They attacked your village day before yesterday—one man killed, several horses stolen." Jubal hesitated, clearly hating what he had to say next, then he looked Raven's Heart in the eye. "I'm as sorry as hell to tell you this, Raven's Heart, but they took Sparrow."

Joseph ended his translation, then fell silent, sick at heart. *Not Sparrow, the only child of Raven's Heart and his beloved wife, Little Leaf.*

His grip on Annie Rose's hand tightened even more. Eleven years old, Sparrow was a precocious and lovely child on the verge of womanhood. Through his mother's family, Grey Eagle was the only Beaudine who could claim her as blood kin, but all of the Beaudine siblings considered Sparrow a beloved niece.

It appeared that Raven's Heart could not speak.

"What is being done?" Grey Eagle demanded hoarsely.

"The Hunter's already on the trail," Jubal said. "That's why I'm here—to get the message to you. We're to catch up to him as soon as we can."

"Go at once," Joseph urged.

Grey Eagle looked at him, upset, frowning. "What of you? What of the Norseman? What of the Golden Mare?"

"Go!" Knute ordered. "We will manage."

"We will, Grey Eagle," Annie Rose assured him. "Find the child. Bring her home to her mother." She turned sympathetic, tortured eyes on Raven's Heart. "Help her father bring her home."

Grey Eagle spoke rapidly in Cheyenne. Knute reached for Raven's Heart's hand, took it in a quick grip, then released him. His facial expression frozen in a stoic, unemotional mask, Raven's Heart hurried to his horse. He returned a few minutes later, leading Grey Eagle's mount as well as Jubal's.

After a few quick words to a teary-eyed Sweet Water, Jubal swung up into his saddle. "Good luck to you, Joe. See to that mare and her foal, then wed up with that woman. Don't you mess up, now."

Even under such dire circumstances, Joseph fought a smile as a rush of affection for the old man filled him. "I won't, you old coot." Then he sobered. "Find Sparrow."

"We'll do our damnedest." Jubal looked at Annie Rose and touched the brim of his disreputable hat. "Welcome to the family, Annie Rose, even if it does mean that your old grandpa is gonna be kin now." He flashed Knute a teasing grin, then jerked a thumb in Joseph's direction. "I'm pleased as hell you're weddin' up with this rogue. 'Scuse my swearin'."

Annie Rose blew him a kiss. "Go with God."

"Yes, ma'am." Jubal touched his hat again, then was gone, with Raven's Heart at his side.

Grey Eagle approached Joseph and Annie Rose. He reached for Annie Rose's free hand. "You and Joseph must take Aurora now, little sister," he said quietly.

Annie Rose met his concerned gaze. "I know. All will be well, big brother. You go with God also." She hesitated. "Or the Great Spirit."

Instantly aware that Annie Rose feared she had made a mistake and perhaps offended Grey Eagle—certain that she had not—Joseph added, "Or both. May as well stack your deck."

Grey Eagle nodded, then vaulted into his saddle. "See you at Laramie in a few weeks. With luck, we'll both have happy tales to tell."

"Farewell, brother." Joseph held his hand up and Grey Eagle grasped it near the elbow. "Bring our Sparrow home."

With a nod, Grey Eagle touched his heels to his mount's sides, and, like Jubal and Raven's Heart, was gone, his long black hair streaming out behind him.

Still clinging to Annie Rose's hand, Joseph turned to Knute.

"Things have changed," he said. "Our plans must change, too."

"Ja." Knute wearily leaned back on his travois. "This is what must be done now." He waved in the direction of the Army detachment. "Thomas, Sweet Water, Erik and I, we and our animals and belongings go with Captain Rutledge to the fort. Hunter's bride Sarah and their infant son should not be alone." He pointed at Joseph and Annie Rose. "You two will take Aurora and Thor away, at once, before the restless young men of the Cheyenne and Sioux nations have an opportunity to change the minds of their wise men."

Joseph glanced at Annie Rose and caught her looking at him, a worried look on her face.

"Alone, Knute?" Joseph asked. "You want us to go alone?"

"Who else? Aurora is injured, upset. She may not let anyone else near her. Annie Rose must go. You know where this place Grey Eagle spoke of is, and you can protect my granddaughter and the horses. You two must go."

"Can Sweet Water come with us?" Annie Rose asked. "Or Thomas?"

Knute wearily shook his head. *"Ja,* I understand your concern, *datter,* but Sweet Water must go to Laramie and take care of some things for her husband, then she goes to the Cheyenne village to be with Little Leaf, wife of Raven's Heart. And I need Thomas with me."

Joseph scanned the gathering of people, which was finally beginning to break up. "I wonder if there is anyone here who can marry us right now."

Startled, Annie Rose looked up at him. "Marry us now?"

"It isn't exactly what I'd planned for our wedding, but if it will make you feel better about being alone with me, I'll do it."

"You would do that for me?" she asked incredulously.

Deeply touched by her obvious vulnerability, Joseph raised her hand to his mouth for a kiss. "Gladly." Then he frowned. "But I don't think anyone here can perform a legal marriage ceremony. I know Captain Rutledge can't, because I couldn't when I was a captain."

"There will be a nice wedding later," Knute said firmly, and a little impatiently. "Today, we must think of the horses. You two are the only ones who can take them to safety." His old blue eyes bored into Joseph. "When you return, you both will honor the vow you have made to wed. Now we must go. The captain is ready to leave."

"Have you spoken with him yet?" Joseph asked.

Knute shook his head.

"I'll make the arrangements." Joseph released Annie Rose's hand and hurried away.

Annie Rose watched him go, her eyebrows drawn together in a frown. Then she turned to her grandfather. "I need to talk to you."

"Ja, I know, *datter."*

She looked at Thomas. "Would you mind helping Sweet Water make sure the packs are secure, so that Gramps and I can have a few minutes alone?"

"Sure, sister." Thomas straightened. "Come on, Maggie." The boy sauntered off, with the dog trailing behind him.

Annie Rose knelt down beside the travois, then sat back on her heels. Her blue skirts pooled around her legs, and her hair blew in the cool wind. "Do you really think it wise for Joseph and me to go off alone and unwed, Gramps?" she asked bluntly.

"What is it you fear, Annie Rose?" Knute watched her, his expression one of love and understanding.

She dropped her gaze to her lap, where her hands lay entwined. "I fear we will love," she said quietly.

"And if that happens, then what do you fear? That Joseph Beaudine will not honor his word to marry you? That he will leave you disgraced, perhaps with child?"

She closed her eyes. When spoken aloud, her fears seemed so stark and ugly.

Knute covered her hands with one of his. "Annie Rose,

do you really believe him capable of such a thing? If so, then you do not trust him, and you should not marry him."

At that, she opened her eyes and stared at her grandfather. "I do not doubt my decision to marry him, Gramps."

"Do you trust him to keep his word?"

"Yes."

"Then take Aurora and Thor away to safety. That must be your first and foremost concern. That is the reason you make this journey. Perhaps you and Joseph will find that you wish to wait until your marriage; perhaps you will not wish to wait. Always be respectful to each other, treat each other with kindness and love, and nothing you ever do together can be wrong." He smiled at her. "There are several things I would say to you, beloved granddaughter, if you will tolerate the ramblings of an old man for a few minutes."

"You know I will," Annie Rose answered softly.

Knute squeezed her hand. "The actual ceremony of marriage, the public claiming of each other, is very important to you, and I know that is because of the shoddy manner in which your father treated your mother. But marriage vows do not necessarily keep a man from abandoning his family, Annie Rose. The frontier is filled with men who left wives and children behind. A man stays with his family, or he doesn't, because of what is in his heart. So don't think that marriage is a guarantee of anything."

Annie Rose stared at him. She had never considered that perspective before.

"Next," Knute continued, "remember that true marriage is forged in the hearts of two people, not created by a preacher and a piece of paper. I believe Joseph Beaudine has already made you his bride in his heart. He will not abandon you."

Those words brought a swell of joy to Annie Rose's heart. She recognized the truth in her grandfather's words, and the truth gave her comfort. She would go into the wilderness with Joseph, and treat him with respect and kindness—and with love.

* * *

Annie Rose sat atop Calypso once again, her hair repinned, her hat in place, her grandfather's rifle in its scabbard at her thigh. The crowd had broken up. A few of the Cheyenne warriors had followed Grey Eagle, intending to offer their assistance in the search for Sparrow, while the rest of the Cheyenne and the band of Sioux had left for their separate encampments. Now, from the top of the rise, she watched as the column of soldiers headed east past the lake, bound for Fort Laramie. Her family followed the soldiers, along with their animals and the string of packhorses that carried their belongings. Some of the frontiersmen who had come out for the auction travelled with them, giving Thomas a hand with the horses. Erik's lone figure could be seen at the very end of the line.

Even from this distance, Annie Rose could hear Maggie's excited barking. She felt a pang, and was torn. A part of her longed to be with them, to see to her grandfather's care, to help get the family settled. Another part of her was overjoyed and more excited than she had ever been about anything in her life to be heading into the wilderness with Joseph Beaudine.

He stood next to Calypso with Grace's reins in hand as he, too, watched the caravan in the distance. She could have reached out and touched him.

Earlier, Joseph had returned to Knute's travois with the news that, as he suspected, no one present had the authority to marry them. In fact, he learned that a chaplain had not yet been posted to the fort. It could be some time before they were able to marry, whether they took Aurora and Thor south now or not. His concern for Annie Rose's feelings in the matter had deeply touched her. He looked up at her now, his brown eyes intense, his expression serious.

"I swear to you, Annie Rose, I will not dishonor you on this journey, nor ever in our lives together."

Annie Rose looked down at him in amazement, and remembered that they had not yet had a chance to speak in private since the decision had been made for them to travel alone. Perhaps he thought that she was still worried about things which no longer concerned her. She climbed down from the saddle and stood before him, taking his hand in hers.

"Joseph, you could never dishonor me. That I know, here." Annie Rose placed his hand over her heart, saw his eyes widen in surprise at the intimate contact. His hand lay across her breast, not resisting, not fondling. She continued. "My grandfather said that we should always treat each other with respect and kindness and love. He also told me that if we do that, nothing we do together can be wrong." She moved his hand so that she could hold it between both of hers. "I don't know what will happen between us on this journey, and I refuse to worry about it. Let us concentrate on getting the horses safely to their winter grounds, and see what happens. Above all, I want us to be comfortable with each other. No expectations, no restrictions. Agreed?"

Joseph gave a small sigh of relief, and his lips curved into a smile. "Agreed." He looked up at the sky. "We still have a few hours of daylight. We'd better get as far from here as we can before dark. Your grandfather might be right about some of the Indians changing their minds."

He did not mention Abby Baines, but Annie Rose knew that man was on Joseph's mind as well. Perhaps the arm wound she had given Baines would force him to seek medical attention, and buy them a little more time.

Joseph helped her into the saddle, vaulted into his own, and took up the lead on the single packhorse that carried their supplies. Annie Rose led Aurora; Thor followed his mama, and the grey mare, who needed no lead, brought up the rear. They turned south.

"I think the journey will take all of two weeks," Joseph told her. "The Medicine Bow Mountains are about one hundred miles from here, and we have to travel easy, because Thor is so young, and because I want to avoid leaving an obvious trail, especially these first few days. The return trip will be faster, but I'll want to come back a different way."

"That sounds like a good plan to me," she said, falling into position behind him, knowing that any who found their trail would have a difficult time guessing how many were in their party if their horses' tracks covered one another's.

Annie Rose spoke little for the rest of the afternoon, wanting to give Joseph the freedom to plan their path without distraction. She followed his lead without question, trusting him as implicitly as she had always trusted her grandfather. They travelled slowly, often following an established game trail or splashing along a narrow creek, and stopped frequently, to allow Thor to rest, to give Joseph time to scout their back trail for signs of pursuit, to camouflage any obvious evidence of their passing.

Finally, after the sun had disappeared behind the distant mountains and the wind had taken on a definite chill, Joseph signalled a halt near a small stand of cottonwoods, the only vegetation other than dried prairie grasses visible in any direction. Annie Rose knew he chose the site because the cottonwoods indicated nearby water. She also worried that the tall trees might draw the attention of anyone else in the vicinity for exactly the same reason.

"We'll water the horses here, then move out maybe a quarter of a mile." He pointed to the west. "Behind that rise. We'll be close enough to come back for water again in the morning. By noon tomorrow, we should find the Laramie River, and we'll follow it as far as we can. At least water won't be a problem then."

She smiled as she climbed down from the saddle, careful to keep her head turned from Joseph, for she did not want him questioning her about that smile. The Beaudine brothers were legendary for their knowledge of the frontier; she was pleased to know that their reputation had not been exaggerated. But then, she had never believed it was.

Joseph found a seeping spring and dug it out enough to water the horses. Annie Rose declined any of the muddy water, deciding that no matter how stale the water in her rawhide water bag was, at least it wasn't laden with dirt.

They moved past the rise and ate a cold supper. Joseph would not allow a fire, even for coffee, and he would not put up the Army tent Grey Eagle had left for them, claiming that its whiteness would be too obvious in the dark. With a promise that he would relax the uncomfortable conditions he was enforcing upon them when they were farther away from the scene of the unsuccessful auction, Joseph rolled into a buffalo robe, and, as far as Annie Rose could tell, was quickly asleep, leaving her alone to watch the constellations on their eternal journey.

Because Annie Rose understood the reasons for all of his decisions—indeed, approved of them—she fought a vague sense of disappointment. She didn't know what she had expected, but she had expected her first night in the wilderness alone with Joseph Beaudine to be different. After what seemed like many surprisingly lonely hours, she fell into a troubled sleep.

The next day passed without event. Just as Joseph predicted, they reached the Laramie River shortly before noon, and from then on travelled within sight of the low, sluggish river. Late in the afternoon, they spotted a small herd of wild horses grazing perhaps a mile to the west. Annie Rose wondered if The Paint was with them.

When the second evening was spent much like the first— no fire, cold supper, little conversation, Joseph rolling into his robes as soon as the light was gone from the sky—Annie Rose began to fear that something was wrong.

By the third evening, she was convinced of it.

Joseph decided they were far enough away from the fort to allow a regular camp. He selected a pleasant site among a stand of box elders and cottonwoods, perhaps two hundred yards from the river. The light and warmth of the fire and the hot coffee were most welcome, as was the rabbit Joseph roasted over the flames. He set up the small Army tent for her, and she took her soap to the river and indulged in an actual bath.

Later, she sat before the fire, wearing only her chemise, drawers, and petticoat, her thick red blanket wrapped around her, and worked her brush through her damp hair. She was very careful to keep the blanket from slipping off her shoulders, which made the brushing awkward work.

Joseph sat across the fire from her, oiling his rifle.

The silence between them grew long. Finally, Annie Rose spoke. "It was nice to bathe again, but I sure do miss the heated water of our bathing pool." She did not mention her disappointment that they would never share its inviting waters.

"The pool was an enjoyable luxury," Joseph commented in agreement. His tone was pleasant enough, but he said nothing more.

Annie Rose tried again. "How many miles do you think we travelled today?"

"Perhaps twenty." Silence again.

Her grip tightened on the brush handle as she looked down at her lap. "What is wrong, Joseph?"

"Nothing's wrong."

Annie Rose raised her head and stared at him across the flames. He met her gaze. "Something is," she argued gently. "You will hardly speak to me. Have I offended or angered you in some way?"

His expression softened. "Not at all, sweetheart. I'm sorry. I've been concerned about getting you and the horses safely away. I didn't mean to be unkind." He got to his feet. "The idea of a bath sounds good. I'll be down at the river for a few minutes." His rifle in one hand, he patted her shoulder as he walked past her. A moment later, he disappeared into the trees.

"He patted me like he does Maggie," Annie Rose whispered at the unresponsive flames. Annoyed, she glared over her shoulder in the direction Joseph had gone, very tempted to follow him and give him a piece of her mind.

But he was bathing.

Her mind flashed back to the night she had seen him by the pool. He had been so beautiful to her, exposed in the soft light of the lantern. How she had longed to touch him, to lay her hand over his heart. Later, she had, briefly. Too briefly. Annie Rose trembled, and it had nothing to do with the cool night air caressing her damp hair. With a groan, she dropped the brush to her lap and buried her face in her hands, allowing the blanket to slip off her shoulders.

More than anything, Annie Rose wanted to follow Joseph to the river. She ached to slip out of her petticoats and drawers, to tear off her chemise, to press her naked breasts against the solid strength and warmth of his bared masculine chest. She wanted him to fulfill his promise of moving his mouth all over her body, and she wanted to do the same to him. She wanted him in her arms, and in her body, just as he was already in her heart.

Even though she was alone, Annie Rose blushed at her wanton thoughts. Joseph had rarely touched her in the last three days, and then only when necessary—as when he helped her down from the saddle—or by accident. He had made no attempt to hold her hand, to hug her, or to kiss her, as he had often done when they had been surrounded by her family. Now they were completely alone, and it was as if he had no interest in her whatsoever.

Tears pricked her eyes as she stared into the flames. "I don't understand," she whispered brokenly to no one.

She would not go after him, for she would not be able to bear it if he spurned her affections.

Annie Rose scrambled to her feet, grabbed the blanket and the brush, and retreated to the lonely safety of the tent, for she doubted she could look upon Joseph Beaudine and not feel compelled to touch him, no matter how cool his attitude was toward her. As her mother had been with Blaine Coburn, Annie Rose was desperate for Joseph's touch. She found it terrifying that she was so close to shaming herself, just as her mother had done with her father.

From the trees, Joseph watched her forlorn figure. She put her face in her hands and leaned forward, which caused the blanket to fall off her shoulders, revealing the wide straps of her chemise. How he wanted to go to her, to take her in his arms, to kiss the lines of worry from her forehead, to kiss her soft shoulders. Annie Rose had been right—something was wrong, but not in the way she suspected.

Joseph didn't dare talk to her too much, for surely they would move onto intimate topics sooner or later. He didn't dare touch her, for then he would only want to touch her more. It took all of his considerable willpower to keep himself in check. There were times he thought he would explode if he did not tell her again how he loved her, if he did not caress the softness of her cheek, kiss her enticing lips.

But he did not.

Nor would he discuss his feelings with her, for he was terrified that she might glimpse the simmering passion that he was barely able to keep under control. Since they were not yet wed, his powerful feelings might frighten her, might cause her to doubt that he could control himself. Once, she had been frightened of him. Never again did he want to see fear of him in her beautiful green eyes. Better that she be angry with him than afraid of him.

When this blasted journey ended, Joseph silently swore he would make it up to her. He would marry Annie Rose as quickly as possible, and spend the rest of his life telling her and showing her how much he loved her.

He watched as she rose from her position near the fire. The blanket fell off her completely, and he saw that she wore only her petticoat and chemise. Joseph shuddered as an unbearably intense wave of desire roared through him, leaving him hard and lonely. Annie Rose ducked into the tent, and Joseph fought the urge to rush to her side. Instead, he turned back to the river in the hope that another dip in the cold waters would calm his body and clear his mind. He prayed that she could forgive him for the distance he felt he had to put between them.

The next morning passed with no easing of the strange tension between them. When the noon meal was finished,

Annie Rose crouched on the bank of the river, the coffeepot in hand, while Joseph worked a short distance away, securing the pack carried by the patient packhorse. As she rinsed the battered pot in the water, the fact that she and Joseph had spoken no more than a few words to each other all day grated on her until she could bear it no longer. Annie Rose jerked the pot from the water and straightened, whirling about to face Joseph.

"If you have lost interest in me, Joseph Beaudine, I'll not hold you to your promise to wed me." There. The awful words were out. With bated breath and pounding heart, Annie Rose watched him, impatient for his reaction at the same time she dreaded it.

Joseph stiffened as if she had struck him with a rock, then slowly he turned to face her. "Not interested in you?" he repeated incredulously. "You think I'm not interested in you?" He stormed toward her.

Annie Rose watched him come, her eyes wide. She wasn't frightened, yet she found herself wanting to step back. She raised her chin and stood her ground.

Joseph grabbed her shoulders, tight, but without hurting her. "My God, woman, for days I have watched you, wanted you, ached for you. I've been afraid to touch you in any way, at first because I wasn't sure you wanted me to, now for fear I won't be able to take my hands off you until I have touched you everywhere, kissed you everywhere. Not interested? How could you think such a thing?" He gave her a small shake. "I'll show you how interested I am." Joseph pulled her to him and kissed her hungrily, voraciously, until she could hardly breathe. His lips ground against hers, nibbled, sucked, teased. His tongue didn't ask for entry to her mouth this time, but demanded it, and Annie Rose gladly gave him access. She had not known it was possible to be kissed like this. The coffeepot fell from her grip and she melted against him, holding him close, reveling in his strength.

He moaned, and his hands moved up to work through her hair. Then one hand stroked her back, her hip, and lower, until he cupped her bottom and pulled her even more intimately against him. She shivered at the feel of his hard maleness.

"That is how interested I am, Miss Annie Rose Jensen," he said hoarsely, his own breath coming fast. "I can't wait to show you with my hands and my body how much I love you, to truly make you my wife. But I will wait until we stand before a preacher, for your sake." He set her back from him, and the tender expression on his face belied the passion that still burned in his eyes. "Don't ever let me hear you insult yourself again by assuming I am not interested in you, my beautiful woman." With that, he spun around and walked away.

Stunned, Annie Rose watched him go. She trembled from head to foot, her mouth felt swollen from his onslaught, her breasts tingled and ached for his touch, and a strange fire glowed low in her belly. She longed to call him back, to ask him, to beg him if need be, to fan the coals of that low-burning fire into the flames of passion she knew had threatened to consume him. She wanted to feel the full force of those flames, too.

"We've got a distance yet to cover today," Joseph said, his tone determinedly casual. He swung into the saddle. "Let's go."

Annie Rose reached for the coffeepot with shaking hands and forced her leaden feet to move, one in front of the other. She stuffed the pot in her saddlebag, then struggled into the saddle. Without a word, she followed him, her mind tumbling from one thought to another.

Joseph loved her—she knew that, had known it for a long time. It was a revelation to her how desperately he also wanted her. He had been restraining himself for her sake, determined to marry her before he took her to his bed, because he thought that was what she wanted.

At one time, she had.

Things had changed.

Somewhere along the way, the love she felt in her heart had become much more important than a marriage certificate. The love Joseph offered her meant more than the name he offered her. Their marriage was still important, but she knew he would honor his vow to her, whether she returned from this journey a virgin or not.

Her grandfather had put her mind at ease about the love she and Joseph might choose to express with their bodies, just as he had calmed her ridiculous fear that Joseph might not honor his promise of marriage when they returned to the fort. After that, Annie Rose had feared above all else that she and Joseph would become uncomfortable with each other on this journey.

It had happened.

Somehow, someway, she had to—she *would*—fix that.

Twenty-three

"We'll be turning in a more southwesterly direction tomorrow, away from the river," Joseph announced that night. They had just finished a tasty supper of fried fish and potatoes, and now both Joseph and Annie Rose sat near the fire, resting against their saddles as they sipped coffee. The sunset spread a blanket of glorious color over the distant mountains. "You may want to bathe again; I don't know how soon we'll come upon another river or a lake."

Annie Rose nodded. "I'd like to wash some of my things, too. I'll go do that now." She rose and set her cup near the fire, then gathered her soap, a few underclothes, and a soiled bodice. About to set off for the river, a thought occurred to her, and she hesitated. "I'd be happy to wash your white shirt for you, Joseph," she said shyly, knowing the dirty shirt was stuffed in his saddlebag.

"That's real nice of you, Annie Rose," Joseph responded.

She was relieved to hear a note of genuine warmth in his voice. Since the episode at the noon stop, they were still cautious with each other, but some of the tension between them had lifted.

Joseph handed her the shirt, and she hurried toward the river. She'd have to work quickly in order to be finished by the time full darkness was upon them.

A half an hour later, she returned to the camp. Because most of the newly washed items were her underclothes, she modestly declined Joseph's offer to help her drape the clothing over nearby bushes and tree branches. Just as Annie Rose had hoped he would do, he announced that he, too, would take this last opportunity to bathe, and disappeared in the direction of the river.

She watched him go, then took a steadying breath. Did she have the courage necessary to put her daring plan into action? Annie Rose leaned against the tree near which she stood and closed her eyes, bringing to mind the picture of Joseph's face this afternoon—his beloved handsome face, his expression so intense as he told her he loved her, his brown eyes fairly burning with passion and suppressed need.

He loved her.

She loved him.

Nothing else mattered.

Annie Rose threw the last of the wet clothes over the nearest branch and hurried back toward the fire.

Joseph finished his bath, and decided to check the horses one last time. Thor was holding up well, considering the miles the little guy had to cover each day, and Aurora looked like a completely different animal than the terrified, maniacal beast Annie Rose had calmed that day at the lake. The little cuts that had covered her coat were healing nicely, the rope burns had faded, Annie Rose had coaxed the mats out of her long white mane and tail, and the mare had put on a little of the weight she had lost during those three days with Baines.

Aurora nickered contentedly now when he approached. "Hey, girl," Joseph murmured. She nuzzled his shoulder, and he scratched her forehead. "I reckon we'll be there in two days—three at the most."

As he stroked Aurora's neck, Thor stepped closer and nosed him. With a smile, Joseph caressed the colt's neck as well, and he thought how fortunate he was to be a part of this journey, to be involved in Annie Rose's quest to keep the Golden Mare and her colt free. The cause was a worthy one.

A low rumble of thunder reached his ears, and off to the north, over some distant hills, he saw a flash of lightning. The sky directly above him was clear, and he hoped it stayed that way. Joseph did not relish the idea of trying to sleep in the rain, and he would not intrude upon Annie Rose in the tent. That shelter belonged to her, and it would be up to her to offer to share it.

"Good night," he said to the horses, and headed back toward the fire.

He drew near to the welcoming light, but saw no sign of Annie Rose. Disappointed that she had already gone to bed, he hunkered down by the fire and added a few more lengths of wood. As much as he wanted to look upon her lovely face, it was probably best that they not spend too much time together. To see her, to have her so close, and yet not be able to touch her, only added to his torment. He reached for the coffeepot.

"Joseph." Her soft voice came out of the darkness, from the direction of his makeshift bed of buffalo robes spread on the ground.

Startled, he looked there, and almost dropped the coffeepot. Afraid he was dreaming, he hurriedly set the pot on the ground and stood, then took a few steps forward, squinting into the night. His eyes adjusted, and Joseph caught his breath at the sight before him.

Annie Rose was in the middle of his bed, kneeling, sitting back on her heels, her pale form a sharp contrast to the dark buffalo robe. As far as he could tell, she wore only her thigh-length chemise, for her exposed knees were bare. Her golden hair was down and free, falling over her shoulders and breasts to her lap, where her hands were demurely placed. She looked up at him, her expression now readable, the love he saw there unmistakable. His heart rate accelerated and his loins tightened.

She held her hand out to him. "Come to me," she whispered.

Joseph saw that her hand trembled, and he realized that she was afraid he would refuse her. In an instant, he was on his knees of front of her, clasping her cold hand. "My love."

"There is only one thing I would ask of you, Joseph Beaudine." She cupped his cheek in her other hand.

"Anything." He brought the hand he held to his mouth and pressed a kiss to the palm.

"Did you love your parents?"

Joseph stared at her, perplexed. "Very much."

"Then I ask you to swear, on the graves of your parents, that you will claim and support any child I may bear you, even if you do not wed me."

Anger that she still doubted him flashed through him, and his hold on her hand tightened involuntarily.

"No," she soothed, rising to her knees. "Do not misunderstand me. I believe you will marry me, Joseph. It's just that I know I will accept whatever you offer me, marriage or no. I love you that deeply, that completely. But I must know that my children will have a father who will claim them, that they will be wanted and loved and cared for."

Thankful that the firelight allowed him to see her, and her to see him, Joseph grabbed her other hand and looked into her eyes. "Annie Rose Jensen, I swear that I will publicly wed you as soon as possible, and that I will proudly claim and dearly love any children you may give me. Tonight, however, is the night I will truly make you my bride, if you are agreeable."

She nodded, her eyes bright with tears—of happiness, he hoped. "I am agreeable."

He pulled her close, simply to hold her, not needing yet to even kiss her. He felt the soft mounds of her breasts pressed to his chest, felt her hands as they moved over his back. His own hands, at last, played with her long, fragrant hair.

"This is in the way," she said, her voice muffled against

his shoulder. He realized that she was plucking at his buck-skin shirt. "I would have it gone."

A shock of erotic pleasure rocketed through him. "Yes, ma'am." He leaned back away from her, amused at her efforts to help him remove the shirt. She loosened the lacing at his throat, then grabbed the hem to assist in pulling the shirt over his head. Because he had not dried off after his bath before putting the shirt back on, the buckskin stuck stub-bornly to his damp flesh, causing them both a little frustra-tion. Finally, the shirt came off, inside out, and he flung it away. Annie Rose smoothed his long, wet hair, then put her arms around his shoulders and kissed him.

As he had never before been kissed.

She held nothing back, and he immediately noticed the difference. She was reaching for his heart, as she reached for the hearts of the horses, and he gave it to her. This time it was her mouth that took his, her teeth that nipped and nibbled, her tongue that prodded and explored. Joseph couldn't breathe. He tangled his hands in her hair and let her feminine power wash over him.

She released him then and leaned back, panting. Her eyes, hot with passion, searched his. His hands found the hem of her chemise, and she raised her arms over her head. The garment was gone in a flash, leaving her naked, and again she pressed herself to him, moving against him.

"I have wanted to do this for weeks," she whispered hoarsely. "To feel your chest against my breasts, to feel your heart next to mine."

Their mouths met again, fiercely, then Joseph moved to her ear, where he blew lightly and nibbled that delicate shell. He felt her nipples harden against his skin, and he hardened even more himself. As he had promised, he kissed his way down her long, lovely neck, taking great pleasure from her moans of pleasure. She clung to his shoulders and arched her back, offering her breasts to him—a treasure he could not refuse. Moving slowly now, he kissed his way down from her collarbone, down her chest, over the soft mound of her left breast, closer and closer to the nipple, then at last latched on.

Annie Rose cried out, her fingers digging into his shoulders, as Joseph lovingly explored that fascinating little bud with his tongue, his teeth, and his mouth. She ground her hips against his, ground her stomach against his hardness, exciting him almost beyond endurance.

When he finally showed her some mercy and moved back up to her neck, she tugged at the waistband of his pants and said breathlessly, "I would have these gone as well."

Breathless himself, Joseph responded, "Yes, ma'am," and moved away from her to stand.

She sat back on her heels and watched him, her long hair laying wildly about her, her eyes hot with interest. He found that simple act of watching wildly arousing, amazed that he could feel her so strongly when she wasn't even touching him. Knowing that she soon would be, Joseph hurriedly removed his moccasins and buckskin pants, then proudly stood before her, as naked as she was.

He took masculine pride in the way her eyes widened as her gaze travelled over him. Her lips parted, and she moistened the lower one with the tip of her tongue.

That was his undoing.

Joseph dropped down to his knees and guided her onto her back, then stretched out beside her. The firelight played over her pale body, revealing long shapely legs, slightly flaring hips centered with the intriguing triangle of hair, a narrow waist and flat stomach, rounded breasts with peaked nipples that seemed to plead for his touch. He looked into her eyes.

"You are so beautiful, Annie Rose," he whispered, and gently kissed her mouth.

"Do I please you, then?" she shyly asked.

"Oh, yes." He gathered her into his arms and she clung to him.

"You please me, too, Joseph Beaudine."

Their mouths met again, briefly, then Joseph whispered against her lips, "I haven't begun to please you yet."

At that moment, the power between them shifted, and they both knew it. Annie Rose lay back on the soft robes and gave herself to him. Joseph accepted her gift. His strong hands caressed her from shoulder to knee, while his mouth caressed her neck, then her breasts. The teasing tickle of his mustache and the rougher scrape of his growth of beard sent shivers through her and contrasted sharply with the wet warmth of his knowing lips and clever tongue. Annie Rose could do no more than lay there, helpless under the loving onslaught of his touch, overcome by feelings of pleasure she had never dreamed existed.

Then, when she thought she could bear no more, when she was certain that she would explode from the ecstasy, his hand moved between her legs and showed her that she could indeed bear more.

She gasped at the intimate touch, then shifted her legs farther apart for him. He moaned when his fingers found her, why, she did not know. Joseph's breath came faster now, as hers did, and to her surprise, she did explode from the ecstasy. Annie Rose cried out and clung to him, shaking. He held her close, his face buried in her hair, and whispered words of love.

Gradually, the tiny spasms deep inside her subsided, and her breathing slowed. Hungry now to know as much of Joseph as he knew of her, Annie Rose deliberately moved her hands over him, stroking and pressing and caressing. She felt the strength in the muscles of his back, found the smoothness of his buttocks an intriguing contrast to his powerful, hair-roughened thighs, enjoyed the fact that his breath caught when her hand wandered over his hip to his abdomen. Boldly, Annie Rose searched lower, and was thrilled to hear him gasp when she took his throbbing maleness in her hand. He was so hard, so powerful, yet the taut skin covering that hardness felt like hot satin. How fascinating was Joseph's male body, and how beautiful.

"Give me all of you," she whispered. Her hand moved to his hip and pulled, urging him closer.

"Yes, ma'am." Joseph settled on top of her, his hips between her legs, his hardness poised before her softness. "Look at me, Annie Rose," he commanded. "Look into my eyes."

She obeyed, working her arms under his so she could hold him. The intensity in his eyes heightened as he slowly pushed into her. She gasped at the pain of her virgin body's resistance, but did not take her eyes from his, and the pain soon subsided and was replaced with the wondrous feeling of him stretching and filling her. So slowly, he moved against her, in her, giving her time to adjust to his presence, to match her rhythm to his. It was much like riding a horse, Annie Rose decided, to find that rhythm and move in synch with each other—a dance, almost. But so much more than a dance, so much more than riding a horse.

Together, they found the rhythm, and again the pleasure built, higher and higher, until again she cried out, and his hoarse cry joined in. Joseph and Annie Rose clung together, heart to heart, soul to soul, truly connected at last.

The night wind cooled their heated bodies, and Joseph pulled a blanket over them. They still lay in each other's arms, their legs entwined. She kissed his chest; he stroked her hair.

"You are my bride, Annie Rose." Joseph kissed her forehead. "Your name is Beaudine from this night forward." He felt her smile against his shoulder.

"Annie Rose Beaudine. I like it." She kissed his jaw, which he knew was covered with several days' growth of beard.

"I'm sorry I didn't shave," he said. "I didn't know what you had planned for tonight, or I would have. I hope I haven't hurt you with that stubble."

"No." She nuzzled him. "I like how it feels."

"I like how all of you feels."

She giggled, then sobered. "I can't believe I was fearful of this." Her fingers toyed with the hair on his chest.

"I can understand why, though." Joseph kissed her again. "I'm glad you're not any longer."

"Not at all. But I warn you, sir." Annie Rose poked his chest. "I may need to experience this pleasure fairly often, just to ensure that the old fears don't return." She draped her leg over his hip.

"Anytime, Mrs. Beaudine." Joseph pushed her hair out of the way and nipped at her neck. "Just crook your finger, and I'll come running."

Annie Rose moaned and arched her neck for him. "I'll hold you to that, Mr. Beaudine."

Annie Rose awakened early the next morning, the sounds of nickers and munching drawing her from a deep, contented sleep. Once she opened her eyes, it took awhile for her to get her bearings.

Rather than in the tent, she was outside, the sky overcast, the morning air on her face very cool. Under a buffalo robe, she snuggled against Joseph's naked heat. The wonderful, erotic memories of the night before washed over her and infused her whole being with a warmth that had nothing to do with Joseph's protective nearness. Never before could she remember waking with such a feeling of peace and well-being.

During the night, the hobbled horses had drifted closer to the campsite, and Annie Rose now saw that all six animals were within close proximity, which explained the horsey noises that had awakened her. Thor actually nosed the blanket and blew, then shook his head. She could not stifle a laugh.

Joseph, instantly awake, sat up and reached for his rifle.

"It's all right, Joseph," Annie Rose said happily. "We have company, that's all."

He blinked and looked around, then released his rifle and relaxed. "Pesky horses," he growled good-naturedly. "They have their nerve." He looked down at her, and his eyes lit up with carnal interest.

Annie Rose reached for the robe, which Joseph had pulled off her when he sat up. As if her nipples—puckered by the cool morning air—hadn't already told her, she was exposed to the waist. She clutched the robe to her throat and stared into his eyes, then slowly, so slowly, crooked her index finger.

Joseph pounced on her. Her peals of laughter quieted to giggles when his head disappeared under the robe, and, a short time later, to gasps of pleasure.

Aurora pricked her ears, then continued munching the dew-wet grass.

Their journey continued, and all awkwardness between Joseph and Annie Rose disappeared. Where before she had found the days of silence long and lonely, and the nights even worse, now the days passed much too quickly, and the nights, filled with joyous loving in Joseph's arms, flew by. The Medicine Bow Mountains appeared on the distant horizon and grew in size until they towered over the land and the little group that approached. Snow appeared on the highest of the peaks, reminding them that winter was not far off.

For two days, when checking their back trail, Joseph reported seeing a small band of wild horses in the distance, but he couldn't be certain it was the same band. Annie Rose wondered if The Paint was following them. It wouldn't surprise her, for hadn't he once come to her grandfather's valley seeking Aurora?

As the mountains drew near, so did the time when Annie Rose would have to say goodbye to Aurora and Thor, and the knowledge tore at her heart. How she wished she and Joseph could simply stay with the horses, shut out the rest of the world, and live in peace and bliss.

But no such plan would work without Thomas and her grandfather with them, and the practical part of her mind knew that the fantasy was just that—a fantasy. Still, she wished with all her heart that there was a way to keep all those she loved close to her, safe and happy. That could not be with Aurora and Thor, who needed to be free. Painful as it was, she knew her original decision was still the best.

Joseph unerringly led them up into the mountains and to

the top of a low pass. Before them spread a valley. No heroic efforts would be needed to reach the sanctuary, as had been the case with Knute's valley, but, in terms of beauty, it closely resembled the home Annie Rose had known for the last seven years.

She sighed happily as her gaze wandered over the valley. It was larger than Knute's, perhaps fifteen miles long and five to six miles across. Lush meadow grasses, turning yellow now, a swiftly moving stream, protective groves of fir trees, a low enough altitude that the winter snows would not make grazing impossible, no sign of mankind—the place was an ideal retreat for Aurora and Thor.

"It's perfect, Joseph." She looked at him and smiled.

"It is, isn't it?" He leaned forward, his hands on the saddle horn. "Makes me want to stay here with them."

"Me, too."

Joseph studied her. "I don't know why we can't stay a day or two." He shrugged, his expression serious, but Annie Rose detected a lascivious gleam in his eyes. "You know, to make sure the horses get settled and all."

Annie Rose fought to keep her own features schooled in a solemn expression. "Seems like the only responsible thing for us to do."

A wide grin split Joseph's handsome face. "Good. Let's scout around for a good campsite." He led the way down to the valley floor.

They set up the tent near a small stand of fir trees, not far from the clear, cold stream. Annie Rose loved the soothing noise of the wind as it moved through the boughs of the trees, and of the water as it gurgled and laughed over the rocks in the streambed. The sounds of nature were an eternal lullaby, one of which she would never weary.

The horses loved the freedom of the valley, for Joseph did not hobble them. He explained that Grace was trained to come at his whistle, and if necessary, he could recapture Calypso and the packhorse when the time came to leave.

The hours flew by, and so did their two days. Annie Rose

desperately wanted time to stop, but of course, it would not. She and Joseph put the precious time to good use, though. They explored the valley on foot and on horseback, feasted on fresh trout and wild onions, marveled at the beauty of the sunrises and sunsets, and made love with wild abandon whenever the urge struck one of them—which was often. They simply could not get enough of each other.

The complete safety and isolation of the valley gave them a sense of freedom neither had ever before experienced. Annie Rose left her hair down throughout the day, much to Joseph's delight, and, in the warmth of the lazy afternoons, wore no more than her chemise, drawers, and petticoat.

Joseph watched Annie Rose blossom with a joy that healed her spirit and reached to her soul, and his heart was warmed by the knowledge that his love for her had contributed to the change in her.

Annie Rose held Joseph's hand and listened intently as he spoke of his dreams for the future, how he hoped he could accomplish something of value in the strained relationships between the Indians and the white man. She knew that he had found a more definite direction for his life since that day when he had first come to the valley with her grandfather.

The love each felt for the other had healed them both.

On their third morning in the valley, they awakened to frost on the grasses and a chilling mist that obscured the mountains ringing the meadow.

"We must go, Annie Rose," Joseph said reluctantly. "It's early October—not too soon for a surprise blizzard. We need to get back to Fort Laramie."

"I know." Annie Rose snuggled against his warmth for a minute longer. "These last two days have been heaven, Joseph. You've given me a wedding trip I will always treasure."

He kissed the tip of her cold nose. "Now I'd better give you a wedding you will always remember, huh?"

She giggled, amazed that she could find humor in a topic she had always taken so seriously. "You'd better."

"Besides," Joseph added with a teasing smile, "I don't want your grandfather to kill me."

Annie Rose lifted up on one elbow. "Did he threaten to if you didn't marry me?" she demanded.

"Yes, ma'am, he sure did. Said that if I accepted your love then didn't do right by you, he'd kill me. I told him he'd have every right to." Serious now, Joseph looked into her eyes. "I meant it, too, Annie Rose. I'd expect your grandfather to come after me if I betrayed you. But it won't be necessary. I won't let you go, even if you wanted to. We're meant to be together." He reached out and placed his hand over her exposed left breast. "The heart that beats here belongs to me, and I treasure it."

Overcome by love and emotion, Annie Rose lay her head on his chest, right over his heart. No further words were necessary.

By the time they broke camp and prepared Grace, Calypso, and the packhorse for the return journey to Fort Laramie, the morning sun had burned away the mist and melted the thin layer of frost. It could be put off no longer. The leave-taking was upon them.

Annie Rose stood with Aurora, her arms around the mare's neck, fighting tears. "I didn't know it would be this difficult," she said mournfully to Joseph.

He squeezed her shoulder in silent understanding. "I'll bring you back in the spring," he promised. "For a visit, and to be certain they made it through the winter."

She nodded against Aurora's clean, horsey-smelling coat and closed her eyes. Her aching heart sought comfort from Aurora's heart.

Annie Rose heard the beating of the mare's heart, and focused on that steady rhythm. Deeper she went, and deeper. This time it was her spirit that needed calming.

She felt Joseph's arm go around her waist, knew without seeing that his other arm was on Aurora. Thor nuzzled her side, and she moved one hand to the colt's neck. They stood together—the man, the woman, the mare, the colt—connected in a circle of perfect love.

The silence of the valley was broken by the wild call of a stallion. Annie Rose blinked her tear-filled eyes and looked toward the sound. Aurora nickered, but, surprisingly, did not move away.

"It's The Paint," Joseph said wonderingly. "He's found her again."

"Of course he did," Annie Rose whispered. A new sense of peace filled her heart. As much as she loved Aurora and Thor, they were meant to follow a different path. She smoothed the white forelock that fell over Aurora's forehead and kissed the mare's velvety nose.

The Paint called again.

"Go to him, Aurora," Annie Rose urged. She patted Aurora's shoulder and the mare turned away, taking a few hesitant steps. Annie Rose took Thor's head between her hands and placed a kiss between his big brown eyes. "Go, little one. Go meet your daddy." A light smack on Thor's rump was all it took to send the colt dancing after his mother. Aurora broke into a trot, then a gallop, and she raced away, her mane and tail streaming out behind her, Thor scrambling after her.

Joseph put his arm around Annie Rose's shoulders and held her close. A few tears trailed down her cheeks as she circled Joseph's waist with her arms. Together they watched the reunion of the Golden Mare and her mate, saw Thor peek under his mama's tummy at his awesome sire, saw The Paint's curious nuzzling of his son. The Paint's triumphant call echoed across the valley.

Annie Rose's quest was completed.

Twenty-four

"Are you sure you're all right?" Joseph asked. Concerned, he studied Annie Rose's lovely face. They had halted at the top of the pass that would lead them out of the valley, and she now watched the herd of horses that grazed peacefully on the valley's floor. The Paint had not come alone; perhaps a dozen other horses would spend the winter with him and his little family.

"Truly, Joseph, I'm fine." Annie Rose's voice was soft but clear, and there was no hint of more tears in her green eyes. "I wish there was a way we could all live together in peace, but we can't. This is as it should be." She smiled, a small smile, but it was enough to cheer him.

Joseph leaned out of the saddle and placed his hand over hers. "You are a wise and courageous woman, Annie Rose. Giving Aurora up was one of the bravest things I have ever seen anyone do."

Her eyebrows drew together in a puzzled frown. "I don't feel brave. I feel that it was the only thing I *could* do."

"No. You could have been selfish. You could have kept Aurora and Thor, saddle-trained them, used them as most people use horses. You had the opportunity to do that."

"I wouldn't have," she exclaimed. "I *couldn't* have."

"I know, sweet woman. That's one of the reasons why I love you." Joseph patted her hand and straightened in his saddle. "Are you ready?"

One last time, her gaze travelled over the valley. Then she nodded. "I'm ready."

Joseph started Grace down the pass, leading the pack-horse, and Annie Rose followed.

As he had warned her, Joseph took a different route on the way back. They headed in more of an easterly direction instead of angling to the northeast, and, without making all the stops that had been necessary when travelling with Thor, made excellent time. Joseph still was careful about leaving as little evidence of their passing as possible, but even with that caution, they reached the Laramie River by sunset. They saw to the horses, put together a quick camp, ate an early supper, and turned in. Later, when a cold rainstorm blanketed the area, they were grateful for the shelter of the Army tent.

At sunrise they were up again, and soon on their way. They followed the river for only a few hours, then forded it and turned northeast, heading across the desolate plains on a relatively straight line to the fort. The farther away they got from the Medicine Bow Mountains, the more anxious both Joseph and Annie Rose were to reach Fort Laramie, and not just because of the weather. Concerns that had been left to rest for a while came back to the forefront—concerns such as Knute's wounded leg, Erik's injuries, housing for the family for the winter, the return of Sparrow to her people.

A wedding.

Annie Rose was surprised that her feelings about the wedding ceremony did not have the same sense of urgency they had before. Deep in thought, she watched Joseph as he rode in front of her, and she realized that her grandfather's words were true. Marriage was forged in the heart, not in a ceremony. Joseph had given her his name as well as his body. She already considered him her husband. The thought made her smile. She still wanted a wedding, but all of her impatience and fear had gone.

At mid-morning on the last day of their journey, Joseph pulled Grace to a halt and stared into the distance. Annie

Rose guided Calypso to his side. The expression on his handsome face troubled her.

"What is it?" she asked, speaking in a low voice, even
though they were completely alone.

"Company." Joseph slid his Hawken from its beaded scabbard.

Annie Rose put a hand to the brim of her hat and squinted
into the afternoon sun. Perhaps a mile away, she saw three
men on horseback, one leading a packhorse, all of them heading west. From that distance, she could not tell if they were
white men or Indians. She drew her grandfather's rifle from
its case and cradled its comforting weight in one arm.

"Have they seen us?" she asked.

"I think so. We came over the top of this rise the same
time they topped that hill."

Sure enough, the group of riders in the distance changed
their direction.

"Who could they be?"

Joseph shrugged. "It's not a war party—they could be
Cheyenne or Arapaho, going to join their encampment. Or
they could be frontiersmen scouting for the Army or looking
for a place to winter. Or it could be Baines, hunting us and
Aurora."

Annie Rose looked at him. "If they are Cheyenne, they
may have news of Sparrow. The same could be true of scouts
or frontiersmen, because they most likely came from the fort.
If it's Baines, we may be able to throw him off the track, or
discourage him from going any farther."

"I'd like to kill him," Joseph said darkly.

Annie Rose returned her gaze to the distant riders. "So
would I, if for no other reason than for what he did to Aurora."

Joseph stood in the stirrups, staring. "They're white men,
for sure, and that horse in the lead could be Baines's." He
looked at Annie Rose, his expression grim and determined,
and he spoke to her in a commanding tone that he had never
before used with her. "If I'm hit, or if I tell you to, ride,
Annie Rose. Don't argue with me, and don't wait for me.

Ride for the fort. If I can be, I'll be right behind you. If I can't be, I don't need to be worried about you, too. Is that understood?"

She nodded. "Yes." *As if I'd leave you, Joseph Beaudine.*

He pointed to a small rise a short distance away. "We'll wait for them there. Position yourself so the sun will be in their eyes."

Again she nodded, and followed Joseph to the rise. They waited, rifles balanced and ready. As the riders drew closer, Annie Rose saw that the man in front was indeed Abby Baines. Painted Davy Sikes followed, leading the packhorse, then came a third rider she recognized as a frontiersman named Will Mayhew. That she found puzzling, for Mayhew had a decent reputation. What was he doing with scum like Abby Baines and Painted Davy?

Apparently Joseph had the same thought. As the three men closed the distance between them, he called out.

"Will Mayhew! How are you, man? Thought you had more sense than to ride with those two."

Will was a big man, tough and weathered, wearing dirty buckskins and sporting a full beard. "Howdy, Joe. Baines keeps mouthin' off about that Golden Mare. Got back last week from Fort Kearny and didn't have nothin' else goin', so thought I'd try to get a look at her. Just once 'fore I die, I'd like to see me a real spirit animal." He took off his hat, revealing a full head of greying brown hair that was just as bushy and unkempt as his beard, and nodded at Annie Rose. "Ma'am. You must be the Norseman's granddaughter. Word is out all over about you. You're just as pretty as they said you was."

Still unused to compliments, Annie Rose fought a blush as she inclined her head in greeting. "Pleased to meet you, Mr. Mayhew. I've seen you from a distance when you met with my grandfather. He has always spoken well of you." She pointed to Abby Baines. "You should know that his intentions toward the Golden Mare are less than honorable."

"Mind your own business, missy," Baines growled, insolently running his gaze over Annie Rose from head to foot.

Joseph leveled his rifle at Baines. "That's 'missus' to you, Baines, and be real careful how you look at my wife."

Baines spat a stream of tobacco juice to the ground as he shifted his hate-filled gaze to Joseph. "You won't take that mare from me again, Beaudine, neither you nor your woman." He spat again.

"You won't find the mare again," Joseph calmly said.

"I'll find her. You and your gawddamned brothers aren't the only ones who can track."

Will Mayhew smacked Abby's arm with his hat. "Don't swear in front of the lady. And take off your hat." He glared at Painted Davy, who hurriedly removed his scruffy hat.

"I ain't takin' off my hat," snarled Baines. "Don't push me, Mayhew."

Will shrugged. Painted Davy put his hat back on.

"You can't track a ghost horse," Joseph said. "Not even the Hunter could do that."

"We ain't trackin' no ghost horse," Painted Davy argued. "I seen her with my own eyes, had my own rope around her neck."

Anger started boiling up in Annie Rose at Painted Davy's words. She bit down on her lip and noticed that Baines stared at Joseph with an expression of worry growing on his dirt-smudged face.

"Whatever you say." Joseph glanced at Annie Rose. "Let's be on our way and leave these men to their hopeless search. Good to see you again, Will. Watch your back."

Annie Rose nudged Calypso to a slow walk. Joseph followed.

"Beaudine!" Baines shouted. "What're you sayin'?"

Joseph halted and looked back at him. "I'm saying you won't find the Golden Mare, Baines. She's gone, safe in a place beyond your reach."

Baines gaped at him. "You killed her?"

A swell of admiration and pride in Joseph's ingenuity

filled Annie Rose. She turned Calypso around so she could face Baines. "Death is preferable to what you would have condemned that mare to." She deliberately added a righteous note to her tone. "I told you the Golden Mare had to be free. Now she is."

"I don't believe you!" Baines shouted. "You wouldn't kill that mare!"

Still clutching her grandfather's rifle, Annie Rose used her knees to nudge Calypso closer, her eyes narrowed, her lips tight with anger. "Mistake me not, Abby Baines; I would do *anything* to protect that mare. She is forever safe from you, whether you believe it or not."

Baines blinked, and his face drained of color.

"Aw, hell!" Painted Davy said as he slapped his thigh in frustration. "I just knew this was a gawddamned dumb idea, what with winter comin' on and all." At Will's thunderous expression, he quickly added, "Sorry, ma'am."

Joseph caught Annie Rose's eye. With a motion of his head, he indicated that he wanted her to leave. She nodded and turned Calypso back in the direction of the fort. Again, he followed.

Painted Davy's whining voice reached her ears. "Now what're we gonna do, Abby? You said them Sioux buddies of yours would pay us well for the mare, let us winter with 'em. Now what?"

Annie Rose strained to hear Abby's response, but she heard nothing. A bad feeling—a warning—settled in her gut, and she fought the urge to kick Calypso to a gallop. She glanced back over her shoulder. Joseph was at her right flank, the packhorse behind him. Farther back, Abby and Painted Davy sat their horses, side by side, watching them go. Annie Rose could feel Abby's evil hatred as distinctly as if it were a hot wind from hell. Will Mayhew waited a little off to the left.

"Keep going, Annie Rose," Joseph said quietly.

She nodded and faced front, but caught a glimpse of something out of the corner of her eye. She looked. Another rider approached from the north.

"Joseph."

"I see him. Keep moving. When we top this hill, *ride.*"

Annie Rose held the rifle in a tight grip and made certain her skirts were hiked up enough to allow access to the knife that nestled in her calf-high moccasin. The very wind seemed to scream of danger.

"Beaudine!"

Annie Rose recognized Will Mayhew's voice. A gunshot echoed through the air, then she was knocked from the saddle. Another shot sounded. Annie Rose landed hard, with Joseph on top of her. Knute's rifle flew from her hand and fired harmlessly when it hit the ground a few feet away. Calypso screamed, then bolted, with the packhorse right behind her. Grace trotted off, but stayed fairly close.

Instantly, Joseph was on one knee in front of her, facing their assailants, his Hawken ready. "Are you hurt?" he asked tensely over his shoulder.

"No." She scrambled to her knees beside him, breathing hard, her knife in hand. "Are you?"

"No."

Annie Rose stared at the men and horses a short distance away. Both Will and Painted Davy were still in their saddles. Abby Baines lay on the ground near his horse. The mysterious rider came closer, heading toward the other men.

"What happened?" she asked.

"I'm not sure." Joseph straightened and helped her up. "Will shouted my name, and I saw Abby taking aim at us. I wanted to get you down." He looked at her. "There was no time to warn you. Are you certain you're not injured?"

"A few bruises may show up, but I'm fine." Annie Rose slipped her knife back in her moccasin, then retrieved Knute's rifle.

Joseph took her elbow. "Let's get this figured out."

They walked back to where Will and Painted Davy waited.

"I didn't have nothin' to do with it, Beaudine," Painted Davy hastened to say. He held up his empty hands. "It was like somethin' in ol' Abby snapped. I didn't have time to even try to stop him."

Joseph halted at Abby's side and crouched down, although the huge wound in the man's chest told Annie Rose he was beyond human help. "He's dead," Joseph said as he stood. "Who shot him?"

Will nodded toward the rider who slowly approached. "That man there."

Numbly, Annie Rose lifted her gaze from the body of Abby Baines, then she stared. "Erik?" she whispered. The man had lost some weight, and trimmed his red beard shorter, but it was her cousin.

Erik pulled his horse to a stop. "Hello, cousin," he said quietly. An old buffalo gun rested across his thighs.

Annie Rose closed the distance to Erik's horse. She stopped at his side and looked up at him. "What is this? Why are you here?"

Erik shrugged. "I overheard Baines and Painted Davy making their plans. You and the captain weren't back yet, and I didn't want Baines to find you. I tracked them from the fort, always staying just out of sight." He looked past her to Joseph. "The Beaudines aren't the only ones who can track." He paused, then admitted, "Of course, it wasn't that difficult. Baines left a trail as easy to follow as a herd of buffalo."

"Well, we wasn't tryin' to hide from no one," Painted Davy protested defensively.

"We're obliged to you, Erik," Joseph said.

Erik shrugged again. "I couldn't let him murder you." He glanced at Annie Rose. "Either one of you."

Will stepped down from his saddle. "I reckon we'd best bury the fool," he said. "C'mon, Painted Davy. If we hurry, we can still make it back to the fort by sundown. Take your woman and get, Joe. She don't need to be seein' this."

"Thanks, Will." Joseph held out his hand, which Will shook.

"Yes, thank you, Mr. Mayhew," Annie Rose added.

Will tipped his hat and nodded at her. "Ma'am." He moved to the packhorse, where he extricated a short-handled shovel from a pack, then he and Painted Davy walked to a site not far from where Abby Baines lay.

Joseph approached Annie Rose and Erik, his eyes on Erik. "Thank you for watching out for us," he said.

Again, Erik shrugged. "It was nothing. Is the mare safe?"

"She is."

"Good." Erik repositioned his reins.

Annie Rose stepped back to Joseph's side. "How is Gramps?" she asked Erik. The closed, defensive look that settled over her cousin's face broke her heart.

"All right. His leg is getting a lot better. That new surgeon—Doctor Murdoch—he knows what he's doing."

"Good. Any news of Sparrow?"

Erik shook his head. "Jubal sent back word. There was a hellacious storm up north that wiped out the tracks. They were going to try to pick the trail up, but they're getting close to Crow and Blackfoot land, and they're not supplied as a war party. It doesn't look good, at least for now."

Annie Rose glanced at Joseph, saw the sorrow in his face. She squeezed his hand in sympathy.

"Well, I'll be on my way." Erik pulled his horse's head around.

"We'd be pleased to have you ride back with us," Joseph said.

Erik looked up, surprised.

"Please, Erik," Annie Rose added. "That is, if you're going to Fort Laramie."

"I am." Erik nodded. "Thank you for the invitation. I'd be pleased to ride with you."

Annie Rose smiled, relieved and happy. Perhaps more of Erik had healed in the last few weeks than just his bruised face.

Joseph whistled for Grace, who obediently trotted to his side.

"I'll help you retrieve Annie Rose's horse, Captain," Erik offered.

"On one condition," Joseph said sternly. He handed Annie Rose his rifle, then swung up into the saddle.

"Yes, sir," Erik nervously responded.

"Call me 'Joe.' "

For the first time in over a year, Annie Rose saw her cousin smile.

"Yes, sir," said Erik, then quickly added, "Joe."

Joseph took up his reins. "I'll go after Calypso if you'll find our packhorse."

"Let's do it."

Annie Rose shifted the two rifles she held to a butt-down position on the ground and watched her cousin and her lover ride off. Never would she have guessed that Joseph and Erik would be able to work together again after all that had happened between them, yet they were. There was much to be thankful for. She smiled, and a sense of peace stole over her.

If Sparrow could be found, the Hunter would find her.

Aurora and Thor were safe with The Paint.

They were all safe from Abelard Baines.

Erik seemed to be recovering from both his physical and emotional wounds.

Her grandfather still lived, and soon she would see him, along with her beloved brother.

She and Joseph would marry.

There, on a small rise in the middle of the endless prairie, Annie Rose waited with the rifles, as the cool wind blew her skirts against her legs and whispered to her the promise of winter.

No, she corrected herself.

The promise was for the future.

Twenty-five

As other dancers continued to whirl past her, Annie Rose Beaudine fell breathlessly into a chair, careful of the hoops under the skirts of her exquisite silk and lace gown. "I must rest!" she gasped, and smiled up at her husband. She still could not get over how beautiful he was to her, on this, their wedding day.

Joseph wore a black broadcloth suit, complete with a frock coat, a white shirt, and a gray silk cravat. His hair had grown past his shoulder blades, and she liked it long. He smiled down at her, his teeth very white under his dark mustache. "Forgive me, wife." His voice was low and warm with love. "I've wanted to dance with you since I met you, and now that I have, I don't want to let you out of my embrace." He hunkered down next to her and captured her left hand in his. "Wife. I love the sound of that word." He placed a kiss on the gold band that encircled her third finger.

Love swelled in Annie Rose's heart. "Husband," she whispered, and stroked his long hair. "Thank you for giving me such a fine wedding."

"I wanted to do it right." Joseph maneuvered into the chair next to her, still holding her hand.

"You did," she assured him.

They fell silent and looked out over the group that had

gathered in the fort's mess hall to celebrate their formal marriage. The room was crowded with soldiers, frontiersmen, friends—such as Will Mayhew and the sutler, Miles Breen—and various family members. All wore their best, be it dress uniform, tailored suit, fancy gown, elaborately beaded buckskin, or, as in the case of Jubal Sage, an eclectic mixture of fashions.

The music quieted for a moment, and as the dancers vacated the center of the room, Annie Rose looked across the way. With a curious expression of concern mixed with pride, Thomas perched on the edge of a chair and cradled the infant Henry Jedediah in his arms. Next to the boys, Knute sat with Joseph's stepmother, Florence Beaudine, who, along with her two pretty daughters, had finally arrived from St. Louis three weeks earlier. Knute and Florence sipped on punch as they carried on an animated discussion, and Annie Rose's heart filled with joy to see her grandfather looking so well and happy. For a moment, her thoughts dwelled on the fort's new surgeon, Doctor Gideon Murdoch, who had taken such competent care of Knute over the last two months. The good doctor suffered from a chronic ailment and had been feeling poorly, so he had remained at home today, with his grown daughter, Diana, watching over him. Annie Rose missed the amiable presence of both Murdochs, and was sorry they couldn't be here.

Grey Eagle and Orion stood nearby with their sisters, Juliet and Cora. Sarah Beaudine's arm was looped through her husband's, and Raven's Heart and his soft-spoken wife, Little Leaf, were there also, both resplendent in their Cheyenne finery. All in that group laughed when Jubal Sage led Sweet Water past them in a galloping rendition of a new dance called the polka. Jubal exhibited more enthusiasm than skill in executing the dance steps, and Annie Rose was impressed that Sweet Water did such a good job of keeping up with her husband.

Only two notes of sadness marred this otherwise perfect

day: Erik's absence, and the fact that the kidnapped child Sparrow had not been rescued from her Crow captors.

Although her cousin had reconciled with his family, Erik was still determined to work his way to the gold fields of California, and so had departed the week before with an Army detachment bound west for Fort Bridger. Before he left, Erik had given Joseph and Annie Rose his sincere best wishes, as well as a beautifully carved wedding chest, which he himself had made in an attempt to atone for the heirloom chest that had been lost in the cabin fire.

As for Sparrow, the tormenting worries about how her captors were treating her—in addition to the knowledge that she might never be seen again—weighed heavily on the entire Beaudine family. Annie Rose said a silent prayer for the safety and well-being of the young Cheyenne girl she had never met—a girl who was now her niece.

She sighed and smoothed the skirt of her silk wedding gown with her free hand.

"Why the sigh?" Joseph asked.

Annie Rose raised her head to find his dark, intense gaze on her. "I was thinking of Sparrow and Erik," she answered. "This day is perfect but for their absence."

"I know." Joseph raised her hand to his mouth for a quick kiss. After a moment of compassionate silence, he added, "Have I told you how beautiful you look in that gown, Mrs. Beaudine?"

Even as she smiled, Annie Rose could feel a faint blush heat her cheeks. Would she ever get used to Joseph's open admiration for her? "Many times, Mr. Beaudine, but you can tell me as often as you like." Again, she stroked the soft, ivory-colored material. "This is the loveliest gown I have ever seen, let alone owned. And it is all the more special because it came from you and your family—you ordered the materials, and Mama Florrie and your sisters made it for me." Her fingers tightened on Joseph's hand. "You really did give me a wonderful wedding, husband, and I thank you for it."

"You deserve it, Annie Rose. I'm glad you are pleased.

But as wonderful as this wedding is"—he placed his mouth near her ear and his voice dropped to a low, sensual whisper—"I'm getting anxious for our wedding night."

A shiver of delight raced through her, and Annie Rose closed her eyes. The many weeks that had passed since their return from Aurora's new home had left them both taut with sexual frustration. They considered themselves wed, but, out of respect for their families, until today Joseph had bunked with Knute and Thomas, while Annie Rose shared Florrie's small quarters. Except for illicit minutes of intimacy, stolen during horseback rides into the countryside or late-night strolls along the river, their physical passion for each other had been suppressed. As the days passed, their frustration intensified, following as it did the freedom they had enjoyed during their trip with the horses. Their bedroom, which had been added onto Orion's home, had been finished for days, and the wide, comfortable-looking bed therein called to them both, but neither had been willing to sleep there without the other.

Tonight, they would share that bed.

At the thought, Annie Rose shivered again. "How soon can we leave without appearing unseemly?" she whispered.

"How about right now?" he whispered back, and nipped her ear.

Her lips curved in a smile. "In the middle of the afternoon?"

"Captain and Mrs. Beaudine?"

Annie Rose started, and her eyes flew open. An officer she recognized as Captain Adam Rutledge stood before them in his dress uniform, a folded paper held in one gloved hand.

"I'm sorry I couldn't be here for the ceremony, but the detachment from Fort Kearny had just arrived," the captain said.

"We understand." Joseph stood up. "Hello, Adam." He shook the captain's hand.

"Congratulations on your marriage, Joe." Captain Rutledge nodded at Annie Rose. "You, too, ma'am."

"Thank you, Captain," Annie Rose replied. Since the day she first met him, when he stood between her and Abby Baines at the aborted auction of the Golden Mare, she had liked the handsome captain. With his blonde hair, neatly trimmed beard, and eyes that on a man were a startling shade of blue, Captain Adam Rutledge cut a dashing figure, especially in his uniform, and Annie Rose wondered why he had not yet married. She knew he had once been engaged to Orion's wife, Sarah, but that had been over a year ago. Of course, she mused, there weren't many available women in the vicinity of Fort Laramie. Her thoughts were cut short when the captain handed Joseph the paper he held.

"This message came for you with the detachment, Joe," said Captain Rutledge. "I wanted to get it to you right away."

"Thanks," Joseph replied. "I hope you can join the party now. There's some punch on the table over there by the Norseman, and a keg of brandy out back, if you want something stronger."

"Sounds good to me. I'll leave you to read your message." Adam bowed to Annie Rose. "Mrs. Beaudine." He turned and left them.

The band came to the end of its song, and the large room suddenly seemed quiet. Annie Rose watched Joseph's face as he read the message. His expression was somber, and a small kernel of worry formed in her stomach.

"I'll be damned," Joseph muttered, and sank back down in his chair.

"What is it?" Annie Rose asked.

Joseph turned to her and reached for her hand. "I did something without your permission, Annie Rose, and I need to tell you about it."

The kernel of worry blossomed. Joseph looked so serious! "Then tell me, please, Joseph. You're frightening me."

"Do you remember when Jubal came down to the fort with messages for Orion, when we'd made the decision to winter here?"

Annie Rose nodded. It seemed so long ago now.

Joseph continued. "I asked Orion to do a couple of things for me. One was to order the material for your gown. The other was to send a message to a friend of mine back East." He hesitated.

"And?" Annie Rose prompted.

"I asked my friend to make discreet inquiries about your father, Annie Rose. This message is his reply. There is also a letter here for you, from a man who claims to be your half-brother."

The blood pounded in Annie Rose's ears, drowning out the sounds of the celebration. Shocked, she stared into Joseph's brown eyes and saw the compassion there, the worry, the fear. He had acted out of love for her, of that she had no doubt. Her fingers tightened on his. "Perhaps my grandfather and my brother should hear this."

"You're not angry with me?"

"No, dearest. I'm surprised, that's all."

"I was afraid you'd forbid me to do it if I asked you."

Annie Rose shrugged. "I may well have." She sighed. "But it's best that we know the truth. Perhaps everything can be put to rest then."

Joseph stood and pulled her to her feet. Her legs felt strangely weak, and she took a calming breath. No matter what the letters said, her father could not hurt them now. She focused on her grandfather's beloved face, aware of the unfamiliar hoops that swayed around her legs as she walked.

Knute's gaze fell on her, and he rose from his chair.

"Gramps." Annie Rose placed a kiss on Knute's cheek, then motioned to Thomas. "Joseph has some news for us."

"This sounds serious," Florrie Beaudine said cheerfully. She stood up and turned to Thomas. "Give me my grandson, young man," she commanded kindly. "Your family needs to discuss something in private."

Thomas obeyed, and, as Annie Rose watched Florrie walk away with Henry in her arms, she could not help but think that it was impossible for the slight, pretty woman to be a grandmother. Florrie Beaudine didn't look much older than her own daughters.

Joseph herded Annie Rose and her family to a relatively quiet corner and told Knute and Thomas the same thing he'd told her.

Knute's mouth tightened under his white mustache, and Annie Rose feared he was angry. But her grandfather's voice was calm when he spoke.

"Tell us what you learned, Joe."

"Blaine Coburn died two years ago from a failure of the liver." Joseph stared at Knute, and Annie Rose sensed that he meant his next words for her grandfather only. "There were no other contributing factors in his death. Until his final illness, he remained an astute businessman, and left his family—I should say, his *other* family—well situated."

Knute took a deep breath and momentarily closed his eyes.

Annie Rose frowned, certain that Joseph had just told Knute something private. What secret did her husband share with her grandfather?

Joseph continued. "Coburn's other family consists of his widow, a son, and two daughters." He turned to Annie Rose. "The son—your half brother—named Daniel, has written you and Thomas a letter." He pressed a folded paper into her hand, then guided her to a chair.

Thomas pulled another chair closer and sat down. "Read it, sister," he urged, tugging irritably on the cravat that encircled his neck.

Annie Rose unfolded the paper. A rather long message written in a neat script stared back at her. She cleared her throat and began to read aloud.

"Dear Sister Annabella and Brother Thomas. I hope this missive reaches you. The gentleman making the inquiries about my father—our father—is most secretive, and will not tell me where you are.

"Before our father's death two years ago, he confessed to

me the truth about his relationship with your mother, Thora Jensen. Imagine my astonishment to learn I had a sister and brother about whom I had known nothing. I was mortified to hear how my father had treated the two of you and your mother. Father was a hard man—indeed, cruel, on occasion—and loath to demonstrate affection even toward those he loved most dearly. In the hope that it will offer you comfort, I have the very strong impression that our father cared deeply for your mother and, at the end, was haunted by his unkindness toward her and you."

Annie Rose paused, unable to believe the words she had just read. Then she continued.

"For years he searched for you, as I have done since his death. Your grandfather is to be complimented for hiding you so effectively. I understand why he felt he had to protect you, and I have no doubt that, at the time, he made the right decision. However, times have changed. When Father realized he was dying, his greatest wish was to see the two of you again and atone for his past cruelties. He did not have the chance to do so in person, and commanded that I act on his behalf.

"Should this letter reach you, and you have no wish to respond to me, I shall be disappointed, but I will understand. You have two sisters and a brother—me—in Baltimore, should you ever desire to meet us. Also, Father left each of you a settlement in his will. If nothing else, please send instructions to the family solicitor (Mr. James Baldwin, Esq., High Street, Baltimore) as to what your wishes are for your respective inheritances.

"It is my fondest hope that we can one day meet, Annabella and Thomas. For all our sakes, the past should be reconciled.

"I remain affectionately yours, Daniel Coburn."

* * *

Annie Rose clutched the letter and allowed her hands to fall to her lap. Tears formed in her eyes, and she felt as if a great weight had been lifted from her shoulders.

The silence was broken by Thomas's skeptical voice. "Do you think he's telling the truth?"

"About what?" asked Joseph.

"About all of it—our father's change of heart; our inheritance; wanting to meet us." Thomas shoved long, unruly blonde hair back from his forehead and frowned. "This sounds too good to be true."

Joseph shrugged. "Maybe it is, Thomas." He waved his own letter. "But, for what it's worth, my friend came away from the meeting with Daniel Coburn convinced that the man was sincere."

Annie Rose looked up at her grandfather. "What do you think, Gramps?"

Knute stroked his mustache as he slowly shook his head. "I don't know, *datter*. That young man is not describing the Blaine Coburn I knew, but the thought of soon meeting one's maker can change a man real quick."

"I'm glad our father is dead," Thomas declared fiercely. "The bastard!" He jumped up from his chair.

"Thomas," Annie Rose said pleadingly, reaching for her brother's hand.

Thomas tolerated her touch, then pulled away. "Well, I *am* glad. Now we can live in peace, without always having to worry about him coming after us. And that man Daniel is no brother of mine. I want nothing to do with him or the Coburn money." He spun on his heel and left.

With an aching heart, Annie Rose watched her brother stomp across the room and out the side door.

"I'll go after him," Joseph offered.

"No." Knute wearily sank onto the chair Thomas had just vacated. "He's entitled to his feelings. Let him blow off some steam."

"What do you think we should do, Gramps?" asked Annie Rose.

"That will be for you and Thomas to decide, *datter.*"

"And there's no need to decide today," Joseph firmly interjected.

Annie Rose smiled up at her husband. "No, not today." Then she frowned, and looked from Joseph to Knute. "Something was going on between you two," she accused. Her gaze settled on Joseph. "What were you telling Gramps about how my father died?"

Knute somberly answered her question. "He was telling me that I didn't kill your father, Annie Rose."

She stared at her grandfather. "Of course you didn't kill him."

"I didn't know that until a few minutes ago." Knute reached for her hand. "The day we left for the West, do you remember that I told you I had to run an errand?"

Annie Rose nodded, feeling numb and confused.

"I went to see your father, to tell him what I thought of him." Knute's expression grew grim. *"Ja,* it was an ugly scene. His poor wife was there, shocked and crying. Coburn said terrible things about your mother, threatened you and Thomas, threatened to have the law after us, and I lost my temper. I hit him as hard as I could, Annie Rose. He struck his head on the marble mantel and went down. I left, not knowing and not caring if he was alive or dead. I didn't know until today." He paused, and his fingers tightened on hers. "I would have killed him to protect you and your brother, but I'm relieved that I didn't."

"I'm glad you didn't, too." Annie Rose placed an affectionate kiss on her grandfather's pale cheek. "It's over now, at least as far as you and my father are concerned." She folded Daniel Coburn's letter and handed it to Joseph. "Thomas and I will decide later what to do about our new 'family' and our inheritance, whatever that might be. And I most certainly will respond to my half brother's letter. But, right now, I wish to dance with my husband."

"I am at your disposal, wife." Joseph put the letters in his breast pocket and took the hand she held out to him. "A bride's wishes should be fulfilled on her wedding day," he said as he gallantly bent over her hand to kiss it. His kiss was not a chaste one, and Annie Rose was again amazed at how aroused she could become with Joseph's fingers and mouth touching only her hand. She stood up, as did her grandfather.

Knute placed his gnarled old hand over hers and Joseph's joined ones. *"Ja,* this marriage is blessed," he said, his eyes suspiciously watery. "May you always love each other as you do today."

Annie Rose's own eyes watered, and she put her free arm around her grandfather's shoulders. "We will, Gramps."

"Ja, I know, I know." He shooed them away. "Go to your dance now."

With a quick kiss blown from her fingertips to Knute, Annie Rose allowed Joseph to lead her to the center of the room. The band had just begun a waltz. As her husband took her in his arms, Annie Rose felt a sense of contentment and peace she had never before experienced at such a deep emotional level. It was as if she were connected to the spirit of a beloved horse, but this was more profound.

She was connected to Joseph.

Perhaps he felt it, too, for his arms tightened around her. He lowered his head so that his mouth was close to her ear. "Just to warn you, wife," he whispered throatily, "this waltz is going to be one of short duration."

Annie Rose shivered in sensual pleasure and pulled back far enough to look into Joseph's eyes. "Very short," she agreed, and suggestively ran the tip of her tongue over her bottom lip.

With a low moan of desire, Joseph waltzed his bride right out the door.

Later, Joseph held Annie Rose close as they dozed on their new bed, covered by a beautiful quilt made as a wedding gift for them by the other women in the family. The past two hours had been spent in sensual bliss as they celebrated their wedding in true carnal fashion. Now, Joseph stirred and looked around. The light behind the calico curtains at the window had faded, telling him that dusk had fallen. He thought idly about lighting the candle that rested in Annie Rose's brass candlestick on the nightstand, then discarded the idea. He did not want to move.

Annie Rose shifted and nuzzled the underside of his chin. "Mmmm," she murmured sleepily. "I've missed loving you like this." She pressed her naked breasts more firmly against his chest.

"Not as much as I missed it." Joseph ran his hand down her back and stroked her femininely rounded bottom. "You are positively addictive, woman."

"I think it's a mutual addiction, Joseph Beaudine." Annie Rose nibbled on his neck, and her hands began to wander over him. Over all of him.

Joseph was astonished to feel himself stirring again under the enticing touch of her fingers. Her loving heart and sweet body encouraged him to performance levels he had not thought possible, while her eager acceptance of his body within hers touched his soul. Never had he felt so welcomed, so loved. He gave in to the demands of her small hands, but this time pulled her on top of him. Their mouths met, and she brushed his hair away from his face even as her long golden locks fell in a curtain around them.

"This is different," she whispered, sliding her body against his, parting her legs over his hips. "I like it."

"I . . . like it, too." Joseph pushed her hair behind her shoulders. "I want to see you, wife. Light the candle."

"Mm. Good idea." Annie Rose leaned over and lit the wick with the first match.

Pale light filled the room and seemed to bathe her in gold. Joseph stared at her as she again settled on top of him.

"Thank you for teaching me that physical love can be fun, Joseph Beaudine." She ran her tongue lightly over his lips.

"You're welcome," he managed to mutter, then gasped when she shifted over him.

Her next words came out in a sultry whisper. "Let me lead this dance, Joseph."

"All . . . right."

Her fingers held him lightly, guided him home, and slowly, so slowly, she slid down his straining length, enclosing him in her wet warmth until he could go no deeper. She moaned with pleasure as she sat up straight, keeping him tight inside her. Her head fell back, causing her breasts to thrust out proudly and her long hair to brush his thighs behind her.

"This is so nice," she whispered.

Although he agreed with her, Joseph could not speak. He looked up, saw his wife in the throes of passion, in the act of loving him, and he felt that he had never seen anything more beautiful. He caressed the peaked tips of her breasts, pleased to hear her moan again.

Finally, she looked down at him and began to gently rock. "This is like dancing, Joseph, or riding a horse, in that you have to find the right rhythm." Her rhythm changed, quickened, and so did his. He stayed right with her.

Dancing.

She was right.

Love was a dance, a dance of life. Sometimes fast, sometimes slow, sometimes joyous and unrestrained, sometimes sad and hurting, but a dance all the same.

Joseph loved to dance, and from the look in Annie Rose's beautiful green eyes, from the beating of her precious woman's heart under his hand, he knew that she did, too.

He had found the dance partner—indeed, the very song—for his life.

That song was Annie Rose.

Dear Reader,

The legendary Golden Mare described in *Joseph's Bride* is a creation of my imagination, although the Native Americans held powerful beliefs about spirit animals such as Aurora. As was depicted in this book, the Indian tribes and men like Knute Jensen had access to wild horse herds. To this day, descendants of horses who escaped from the Spanish conquistadors live in wild herds throughout the American West. Periodic round-ups are done in an attempt to avoid overpopulation of the herds, and many of the captured horses are offered for adoption.

I hope that you have enjoyed this part of the saga of the Beaudine family. Now that both Orion and Joseph are happily wed, I will turn to the story of their brother, Grey Eagle, a tall, imposing man who is caught between the conflicting worlds of his beloved Cheyenne mother and his equally beloved white father and siblings. It will take a special woman to capture this man's heart, and Diana Murdoch, a gifted healer who shares an unusual friendship with an eagle, is a special woman, indeed. *Grey Eagle's Bride* is scheduled for an October 1998 release.

One of the reasons I write romance novels is to try to combat some of the unhappiness I see in the world around me. It is my hope that my stories offer you an enjoyable escape from your own concerns, if only for a while, and that they help keep alive the belief in the healing power of love.

Jessica Wulf
P.O. Box 461212
Aurora, Colorado 80046
(If you write, an SASE
is appreciated.)

ABOUT THE AUTHOR

Jessica Wulf is a native of North Dakota and has spent most of her life in Colorado, where she now lives with her husband and two dogs. She has a B.A. in History, as well as a passion and fascination for it, and often feels she was born in the wrong century. *Joseph's Bride* is her fifth novel.